THE REVERENT CREED

THE TRANSCENDENT GREEN
BOOK FOUR

MATI OCHA

Robot Dinosaur Press
robotdinosaurpress.com

The Reverent Creed
Copyright © 2024 by Mati Ocha
All rights reserved.
Published by Robot Dinosaur Press.
Cover art by Uzuri Art.
Cover design by Novae Caelum.
Paperback cover design by Sarah Loch.

This is a work of fiction. The names, characters, incidents, and places are products of the author's imagination and are not to be construed as real except where noted and authorised. Any resemblance to persons, living or dead, or actual events are entirely coincidental. Any trademarks, service marks, product names, or names featured are assumed to be the property of their respective owners and are used only for reference.
There is no implied endorsement if any of these terms are used.

The author and editor have taken great effort in presenting a manuscript free of errors.
However, editing errors are ultimately the responsibility of the author. This book is written in Scottish English and includes relative diction as well as instances of Scots spellings. We trust you'll keep up.

Do Kirsteen, a' cuimhneachadh oirre le tòrr ghràidh. Thig crìoch air an saoghal, ach mairidh gaol is ceòl.

Tha sinn gad ionndrainn, is tu beò nar n-òrain gu bràth tuilleadh.

For Kirsteen, with love and remembrance. A life may end, but love and music remain.

We miss you. You live on in our songs forever.

THE ASCENSION THUS FAR

The ascension has begun to mean more than simply the addition of magic to Earth.

In Calum's path home to Oban, he was among the first to find evidence of threats both within the world he knew —and invasive.

A twist of fate put him in the path of his ex's best friend and soon after, a nineteen-year-old girl and a helpless, endangered Scottish wildcat kitten.

What began as a reluctant and antagonistic partnership born of necessity has evolved, not just into a partnership of choice, but bonds of genuine love and affection that grew deeper as this unlikely trio and their tiny fur ball discovered the darker and more sinister forms of magic: the arcane as a weapon not just for physical damage but to control the minds and usurp the agency of those it targets.

And in the process, Calum, Eilidh, and Rhona discovered something even more insidious: a creeping corruption that turns the ascension-mutated animals into mindless monsters bent on violence—and who seem to find their little group wherever their path leads.

All across the world, communities have begun to see the truth of the ascension directive: that strength lies in collaboration, communication, and cooperation.

In Argyll, this has never been more true. Having defeated the rogue mage Lord Edwin Thomas Sackington—more vehemently known as Lord Bawbag—Calum was faced with an altogether different threat from the depths of the sea. Just as the people of Oban began to make connections again with the isles of Mull, Iona, and beyond, a kraken emerged from the mysteries of the deep to wreak havoc on the communities only beginning to find their feet in an ascending world.

Only through their combined efforts and working in tandem with a select group of others seemingly called by spirit itself to serve their homelands could such a threat be neutralised.

With the defeat of the kraken that hounded the seas around Oban and the Inner Hebrides for weeks, an all-new form of ascension has begun. Calum and his comrades have unlocked a daunting specialised affinity: Pantheon.

They now have received the blueprints for something called the Resplendent Throne, which can only be built by an ascending community where members have unlocked the Pantheon affinity.

Their community, under increasing threat from the corrupting influence of the anomaly that has already claimed one of their own, has become a ticking time bomb. And it seems that time is running out.

PROLOGUE

There was something absolutely delicious, Will Grayson thought, about watching an arsehole of the first degree vomit bullshit all over everyone and call it gold nuggets—at least when you had a running countdown to revealing it all as gilded turds.

"I can't believe him," Moira muttered beside Will, her voice rife with disgust so profound, Will wondered if she'd thought of the same analogy.

"Aye, that one'd throw a baby in a cesspool and call it the fountain of life, and I reckon the sycophants at the front of the crowd would applaud and believe it."

The tow-headed Scot sniffed in disdain, glancing over at Nalin, his former colleague turned comrade-in-arms.

Jackson, of all the people around Will for this little showdown, would know. He'd worked for Zeke Bosworth as a bodyguard with Nalin. And, in classic Zeke Bosworth fashion, the man had rewarded him by sending them both off to die along with Will himself.

Twilight fell over the square, lit only by the soft glow of candlelight from the vigil they were crashing. Normally,

Will wouldn't crash a vigil, but since it was, you know, *for him*, he figured he had a right. The golden glimmers of flames flickered against the faces Will could see in profile from where he stood at the fringes of the crowd with his friends. The other half of their group would be on the opposite flank, waiting for the same signal as Will.

But Bosworth, like most politicians, was so delighted with the sound of his own voice that he was taking aeons to get to the bloody point. Will stifled the urge to yawn at his own funeral.

"We must never forget the tragic losses Leeds has seen in recent days, but I know our valiant fallen heroes would want us to come together here, now, so that Leeds may rise from the ashes as a beacon of hope to all of England!" Bosworth's voice boomed out again after the brief pause, his face taking on a tragic air as he raised his hand to his heart. When he began speaking again, his tone shifted to conciliatory, to hammer home his ham-handed point that he stood amidst fellow mourners. "I myself lost three good men, three heroic men, to make Kirkstall Abbey once more safe."

Will was already sick of his patter.

Behind Bosworth was the hulking Barbosa, Bosworth's right-hand man who had buggered off as Will and his comrades battled for their lives against a literal legendary Loiner werewolf, of all bloody things.

Bosworth kept on talking, his cadence rising and falling as he regaled the crowd of a spectacular battle that had never happened.

It did make Will sound quite heroic, he'd give the tosser that, but Will would have much rather fought the trio of jacks-in-irons the way Bosworth was describing than the reality of descending into hell among legions of ghosts and mutated corrupted monsters. Bosworth didn't even have the imagination to come up with something original—the battle he was prattling on about was a trumped up version of the jack-in-irons they'd fought together, with a few gabble retches sprinkled in for good measure. Snore.

"Be ready to move," Will muttered to Moira. "Just a few moments longer."

Bosworth was going on longer than he had expected, which worked in Will's favour—the more Bosworth regaled the crowd of his magnificence and glorious self-sacrifice, the more daft the bugger would look when it became obvious he was talking out his arse—but it didn't do much for Will's nerves.

Just to be safe, he reinforced the weaves of spirit he'd cast into his Shadows ability. Having a group stealth skill had saved their lives more than once in the tunnel dungeon beneath Kirkstall Abbey, and he was not above using it to be enormously petty today.

Because that, of course, was what they were going to do here.

Bosworth had told all these people they were dead. He'd told everyone here that no one but his own gaggle of now-depleted fighters had survived. That meant Ngozi Henderson, Moira's mother, was standing towards the front of the crowd, silently weeping because she believed her daughter was days dead.

It meant Dex and Angie, who had helped Will and sheltered him, each had an arm around Ngozi to comfort her.

It meant that everyone in this crowd who knew someone who'd gone north into the abbey was grieving—and most of them would *not* get good news today. But they deserved the truth. Not that their neighbours and loved ones had died to run-of-the-mill ghosts to pad a politician's ego, but that they'd fallen to the biggest threat Leeds had seen in this ascension: the anomaly Will was devoting his entire being to fight.

If he thought too hard about it, he would vibrate into a rage so strong, he might actually combust.

So instead, he focused on the task at hand, which was skirting the edge of the gathered crowd to make Zeke Bosworth look like exactly the type of liar he was: a supreme tit.

Will knew the other half of their motley crew would be getting into position themselves with Xander's help, just as soon as Bosworth did what he had called this rally to do.

Even as Will thought it, his ears picked up a shift in Bosworth's tone again, to supreme reverence.

"Join me in a moment of silence as I read the names of the fallen," he said. "Let us honour their memory, that they will not have died in vain."

"Boak," Jackson said under his breath, blowing out his cheeks like he really might gag.

"Nalin Singh," Bosworth said, beginning his prepared litany.

That was it. First name was the signal.

Beside Will, Nalin pretended to sniffle and gave his own departed spirit the three-fingered salute from *The Hunger Games*.

Moira rolled her eyes as Will signalled them to move.

It was easy sneaking in the twilight. The shadows gave his skill of the same name plenty of juicy cover.

One by one, Bosworth read out names. Will Grayson. Rachel Maloney. Moira Henderson. Alexander Hamilton.

That one got a few unexpected titters—quickly stifled —from the crowd. Xander was probably on the other side of the square rolling his eyes.

If only they'd had full orchestral backing and could play the signature theme from the Broadway musical just as Xander leaped into the middle of the makeshift stage.

Will snorted at the thought.

They made their way quickly around the edges of the crowd, glad this rally hadn't drawn as many people as it could have. Probably because so many people really *were* dead.

Keen Eye assured Will that they were in little danger from any actual fight, but he still wanted to avoid violence. Bosworth was enough of a coward that Barbosa beside him was the highest level in his crew of flunkies at a now-measly level six.

Will and his pals? Closing in on level thirteen and fourteen.

A small trill from high above, easily mistaken for a songbird, told Will the others had made it to their ambush point.

Another thirty seconds and so had Will's contingent.

He gave Moira a knowing look, and at her nod, triggered his extra stealth ability and left her and the others behind.

Bosworth had finished reading names and was now standing in silence as Will slipped between him and Barbosa to lean against a statue not far behind Bosworth's right shoulder.

At another trill from Will's airborne comrade, he felt a wave of spirit from Rae, one of the companions who had made their way in from the other side.

The silence around him felt sombre, as it probably should. Will felt bad about what he was about to do, just not for Bosworth's sake.

Will let Shadows drop away.

"What a lovely eulogy, Zeke."

Will, still leaning against the statue's plinth, made a small show of examining his fingernails as Bosworth spun to face him and gasps of surprise filtered through the crowd at his sudden appearance. They wouldn't know who he was, not yet—but Bosworth did. So did Barbosa. But aside from spinning like he was on a lazy Susan, neither of the men could move, thanks to Sammy and Rae's magic.

Will went on, straightening up and taking a few steps to close the distance between himself and Bosworth. "Truly chuffed to be remembered, but honestly, when you leave people to die, you might want to actually make sure they're dead before you arrange the memorials. Bit awkward, really."

Bosworth's mouth moved, but no sound came out. The shape of his lips and eyebrows looked suspiciously like he was trying to play surprised and relieved, but the veins bulging out in his neck and temples told the real story.

Will's companions all stepped out from the wings, and Ngozi let out a strangled cry at the sight of Moira.

The two women flew into each other's arms, and this time, the surprised gasps in the crowd turned to murmurs.

"Allow me to introduce myself and my comrades," Will said. "My name is Will Grayson. My friend there, who is very much alive, is Moira Henderson."

One by one, his friends joined him, and as his introductions brought his companions back from the dead, murmurs in the sea of people in front of him turned angrier and angrier.

"Why'd you tell us they were dead?" someone finally yelled.

"We'll let Bosworth speak for himself again in a moment," Will said. "But I think he's had enough time to blow hot air at you all, so first, you're going to listen to us. Then you can decide after that whether you fancy polluting your ears further with his bullshit."

Will took a breath. Here went nothing.

But first, he turned to Bosworth, because there was something he'd been itching to say for the entirety of the time he'd known the man.

"You should know," he said softly to Bosworth, knowing that despite the quiet volume of his words, every syllable would carry through the entire crowd, "that your son Ezekiel is a brave man who has looked in the face of the dangers we fought in the abbey's tunnels without flinching. He's battled worse than you can even conceive and did it while protecting me. He's the reason I came to Leeds at all, and he's the reason I'm moving on to keep fighting the real enemy. You are barely worth my time, and the only reason we came here today is to make sure the people of Leeds know the truth about what we're up against. And they can't protect themselves while you're blowing smoke up their arses."

Bosworth, muzzled by Sammy and Rae's magic, wasn't even trying to hide his rage now. His face contorted in pure fury, veins throbbing and muscles straining as he tried in vain to break free. His pale skin grew mottled, and spittle gathered at the edges of his mouth as he shouted abuse.

It was like watching a muted drama on the telly.

Will had had a very, very long week, but there was one more thing he had to say to this man.

"The real strength and power is being willing to own up to your own shit and learn to be better. You've spent a lifetime trying to make your son feel like less of a man so you could puff yourself up, but for all you've done, the harm you've caused to him and countless others, you're just a pathetic little liar." Bosworth's eyes bulged out to the point that Will half-expected him to pass out. Will met that furious gaze without blinking. "Ezekiel is a thousand times the man you'll ever be."

With that, he turned back to the crowd, in time to see Moira's flinty gaze locked on Bosworth's face as she nodded in agreement. After a moment, she glanced at Will and looked out over the crowd.

"If you're willing to listen, we would like to share with you what really happened in Kirkstall Abbey. Will you hear us?" Moira gestured at Will and the rest of their friends. "Rest assured also that those who have doubts can now go to the abbey and see for themselves."

"Tell us!" First one voice, then others.

Will nodded, gathering himself.

Soon, he and his friends would go north to seek out a seer and a witch. Soon, he'd use his new magical compass to track down Evelyn, just as Ezekiel told him to. Soon, soon, soon.

For now, he would tell his story. With a little luck, they'd leave Leeds behind with the tools the city needed to protect themselves through the ascension's growing pains.

Will could only hope it would be enough. The anomaly had moved on, and he and his friends would continue following it north until they could figure out how to stop the corruption.

That didn't mean the corruption was done with Leeds.

So Will began. He started, as is fitting, with the tale of Barbosa and Bosworth's betrayal.

Time would tell where this tale would end for any of them.

CHAPTER
ONE

The scratches on Iain's face may have been healing, but the wounds to his pride? I was beginning to think those might just last a lifetime.

Eilidh, for her part, was doing an excellent impression of truly heroic stoicism as she tilted her head to one side, light from the campfire casting her face in gold with a ruby halo that turned her hair to flame.

"A giant—" she began, but Iain cut her off.

"Don't bloody make me say it again."

"It was a giant chicken," Meeksy said helpfully, his attention half on spinning a net of Purifire to cleanse the rag in his hand of Iain's blood. "It was absolutely and without any doubt a giant fuck-off chicken."

"You know what? I hate you all." Iain pointed at Meeksy. "I *was* going to give you the drumsticks from the giant fuck-off chicken, but no. You'll be lucky to get the gizzard now. None of you deserve delicious drumsticks the size of yer legs."

"It could be worse," Eilidh chimed in. Her face showed

hairline cracks as the corners of her lips trembled with the Herculean effort of holding back laughter. "It could have killed you."

"At least then I'd be dead! Now I just wish it had pecked me clean through the heart," Iain shot back.

"But your *cause* of death would be 'giant fuck-off chicken,'" Eilidh pointed out.

Iain threw up his hands just as I—in complete innocence, naturally—started to cluck under my breath with a *bawk-bawk-ba-gawk.*

He took one look at me and stumped away from the relative safety of our small campfire and into the twilit forest.

Then he made a noise that at first I took to be clucking himself, but I made out the word *fuck* instead of my *bawk-bawk-ba-gawk.*

"Fuuuuuuuck-fuck-fuck-fuck-fuck-fuck-fuck-*fuck off.*"

Iain threw up two fingers on each hand as he vanished on the last syllable. And that was the end of any semblance of contrition.

The small Argyll glade rang with our veritable howls.

We all knew Iain—he'd dish it out and take it right back with equal facility—but when our torrents of laughter finally died down, he still wasn't back.

"Should I go fetch him?" Meeksy asked. "He wouldn't go far."

Eilidh, still wiping tears from her eyes, went quiet for two ticks before saying, "He's on his way already. No need."

Sure enough, he came back into the camp two minutes later like a walking boulder somehow carrying an armload of firewood, and just like I'd expect, he grinned. "That'll be a tale for the bàrd, aye?"

Iain dropped the firewood near the rest we'd gathered, coming over to stand by me.

"Finn will be delighted, even if it's not perhaps his usual oeuvre," I assured him. "Or...oeuf-re."

"Well, you can lead a pope to the woods, but you cannae make him shit," Iain replied sagely as he high fived me for my terrible French pun, his tone bordering on breezy, which made Meeksy choke on his mouthful of water.

Meeksy was still spluttering—whether about Iain's malaphor or my egg pun, I don't know—when the communications crystal in my bandolier chimed. I jumped. Bloody rockie-talkies. You'd think that coming to the ascension from the twenty-first century of smartphones would mean I didn't jump at every crystalline ping, but you'd be wrong. I always had those things on silent, but we've yet to discover a do not disturb setting for literal rocks.

"Rhona, that you?"

"Claro que sí," came her annoyed voice.

"Are you sure?" I didn't think I'd ever heard oor Rhona speak Spanish.

"Get tae fuck, Calum, I just learned Spanish and I'm having fun. Don't pretend I spoke Klingon. Yo sé que tu entiendes, for fuck's sake."

Rhona paused, and I could almost see her face in its signature scowl despite her being miles away in Oban. We were all still getting used to learning new languages with the same ease you might learn dropping a bowling ball on your foot would hurt. But she was right—I did understand her just fine. Klingon was not one of the languages in our growing archive, but we had both Castilian and Cuban Spanish so far.

"I've got bad news," Rhona went on in English. "They tracked Ronald to what they think is the last place he camped. It's near Dalmally, but he's already moved on. Bastard's still alive, at least. But he seems to be zigzagging all over the shop."

"That's unsettling."

"Is there anything about this that's not?"

I exhaled slowly. We'd been looking for any sign of Ronald for two days after a slim lead sent us haring out of Oban, and it didn't bode well that someone found traces of him before we did. Or that those traces were behind us, since we passed Dalmally earlier today and were now just past Inverlochy. Not far from where I first encountered the beithir in the earliest days of the ascension.

The others were all watching me through this exchange, any semblance of crosstalk already dead. Iain had gone back over to Meeksy and was stretching his triceps. I gave them a light shake of my head so they wouldn't think someone had gotten eaten or corrupted, and Eilidh and Meeksy both relaxed. Iain just belched.

"I heard that," Rhona said. "Weak. I've done better."

"I'll make sure to pass that on," I told her dryly. "Guess we're turning around. Was there anything else?"

"Erm, yes. But it's a rumour and sounds kind of ridiculous. You know the swingers?"

"How could I forget?"

Rhona barrelled on as if she hadn't heard my remark. "Well, one of them went to meet some of their less swing-y cousins or something who were coming this way from Gleann Orchaidh and they said they ran into some very strange people."

"I'm honestly intrigued as what that could possibly mean," I said.

"The swingers are boringly normal," Rhona said. "Don't be catty."

"I didn't mean it that way, Rhona, I just meant that it's the apocalypse and there's all sorts of very strange things happening, but we're mostly past the point of finding things notable enough to write home about." I scrubbed my hand through my hair and instantly regretted it since the right side of my curls would now be pure floof. "Please tell me you have more information than just *very strange people* if it's worth calling me on a rockie-talkie."

"Oh, I do, it's just—fine, you know what? They said there were giant blue people like that obnoxious movie, what was it? Ugh, it doesn't matter. Giant blue people. In Gleann Orchaidh. I told you it sounded ridiculous!"

I blinked, genuinely surprised. It was nice to know I could still be truly surprised by something in this brave new world.

"Calum?" Rhona pronounced my name gingerly, like she was afraid I was going to dive through the communication crystal and laugh in her face.

"Erm, you're right, that qualifies as very strange. On a scale of swingers to our friend the glaistig, I've got to say, giant blue people fall somewhere after the glaistig. At least she's someone we know from our cultural history. Not that movies *aren't*, but—"

"Exactly." Her sombre tone should have made me laugh, but it instead only made my stomach flutter with sudden nerves. "So you'll go check it out?"

Three *very* interested faces stared at me around the campfire.

"Aye, we'll investigate," I told her. "If nothing else, it's a better story for Finn to immortalise in song than a the giant chicken that almost ate Iain."

"Rude," Iain muttered from the other side of the fire.

"Only if you find them," Rhona said, then brightened as she went on. "The chicken would suit a puirt-a-beul."

"I'll leave that in your capable multilingual hands," I told her.

We said our goodbyes, leaving me to try to explain what we were meant to do to three very baffled friends.

After a fair—accidental—imitation of Rhona's own floundering, I gave up and just wiggled my fingers in the air.

"Aliens." I shook my head. "I think we're supposed to go find aliens."

From Iain's narrowed eyes and Eilidh's confused frown, I think they'd both prefer giant chickens.

Meeksy, however, had lit up like a child seeing a surprise birthday cake, his eyes reflecting back the firelight.

"Really?" He actually gave a little bounce. "We're going to go look for real aliens?"

Why did I feel like Earth just got punted into a whole new bin fire?

Gleann Orchaidh—or, as anglicised, Glen Orchy—wasn't exactly a small place to search for aliens.

The glen runs from Dalmally to to Bridge of Orchy along the River Orchy, so it made sense for us to at least take a gander up the glen before going back to Dalmally to see Ronald's abandoned campsite. We'd turned northeast at Inverlochy and into the glen from there. I'd gone walking and camping in Gleann Orchaidh plenty of times with Mum. Once, we got caught in a torrential downpour whilst investigating a ruined old farmhouse that looked touched by the faeries, its crumbling stone walls blanketed in shamrocks under a canopy of trees. We'd stumbled down the hill and into the inn looking as if we'd fallen in the river or taken a shower under the raging falls.

I wondered what Mum would make of this new adventure.

I wasn't sure exactly how we were supposed to find Rhona's big blue aliens any more easily than we were to find Ronald, but here we were anyway, staring up the River Orchy from the vantage point of its biggest and eponymous waterfalls, Eas Urchaidh.

The waterfall was plenty impressive. At some point, I'd probably known more about the geology that split what seemed like solid rock into terraced stone cascades and potholes. At the moment, it didn't much matter what type of stone it was—water crashing over it made an ongoing roar, and the holes worn in the enormous sheets of bedrock formed pools and eddies, depending on the level of the river.

At this point in the early summer, it was running lower than spring flood stage but still high enough to fill the crevasse of rock with whitewater rapids.

Connection was giving me bugger all about the aliens, but I figured that at least wasn't too much of a surprise. I *had* no connection to any alien lifeforms that I was aware of, so why would it?

"We're running around like headless chickens ourselves," I muttered.

Eilidh glanced at me from where she crouched on a wide outcropping of rock overlooking the falls. Meeksy and Iain were a bit farther upstream, Meeksy pointing at something in the distance.

"It'd be easier looking for a needle in a haystack," Eilidh

agreed. "At least you can be relatively sure the needle isn't moving of its own accord. Whatever Rhona has us tracking is probably mobile."

"Aye, exactly." I blew out a breath. "We could comb the glen for a year and not find them."

"What do you want to do?" she asked. "Back to the original plan?"

I grimaced. *Want to* was a stretch, but considering finding Ronald was a very high priority, I couldn't much think of a better idea. At least we knew where he'd been, and I had a solid connection with the string bean, so once we got to his last campsite in Dalmally, I might actually stand a chance of finding where he went next.

For a former primary school teacher, he was proving annoyingly slippery. I supposed he *was* an ultramarathoner, but he didn't seem to be making a dash for anything from the hodgepodge of locations our scouts had discovered.

"I think that's our best bet if we don't want to run laps up and down the glen for nowt," I said.

Eilidh nodded, getting to her feet, and made her way towards Iain and Meeksy to rein them back in.

I couldn't shake the feeling that I was missing something—or maybe it was just the irritation and frustration of not knowing what to do next. For the past few weeks, we'd had pretty set plans: get the ionadan-siubhail sorted so we could be more connected, make contact with Morvern and Ardnamurchan, find out what the hell was going on in the Outer Hebrides, get more people in communication.

That was all moving along as it should be, with a few hiccoughs from ascension-mutated monsters and surprises, but it was also all stuff I could—and should—delegate.

Which left me with the biggest and most elusive problems.

When the others made it back to me, we turned back towards the southwest and Dalmally.

Whether or not Ronald had left clues as to his whereabouts was secondary to at least having a direction to aim in. With my luck, he'd probably have already moved through the glen to Bridge of Orchy and we'd just have to turn around and come right back here, but at least we'd know more than a simple guess.

I was so focused on my circular internal grumbling that I almost missed the ripple of movement through the trees to my left on our side of the river.

Stopping short, I cast Connection out of reflex, allowing my now-familiar tendrils of spirit to seek out the disturbance.

"There's something out there," I said in a low voice to the others, who all came to a halt at my words. "I don't think it's friendly."

That impression was sheer instinct; I had nothing to go on other than the way spirit seemed to slip right off the edges of whatever it was, and that felt like warning enough.

"Which way?" Iain asked.

I gestured, pulsing Connection again as if it might give me something more to work with than *over there*.

The four of us made our way carefully down the bank of the river until we could pick out a path through the underbrush. I led them until we were right on top of whatever I'd seen, but nothing revealed itself. Not with my usual senses, not with Connection, and not from the trees when I reached out to an old Scots pine to see if anything had disturbed it. Only the same awareness of *something*—which I suppose was helpful.

We combed through the chunk of forest for the better part of a half hour, finding nothing that shouldn't be there. No corruption, no people, no monsters. Nothing but the pervasive feeling of being watched.

At least the trees felt it too.

Never in my life did I think talking to trees would make me feel *less* crazy.

"This is where he camped, all right," Eilidh said, nudging at the dug-in fire pit with the toe of her boot. "At least he was responsible enough to not set the forest on fire."

We still had people out searching for Ronald beyond our little quartet, of course, but I supposed it was worth trying ourselves, to humour Rhona if nothing else.

"Now what?" Iain asked with his usual bulldozer-like subtlety. "He's not here and we don't know where he went."

Meeksy crouched next to the fire pit, grabbing a small stick from nearby and using it to poke at the dew-damp ashes. "I don't think he was here very long."

"Oh, well spotted," Eilidh murmured. She squatted next to him to look closer. "Either he only lit it for an hour or so on purpose or he left in a hurry. There's almost no ash buildup."

I turned in a small circle, scanning our surroundings. Not far from the clearing with the fire pit was a young tree with bushy branches, under which lay a small pile of firewood.

"I think you're right," I said to Meeksy. Motioning at the pile of wood, I let out an irritated sigh. "He had enough wood there for a whole night and didn't take it with him."

That latter bit was more telling than anything else, I thought. In an ascending world where we had instantaneous stashing powers to chuck things in inventory, if he bolted without taking it, that said something.

"So he took the time to douse the fire but not to grab his firewood?" Iain kicked at a bedraggled pinecone, launching it into a nearby tree trunk. "Environmentally conscious priorities, I guess."

"Might have had a bucket handy," I said with a shrug. "Or he heard something and smothered the fire first to conceal his location and *then* had to leave in a hurry."

"Nothing that man does makes sense," Iain muttered.

"It does tell us that he hasn't gone feral yet," Eilidh said, rising back to her feet with Meeksy doing the same a moment later. "I doubt he'd have enough presence of mind to put out a fire—or build one, for that matter—if he was corrupted."

"Alison still seems relatively human," Iain pointed out. "Just extra creepy."

Eilidh shrugged. "We're all flying blind in this. I don't know how to explain any of it."

"What now, Calum?" Meeksy asked. "Do we stay out here and keep looking?"

I paused for a moment before responding, my mind rifling through the seemingly endless list of things to prioritise.

We had the anomaly threatening, well, everything. We

had a blueprint for the "resplendent throne" but no context for what that meant other than the tantalising-if-terrifying hint that crafting it would allow us to access the specialised affinity some of us had unlocked: Pantheon. We had skipped UFO sightings and gone straight to reports of giant blue aliens. We had rumblings filtering in slowly about upheaval in Dundee. We had communications networks to create and fast travel points to expand. And we had further incentive to craft the communication beacon promised alongside the throne, which might very well restore the semblance of *global* communication, since communities on at least four continents had also earned those blueprints.

And here we were, scouring an abandoned campsite in Argyll for a defecting community member who may or may not have gotten corrupted in his proximity to our very own anomalous Alison.

"Earth to Calum," Iain said, chucking a pebble at me.

It bounced off my armour, and I gave Iain a withering glance. "I'm trying to answer with an actual answer that isn't just *fuck if I know*, if you don't mind."

"Oh. Oan yersel', then."

"I only got as far as *fuck if I know*. I don't know what to do now." I blew out a gust of a sigh. "I am open to suggestions."

From the answering silence, it seemed I wasn't alone in my overwhelm.

I wished Sailean had come with us, but our furry wee wildcat kitten—quickly becoming gangly wee wildcat adolescent—had opted to stay in Oban with Rhona. A purring fur ball would be a boon right now.

Before anyone could work up a sentence or their own *fuck if I know*, my rockie-talkie pinged again.

"Me again," Rhona's voice said as if I'd summoned her by thinking her name. "Trackers found another campsite, this one just before Tyndrum."

I stifled a groan. Right back the way we came. "I swear, if this is just a way of making us run up and down the road for days, I'll never forgive you."

Rhona went on as if I hadn't said anything. "Not just one, either. There's one up by Auch and they found another between Tyndrum and Arrivain, and from the sound of it, the newest one is that last spot."

My brain felt like mush trying to mentally picture the map of this part of Scotland. "Wait. Auch—that's north of Tyndrum, yeah?"

"Halfway between there and Bridge of Orchy."

"So you're saying Ronald went from Dalmally east to Tyndrum, then north from there to Auch, then back through Tyndrum almost to Arrivain?"

The others, listening to my half of the conversation, all frowned as they did the same mental gymnastics.

"He's retracing his steps?" Eilidh asked me.

"Sounds like it," I replied.

"What?" Rhona said.

"I said it sounds like he's retracing his steps—the others can hear me, but they can't hear you." I had only been joking about running laps up and down the glen, but it looked like we were going to literally have to do just that. "Thanks, Rhona. We'll let you know if we have any news."

No way was I going to want he battle against the sigh that sought escape, so I let it out, childishly enjoying the lip flap at the end as it turned into a raspberry.

"That's us back the other way," I told the others, though I was pretty sure they'd caught that drift already. "Is this just Ronald's way of making us all train for an ultra-marathon?"

From the small chorus of snorts in response, I wasn't about to rule it out.

❖

Clouds had rolled in by the time we made it to the spot Rhona had mentioned outside Arrivain, and a light mist fell over the hills to cloak them from view.

The little Peugeot I'd seen in my initial flight from Glasgow still occupied the same patch of road a little less than a mile outside the village. Just the memory of what the beithir had done to its owners still made my stomach slosh.

It felt like an aeon ago and not a bare few weeks.

We walked another ten minutes or so without stopping. The road into Arrivain ran like a black river through the pale mist, and I couldn't for the life of me figure out why Ronald would have come here. Connection gave me no real clues.

Our scouts had left a small, glowing cairn of stones to mark the path to Ronald's campsite. We picked our way off the road and followed the guides to the crook of the River Lochy that cut almost a ninety-degree angle away from the A85, finding the campsite on a bit of high ground ten metres from the river itself.

There wasn't much to differentiate it from the last one, other than the lack of firewood. The fire again seemed like it had only burned long enough to go through the equivalent of a single log. A smattering of bones lay amid the ashes.

"I think he only started the fire for cooking," I said

slowly. "Why'd he do that here and not in Tyndrum or Auch?"

"I wish I knew," Meeksy said.

"Maybe he liked the view." Iain shrugged, shifting his weight. "Chan eil fhios am, a chàirdean. Tha e craicte gu tur."

"He might be a lot of things, but I don't think crazy is one of them." I frowned, seeking out Eilidh for her opinion, but she stood about five metres away, her gaze trained on something in the distance. "Eilidh?"

"There's something over there," she answered absently. Droplets of mist clung to strands of her auburn hair. She seemed to shake herself out of a trance and looked over at me. "I don't think it has anything to do with Ronald. Not directly, anyway."

"What is it?" I squinted in the direction she'd been concentrating, but all I could see was mist.

"I don't know, but I think we should find out."

Without needing further prompting, she motioned at me, and we made our way through the heather with Iain grumbling behind us.

"This feels like the perfect setup for a horror film," he said.

"Just be thankful the beithir's already dead," I told him over my shoulder. "Last time I was here, there was nothing cinematic about the horror. Just...entrails."

It didn't take me long to see what Eilidh had spotted, though *how* she had spotted it through the rapidly increasing mist was a mystery for another day. My first thought was the simulacra we'd faced, the bizarre, semi-sentient jellyfish spies Lord Bawbag had used as puppets before getting inspired to try the same with human beings.

The object of our attention was similarly transparent, but that's where any commonality stopped.

Unlike the simulacra, this was not corporeal. It was almost like a hand-width curtain of water stationed midair, distorting the mist around it. And in the centre...

In the centre was a veiled view of reddish dirt and indigo sky. It looked like early machine renderings from when the art generators just spat out impressionistic dreamscapes, before whoever trained them glutted them on the entirety of the internet with dubious legality.

But what made my vertebrae itch wasn't that it seemed we were looking into another place—it was the dry and unfamiliar odour with an undertone of rust that wafted from the rift and the certainty that grew stronger every passing second that whatever we were seeing was *not* Earth.

"Gasta," Iain said. "This is just great. Now it's even creepier."

"Do we think the aliens came from...there?" Meeksy asked, his mind clearly having come to the same conclusion as my own. "Is that how they got here?"

Until he said the quiet part out loud, I had been quite happily occupying a small eddy in the current of De Nile. My brain had compartmentalised aliens memes somewhere in my skull, probably to protect me from adding yet another layer of existential dread to my already impressive Everest.

"If they did," I said slowly, "this isn't the only one they came through. I think I spotted another like it near Eas Urchaidh, when I told you all something was out there."

"You said it was something unfriendly." Eilidh tore her gaze away from the rift in reality to meet my eyes. "What made you say that?"

"Just a gut feeling," I replied. "Better safe than that other thing."

It was a good question, one I couldn't readily answer, but all that skated right out of my head when something flew through the air past my head and into the rift.

And there was no quiet thump of whatever it was hitting the heather, no rustle, nothing.

"Erm," I said, "what was that?"

"Chucked a rock at it," Iain answered without missing a beat. "That answers my question. Rock definitely did not stay here."

"I would prefer not to repeat that experiment." The itch in my vertebrae seemed to be spreading across my body with every passing moment, and I had to resist the instinct to shake myself all over to dispel it. "For the sake of not fucking with things we absolutely do not understand, let's just assume that what goes horizontally one way can also go horizontally the other way."

"Aliens," Iain agreed.

Meeksy, who had seemed very excited about aliens until the porthole off our own mothership Earth appeared, started to take on a tinge of grey under the usually warm brown of his skin.

"Calum," Eilidh said urgently, drawing my attention back to the hole.

Which was changing.

Or, more accurately, shrinking.

I felt a ripple in the ambient spirit surrounding us, one that sent my skin prickling into gooseflesh.

As the four of us gaped at it, standing stock still in the rain, it was as if someone had taken a length of fabric with a hole slashed in it and pulled it taut. The edges drew together until the rust-red and indigo colours muted into the silver-grey of Scottish mist.

Then it was gone.

"Well," Iain said, "I would like to be the first to say it."

"Say what?" Eilidh asked him warily.

Iain pressed his lips together and folded his arms across his muscular chest. "Fuck."

THREE

My head felt like it would explode.

Not just from the strange wooziness that had followed the rift's closure but from the sheer number of competing crises. "Rift" was the word we'd landed on as the best descriptor before we'd relayed the experience to Rhona, and I couldn't blame her for her blunt response of, "Are you taking the piss?"

I sat in our small campsite, attempting to meditate. We'd buggered off out of Arrivain and into Tyndrum and politely refused hospitality from the handful of locals, mostly because we didn't think we were capable of having normal conversations with people when the only real news we had was enough to make even the most levelheaded person have a full-on panic attack.

It was strange to be back here, where I could see the Green Welly across the road from the field we occupied. I wondered if that bloke who nicked my bike made it where he was going. I had to admit that I hoped he had. I hoped he'd found who he was so desperate to reach and that they were safe.

I tried to turn my focus back to the task at hand, counting my breaths along with the flow of spirit through its myriad channels.

Cycling through spirit in time with my breathing usually calmed me, but today, I couldn't escape the itchy spine feeling. If we had the anomalies on one front and literal aliens on the other, plus the run-of-the-mill ascension surprises like a beithir or fuath or kelpies or great big killer rabbits—or exciting combinations of the same, as we'd already experienced—the hope I'd been so doggedly cultivating through our Argyll community's ascension? It was in danger of getting squished.

I tried to calm myself by looking at my progression, as if seeing how far I'd come from pathetic himbo hamster to apparent deity-in-waiting might cheer me up, but it only made me realise how close I was to another class specialisation. Talk about adding to the overwhelm. It would be more exciting if it wasn't another choice upon which lives might hang in the balance.

Name: Calum Green

Age: 36

Level: 26

Class: Draoidh (Further class specialisation at Level 27)

Affinities: Nature (Level 21), Healing (Level 8), Synthesis (Level 14), Staves (Level 20)

Specialised Affinities: Wild (Level 17), Coimhearsnachd (Level 8), Justice (Level 2), Pantheon (available with activation of the Resplendent Throne)

Marks of Esteem: Life, Connection, Justice, Passage

· · ·

Alteration:
  Strength: 47
  Dexterity: 56
  Agility: 65
  Mind: 137

Regeneration:
  Constitution: 44
  Stamina: 82

Manipulation:
  Spirit: 133
  Pathos: 51
  Will: 55

Boons:
  Blessings
  Làmh na Glaistige
  Glòir a' Ghiuthais
  Blàr Ghaineamhain

I couldn't pretend to understand how the attributes actually worked. Early on, a single point into Strength had made me burst a seam on my shirt. Now I'd quadrupled that stat, but I could still fit through the average door just fine. I'd gone from being somewhat medium height to downright tall; my muscles hadn't exploded.

The only vague hypothesis I had for that was that increased use of spirit had very clear effects on the items I crafted with. It stood to reason that bodies might be similarly strengthened, honed, and streamlined. Plus, Eilidh's Strength stat was over a hundred, and while I'd no doubt she could chuck Iain from here to the Green Welly's gift shop, she didn't *look* like a walking, talking trebuchet.

We hadn't had to do battle much in the days since the kraken, and my crafting had been limited to small things, nothing that would have increased my experience into spitting distance of level twenty-seven.

I didn't need to be a walking, talking trebuchet, but physical strength wasn't the only kind of strength.

And I needed to get stronger.

Fast.

Unlike my seeming ability to summon Rhona via rockie-talkie, my growing urge to fight something did not manifest anything overnight.

No, the threats waited until we had just set foot on the road to head north to Auch to see the last of Ronald's fruitless campsites.

As usual, it started with the sound of someone yelling.

The Green Welly was still the hub of traffic in the ascension that it had been as a tourist stop, and we quickened our pace to reach the clamour.

"Please," a voice was saying, the speaker hidden in a crowd of gathering people, "I don't know what's wrong with him."

A slick, oily feeling slid into my gut.

I didn't wait for the others. I broke into a sprint, casting Connection with a reflex like breathing.

I already knew what it would find, but even so, the

tendrils of my spirit pulse recoiled as they wound through the crowd.

No, no, no, no, no.

"Let me through," I barked when I reached the wall of onlookers.

"Hey!"

Someone tried to protest as I shouldered my way between them, but they must have seen something in my face, because they did a quick hop-skip away to let me pass.

When the final line of people drew back, my eyes sought out the prone shape lying on the ground. The distraught male voice I'd heard calling out belonged to a young man, and he cradled another man in his arms. They both had dark hair and eyes and pale skin, their features similar enough to mark them as brothers.

The one lying on the floor and twitching was covered in the now-familiar grasping tendrils of corruption.

Those minuscule, hairlike energetic growths clung to the healthy man, seeking purchase with a hunger akin to tens of thousands of tiny leeches.

"You should back up," I said to the bloke, trying not to gag at the sight. "It's not safe to touch him."

"Do you know what's wrong with him?"

The panic in his voice spread palpably from his words in a ripple of movement as the crowd around us took several steps backwards.

"Yes. Eilidh!" I turned my head to look over my left shoulder, but she was already pushing her way through the gathered people with Meeksy right behind her. Looking back to the young men in front of me, I motioned to the uncorrupted one and began pulling threads of spirit into a weave of Purifire and Spèird. "Back up. Now."

"But—"

"Do it. I'll explain in a minute, but first we have to contain the danger."

The bloke's eye's widened, and he scrambled backwards without standing. As soon as he was out of contact with his brother, I loosed my spirit into a fine mesh of a net in an oblong egg shape to surround the downed lad's body.

Eilidh reached the other brother, who kept swallowing —or trying to—his Adam's apple bobbing in his throat.

One of her new abilities was called Sgùr, or Purge in English, and it was meant to cleanse someone of more mundane contaminants, but we'd taken to using it as a precaution any time we came up against an anomaly. The word was similar to the English *scour*, and it gave off precisely that sensation when Eilidh used it. She'd used it on me to test it. Felt like the time I'd gone to a hamam in Marrakech and got scrubbed within an inch of my life from head to toe and everything in between, but...spiritually as well as physically.

I slowed my breathing, lowering myself into a crouch and then to a crosslegged position next to the corrupted man's side. I needed to assess how far gone he was and thus how much of a threat he posed to everyone here.

"What's happening?" someone asked from behind me, and Meeksy began to explain as Eilidh spoke to the frightened brother.

"What's your name?" she asked. "I'm Eilidh."

"Kev," he said. "My brother's Aidan."

I tuned out as Eilidh began to describe what she was about to do, focusing only on Aidan and the sensations permeating my body.

The concrete where I sat was rough beneath me, smoother than tarmac but gritty. Breath. Heartbeat.

Bit by bit, I found the rhythm I sought, pushing

Connection like my pulse through a pattern of short-long, short-long. My heart eased into this rhythm, and with it, all the meridians of spirit that fed into and through my bodies both physical and energetic tingled to awareness.

Like with Alison, Aidan's skin seemed to have lost its collagen, the thinnest layer of epidermis covering musculature in a way that wrinkled and rippled bizarrely. The best way I could explain it was the film that forms on top of hot milk as it cools where the wrinkles lack substance beneath them and create strange ruching when disturbed with a spoon.

Human skin should never look like that.

That thought threatened to shake my resolve and focus, so I batted it away as best I could. Breathing was key here.

I'd learned that the yogic ujjayi breath fit well with this practise, a controlled and purposeful use of audible inhalation and exhalation that helped regulate the nervous system and move us from fight-flight-freeze-fawn to the elusive rest-and-digest mode. I wasn't trying to rest, per se, but I did need to get myself into the zone where my body was secondary to spirit.

Within ten breaths, I sensed the shift at the entry points for spirit in my physical body. My third eye, the pineal gland between my eyebrows, cooled noticeably, the biggest draw for circulating ambient spirit through my system.

After thirty breaths, the rest of the world fell away.

Once again, my awareness seemed to lift from my physical body as my consciousness shifted to somewhere above us, looking down. The dance of those infinitesimal filaments that made up everything continued to amaze me, but one thing tried to steal my focus: like it had with Rhona, where my energetic body brushed against Eilidh's, those filaments *ignited*. They seemed not to pull at each other but to enhance one another, a dance both beautiful and electric. Elegant.

But that wasn't what I was here to observe.

With dread, I dragged myself to concentrate on what I already knew was there. The anomaly, just like in Alison, extended far beyond the physical boundaries of poor Aidan. My containment net had done its job, limiting the scope of its grasping, ravenous cilia, but if anything, their prison made them even more desperate.

That he was so out of it was not like Alison. She'd been corrupted through something Ronald had done in trying to study the anomalies; she'd been lucid when she asked to be put in a cage. Her choice.

This—this wasn't like that.

From my preternatural vantage point, I could see, in the clarity of infrared-like mapping, the density of corruption in Aidan's body spreading from a single point.

It had already encompassed him, and no wonder. Whether bite or blade or beak or claw, something had gotten the anomaly's sickness right into his body, past every defence and every hope of staving off the effects.

We'd learnt that the corruption was a degenerative disease, for lack of a better term, so if he was this bad this fast, well. It didn't bode well.

This was bad.

This was very, very bad.

I made myself reenter my physical body with reluctance. I'd discovered in practicing that doing so quickly would give me vertigo enough to make me boak, so going slowly was a necessity. Even so, every breath struggled to remain deliberate when the urgency of the situation had officially skyrocketed to full-on red alert.

When I opened my eyes, blinking to resolve the

disparate nature of wider scope I'd had in my out-of-body awareness, Kev sat in a ball with his knees pulled up to his chest, a containment weave around him as well.

Fuck.

This time, my exhale felt like clearing away all the rubble in preparation to break ground on a project so ambitious it'd be seen from space.

Eilidh stood a few paces away from Kev, speaking in a low voice to the crowd, where tension tightened every single body to the point I feared hearing an imminent crunch from someone's joint cracking under the stress.

"Kev," I said quietly to the young man, watching him rock back and forth. Poor sod. "How did this happen?"

"Birds," he said, his voice raw. "It was—there were birds. We tried to kill them, but some got away."

My gaze rose reflexively to the sky as if just the thought could summon them here, draw them to me where I could end them in a Purifire immolation.

I pushed myself to my feet and moved to sit again, this time in front of Kev about a metre from the border of his bubble. "Tell me everything."

CHAPTER

FOUR

Despite their presence on the north side of the Green Welly, the lads had come from the south. They'd been trying to make it to Bridge of Orchy, which was still miles away, when Aidan collapsed.

Eilidh and I left Meeksy and Iain to keep watch over Kev and Aidan, and together, we hoofed it down to the address Kev had given us, which sat a stone's throw away from Tyndrum Lower rail station.

We remained silent as we ran, our ascended bodies more than up to the task of covering the distance at a near sprint.

What we didn't expect was the sight that greeted us upon our arrival.

A gaggle of children stood around a rift, chucking pebbles into it and giggling as the pebbles vanished into what appeared to be a view of a tropical black-sand beach. I could only hope none of them had tried to stick a hand in there.

"Thighearna," Eilidh said, skidding to an ungraceful

stop as the weans spun to see who was approaching with wide eyes.

"Dè nì sinn?" I asked in a low murmur.

How was I supposed to tell someone else's kids what to do when the stakes were life and possibly-getting-yeeted-into-another-world death?

Thankfully, Eilidh's brain kicked into gear before I could say the exact wrong thing and blurt out something about portals.

"Hiya, can you go get your parents right away? It's an emergency."

Something about the tall, armour-clad ginger woman with elf ears must have struck awe into the children, because after a moment of open-mouthed gaping, the kids let out little squeals and took off running.

"Good shout," I said to Eilidh. "My mind went completely blank. I think I'm broken."

"Chan eil thu briste," she murmured. "This is—a lot all at once."

The hitch in her voice between *this is* and *a lot* felt all too relatable to me.

It didn't take long before a handful of adults approached, kids dragging them by the hand or trotting alongside and pointing at us.

"Oh, what the…" A dad groaned and raised his hand to his face in a gesture I understood keenly. "You've got to be kidding me."

"I honestly don't know if you mean our ears or the hole in the air or everything all at once, but let me just say *same*, pal." I gave him what was probably a crooked smile, hearing someone's mum snort and another one mutter "Christ, it's bloody Galadriel and Elrond. What next?" just as someone else choked on a "A *what* in the air?"

I hurriedly ran us through introductions with a warning to keep the kids away from any rifts they found. Answering their questions felt a bit pointless, since aside from *probably dangerous*, we didn't have anything definitive we could tell them. After a short while, Eilidh turned to me and said in a quiet voice, "Cumaidh mise aire na cloinneadh—bruidhinn rim pàrantan."

With a nod, I paused while Eilidh did as she'd promised, asking if she could take the kids a bit down the road—still in sight—where I could speak to the parents about something "boring", as she put it, with a great show of yawning for the kids' benefit.

That was one way of getting them to go, but the real kicker was when she conjured a small golden light in her palm and led them away like an elven Pied Piper.

At least I was certain she was taking them away from danger and not into its maw.

When they were far enough away, I pulled threads of spirit into a simple ward that would keep any stray outbursts from drawing the attention of little ears.

Three parents, a dad and two mums, had come out to greet us, and I saw a man's face peering out the window of the nearest house. One of the women with me, a middle-aged brunette who looked like she had invented pilates, turned to him and waved him off.

"What is this about?" The first dad, whose name I'd already forgotten, rubbed a hand through his receding hairline. Or it had been receding before the ascension—now he had little wisps of regrowing hair. "We're managing okay around here, but barely. Have you heard anything from the government?"

I had to stifle a snort at that, but I managed to keep a straight face and shake my head. "Unless you count Lord

Bawbag—erm, Sackington—as a representative of the House of Lords, but he's rather...dead now."

"We heard about that," said one of the mums, looking harried. No one had blinked at my use of *Lord Bawbag*. "I'd be horrified, but if he really killed all those people, good riddance."

"He did," I said flatly. "And worse. But that's not why I'm here. A pair of brothers turned up at the Green Welly in a bad way. Kev and Aidan. Do you know them?"

The first twinges of alarm filtered through the trio's expressions, with Bald Begone and Pilates exchanging a worried glance. The third, a blond woman who seemed to be about my age but plump where Pilates was lithe, was the first to speak.

"They're neighbours," she said in a distinctly Edinburgh accent. She reminded me a tiny bit of one of my old primary school teachers. "There was a big racket this morning, but they said they'd taken care of it."

"Can you show me where it happened? Do they live alone?" I met her blue eyes, which tightened at the corners as she gave me a reluctant nod.

"Yes to the first part," she said. "And I suppose also to the second. Their parents died in the first days of the ascension. Mutated stoats."

"Okay. Show me the way, and I'll tell you as we walk. It's imperative that I make sure there's nothing left that can hurt anyone," I told them, letting the ward fall since we hadn't yet figured out how to make them portable.

Luckily, she started walking in the opposite direction to where Eilidh was, and Pilates paused to wave at the window once more. When the man I'd seen peeking out poked his head out the door, she called to him. "Watch the weans!"

I saw him nod as I turned away, following Primary Teacher down the street. She turned left at a small junction, motioning at a bed and breakfast with a sign that said Tigh-na-Fraoch. Mum would gripe about the grammar, but right then, I couldn't be arsed.

"They lived at the B and B?" I asked.

Bald Begone nodded. "I think the shakeup happened in the garden between the house and next door. I didn't see much, just heard a lot of yelling and squawking."

Bracing myself, I let him take over the lead. The garden was more of a strip of grass cut by a small burn that ran in a rivulet between its steep banks. A tidy brown wooden bridge crossed it, and we walked over that.

I immediately saw the disturbed earth where Kev and Aidan's feet had churned the grass and cut into the sod. And just as immediately, I spotted the blood.

"Stay back," I cautioned the locals. "I need to burn anything with blood on it."

"Burn?" Primary Teacher protested. "That's dangerous."

"It's far more dangerous to leave it where anything could get infected."

At the word *infected*, I heard her mouth snap shut and someone let out a low whistle.

I pulsed Connection, falling into my routine to catch the extent of the corruption. This was, as far as I knew, the first time it had been left to fester anywhere. We'd always been careful to kill it with fire.

But here, it had sat in the grass for hours.

Sickness spiralled through my belly as Connection picked up the grasping filaments that identified the anomaly. Though the blood on the grass maybe spanned a two-metre radius, the corruption hungered. It *wanted*. It clawed and it grabbed and it reached, always reaching for something new to latch onto. With the absence of any mobile sentient of sapient life, it had—for the first time in our experience—sunk into the grass.

And grass? Grass had roots.

Roots that connected it to *everything*.

"Shit," I muttered. "You're going to need to back up. Now."

To their credit, they practically leapt backwards.

Without wasting another moment, I wove Purifire into a thin plait and threaded it through the grass, tracing the outer boundaries of the corruption where it stopped a mere foot in front of my feet under seemingly healthy and untouched grass. I swallowed as the thread skated in an amoeba-like shape, sometimes curving outwards, sometimes back in as it followed the outermost edge of the anomaly's taint.

I had to forcibly keep myself breathing. The impulse to hold my breath kept clawing at me as my Purifire sketched out the perimeter. When it finally connected, I let out a shaky exhale, tugging at spirit to expand it to a perfect circle with every sliver of toxic corruption well within the edge. No cock-ups here. No margin of error.

The circle lit up in blue-green, drawing gasps from the people behind me, which I ignored. Smoke rose.

I could simply ignite the whole circle, but I didn't think it was enough; the corruption wasn't just on a single plane but *beneath* the earth. In the earth. In the root system of the grass and other plants.

Where there was also mycelium.

Fuck.

The mycelium was a vast network, far beyond the connectivity of plants' roots. If the anomaly could seed itself inside the fungi? It would be like infecting the entirety of the internet with a debilitating virus. Maybe later I'd have time to assess how the corruption hadn't simply leapt to envelop the entire plot of land, but for now, I had to eliminate what *was* there.

Because of that, I couldn't risk something as simple as a two-dimensional burn. I gritted my teeth, pouring more spirit into the plaited threads of Purifire.

I watched as the circle expanded above ground, knowing it also delved into the soil. Not a flat circle. A sphere.

With a push of my mind, the sphere ballooned into a glowing dome, the other half of it invisible underground but just as present, just as effective.

Inside that sphere, heat built. I heard the others take more stumbling steps back as the blue-green flames took hold, growing into a burning furnace contained by my will alone.

Seconds stretched out into minutes. My spirit drained steadily, and I cast Fuaran to get it replenishing again, but the pull remained more than the influx.

I wasn't satisfied my regular pulses of Connection turned up nowt but now-dead soil. When the flames dropped, cool air washed across my face like water, and a thin blanket of pale grey ash dropped into a perfect circle like a fairy ring, smooth like sifted flour for one brief moment before the tiniest breeze stirred it into a cloud that billowed into the air with the smoke.

Earthworms, beetles, spiders, ants—everything that had lived in that patch of dirt was now dead.

And finally, I could breathe easier.

I turned back to the neighbours, trying to allow as much spirit as I could to replenish. I'd grown in power and my magical abilities, but the need to be so thorough had depleted me. My legs wobbled like I'd just stumbled across the finish line of one Ronald's ultramarathons.

All three of the locals stared at me as if I'd done just like that but dressed as the giant chicken that had almost gotten Iain deid.

"First of all," I said to them, clearing my throat of its hoarseness. Absently, I pulled a water bottle from inventory and downed half of it before continuing. "First of all, if anything like that ever comes here again, it's imperative that you take no chances. I cannot stress enough that this sickness, this anomaly, is the biggest threat any of us have ever faced. Think virus as infectious as COVID but intelligent and hungry, and you'll be halfway there."

At their horrified looks, I gave them a tight smile.

"The second thing you need to know is how to contain and destroy it—and how to teach others to do the same."

A quick cast of Keen Eye—shockingly easy with the level differential between us—told me they were all barely level eight. Bald Begone was the lowest, still only level seven.

I think we'd just found priority one.

CHAPTER
FIVE

By the time I made it back to Eilidh, the rift the children had been playing with had already closed up. I couldn't tell whether that made me want to laugh or cry.

Maybe both.

The parents trailing along after me were a bit shell-shocked from their crash course in corruption prevention, and when Pilates's husband left Eilidh and the kids and came trotting up to us, he gave me a dirty look. "Someone better tell me what's going on."

"Your wife will fill you in. Right now, Eilidh and I need to get back to Kev and Aidan at the Green Welly and figure out next steps." I waved to Eilidh, who didn't acknowledge the gesture except to clap her hands and start leading the kids—whose plaintive protests I could hear from here—back our way. "And look, I don't know how to explain the rifts, but it might be a good idea to keep the kids under heavier supervision than usual. The last thing any of us need is people falling through holes in the air into bloody Narnia or Mordor and never coming back."

"*What?*" Husband's brown eyes almost bulged out of their sockets. "Fucking—fuck."

"My thoughts exactly. The kids were throwing rocks through one when Eilidh and I arrived, so maybe... discourage that, if you can. For all we know, something could come *out* of them." I pressed my lips together in a grimace. I hadn't told them about the aliens. That could probably wait. "Like I said, the others will fill you in. If you want a bit more security, we have a good community in Oban, and the Muilich"—at their confused look, I clarified in English—"the Mull folk have the island well in hand as well, as do Kerrera and Lismore and Coll and Tiree."

"What are you going to do?" Primary Teacher asked me, pushing an errant lock of blond hair back from her face. "Do you really think you can stop this...anomaly?"

The hesitation before she said the word accompanied another wild-eyed look from Pilates's husband.

"Do you want the truth or a comforting lie?" I asked, wincing because Eilidh and the kids were well back in earshot. I chose for them. "Truth is, I don't know. It's a brave new world out here, and we're all just trying to survive as best we can. But we're going to do our best."

"Doing our best is important!" chirped a wee girl, who was probably only five or six from her size.

The parents all just stared at me, but I gave her an encouraging smile. "Aye, it is."

"Sorted?" Eilidh asked me.

I nodded. "For now."

Eilidh glanced at the adults, who still looked a bit lost, and the kids were starting to take notice.

"Mummy, what's wrong?"

I didn't see who said it, just heard Pilates murmur "Wheesht" to quiet the child.

"You all need to get your levels up," Eilidh said bluntly. "However possible. Crafting is safest. If you don't know how, say so, and we'll send a crafter from Oban who could be here by tomorrow to teach you, but you should be in the teens by now. Do you know how to craft ascension style?"

By the blank looks, that was a no.

"We'll send someone straight away," Eilidh decided.

"Offer stands if you decide to go to Oban, too," I told them. "I understand the risk, believe me, but the risk in staying here is not negligible."

"We're not leaving," said Husband, but Bald Begone shook his head so sharply that the other man fell silent.

Eilidh put her hand on my shoulder, making eye contact.

I glanced back at the small gaggle of survivors, my gaze lingering on the kids, whose spider senses were clearly in full tingle now.

"Think about it," I said as we turned to leave. "For their sake."

We walked back to the Green Welly instead of sprinting, and I filled Eilidh in as we went. I could almost see the gears in her head turning as she pondered what I'd told her about the corruption spreading to plants, but she didn't say anything, so I took the opportunity to call Rhona on the rockie-talkie.

I walked her through what had happened and the two infected young men—to a litany of curses in several languages—and asked her to send a crafter down this way with an escort to teach the folk of Dalmally how to level up with less risk of violent demise.

When I was finished, Rhona grew quiet. Eilidh and I had just reached the public toilet at the side of the A82 with a crowd still visible across the street at the Green Welly a hundred or so metres away. I paused, sensing Rhona had something else to report. The sun had just peeked out between clouds, and it warmed my face, its rays sparkling on morning dew atop the leaves of nearby foliage.

"I was going to call you anyway, but you beat me to the bad news one-two punch. One of the tracker groups said that they'd lost all sign of Ronald but *did* find a badger sett near Crianlarich and needs help containing it." Rhona's voice sounded far more world weary than her nineteen years should impart. "Anomalous, obviously."

I closed my eyes, feeling the sun's heat against the lids as its brightness turned my darkened vision red.

"I guess we're going to Crianlarich, then," I said, feeling as weary as Rhona sounded.

"Aye, you should do that. Who knows, maybe I'll see you again someday."

"Drama queen."

"I *am* a banshee." With that, the connection vanished.

Eilidh gave me a rueful smile. "Crianlarich?"

"Crianlarich. More anomalous badgers this time."

We started walking again.

I gnawed on the inside of my cheek. There was a woman I met here in Tyndrum with her daughter the day after the ascension began. She was from Crianlarich and had invited me to stay with them if I needed to. Possibly out of guilt that she'd been watching my bike when it'd been nicked, but she seemed like a good sort anyway. What was her name? Helen. That was it. I had her address.

That might be a good place to start, assuming she and her daughter had made it home alive.

"You can't just keep people locked up forever! They're free citizens!" A stocky man with an American accent was shouting this at Meeksy as Eilidh and I walked up, and he turned to see the two of us, his pale face ruddy and flushed. "Lockdowns are over, and if you think you're going to put these boys in quarantine—"

"We could put you in with them and have you report back on the danger," I said loudly, drawing a solid ten head swivels as people turned to stare at me. "If you're the sort who thinks individual freedom gives folk the right to literally cause hundreds or thousands of deaths, I might just have help chucking you in there with them. But honestly, these lads have been through enough without your presence."

I had just about exhausted my patience for the day with the anomalies and impromptu arcane training basics, and my tact? A dim memory. I knew—and was fond of—a lot of Americans. Right now, I was fervently wishing I was face to face with any of the few hundred million who were not going to be an absolute twat about containing an arcane contagion we didn't understand.

Iain, who was at his partner's side looking ready to do damage, had his mouth open, but I'd gotten there first, and he closed his lips with a relieved nod in my direction.

"Look. I'm not actually trying to be a dick," I said, and when the angry American opened his mouth again, I looked straight at him, cast Keen Eye—he was a level nine hunter—and snorted. "Naw, mate, if you don't let me talk, I will literally have Eilidh and Iain gag you. I am having a very bad day, and I've just found out I have to go to Crianlarich to put out more fires. Or burn anomalies with fire so they don't infect more people. Shut yer damn gob and stop being a walking stereotype. Save the freedom bullshit for the Aussie with the crap Scottish accent. You're embarrassing yourself and your entire country."

To his meagre credit, he did shut up, more cowed I think by the few muttered instances of "Hear, hear" that filtered through the crowd than by my rudeness. Though he did look like a cartoon thermometer with his head so red I was concerned it might actually explode.

Because of the level of bluntness I was about to loose, I quickly cast a ward to exclude Kev and his brother in their Purifire bubbles with an apologetic glance at Meeksy, who went to Kev to explain without me needing to ask him. Kev didn't deserve my dubious bedside manner telling him he was going to kill a bunch of people before we had to kill him if we didn't lock him up.

"This isn't 2020, folks," I said when the ward was cast. "What Kev and his brother have is just as contagious as COVID, incurable, and has a hundred-percent chance of eventually turning you into a mindless murder machine. There's nothing dead or undead about it, because the anomalies are still alive, but I'm pretty sure they *wish* they were dead, if for no other reason than because having a front-row seat to your meat suit becoming a mindless murder machine is shite."

I saw a couple nods in the crowd—as well as the subtle shift as people drew back from the American. In some ways, I couldn't blame the bloke. He likely was having an absolute shit holiday with no current hope of getting home. Even so, I would be a tyrant about this if it saved lives.

"And we're just supposed to believe you?" he asked sullenly after a long pause.

"Mate, I don't really care either way, but I've got enough on my plate without worrying that someone like you is going to be ground zero for a plague that will make the Black Death look like cosy family fun." I blew out an exasperated sigh, about to go on, but Meeksy's voice got my attention.

"Calum," he said. "Kev has something to say."

I dropped the wards with a flick of spirit. "By all means."

"Listen to them," Kev said. He still sat with his knees drawn in, looking younger than a man in his mid-twenties should. "Whatever this is...I can feel it. I could feel it when it started changing my brother. And the birds—"

He broke off when his voice cracked. Kev shook his head violently before seeking out the American's face. His eyes seemed glazed, unfocused, but they homed in on the bloke's eyes with an eerie, unblinking precision I knew too well from seeing it in Alison. A murmur of unease went through the gathered people; even if they didn't know for sure what was happening, they could sense the wrongness. It seeped into the air around Kev like the odour of rot that would eventually haunt his every step.

"You don't know what the fuck you're talking about," Kev said with surprising venom. "And I hope you never have to learn."

And then he passed out where he sat.

Crianlarich lies only a bare five miles from Tyndrum, southeast on the A82. Some of the cars along the road had been pushed to the side since I'd cycled through, but they were sparse to begin with, and Eilidh and I took the entirety of the journey at a run.

We slowed when we reached the roundabout where we had to veer onto the A85. Helen's house was probably easier to reach following the A82 southward, but the badgers were to the north, apparently in a stand of trees just on the other side of the River Fillan.

"Was it right to leave Iain and Meeksy with them?" I asked when we stopped. "I know they can take care of themselves, but that bloke looked ready to blow a gasket."

"It'll be fine," Eilidh reassured me. "You may not have been able to see everyone's faces when you were mid-rant, but everyone there saw in real time how quickly Kev's infection progressed. They're not going to take any chances."

Then she snorted.

"What?" I asked.

"Just laughing at your reference to a certain famous film," she said. "I wonder how Australia's getting on, come to think of it."

"I'm not sure I want to know. Can you imagine a giant anomalous huntsman spider?"

Eilidh shot me a sour look. "Thanks for that nightmare."

"You're welcome."

A few people waved at us warily when they saw us coming into the village. When we reached the hotel on the right side of the road, an elderly woman with blue hair in a mop of curls, an enormous pink jumper, and a sword held in one hand waved her blade above her head.

"You the Oban folk they're waiting for?"

"Aye!" I called out.

"Take the first left at the level crossing and go over the

bridge on the train tracks!" The cailleach lowered the sword and held her empty hand up to her eyes to shield them from the morning sun. "Pop by the hotel once you're done for a cuppa."

Bless her.

"Cheers!"

"What a time to be alive," Eilidh murmured. "Go kill some badgers and pop by for tea."

"You're not wrong," I said in full agreement.

We made it to the turn and followed directions, increasing our speed again to a jog. Gravel crunched under our feet whenever we landed on that instead of a railroad tie. At least we knew the chance of getting smashed by a train these days was nil.

I recognised the bloke waiting for us in the middle of the railway bridge as soon as we drew close enough. Brandon. The sight of him filled me with a small bit of relief I hadn't realised was lurking at the back of my mind. One of our other trackers seemed to teeter on the edge of going rogue at the slightest provocation, and while I didn't think this anomalous badger sett would prove to be make or break, Brandon had a good head on his shoulders.

That head had also almost reached my height—I wasn't the only one growing in this sometimes very literal ascension. He had brown hair, tanned skin, and green eyes just this side of hazel. And right now, he looked like he'd aged a decade in the few days since I'd last saw him.

"Oh, thank god," he said the moment we hit the bridge. Brandon looked around as if searching for more reinforcements, but seeing only us, he pushed his lips against each other for a moment before loosing a resigned sigh. "Hurry. We've already lost one person."

Maybe it wasn't right to leave Iain and Meeksy in Tyndrum, and not because they were in danger there.

Because there was bigger danger here.

Shit.

CHAPTER
SIX

If Brandon's warning hadn't been enough, shouts of alarms reached us the moment we got to the other side of the River Fillan.

Brandon broke into a run, and we followed hot on his heels.

Why the badgers—pre-corruption, I supposed—had decided to burrow so close to an active railway was anyone's guess. Maybe they liked the vibrations, who knew?

All I knew now was that from the flashes of Purifire pinpointing our destination, something had broken out of containment.

Our jog quickly became a sprint, and I thanked my lucky stars that the ascension had improved my agility enough to avoid curb stomping myself on a railroad tie.

The rails curved to our left, but it was to the right Brandon led us, where a low hillock gave off a steadily increasing plume of smoke.

Brac-Meanmna almost leapt into my hands from where I was so used to it magically attached to my armour at my back. The living staff had been quiet for the past few days, but now it woke up, spirit pulling from the ambient energies around us to focus through the weapon I'd crafted with my own magic.

The sound of scrabbling snarls made an undercurrent to the shouts of the quartet of fighters currently straining to keep a net of Purifire trained on the badger sett dug into the hill.

We'd be utterly buggered if that net failed.

With a deep breath, I tuned out Brandon and Eilidh as they readied their own weapons, focusing instead on pulling spirit through Brac-Meanmna, moulding it, refining it, readying it to reinforce what the others were barely managing to maintain.

Connection pulsed with me, seeking out the weak spots in their hasty measures of containment, of which there were many.

Brac-Meanmna had instincts of its own. As a living weapon—the first in Earth's ascension, my first bafflingly enormous accomplishment—it learned like I learned. And it had learned to despise the anomaly and its corrupted spawn beyond anything I could have imparted myself.

As I moved the staff through a simple form, spirit first trickled and then poured through our combined foci. I saw through my second vision as those streams sought spots they could stabilise, and from there, they pulled taut.

Branching spirit twined itself together, reaching up and over to encompass the hillock like I'd done with the corrupted grass, but I knew I couldn't do what I'd done with the grass. Too many badgers.

The elder Millennial in me would have a joke about this if we lived to tell it. Haunted by the internet memes of the early Aughts. Go figure.

My help bolstered the others' efforts, and slowly, the barrier they'd erected stabilised with the influx of my spirit.

I could only see people in my peripheral vision, another four plus Eilidh and Brandon, and to my annoyance, one of the others was George.

After we'd found the anomalous ùruisg—Gaelic for brownie, known as helpful-if-mischievous house goblins, for lack of a better term—George had wanted to kill the creature on the spot. But ùruisgean were sapient creatures, intelligent and canny, and we'd redirected George to other, lower-stakes work to keep him away from the anomalies in Kilmelford. It seemed like he'd found a way to stay away from them by hunting new ones.

This was not the opportune moment to address it.

"How many are there?" Eilidh called out.

Another pulse of Connection found a hair-raising *twenty-six* signatures within the hillock that had to be badgers.

"Twenty or more!" George called back just as I said "Twenty-six!"

George looked over at me with a nod of assent, which I returned, my mind already trying to find a route through this mess that didn't involve a cartoon coyote and a bunch of explosives labelled ACME.

"Any ideas to get them out of there?" I asked, though I dreaded the answers.

"Sure, drop the shield," one of the others said with a sharp, grim laugh. "They'll come out all on their own."

I'd walked right into that one.

"Preferably one at a time," I amended.

"In that case, no idea."

Good. George *and* a brand-new smart-arse. Then again, I was one to talk.

"Could you make a hole in the net?" Eilidh asked. "Anything?"

"Maybe if I'd constructed the whole thing," I said, "but this way, I think it could just bring down the whole thing all at once, and then we'd have the twenty-six-badger problem all over again."

"We can't hold it forever," a new voice said from my periphery, this time a woman. "Honestly, maybe not even for an hour. We almost lost it right before you came."

Think, hamster, think.

"Eilidh, Fanaid?" I wasn't sure what her taunt ability would do to the creatures if they were hemmed in by our barrier, but it was worth a shot.

Eilidh seemed to agree, dipping her head to the side briefly as if waffling before I felt the familiar swirl of spirit as she formed the weave.

Fanaid was a skill Eilidh had used to great effect on everything from anomalies to the beithir, and even when I expected it, the burst of spirit she released felt like a sonic boom of raw, wriggling bait tossed alive into a maelstrom of piranhas.

And too late, I realised we'd moved too soon.

An explosion of movement came tearing out of the dirt, sending clods tumbling down the sides of the hillock as ascension mutated badgers howled, sharp claws rending the earth.

"The barrier!" George yelled, but as usual, Eilidh was two steps ahead.

She threw herself so close to the barrier that I thought she might pitch straight through it into the slavering chaos of twenty furious badgers, but she had the strength and grace to catch herself and make it look easy.

Another twist of spirit and Eilidh bloomed into a searingly bright beacon of golden light.

Tuaineal.

Her stun.

In a split second, the snarls, the snapping jaws, the sound of claws on sod—all of it cut off in an instant.

"Drop the shield!"

I ignored the protests of the others.

My trust in Eilidh was implicit, and as I leaped forwards, dropping the shield as she'd said, I felt the eddies of her spirit meeting mine. Her claymore unsheathed, Eilidh fell upon the stunned badgers like a furious cyclone.

For just one moment, one tantalising moment, I felt something almost ignite in that liminal space where Eilidh's energetic body met mine, but it escaped.

Where Eilidh had blasted the anomalous badgers with blinding light, I had Dubh, the darkness.

Brac-Meanmna seized upon my ability, lashing out at the still-immobilised creatures with pure void, channelling spirit through itself to follow up her brightness with inescapable black.

The others had shaken themselves out of their shock, and bolts of Purifire arced into the mess of badgers even as I moved to give the melee fighters more space.

I pivoted to Fist of Flame, the twist on Purifire a combination of that arcane spark and Spèird, pure force.

The badgers had begun to squall again, unable to see their attackers and fumbling as they shook out of the stun or died on the spot.

And Eilidh's initial stun had missed some of them, likely those who hadn't yet managed to clamber out of the burrows. Even so, we had a major advantage; the first to die made their own barriers.

The anomalous badgers simply had to tear their way through their fallen foes with razor-sharp efficiency.

Moving with spirit as Eilidh's blade clashed with claw and teeth, I cast Fuaran over the lot of us to restore some of our spirit regeneration and hopefully refresh those who'd been struggling with the barrier.

I couldn't keep count of the badgers we killed. Fist of Flame found target after target, and if the first attack didn't smite the anomaly, the second usually did. Eilidh's blade crunched skulls, wreathed in golden fire from another of her new abilities that burned away the corruption as efficiently as my Purifire.

All too suddenly, it was over, with one of the others stabbing through a badger that had darted between me and Eilidh.

"Next time, warn us, pal," George burst out when our vision flashed gold with the notification that the badgers were officially dead. "You could have gotten us all killed."

"What would have killed us all is if they hadn't shown up—or if the barrier had just failed because Tank and Willie and Gemma got too exhausted. You think you and I could have taken out twenty-six badgers alone?" Brandon's voice was steady, cool, as if he were out for an afternoon jaunt and not minutes post battle with monsters. "We'd be dead. Or worse."

George still looked as if he might say more, but I cut in, because he was right.

"We should have had a plan," I told him. "Eilidh and I trust each other and know each other's capabilities from fighting side by side for weeks now, but you all don't have that synergy, and we shouldn't have dived in like that."

Eilidh remained still for a moment, her claymore's

point braced in the dirt as she wiped sweat from her forehead with a towel she'd pulled from inventory, but then she inclined her head.

"Calum's right," she said. "It's been a long day. None of us are making our best decisions, but that's not an excuse."

With the wind taken right out of George's sails, he opened his mouth and closed it several times before finally saying, "Okay."

"Let's get this mess cleaned up so it doesn't spread," I said. "There's a sword-wielding granny at the Best Western who promised us tea."

Twenty-six petrified hearts and several mages almost drained of spirit later, we shuffled our bedraggled arses into the hotel to find the woman in her pink jumper already bustling about.

"Cat saw you coming!" she called over her shoulder as she ushered us through the lobby.

I wasn't sure whether she meant *cat, feline* or *Cat, short for Catrìona or Catherine*, but I was too knackered to care except the thought of any *cat, feline* made me remember just how much I missed Sailean.

The badgers hadn't pushed me into level twenty-seven, and right now, all I could think about was soothing the insistent and acidic rumble of my empty belly with as many scones as I could find. Even if they were stale. I would still eat ten of them.

Sword Granny—I really need to start finding out people's names—led us into what must have been the breakfast buffet area in the pre-ascension tourist world.

Now, it'd clearly been turned into some kind of staging area, half mess hall and half weapons storage. I wouldn't have been surprised if the array of daggers had been crafted out of hotel silverware.

"Sit, sit," she said. Her sword was now sheathed at her hip, and she rested her left hand on the pommel as she peered at us. "For a fight as big as all that, you look fresh as daisies on the outside. Wilted daisies."

"On the inside, I'm pretty much mulch," I admitted to her. "I didn't catch your name."

"Och, I'm Raonaid. And you're Calum Uaine."

I didn't even have enough energy to acknowledge the Gaelic version of my name. The others made their introductions as I zoned out. George and the two women—I wasn't sure if one of them was called Tank or Willie and completely missed as they said it—but

I could sense Eilidh's concern, and from the way she kept stimming with the pad of her index finger pressing against her thumbnail, she was as agitated as I was. Talking freely in front of George felt like a risk. Then again, we might not have much choice. Not if things kept going the way they were going.

Aliens. Anomalies. Rifts. Jeezo.

Raonaid came back out a few minutes later with a trio of helpers that spanned in ages from younger than Rhona to probably older than Raonaid herself, but I only had eyes for the trays of food they carried.

Someone in Crianlarich had clearly gotten the memo on ascension cooking, which was good, since we'd taken great pains to spread the gospel of magic farming from Oban. There were scones—still warm!—and sumptuous clotted cream, along with jam and a spread of sandwiches and veg so fresh I thought I might cry.

I was busy stuffing scones into my gob that I almost choked when Raonaid's words processed.

"Have you heard about the aliens?"

SEVEN

F rom George's guffaw, he had not yet heard of the aliens.

But when he looked around and saw me and Eilidh sitting with neutral expressions, he just groaned.

"Oh, sod it, really?"

The others exchanged somewhat distant glances, which made George turn to Brandon. "You knew about this?"

"Actually, no," Brandon said. "I think I've just lost the ability to be surprised."

"To answer your question, Raonaid, it seems some of us have and some of us haven't," I told the old woman dryly as she pulled up a chair and shooed her helpers away when they tried to help her.

They made their way back into the kitchen with a couple glances over their shoulders, but didn't linger.

"Well, I've seen them myself," she said, shaking her head. "Wouldn't have believed it if I hadn't. Ten feet tall and blue?"

At that, George scowled. "You have to be taking the piss."

"I don't think she is, pal," I told him wearily. To Raonaid, I said, "I've not seen them myself, but we've seen enough oddities today alone that I have, like our comrades here, lost my capacity to doubt. Did they try to approach you?"

"Oh, no, they buggered off the moment they saw me looking at them, like I was the least interesting thing they'd seen in their lives." Raonaid chuckled. "If only they knew."

Eilidh cracked a smile at that, and I noticed Brandon and the two women with their group hiding their own grins.

"Unless they start making trouble, I'm really not sure what to do about them," I said at the same time Eilidh said, "Well, they don't seem to be coming in guns blazing, so that's a plus."

We exchanged a rueful grin.

"Were you the one who alerted us about the badgers?" I asked.

Raonaid shook her head. "Oh, no, that was Bea. She's taken her history of being the biggest busybody in the village to a whole new level now that she's a seer. At least she seems to be using her powers for good. Mostly. Sometimes her idea of *good* has collateral damage."

I was afraid to ask her to elaborate, but considering the badgers had been up a hill off the railroad tracks where there were no houses, I had to get more information. I'd taken another bite of scone and had to wait until I swallowed to ask.

"How'd she even know they were there?" I cleared my throat when a crumb got stuck in my tonsil. "They weren't exactly central—which was fortunate."

"Oh, she did that the old-fashioned way," Raonaid said, gesturing in what I thought must be a relevant direction.

"Which was?" Eilidh prompted.

Raonaid smiled beatifically. "Binoculars out the window of her cottage."

"Thighearna," I muttered, shaking my head.

"We do appreciate the help," Raonaid said as if she hadn't heard me. "Some of the young folk have been talking of dragging us older folks off to Oban where it's safer, but I've been here for sixty years and don't intend to leave it unless I go *whoop*."

At the last word—more of a sound effect, really—she gestured at the sky, but then frowned, looking upwards as if having a small existential crisis about what happens after death in an ascended world.

"Well, with a little luck, it'll be much easier to evacuate and travel soon," I told her, and at her confused look, I hurried on. "Erm, not to heaven or whatever, just to Oban."

"Close enough," Eilidh deadpanned.

George, however, seemed to be growing more and more annoyed with every passing word. "What is *wrong* with you?"

"Rude," the man whose name I didn't know said. Tank or Willie. "Don't be a git."

"You're all just acting like none of this matters!" George burst out.

"To the contrary, I think we're all acting as if *everything* matters, and that's why I'm so tired I could probably out-sleep Rip van Winkle at this point," I said to him. "If you have thoughts on what apocalyptic problem should be our first priority, by all means. Let loose. I'm all ears."

"Obviously the anomaly," he said.

"Great, I agree. How do we find it?"

At that, he blinked. Raonaid grew very still, watching me with a blue-eyed gaze all too shrewdly.

"We're all reacting because there's not much we can do *pro*actively that we aren't already doing," Eilidh said, a hair more gently than my tone had been. "The anomalies appear sporadically, unpredictably. We can't cure the sickness, and we can't protect against it reliably. All we can do is warn people, which we're trying to do, but without telly or radio or anything beyond the rockie-talkies and our own two feet, that takes time and more people than we have. And the person we had with the most information about the anomaly took off and may himself be corrupted."

"I *know* all that," George muttered.

But he'd given me a thought. Or perhaps Eilidh had with her use of the word *proactive* and her mention of global communications.

Raonaid, who was still watching me instead of them, cracked a smile. "I think Calum has an idea."

"I'm not sure it's an idea, since it's nothing we don't already have on the list," I said slowly. I looked to Eilidh, whose eyes—much deeper blue than Raonaid's—met mine quizzically. "You and I have been avoiding the possibility, frankly, for its implications."

Eilidh's eyes widened as she twigged what I was saying. "The communications beacon."

"I'm sorry, you want to what, call *Japan*? Do they even have the anomalies there?"

George's smart-arsery was beginning to feel a bit like shoving acupuncture needles under my fingernails.

"We don't know how far they've spread, and I don't care. The ascension directive, remember? Even if the anomalies aren't there, it doesn't mean they can't help. Our biggest strength is sharing information, skills, resources." I glanced at Raonaid, who smiled and reached out to pat my hand where it rested on the edge of the table.

"Two heads are better than one," she said, then got up and moved over to George, placing one hand on each of his shoulders. "And you, lad, ought to find a way to deal with that anger. Come with me."

George just looked up at her, confusion in his eyes, but he stood obediently. I didn't think many Scots would gainsay a Highland granny, and he was not going to be one of them just because I'd filled his bonnet with bees.

"What—what are we doing?"

"I'm going to teach you to make bread."

Eilidh and I extricated ourselves shortly after—leaving a bewildered George up to his elbows in sourdough with the others happily joining in around an enormous stainless-steel island in the industrial kitchen—but the last thing I wanted to do was run all the way back up to Tyndrum.

"You're sure?" she asked me as nevertheless, we started the trudge at a walk. "What you said in there. You want to go back to Oban?"

"George is abrasive, but I really do think he has a point. We can't just get tossed around by whatever new mess the ascension flings our way, and the best way to stabilise is to actually plan. Train. And...I don't know. If that means we have to build this throne, it really might be our best bet." I rubbed my face with both hands. "I am dreading finding out what that specialised affinity is beyond the obvious, but at this point, it's kind of already done."

"What, you mean you've never aspired to divinity?" Eilidh mock gasped. "Oh, wait, that was Susanna."

"That was proper catty—love it." I snorted, though the

thought of my ex—and Eilidh's ex-best friend—did leave a sober moment of awkward silence hanging in the air.

Eilidh shook her head with a rueful chuckle that almost didn't qualify as any form of laugh at all. "I just about said something worse."

"Hit me with it."

"Everything I learned about being a bitch, I learned from her." Eilidh winced as the words came out, looking at me guiltily through dark eyelashes as she kept her eyes squinted as if braced for my horror.

"Pfft. She didn't teach you very well, then," I said, which got a full-on eye roll from my love.

"Have you forgotten how mean I was to you when we ran into each other?" Eilidh slipped her arm around my waist. "I really am sorry about that, by the way."

"For the thousandth time, you don't need to apologise. I'm a big boy, and Susanna is, as I think I told you ages ago, fuath toe jam." I wrapped my own arm around her shoulders, which was a bit difficult since she wasn't all that much shorter than me, but I managed. "I know the scars from yanking her barbs out of us don't heal all at once in one single go, but at least you and I have each other. She's got *John Frost*, assuming they're still together."

"Hm, maybe she came out ahead after all. What did you say he's the god of?" Eilidh looked up at me sideways with a feigned pensive look. "Och, right, being a massive bam. Naw, I'll stick with my Green Man."

For some reason, her words sent a thrill through me. Not the piss-take, but the last two.

Maybe this whole pantheon thing wouldn't be so terrifying after all. Not if we took these steps together.

I stopped walking and pulled her to me, my hand brushing her hair back from her face as I bent to kiss her.

"What was that for?" she asked when I released her after a long moment.

"Gratitude. If I'm a Green Man, you're none other than Sgàthach, and that's a combination that should put the fear of god—gods—into this anomaly wanker."

Eilidh's eyes had lit up at my likening her to the legendary warrior queen. "Ooh, you know what this means."

"I...do not." I had a creeping suspicion that whatever it was, I might regret starting this conversation. "I'm afraid to ask."

"Sgàthach taught Cù Chulainn how to fight, you know."

"Oh. Oh, no."

"I'm going to teach you how to use a sword when we get back to Oban."

I don't think I'd ever seen Eilidh's eyes that bright and excited. "And here I thought I was done getting punished."

If anything, that made her grin grow wider. "It's not punishment. It'll be fun. Did you know that the legends say they believed only women could truly train men to be warriors and vice versa?"

"Is it too late for me to go find Susanna and John and ask to be a throuple?" I asked the empty air to my right.

"Yes. You're stuck with me. You love me."

"I do. You're right. I think I just gave myself nightmares with the thought of being in a throuple with those two. Fine, you can teach me the way of the sword."

Eilidh, near six feet and capable of throwing a grown man probably farther than any burly Scot could toss a caber, actually did a little bounce. Then her nose wrinkled. "The way of the sword? Really?"

"Pointy-stabby-slash-slash. That better?"

"Maybe I should see about that throuple thing," she

mused, then made a face as if someone had held a dead anomalous rat under her nose and made her take a big whiff. "You know what? Touché. We both get nightmares."

"The couple that dreams together screams together," I told her solemnly.

We both went silent for a moment, and then Eilidh looked around at the empty road. We hadn't been alone in days. Not really since Tiree. To go from windswept beaches and ultramarathons of a different sort altogether to Iain farting in his sleep in the next tent over with a rock digging into my back while Meeksy snored? Bit of a wakeup call.

Eilidh met my gaze with an appraising expression on her face. Perhaps her mind had taken a wee journey along the same path as mine.

"I need to chase those throuple images out of my head." To emphasise her point, Eilidh swung herself up against me to gaze up into my eyes with an intensity that left me in no doubt of what she meant. "We've had a very long day. Perhaps we could make a small detour somewhere private so at least today has one—maybe two or three—nice memories?"

"I couldn't agree with you more," I replied, taking her hand and setting off into the woods.

We didn't make it very far before we started shedding armour and underclothes.

CHAPTER

EIGHT

O ban, it seemed, hadn't missed us at all.

By the time we arrived, a day and a half after the badger incident due to more unexpected—but expectedly fruitless—detours, I was beginning to wish Eilidh and I had just run off into the woods and stayed there rather than rejoining our friends in Tyndrum.

Some of the Oban folk had come to transport Kev and Aidan to Kilmelford where they could be properly isolated with Alison and the ùruisg. That was one of the few boons we'd received.

It took us almost an hour just to get to the Whyte house, where I could feel the presence growing closer of a certain Scottish wildcat kitten I missed rather desperately. Between people clamouring for our attention and chattering at us about new developments—I was certain there were miracles amid all that, which went in one ear and out the other—I could have cried with relief the moment Catrìona opened the door upon hearing our approach.

"Oh, goodness, sin sibhse. Fàilt' air ais, a ghràidh—ooft."

Iain's mum's welcome cut off abruptly as a tiny fur-based missile came hurtling across the hardwood floor only to launch itself into the air and suction cupped itself to my hip. Tiny needle claws like ice crampons scaled the rest of me like I was bloody K2. If not for my armour, I would have been very literally bloody.

Perhaps one small, fuzzy, and endangered bit of Oban had missed us quite a bit, come to think of it.

Sailean smelled of sausage and warm fur as she triumphed over my chest plate and I caught her in the crook of my neck. Her purr had either grown louder in the past few days or she was just that happy to see me.

"Òbh, a luaidh," I greeted her. "Nach robh mi gad ionndrainn!"

"She missed you too," Catrìona said, reaching past me to pull Eilidh into a hug and kiss her cheek, which Eilidh returned. "She's been going out of her mind for the past two hours. What took you so long to get here? Where're my sons?"

I caught the way Eilidh's face went into a helpless pout as she mouthed *Sons!* from behind Catrìona's shoulder. Sailean caught a glimpse of Eilidh and let out a plaintive mew along with a wave of emotion at the sight of her that felt suspiciously, to me, like the warmth a kitten might feel for a maternal figure.

Oh, god. We already had a baby.

I extricated Sailean from my chest and passed her to Eilidh before the wee fur ball could try to fly, and Eilidh promptly cuddled her to her face. Brave. Always brave, my Eilidh, to get eyeballs that close to those needle peets when Sailean was so excited.

"Iain and Meeksy went to pick up some food, but they should have made it here by now," I said.

"Where did they go get food? Iceland?" By Catrìona's tone, I did not think she meant the frozen foods supermarket.

"Then again," I added hastily, "it took us a half an hour to get here from the harbour, so maybe it's no surprise they're not here yet."

Catrìona seemed to take a closer look at us and *tsk*ed. "You two go get comfortable. Rhona said she'd be by later tonight—she's in Kilmelford to help them get ready for the new arrivals—but I've told everyone else they're not to knock unless someone's dying."

"Well, now you've done it," I said. "Someone's going to turn up with a frying pan welded to their head or something."

"Don't be silly. They'd go see Angus for that."

I blinked, afraid to ask why she had said that with such certainty.

"Go, go," she told us, making a shooing motion with her hands. "You've been running mad for days."

I didn't make her tell us a third time and headed for the stairs, only to hear her call out again behind us, underscored by Sailean's rumbly purr.

"All of both of your things are in Calum's room—I thought it might be a good idea."

And the cheeky wee fisher didn't even give us a chance to answer, just skipped out the door and let it slam behind her.

"Well," I said to Eilidh. "Looks like we had a baby and moved in together, in that order."

Sailean just purred louder.

❖

The thing about having big plans to be proactive and make strides towards lofty goals is that inevitably, every being in the universe hears you when you make them and sets out to tar and feather you with the sticky goo of bureaucracy and the million and one tiny wee obnoxious tasks that I was convinced were the true nature of hell.

It took us three days of running from one part of town to the next, up and down the road to Kilmelford, shoving our heads under the surface of Loch a' Phearsain to scream where it would only alarm the fish, and generally getting run ragged every bit as much as we had on the road chasing anomalies, aliens, and rifts.

By the end of the the third day, I was convinced the anomalies, aliens, and rift nonsense had been more fruitful.

We'd seen Kev and Aidan, who were rapidly deteriorating, but neither myself nor Eilidh had been able to face Alison. Not yet. Just the rapid progression for Aidan alone gave us the fear—seeing a friend felt like an impossible ask, especially since Meeksy had warned us there was very little that made Alison *Alison* left to be found. Rhona, for her part, wouldn't even speak of her. An impossible heartbreak, one far more cruel than most.

As it was, Rhona had called us on the rockie-talkie to insist we meet her at Gaineamhan, the site of our battle against Lord Bawbag.

Eilidh looked ready to collapse as we approached the beach, and I didn't blame her. I was half tempted to go lie down in the sea and see where the currents took me. Into a kraken's gullet? Fine. Canada? Sure.

But there was no one on the beach except Rhona, who was busy spreading out...a picnic blanket?

"What's this?" I asked, amused, when we got close enough for her to hear me.

In response, Rhona dropped a rock on one corner and trotted over to throw her arms around me.

"Hey, you." Now I was just perplexed. I met Eilidh's questioning gaze over the top of Rhona's head. "You're making me worried."

At that, Rhona pulled away and punched me in the shoulder.

"Ow."

"I missed you both, jackass."

There she was.

Rhona threw herself at Eilidh next, which resulted in Sailean—who was perched on Eilidh's armoured shoulder—half jumping, half falling from Eilidh's shoulder to Rhona's.

When Rhona pulled away from Eilidh, she gestured at the picnic blanket. "I thought you could use, I don't know, a break. Ealasaid and Finn and Samuel are coming too. They all wanted to see yous. Just not, you know, to have to queue to do it."

"Gang's all here, eh?" Eilidh said, an inscrutable look on her face as she met my gaze.

Not just the gang. The pantheon, if our shared affinity was to be believed.

Even as I thought it, I felt them coming.

I couldn't have described it before the days of the ascension without sounding unhinged.

I wasn't entirely sure I didn't sound unhinged even now inside my own brain. But it couldn't be denied.

Just like I often felt the edges of my spirit melding and fusing with Eilidh's, the presence of the others amplified the sensation. I'd felt it when we faced the kraken, when our spirit blended and gathered strength from all of us, stronger than the sum of our parts.

I felt it again now, knowing even before the boat appeared sailing around the southwestern tip of Lismore that the three of them were in it—and that they were as aware of me as I was of them.

Both Eilidh and Rhona had gone silent as I had, their own gazes trained on the sea to watch the sailboat coming our way.

And they weren't alone.

"Scout!" The eagle's name burst out of me before I could restrain myself, and I ran to the water's edge.

The enormous golden bird cried out in response, soaring ahead of the boat to circle above me in a wide arc before billowing her wings out to land twenty metres down the beach. I jogged after her, fighting the wave of emotion that came with her nearness.

I hadn't realised just how much I'd missed...this.

Unsure even of what I meant in my own mind, I closed the distance to the golden eagle as she turned and hopped on her giant legs towards me in the sand.

"An do dh'fhàs thu?" I asked her incredulously. She seemed even larger than I remembered her.

I felt a ripple of affection from her as she lowered her head to nudge me with her beak. Whether that was meant as an answer to my asking if she'd grown, I didn't know or care. I reached out to stroke her feathers, which she puffed up to let me dig my fingers under them to her skin, trilling ecstatically as I did my best human attempt at preening her the way a nest mate would. I didn't have a beak, but I figured opposable thumbs might count for something.

Eilidh's presence behind me grew closer as she approached almost shyly. Scout's affection rippled outward again as she trilled and this time headbutted Eilidh gently.

By degrees, the tension drained out of me. Not just from me, but from Eilidh and Scout—and Rhona.

Our teenage adopted sister may have been a banshee. She may have been sharp tongued and have a lower tolerance for bullshit than even Eilidh or Iain, but at heart, she was *all* heart.

Then again, most of us shared that little secret.

We also shared something else, and it was that little niggly fact sticking in my throat like an inhaled bit of carrot. We were all classic Gaels, masters of the stiff upper lip.

But it wasn't the truth. Rhona refusing to talk about Alison didn't mean she wasn't devastated.

That's the thing about keeping emotions all bottled up. We could pretend as much as we wanted that they didn't exist, but it was like a toddler throwing a blanket over a mess they made and acting like it had disappeared from the cosmos. Just because we were incapable of expressing them or dealing with them didn't mean they weren't there, ready to kick our arses if we didn't learn how to process them. If there was any criomag of emotional truth I'd learned in the past few weeks, it was that in the long run, bottling it all up solved nothing. It just kept me miserable.

All the best things in this terrifying new world, the highest highs to go with the absolute shite-scraping lows had come because I did the scary thing and let myself feel— and let other people see.

"Hey, Rhona, get over here," I called over my shoulder.

She hurried to do just that, a questioning eyebrow raised.

I stepped away from Scout just far enough to pull Rhona into another hug, but this time, I didn't deflect.

Baby steps.

Sailean clambered from Rhona's shoulder onto mine, purring her wee heart out.

"I missed you too, by the way," I said into Rhona's hair, again meeting Eilidh's eyes over the top of the kid's head. "Rockie-talkies just aren't the same."

Rhona froze in my arms for a moment, not saying anything. After a beat, Eilidh came closer and wrapped her arms around both of us.

I felt a small shake from the banshee between us and realised she was sniffling.

Ooft.

I'd missed the mark a few minutes ago, but I'd be damned if I missed it now.

This was the part I'd usually wall off, crack a joke like I had earlier. And it was also the part where Rhona would deflect and call me a jackass when what she really needed was...this.

Care. Love. Comfort.

Rhona may have been on the precipice of ascending to who knew what kind of pantheon we'd sprouted here in Argyll, but she was also still nineteen years old. She wasn't a child, but she sure as hell hadn't gotten her feet under her as an adult before the apocalypse.

Working for a certified psychopathic murderer probably had not helped.

I heard Eilidh take a shaky breath herself, and I snaked one arm behind her. Never would have thought I'd willingly tolerate a group cuddle, but what was it they said about hugs? Twenty seconds when we realised we were safe enough for our brains to release the happy chemicals?

Even Scout hopped closer, sheltering the three of us under her enormous wings.

That was how our complementary trio found us as they pulled their small sailboat to shore.

Rhona finally squirmed out from between me and Eilidh to greet them, casting a grateful look over her shoulder. Definitely no punch this time.

Emotional intelligence, level up. Look at us go.

Scout waited for us to get a short distance away, then took off back into the air with a few thrusts of her wings. The wind from her departure tousled my hair and blew Eilidh's right into her face, which she batted out of the way.

"You okay?" Eilidh asked me. "If I didn't know any better, I'd think you were feeling at least three, maybe even four separate emotions at once."

"At least," I murmured, taking her hand as we walked to greet our friends. "Remind me to tell her more often that we care."

Part of me thought Eilidh might say something like "She knows," but she didn't.

Instead, she just nodded, a sad smile on her face that I instinctively understood. I'd been lucky to have one parent who loved me and made sure I always knew that—Eilidh hadn't. She knew better than to take it for granted that people know they're loved.

Some of the ponderous mood lifted as we got close enough to see Finn's brilliant smile. Mull's golden boy, a proper Adonis of a man with a sweetness almost treacly but so genuine it was impossible to hate him.

He came towards us with open arms, Am Bàrd Muileach, the Mull Bàrd, scooping Eilidh up in a hug with a chaste kiss on her cheek and then surprising me with the same. That broke any remaining heaviness in the air as both Rhona and Eilidh burst out laughing at what must have been pure surprise on my face.

"What?" Finn said innocently. "It's perfectly normal in half the world to kiss your pals on the cheek in greeting."

He held his hands out to me, and for a moment I thought he wanted me to kiss him on the cheek, but then Sailean mewed and took a flying leap from my shoulder into his hands, and he gave her approximately ten kisses in comparison to the one he'd given me and Eilidh.

"I think we know who he loves the best," Eilidh said, holding a tragic hand to her heart in mock despair.

Samuel's answering laugh boomed through the air like the world's softest thunder.

Eilidh went to the monk and kissed both his cheeks, which made him laugh again, and when I did the same, he almost lost it.

Ealasaid, who had been using her magic to secure the boat so it didn't wash away with the tide, started with Rhona and went down the line, kissing each of us *three* times on alternating cheeks until I thought Samuel might have a stroke laughing. The capstone came when she marched right up to Finn—with whom she'd just arrived—and planted a kiss on each of his cheeks four times, then patted him on the head and stole Sailean.

"It was all a ruse to get the cat," Ealasaid said to me with a wink as she headed toward the blanket Rhona had laid out. "Come on, you lot. We need to talk thrones."

CHAPTER

NINE

The Muilich—and Ealasaid—had brought a second blanket, which they laid out beside Rhona's. I thought that was a good shout. No matter how silly our kiss war had gotten, I didn't think we were quite at the stage of cuddle puddles, especially since one of us was a literal monk.

Samuel, the monk in question, had an actual proper picnic basket he produced from his inventory.

"The community gardens in Iona are just getting started for the year, but we have managed a few specialities with the help of magic," he said, pulling out pots of jam and honey, six miniature baguettes, an assortment of cheeses from Mull.

From the other side of the basket came a smaller basket full of ripe tomatoes and yellow bell peppers, some venison summer sausage, and an enchanted bag of still-crisp lettuce. Samuel reached into one of the pockets of his smock and pulled out a jar of mustard, placing it with the rest.

I wasn't about to ask.

For a while, we all avoided the subject in spite of Ealasaid's preface. We ate luscious tomatoes with sprinkles of sea salt, bread with jam and honey, cold sausage medallions with cheese and mustard. Sailean, as usual, gorged herself on sausage and then fell asleep in a tiny round ball between Ealasaid and Eilidh.

But eventually, not even ascension-encouraged gluttony could exorcise the elephant sharing the picnic blankets with us.

Whilst everyone else was still chewing, I bit the less savoury bullet and pulled up the blueprints for the Resplendent Throne.

The first part of it, at the very least, sounded doable. There were two stages of the task: crafting and activation. I wasn't even going to look at activation until after I read through the crafting bit, since if we had no throne to activate, it would be moot.

To craft the Resplendent Throne, you must gather the following items and assemble the following participants:

   -Native wood from the community of the pantheon

   -Native stone from the community of the pantheon

   -Triune waters from the community of the pantheon (Varies by region. For Earra-Ghàidheal, this consists of: seawater, freshwater loch, rain)

   -Purifire reliquary (additional blueprint unlocked)

   -3 donated animal offerings from sapient, willing participants

   -Guth iomadh-fhillte, aon òran air a ghabhail

. . .

The first three were easy. We could have those tonight. We lived in the west of Scotland; it had to be raining some-where in our network of ionadan-siubhail.

I wasn't sure what a Purifire reliquary was, but without looking at the blueprint, I warily guessed it was something in the realm of my own capabilities.

The animal offerings stumped me. Did it mean we needed to ask Sailean for a whisker or something?

Blinking away the screen, I found the others looking at me.

"I take it you've all read the shopping list?" I asked them wryly.

"Aye," Finn said, stretching to lean back on his hands with his feet straight out in front of him. "Scout's already given us a feather, and you've got the antlers."

I startled at that.

The antlers.

Unbidden, my head turned to look out over the battle-field where we'd defeated Bawbag what felt like an age ago. It'd only been a few weeks, in reality. He had corrupted a great stag, one that ought to have risen to its own heights and even turned into a sick puppet by Lord Bawbag, the stag had borne the name of the Monarch of Glen Etive.

I'd freed the stag from the prison inflicted on him, from the nexus node Bawbag had used to violate his very heart.

Slowly, I reached into my inventory to retrieve the antlers. They'd been in there ever since that night. I hadn't had the heart to move them.

They were, without a doubt, the gift from a sapient, willing participant. As was the feather Finn had placed across his knees, holding onto the pin end to keep it from flying away.

Sailean, still curled up between Ealasaid and Eilidh,

seemed to wake herself up with a little mew, blinking sleepy eyes at us.

Or perhaps she simply sensed my thoughts.

The wildcat kitten yawned, exposing her vicious wee teeth—arch-nemesis of sausages everywhere—and stretched.

All eyes were on her, as usual, but she pushed herself to her feet and stood, all gangly adolescence no matter how round she could be when she curled up.

No one spoke; perhaps they all sensed, like I did, that Sailean herself had something to say.

She gave me one unreadable look. Or it would have been unreadable if I couldn't also feel her complex wee ball of emotions. Through her kitten mind, I could see what was driving her. The comfort of Rhona's face and mine and Eilidh's. How she trusted us even when she was terrified. She had been even smaller not so very long ago, smaller and alone, at the mercy of the very man who had ordered her mother's murder.

Sailean walked on still-sleepy legs over to Eilidh, where she sat and raised one paw to bat at Eilidh's knee.

All at once, it hit me.

I wasn't the only person with something in my inventory that I'd been holding onto. But unlike the antlers in my lap, what Eilidh held had not been a gift.

Or it hadn't until now.

Eilidh's face fell as comprehension dawned. Her gaze lifted to mine, and I didn't have to be psychic to know what she was thinking. *How does she know?*

Ultimately, it didn't matter; Sailean and I were bonded. How much access she had to my thoughts and feelings had to be at least as much as I had to hers, and that was a lot.

Eilidh held out her hands, and a pelt appeared in them.

I hadn't realised that she'd treated it after we'd stolen it from Bawbag's henchies, but I should have known she would show it that respect rather than leaving it raw to dry out and wither.

The tail still hung plush, its blunt tip a view into what Sailean's would one day become.

Sailean sat frozen with her paw still resting on Eilidh's leg. The emotions pouring off the tiny kitten threatened to capsize me, a full-grown adult...elf. Confusion and fear, then outright terror. Grief and loss so intense it could only be felt by a baby, an infant, who hasn't just lost a loved one but the *entirety of their world*.

After a moment, Sailean opened her mouth, but no sound came out, only that of her tiny tongue unsticking from the roof of her mouth. She climbed onto Eilidh's knee, where Eilidh held the pelt in hands that grew shakier by the heartbeat.

Sailean clambered over Eilidh's crossed shins to her other knee, where the head rested. And that tiny kitten we'd rescued, this precious, endangered creature every one of us had loved the moment we laid eyes on her, she head butted the pelt, right against the forehead of what should have been her mother.

That was the thing.

We loved her. To us, she was family. But she was still alone because of Bawbag.

Her next wee head butt was against Eilidh's wrist. Eilidh gently lowered the pelt to drape across her leg and scooped Sailean up to her chest. My partner was not the only one of us blinking back tears. I heard a shuddering breath to my left from Samuel just as Finn cleared his throat.

Then Sailean pawed at Eilidh to get free and jumped

down to come over to me with a mew I understood all too well. I picked her up and held her against my chest.

My job was just to listen.

Like Scout, Sailean could send me specifics. If not in full sentences, in images. In emotions. In sensations.

What she sent to me as she curled against my chest was as complex as any grown adult's desires, a knotted mess of hurt and hope and fear and relief. *Grateful-safe-home.* The last bit came with an emphatic rush, like Sailean had heard me say she was alone and wanted me to know she wasn't, that we *were* her real family, different species or not.

It hurt her, to think of the pelt going with us wherever we went. She understood why; contrary to what humans had thought for ages, animals understood death.

They understood mourning.

And...oh.

Oh.

"She's asking us to use what remains of her mother for the throne so Scotland—" I broke off, my throat suddenly rough. Clearing my throat, I blinked a few times. Damn it. "Sailean wants us, all of us two-legged folk, to remember that she is part of our family and so was her mother."

That was me done for. No amount of blinking would disguise the salt water dripping down my face, but I wasn't about to ruin the moment by being precious about it. This little kitten understood something my mother, my own mother, had instilled in me from childhood.

"Of course, child," Samuel said.

At first, I thought he was talking to me, but then I saw him looking at Sailean.

"Of course, my child," he said to her. "That has always been the point, a point we struggle to remember. There is no separation except that of our own making."

Something in my chest loosened—or perhaps not my chest. Perhaps it was in Sailean's. For a moment, I felt suspended between dualities of my connection with her, of the certainty that the hole of grief with its rigid edges that bleed tension into the entirety of our being felt the same in my chest as it did in hers.

"Tha sinn fada, fada nad chomain," I murmured to her, knowing that to Sailean, it was not our indebtedness to her at all, but hers to us she felt.

We sat in silence for a long while, listening only to the waves upon the sand as the clouds rolled over us. I still held Sailean against my chest, where her exhausted purr faded as she slept, worn out from the efforts of communicating such big feelings as a small kitten.

I was not a small kitten myself, but I found her need to nap highly relatable nonetheless.

After a time, Rhona stood without a word and walked to the water's edge. Into the water a few steps, even, where she bent over briefly and then turned and came back to us.

In her hand was a clear bottle of seawater.

"The loch should be Loch Ba in Mull," Finn said softly. "It's where the Cailleach herself was said to bathe, for renewal."

No one was about to disagree with that, and the ghost of a smile about Ealasaid's lips made me suspect she had done just that.

"I'll collect the rain," Eilidh murmured. "Above the dam, at Cruachan."

"What is that last bit?" Rhona asked. "'Guth iomadh-fhillte, aon òran air a ghabhail'? I understand the words, but I'm not sure what it means. A many-layered voice, one song sung?"

"Ò, a ghràidh," Ealasaid said to her. "Na gabh dragh

mun a sin. 'S ann san Òban a tha sinn—tha còisir Ghàidhlig fhathast a' seinn ann."

Oh, love. Don't you worry about that. We're in Oban, and a Gaelic choir sings here still.

The Mull Bàrd's own lips curled in a smile at our elder's words. "I know just the song."

E ilidh left early the next morning, slipping out of bed whilst I was still trying to accept the need to wake up at all.

"Càit' eil thu dol?" I asked her groggily. I hoped hadn't forgotten I was supposed to be somewhere and she wasn't about to answer with *a meeting with the Island Council* or anything I needed to appear alive for.

"Suas Beinn Chruachain," she said in answer. "Leam fhèin."

That woke me up. I pushed myself to sit up. "You're going up Ben Cruachan alone? Are you sure?" That didn't sound right out loud. "I mean, are you sure you want to go alone. I believe you."

I wasn't sure that was any better.

Eilidh chuckled, coming to sit on the edge of the bed facing me. "You're adorable first thing in the morning before the gears get going in there."

"I'm not made for mornings," I protested. I tried in vain to stifle the head-splitting yawn that wanted to punctuate my plaintive declaration, but it won. They always do.

"To answer your question, yes, I'm sure. I need to do this." Eilidh's smile faded to a pensive half frown. "And I need to do it alone."

She sighed, sending a gust of minty toothpaste breath wafting into my face. Jeezo, she'd managed to make it all the way to the bathroom already. My half-asleep brain had thought she'd only just gotten up.

I waited for her to go on.

"I can't let that pelt be the only thing I contribute," she said after a moment, her voice so quiet it was almost inaudible. "Sailean yesterday—she broke my heart."

"Mine too," I said. "But you know your real contribution, right?"

Eilidh looked at me blankly.

"It's not the macabre gift of a pelt from a skinned family member at all. It's the gift of rescuing our little family before we were even family at all. It's the gift of deciding to be family. Sailean—she understands, Eilidh. She knows just as well as I do that you stole that pelt so it wouldn't be further desecrated. Instead, because of your quick thinking and your empathy, Sailean's mother will be interred forever in something mythical." I paused long enough to scoot close to Eilidh and take her face in my hands, my own morning breath be damned. "She will always be part of us, part of what we've created here. Can you imagine, if she could see the wonders of this new world? Scout and our horse friends and the deer, the starlings and wrens, the wolves. The community here, all of it."

"Thighearna, a Chaluim, bidh mi a' rànail. A-rithist."

Eilidh was right; she was about to cry again. I pulled her close and kissed her. "Thalla suas a' bheinn. Gun toir an t-uisge dhut an glanadh a tha thu ag iarraidh."

She kissed me back and got up, heading for the door. Eilidh paused at the threshold and turned. "Thank you."

"Gaol ort," I replied.

Then she was gone.

I flopped back in bed, certain of at least one thing: she wouldn't feel right until she'd done what she said. The rain *would* feel like a baptism of sorts, a cleansing, and knowing Eilidh, the physical effort it would take to go up the mountain would be in itself a ritual.

She'd be gone at least a day, and as much as I would have rather stayed right where she left me, I gave myself only five more minutes before hauling my sleepy arse out of bed.

We'd both been putting it off since we got back, but I needed to go see Alison.

Even though I was prepared for the compound at Loch a' Phearsain, when I got there, I still hesitated.

Meeksy was nowhere to be seen, which wasn't too much of a surprise if he was in with Alison. The little sign placard that flipped from red to amber to green depending on the state of the warding was flipped to green.

A new building had sprung up, finished just in time for new inhabitants. I truly did not want to know what would happen if we ran out of space. The creeping dread of that seeming inevitability was not a welcome visitor to the inside of my mind.

I wished Sailean was with me, but the cheeky wee bugger had apparently gone with Eilidh. It must have been a surprise to Eilidh as well, since she would have told me if she'd taken the wildcat.

With a little luck, the journey would prove healing for both of them, individually and together.

When someone opened the door of the newer building and turned to look at me, I had to smother a sigh. George. Because of course it was George. I truly hoped his appearance was not an omen about whatever luck I was about to experience for the day.

"Hiya," I said to him carefully. "Who all's here today?"

That felt like a safe enough question to ask. He shrugged and pointed at the door he'd just closed behind him. "Brandon's in there, Farid is in with Alison and the brownie, Magda's in one of the other outbuildings with Jason, and I'm...talking to you."

"Brill, thanks," I said, meaning it. "I'm stalling going to see Alison."

George paused as he walked towards me and grimaced in what I thought was perhaps the first expression of actual empathy I'd seen from him. "She's rough, mate. I don't think there's any preparing yourself for it, but it's only going to get worse."

And that was pure wisdom. I wished George hadn't made me so wary of him by being kill happy with the brownie, because for all his anger, he wasn't clueless.

"You're right," I said after a beat. George scuffed his foot against the gravel track. "I need to just rip the plaster off."

Terrible analogy, considering the situation. The ultimate understatement. Might as well say *I need to rip the leg off*—it'd be closer to reality.

"I'll be down at the pier tonight if you need to get a drink to shake it off," George said, surprising me for the third time in as many minutes. "Wouldn't blame you."

"Thanks." I exhaled in a slow release of air. "I may take you up on that."

His expression made me think of the meme of *Press X to Doubt*. Even so, he gave me an awkward salute and headed past me down the hill the way I'd come.

It made me feel a bit better knowing there were people here I trusted.

Magda and Jason were new faces to me, but Farid was Meeksy's given name. Weird to hear when I was used to his nickname, but I'd always thought it was a nice name. And Brandon, of course. Maybe his steadiness was wearing off on George.

I stood around procrastinating for another few minutes until a light drizzle started. Squinting up at the clouds, I glanced to the east, where Eilidh would likely be at least at Falls of Cruachan by now, probably closer to the dam itself. She'd most definitely get her rain.

A few deep breaths did little to calm my nerves. I'd seen Alison before, but this felt different.

I appreciated George's honesty, blunt or not. I needed to just go. Just walk through the door.

Somehow, I forced my feet to start moving.

George was right.

The stench hit me first when I opened the door at Meeksy's assent, and even though I'd been expecting a smell, I had not been prepared for the intensity.

If I thought the anomalies were bad in the wild, with fresh air and wind, it was *nothing* compared to being in an enclosed space.

Even with ventilation, even with windows and air circulation drawing in fresh air and filtering the internal air through Purifire meshes and the ascension version of the highest-class HEPA, the odour hit me with enough pure, raw stink that my eyes immediately started to water.

I felt a pull on the ambient spirit and braced myself, only to realise it was Meeksy.

"Did you forget I told you to make yourself a bubble before coming in, pal? You're lucky you didn't pass out." He encompassed me in an oblong ball of Purifire, which took the edge off the stench enough for me to breathe, at least. "Too much on your mind."

"You can say that again," I croaked.

Talking was a bad idea; it let the residual smell into my mouth. I gagged.

"Good to see you too, Calum," said a distorted voice barely recognisable.

Oh, fucking hell.

I owed it to her to turn and face her.

I did it slowly, weaving my own web of Purifire and Spèird to filter the air faster in my bubble.

That...was not Alison.

No horror film could have prepared me for the way my brain tried to break.

Cognitive dissonance fell far short, too mild a phrase to describe the creeping sense of wrong. While the shape was recognisable still—that was Alison's straight brown hair, her height, her stature, her cheekbones—it was nowt but a rotting skin suit stretched over a cosmic terror.

Looking at her felt like a million spiders crawling on my skin from the inside out, like my own body had been stuffed with them until nothing remained but legs, legs on every inch of me feeling and prying and pressing for a way to escape. Like someone could draw a razor blade across my flesh and they would pour out, legions of them, replaced from within the moment any left me behind. Inescapable. Permanent.

And that was just the pure fear.

Physically, practically, Alison's skin had sloughed away in patches, baring raw meat that had darkened with black mould.

In the earlier stages of her corruption, I had observed how the anomaly, like the swaying fronds of an anemone turned to desperate fingers, grasped in increasing hunger for anything that ventured near. It latched onto to spirit, to energy, long before it took root in the physical.

Meeksy spoke, jolting me out of my nightmare fuel just enough. "It's best to ignore her, if you can."

His words were meant for my ears alone; he'd grown proficient at shielding them from her hearing.

Because that was *not* Alison driving her meat suit.

It was the enemy.

The enemy knew my name.

She—it—still knew he had spoken. Her rotting lips quirked ironically, like she thought our attempt to conceal his words to be cute.

Part of me wanted to walk right back out that door. I'd done what I came here to do. I'd seen her. Due diligence, tick.

What stopped me was one thing: the knowledge that while Alison wasn't in control, she was still in there. Somewhere. Deep. Buried under everything.

The air in my bubble had cleared enough that I could think again. I reached out and clasped Meeksy's shoulder.

He returned to his post on the other side of the room.

The brownie—the ùruisg—was on the opposite end in their own enclosure. I'd been so distressed over Alison that

I'd missed seeing the ùruisg entirely, and now, they gave me another shock.

I could still tell at a glance that the creature was corrupted; the anomaly was impossible to miss.

But where our people, human and new elves alike, deteriorated physically, the ùruisg remained remarkably hale.

I shot a look at Meeksy, who shrugged. "I've been trying to work it out this whole time. I can't explain why the anomaly hasn't taken hold as deeply with the ùruisg. It's still there, crouching inside like a landmine waiting to be stepped on, but it's stalled somehow."

That was a question we'd need to answer. Maybe it was that brownies were folkloric—but so were elves. While Kev and Aidan still looked human, Alison had been with us through the community ascension. Her body had changed, growing lither, taller, her ears lengthening to points. The science-minded types we had in the community had spoken definitively; we were no longer Homo sapiens sapiens but something else.

Slowly, I settled myself on the floor, crossing my legs and closing my eyes.

Maintaining my bubble whilst meditating would be a new challenge, but it needed to be done. I couldn't predict whether or not I would learn something here, but I had to try.

I steadied my breathing, my spirit. Connection, once more, became my lifeline and my gateway into the state of flow.

It was time to get to work.

❖

When I emerged from Alison's containment room hours later, the first breath of clean air almost bowled me over.

My sinuses felt raw, raw enough that I cast Slàinte, my healing spell, to see if it would help me recover.

I walked a short distance away from the building, needing to put metres between myself and Alison. Even now, I could feel the grasping tendrils of the corruption seeking, seeking, seeking any opening to take hold of me. It hadn't found any; if there was anything I'd learned in there, it was that the corruption needed contact. There might have been some odd fringe cases, an outlier here or there where it seized an opportunistic opening, but for the most part, it needed contact.

There was a pole dug into the ground closer to Loch a' Phearsain, and I aimed my shaky legs at that. When I reached it, I turned to press my back up against the wood and lowered myself into a chair sit, mostly so I could brace my elbows on my knees and stretch my back. Hours of sitting on a hard concrete floor hadn't done my body any favours, ascension healing or no.

Naturally, that was the moment my rockie-talkie came to life.

"Calum!" The voice on the other end was not Rhona this time, but older and male.

"Angus?"

"Aye, we need you at the harbour as fast as you can get here. There's—just get here."

Bloody hell.

That did not sound good. At least there was an ionad-siubhail just down the path from where I stood. I wasted no time. My legs still protested the movement, but step by step, they came back to some semblance of functionality.

The ionad-siubhail had been a triumph not so long ago,

one we'd all taken to with alacrity, but this one was a matter of necessity more than convenience. We needed to be able to get people here in seconds and not an hour, just in case any of the anomalies broke containment.

My mind was still on the anomalies when I stepped through the portal into the big Tesco carpark where we'd established the first of our fast-travel points, I was expecting absolutely anything *but* the sight of ten-foot-tall aliens staring at me.

CHAPTER
ELEVEN

B *reathe, Calum.*

Three of them. No weapons, so I didn't reach for mine, but Brac-Meanmna on my back felt wary and primed for danger.

The beings were truly around ten feet tall, but where they might have seemed stretched out in Earth's cinematic imagination, their proportions were much more similar to our own. These were no gangly streamers of aliens. Bipedal, also with two arms and opposable thumbs. I tried not to do a double take when I realised they each had *two* opposable thumbs on each hand. Their skin was indeed blue, but it had the look of having been painted on.

Like woad. Like the blue the ancient Picts had supposedly used when they went to do battle.

That comparison increased my wariness.

Despite the comparison reports had sparked of a certain James Cameron film, they looked nothing like the beings of his fantasy world. I could natter on all day with an evolutionary biologist about why humanoids had evolved on two completely separate planets or why, bizarrely, even on

Earth, evolution kept trying to churn out exciting new crabs.

But these beings did look like us. Their eyes were slightly bigger, their noses a little flatter. Their ears formed three small points, which struck me as odd until I looked closer and realised they'd been docked like a bloody Doberman's. Full lips. High cheekbones. Long, elegant necks just this side of looking disproportionate to my eyes. Their eyes were deep blue, almost indigo, with round pupils that shifted visibly even from my vantage point.

They wore clothes, not armour, which helped put me a tiny bit at ease after the woad thought. Their clothing was simple, with high-waisted loose trousers in the style we called harem on earth. They ballooned out for easy movement from the knees up and gathered at the calves, tucked into leather boots tooled with script that looked to my eyes like something Tolkien would have devised. Two of the beings had silver hair coiled into intricate plaits secured to their heads, and the third wore theirs loose except for a wide, pale-metal headband etched with the same script.

Angus stood with them, a short distance away. He looked up at them like they might spontaneously turn into pumpkins, and the crowd gathering in the crafting centre closer to the harbour told me news must already have been spreading of their presence.

One of the strange beings, the one with their hair worn loose, approached me holding a stone in their hand. A Clach-Cànain, a language stone.

With only minor hesitation, I reached out and took it when they offered it.

It only took a small rivulet of channelled spirit for the stone's knowledge to wash over me, and the beings before me barely gave it time to work before one of them spoke in a melodic, fluid language that gave me the strangest impression of Welsh, if the Welsh somehow layered their spoken language with polyphonic overtone singing.

"You are the one they call Calum Green," the being who had handed me the stone said, holding out a long-fingered blue hand to take the stone back.

"That's me," I said, my tongue finding the right position to speak their words. *Sui alleiwyth,* as I might write the words. "Who are you? Where have you come from?"

Toh iasia? Cam atosia?

There was a long pause as the beings exchanged glances. I couldn't read their body language; for all I knew, they could also communicate telepathically.

My larynx was not physically capable of producing the polyphonic sounds theirs could—I suspected they had an extra larynx or super-secret additional vocal folds in there that we didn't—but the stone had installed knowledge of a language of hand signs, something that in their world was used much like sign language in ours. Where someone could not vocalise fully or hear the vocalisations, the hand signs could either supplement usual speech or replace it. When I answered them, my right hand swept up my chest and floated outwards and downwards like I was presenting myself. Which I suppose I was.

I wanted to use Keen Eye on them as the silence drew out, but I was not confident they wouldn't know. On top of that, it might be seen as invasive—never mind the fact that they were technically the invaders.

But before I could decide to do anything at all, the three aliens turned and started walking away. No answer, no farewell, only a deliberate and decisive departure.

"Wait," I said. "Where are you going?" *Atisia. Oua thosia?*

One of the beings stopped, but the other two did not. The one who stopped had hair in plaits, and their countenance as they looked down on me gave no expression or hint at their thoughts.

"We were told you were the great power here, but you are inconsequential. We go to seek the truth of who deserves this ascension."

With that, all three of them broke into a run, their size belying the lightning speed and agility as they moved, gone before any of us could react.

I turned back to Angus, who, from his expression, had also used the language stone and had understood what the being had said to me.

"That...cannot be good," I said.

Angus was one of the first comrades I'd met in Oban, back when he had let me and Rhona and Eilidh sleep at his house when we'd evacuated the primary school at Kilninver where we'd met Ronald and Alison. Now, more or less the head of operations for our Argyll community, Angus had even less time for bullshit or dissembling.

"Aye, lad," he said to me. "If they're looking to take themselves to our leaders, it makes me wonder who they'll find."

The crowd over in the crafting area had started to filter our way now that the aliens had gone, and they were going to want explanations I didn't have.

No matter what the aliens were looking for, I knew one thing. The anomaly was the strongest power in these islands.

Perhaps I ought to have taken it as a good thing. If the aliens and the anomaly wiped each other out, that would solve our problems handily.

But somehow, I could not see that happening.

We go to seek the truth of who deserves this ascension.

Suddenly, I wanted to hit something with a sword. And my new swords instructor was up a hill chasing the rain.

Eilidh might have been out of reach, but there *was* a sparring arena we'd built near the old CalMac pier, and that was as good a place as any to burn off steam.

In the few days I'd been gone, the crafters had already upgraded the punching bags and sparring dummies. For a time, I just pummelled the nearest bag, over and over again. No forms, just a rolling litany of jabs, crosses, and hooks until every muscle from my obliques to my traps felt ready to sizzle.

From there, I did press-ups. Pull-ups. Yoga balances and stabiliser strengthening.

What had that alien meant when they said they'd heard I was "the power" here? The obvious answer was the pantheon aspect, but surely then they would have mentioned the others as well. Getting labelled as inconsequential would have stung more if I hadn't thought it might have just saved all our hides.

I wasn't sure what these strange people wanted from us, but I did not think they were hunting all over the highlands of Scotland to find a recipient for a congratulatory fruit basket.

The sun was still high in the sky when Iain found me—this close to the solstice, the sun wouldn't set until after nine at night—and he took one look at my lathered form and sighed.

"I heard we had visitors. Meeksy's gonnae shit a brick when he hears he missed the aliens."

"He didn't miss much," I told him, wiping my face with the towel I'd stashed in inventory. "They literally didn't even tell us their names. Took one look at me, turned up their noses, and buggered off again."

"Well, who could blame them?"

"They'd have bailed faster if they'd seen you first," I told him, blowing him a kiss.

In spite of the lighthearted banter, a heavy silence fell.

After a moment, Iain motioned at the punching bag. "You think they're going to challenge you to a boxing match or something?"

"No. I just needed to hit something." I breathed out hard through my nose and shook my head. "We need to be stronger than this. I don't waiting."

"Yous are working on that throne hingmy, yeah?" Iain asked. "That's something."

"We *think* it's something," I corrected him. "Who knows? It might just end up being a fancy chair."

"I doubt that, and you do too." Iain paused. "If nothing else, the communications beacon ought to help, and we've got everyone working double time to expand our own little network here. Of course, we won't know what the communication beacon even needs until we get the throne crafted, but that's not far off, is it? Mum said Eilidh's hunting raindrops in the hills and Ealasaid is badgering the local Gaelic choir director for an apocalypse mòd."

That made me snort. Now that would be a mòd overhaul that would stun even the most radical folks at An Comunn Gàidhealach, conveners of the Royal National Mòd. Not that they'd ever suggested our Gaelic music annual gathering go any farther than a barbershop quartet and some scat singing. Maybe a beatboxing septuagenarian.

On second thought, maybe I should be talking to Finn to make sure Ealasaid isn't planning any hì-rì hoireann-ò pastiche for the momentous occasion of our ascension to possible deification. I doubt Finn would let her, and he did say he had a song in mind, but with Ealasaid, I never really knew. Mischief of the Morrigan in that one, hide it though she might.

"Calum, did the aliens break you?"

I shook myself. "No, they didn't, but Alison might have," I told him, belatedly realising I'd zoned out. "Throne is happening, beacon after that, but I can't do anything about either of those things right this second, and if I don't have something productive to progress with, I am going to scream."

"Screaming can be very therapeutic."

"So can hitting things."

"Then hit me." Iain flashed me a rakish grin, loosening his shoulders. He'd been a martial arts instructor for years, so he wasn't being a smart-arse. "I've always thought you could stand to be better with hand to hand."

Some little snarky voice rebelled for a moment, probably out of sheer contrariness, but Iain had a solid point, and anything—*anything at all*—would be better than flitting from unfixable problem to unfixable problem while we waited for throne ingredients.

"Mon, then," I said to Iain. "Teach me to fight like the big kids."

❖

Three hours later, the sun was setting at last, and I was bruised from head to toe as I hurried through the door of the Whyte house and up the stairs. Eilidh wasn't back yet, which meant I had time for a shower and perusal of notifications.

And healing. Gods, healing. Even using Slàinte hadn't fully dulled the ache.

In fact, I was vaguely certain the past hours of physical punishment had gone back in time and given me a hiding I'd felt all the way back in primary school.

I took a thorough shower, scrubbing myself from head to toe to rid myself of sweat and grime from alternately pummelling and getting pummelled. Mostly the latter, considering Iain was a fourth dan black belt, and I was Patrick from *Sponge Bob* with a board nailed to my head.

Well. Maybe by this stage I had graduated not hitting my thumb with a hammer.

Even so, I couldn't help the feeling of satisfaction and triumph when I dropped my now-clean body onto the bed and saw the notifications.

Finally. Numbers going up.

Through physical exertion, you have gained a permanent +3 to Strength, +2 to Constitution, and +5 to Stamina. Please note that such increases have diminishing returns as your base statistics grow.

Through physical training, you have unlocked the skill tree: Hand to Hand.

Through physical training, you have learned the skill: One-Two Punch.

· · ·

Through physical training, you have learned the skill: Guard.

It may not have been in my usual wheelhouse, but the notifications filled me with excitement.

Not only had I improved my base attributes with effort, which I had known from the beginning was possible, but I had also unlocked skills without skill points.

That was the real kicker here, a concrete example of what seemed to be a repeatable experiment.

On top of that, it seemed our quest had updated.

And not just updated—it had completed.

Quest complete: Blood From a Stone

The destruction of the anomalous lynx provided you with further information about how the anomalies are changing alongside the ascended world. Alison's corruption, along with the ùruisg and the brothers Kevin and Aidan Murray, has shown you important information about the progression of such anomalies and its effects on different life forms of similar sapience. You have also observed firsthand that plants can fall victim to this corruption, but that it spreads much more slowly in fungi.

Some advanced anomalies seem to have developed the ability to utilise spirit-driven spells and skills, as have the usual shifts in indigenous flora and fauna. As the corruption advances in those you hold in isolation, be mindful of this possibility.

Your ally and friend the glaistig has confirmed also that the originating entity of the corruption is aware of you and your community—and has warned you about the danger.

That danger has now been further realised in the knowledge that another variable has been introduced to your ascending world with the arrival of the Atheani.

. . .

I paused there. The Atheani.

That must have been the name of the beings who had appeared here.

Will Grayson and Ezekiel Bosworth III discovered that the corruption is not immediate, nor is it total, but much more study is needed before there will be any chance of deliberately and unilaterally mitigating its effects, let alone finding a cure.

This has become an evolving quest.

Objectives:

-Create Purification Cages to house any captured anomalies (Complete)

-Capture three different species of anomalous animals (Complete)

-Explore further uses for Purifire (Complete)

-Examine the remains of the conduit anomaly (Ronald) (Complete)

-Contain the corrupted person (Complete)

-Assess the effects of corruption on Alison (Complete)

-Seek out other examples of corruption in sapients (Complete)

Rewards:

-Experience (commensurate with current level progression)

-1 skill point

-1 item (ascension dependent)

-Blood From a Stone: Part II

My vision pulsed with more gold as the experience from quest completion hit.

And there it was, the notification I'd been waiting for and dreading.

You have reached Level 27! You have two attribute points and four skill points to distribute. You may now access: class specialisation or reallocation!

CHAPTER
TWELVE

L evel twenty-seven.

This was the level for advanced specialisation. Whether we could further specialise after this, I didn't know. I wasn't the first person in Oban to hit level twenty-seven, but I was the first among our coalescing pantheon that I was aware of. I had gone through specialisation at level nine, but this felt different. More momentous. Level nine had made me a druid, draoidh, rooted me in wild magic and the rhythms of the earth and stars.

What would level twenty-seven bring?

I needed to find out.

At Level 27, you may choose to continue within your existing class, to choose an entirely new class, or to specialise within your current class.

-Keep existing class: This option will unlock the Àrd-Draoidh skill tree and the Draoidh affinity, and while you will have a further chance to access these paths at Level 81, they are exclusive to those with the Draoidh class.

-Find new class: You will retain access to all existing affinities and skill trees, but depending on your inclinations, this option could require a significant amount of work to be effective. You should only choose this class if you truly feel your current class is a poor fit.

-Specialise (Recommended): You will receive three specialisation options, each with its own skill tree and affinity. These are tailored to your personal experience and choices.

Would you like to keep existing class, find new class, or specialise? Until you have selected and confirmed a new class, if you choose the latter two, you may still return to this choice. Choosing to keep your existing class at this stage is final.

I truly did not know what to do with that.

When I'd hit level nine, it had felt right to explore the specialisations without a thought, but now, some little voice at the back of my mind teamed up with my gut instinct to whisper that now wasn't the right moment to make this choice.

If level twenty-seven had felt like a long way off at level nine, level eighty-one? Well. Literally exponentially more so. How far the levels went, I had no idea, but if it followed that pattern of cubes, the next would be level two hundred forty-three.

No, this was something that would require more thought. Deliberation. I did not think it was a choice to be completed lightly.

That said, I could explore options before picking any of them. I might have to battle with my impulsivity, but I was pretty sure I was resolved enough not to accept the first shiny thing that came along.

The first thing to do was to explore the set options. I knew damn well that going into the "find a new class" screens would come with an entire barge of overwhelm. Like the *Ever Given* in the Suez Canal, that level of barge overwhelm.

Which left the specialisation options.

Your class specialisation options are as follows:

Dìleab an Daghdha—For those who have chosen to walk in the footsteps of the draoidhean of old, this class elevates the draoidh to the role of acolyte under the Dagda, an Daghdha, the father-god of the Tuath Dè Danann.

Just as an Daghdha led in the image of divine masculinity, so would you follow his legacy, lending your strength to the fertility of folk and fields, spiritual guidance, wisdom, and magic.

Dìleab an Daghdha is a class that seeks the support of all for the benefit of all. In combat, their skills guide the flow of the battle outwith the primary struggle where they are able to observe and funnel allies to victory and foes to defeat. As Dìleab an Daghdha, you will unlock the Dìleab an Daghdha skill tree and gain a permanent +10 to Spirit and +5 to Will.

There was little more lofty than a class that, on the surface, looked right up my street. But I had no intentions of staying out of a fight and giving orders from afar. Nor was I particularly excited at the idea of giving spiritual guidance to... whom, exactly? Pilgrims? If I and my friends were indeed on the cusp of ascending to anything resembling a pantheon, the last thing I wanted was a cult to call my very own. No, thank you.

That wasn't an inevitable given if I were to choose this class, but it felt more detached than I wanted to explore. Connection may have been the bottom of the skill tree for mages, but there was a reason it was the skill I relied on most. I wasn't a puppeteer.

Just that thought soured me the rest of the way on the Dìleab an Daghdha class. It was nothing like Lord Bawbag and his attempts to literally puppet people, but I did not want the responsibility of being the one in charge of everyone else, and this felt like it was leading to that. Maybe that's why the Atheani had said I was inconsequential; I had few ambitions to take over the world. And if I was honest, I didn't feel keen to dedicate myself to a god of the past, even if it was my people's Zeus—with less reputation for sexual violence.

Walking contradiction, that was me.

While I could see the logic in the progression, I already knew that option wasn't for me. The bonuses to the manipulation stats felt lofty, a heady temptation if the rest of the class hadn't felt like an ill-fitting shoe to read about. Maybe someone else would find it alluring. There were one or two others among the Òbanaich who shared my class of draoidh.

I moved on to the next one.

Wilder—For mages who have unlocked the specialised Wild affinity, this class offers a chance to harness chaos...or to revel in it. Wilder mages are those who follow their primal instincts in their Manipulation abilities, leaning on Pathos and Will and raw power to achieve the effects they desire.

Not for the faint of heart, the Wilder class demands the mage surrender to patterns they may not be able to predict. Its abilities are some of the most powerful for an ascending mage, but it is a class that prioritises instinct over order, intuition over planning.

In combat, the benefits of having a Wilder on your side are legion; the impact of surprise in the heat of battle cannot be overstated. Wilders are sometimes looked down upon by more stringent disciplines for seemingly lacking structure, but the actual class is full of nuance and the need for deep roots of control in order to utilise its boons. If you choose the Wilder class specialisation, you will unlock the Wilder skill tree and gain a permanent +7 to Will and +7 to Pathos.

That sounded more like a class that was up my street, but part of what had drawn me to the draoidh class was that it was rooted in my culture. I felt a bit like Goldilocks pooh-poohing two solid options because they didn't combine the traits I wanted most. With some luck, maybe the third option would do just that, amalgamate the instinctual wild magic with something that felt personally connected to dualchas, to my people and our history and lore.

Not without some trepidation, I pulled up the third specialisation option.

Làmh Lùgha—Perhaps contrary to first assumption, the Làmh Lùgha class does not refer to acting as the ancient god Lùgh's hand in the world. Rather, as a Làmh Lùgha, you channel the attributes of Lùgh himself.

Lùgh was, in Irish folklore, the epitome of the oft-misquoted adage "A jack of all trades, master of none, but oftentimes better than a master of one". When Lùgh arrived in Tara to join the Tuath Dè Danann, he had to present himself as having a skill that would be useful to the king, but each skill offered had already found representation in the king's service. It was not until Lùgh cannily enquired whether any of the king's devoted can lay claim to all skills at once that he gained entry, earning renown for his abilities as a smith, a master crafter, a hero, a tradition bearer or seanchaidh, a mage, a harpist, a poet.

Within the Làmh Lùgha class, you gain a permanent +10 increase to Spirit, but in lieu of gains to Will and Pathos, you will unlock the following skill trees with an additional three skill points per tree: Bàrdachd (the art and power of verse), Master-work Crafting, and Ceartas (Justice).

I had to admit, I was stumped. Goldilocks or not, the Làmh Lùgha class did appeal to me on several levels, but I couldn't help thinking it was much better suited to Finn. To my memory, Lùgh was said to have been so beautiful that he outshone the sun, that rivals could scarce stand to look upon his face. If that didn't describe our resident golden boy of Mull, I wasn't sure who it would. That class seemed perfectly suited to Finn, who was equally adept at song and story and skirmishing.

Deflated, I exited out of the screens. I couldn't bring myself to face digging through the overwhelming notion of narrowing down a new class from all other possibilities. I supposed it was at least good that I hadn't gotten so tempted that I made a rash decision.

The only problem was that I would eventually have to make one, and the future of my community might hang on my choices.

I had no intention of throwing skill points at the wall

when I would have a new class and skill tree—or three—to explore imminently, but I did want to at least allot my attributes and give them a once over. Maybe it would shake something loose.

A number of my other stats had increased through the gruelling nature of my daily life, and I decided to put my two attribute points into Constitution to bring it to a round fifty.

That meant I had no attributes under fifty now. If I looked back to the first day of the ascension, when an attribute at ten was considered average, it painted a stark picture of my relative strength. Even if it didn't feel like I was making any leaps forwards, I had absolutely made progress.

It was progress. And there would be more.

Name: Calum Green

    Age: 36

    Level: 27

    Class: Draoidh (Class specialisation available) (Further class specialisation at: Level 81)

    Affinities: Nature (Level 21), Healing (Level 8), Synthesis (Level 14), Staves (Level 20)

    Specialised Affinities: Wild (Level 17), Coimhearsnachd (Level 8), Justice (Level 2), Pantheon (available with activation of the Resplendent Throne)

    Marks of Esteem: Life, Connection, Justice, Passage

Alteration:

    Strength: 50

    Dexterity: 57

Agility: 68
Mind: 141

Regeneration:
  Constitution: 50
  Stamina: 90

Manipulation:
  Spirit: 133
  Pathos: 53
  Will: 55

Boons:
  Blessings
  Làmh na Glaistige
  Glòir a' Ghiuthais
  Blàr Ghaineamhain

The quest's completion had also given me an item, and this time, it gave me an unexpected choice between two.

One was a manual on hand-to-hand combat, which had almost certainly been triggered by my little sparring session with Iain. The second seemed a bit more esoteric and far more applicable: *Ascension Epidemiology and Arcane Contagions.*

That was a no-brainer. I could learn hand to hand from Iain the old-fashioned way. We had a fleet of mages in Oban trying to reinvent the wheel on the latter, and maybe this book would save them some trouble rounding out the edges on a square.

Before accepting it and the inevitable wrecking ball to the brain it would cause to absorb its information, I gingerly pulled up the final notification, the one I was afraid would make today's physical beatings feel like a pillow fight with a corgi.

New quest: Blood From a Stone: Part II

With the information you have gained about the anomaly and its varying effects on flora, fauna, and fungi, you have begun to form the foundation for further research.

Containing the spread is imperative; communications with other communities will prove vital to the efforts of preventing epidemic spread.

Objectives:

-Establish a stable network of communications

-Craft and activate a communication beacon

-Investigate the corruption's effects on other life forms: plants, fungi, lichen. (Tip: These life forms do not die immediately when cut off from their roots. It is possible to experiment without risking corruption spreading through established root systems and mycelium.)

Rewards:

-Experience (commensurate with current level progression)

-1 skill point

-1 item (ascension dependent)

-Other possible rewards pending outcome of quest completion

. . .

That last line was a first. And more than that, the last objective was far more informative than any previous quest objective I'd seen since the ascension began. Not that there had been heaps; quests seemed to be limited to issues of dire importance that had the potential to affect a large number of lives. This particular quest most certainly fit that bill. If we couldn't stop this thing, we'd be looking at the second extinction-level event in one year.

There. A cheery thought to capstone my conundrum of how to further specialise.

Peachy.

CHAPTER
THIRTEEN

Eilidh still hadn't returned when I woke the next morning, but a note Rhona had slapped on my door with sellotape told me she'd checked in via rockie-talkie when I was out cold.

I may have been running through the Highlands for weeks on end, but there was something decidedly different about having Iain kick my arse up one side and down the other of the sparring arena for the better part of a day. Or maybe absorbing *Ascension Epidemiology and Arcane Contagions* had just come in for the KO and I'd confused it with a pleasant night's sleep.

Either way, I couldn't afford to lie around in bed.

With the information from that book percolating like my morning coffee, I got myself outfitted quickly for the day. Catrìona was already out on the fishing boat, as usual, and I figured Meeksy was back out at Kilmelford, but I saw neither hide nor hair of Iain.

According to the note, Rhona had gone to Mull to meet up with Ealasaid.

All of this left me to my own devices.

My body had healed as I slept. Feeling fresh as a dewdrop instead of like a pork chop tenderised within an inch of its life after all that pummelling yesterday came as close to a miracle as anything in the ascension. Part of me thought that I'd scoff more at the idea of avoiding lactic acid poisoning than being able to set things on fire with my mind, had I the ability to go back to pre-ascension Calum and deliver portents of his future.

I nibbled my way through a black sausage breakfast roll and a litre of coffee while I prioritised for the day.

Not unlike the pre-ascension cellular towers, our new communications network could be expanded to cover ground farther afield. We already had several reasons to get to work doing just that—the anomaly and the aliens—but now that the system itself had made it an objective of a quest, I had a feeling that was the closest thing we were going to get to a blaring *AWOOGA* that it needed to land on the top of our wee priority pyramid.

With Scout's help, I might even be able to make headway on that today before my repeat date with the local sadist I called a bestie.

The other major priority was obviously the anomaly research. With a little bit of multitasking, I reckoned I could enlist a bird to hit that target as well.

I finished my roll, the last bite of bread and black pudding sticking in my throat until I guzzled the remaining dregs of my coffee.

Right. Time to see an eagle about a field trip.

❖

What better place to give our eagle friends to nest than the highest point in Oban?

The crafters had been busy since the battle with the kraken, finding that the previous perches they'd created down by the harbour were unworthy of the intelligent beings who had, without a doubt, saved our sorry hides.

Now, McCaig's Tower had grown its own watchtowers with the eagles as their guards.

Each of the six eagles had their own stone platform, elegantly designed with both perches and nesting space—and could also deploy a spirit-based shield to protect them from the elements. The nesting space was bowl-like and self-cleaning, enchanted by our crafter mages, who were getting cannier by the day. Perches encircled the nests at two levels, all in sweeping curves of stone like Saturn's rings. It was from there the shield would expand from the loops of rock. And, of course, the rest of the tower's structure provided plenty of perching space when needed.

The eagles didn't use their shield feature much, but it wasn't because they weren't capable; they simply preferred the sensation of the winds blowing down the Sound of Mull from the Minch. I suspected they would find it more useful once mating season brought eggs into those nests. I could not *wait* to see the enormous muppet babies when that happened, but we might have to look into sound dampening for those who sought solitude and quiet under the branches of Craobh an Òbain, the mystical tree at the tower's heart.

Most of the eagles' alcoves stood empty except for enormous nests that could easily accommodate an elephant. Scout, however, sat on the lower level of her personal perch, preening her feathers with meticulous care.

Though I'd released Tàthadh's bond after the battle, such fondness and understanding remained between us that the moment I drew near, she let out a chipper call and fluffed up her feathers before giving them a flap or two as if to ask, *Shall I come down?*

I shook my head, instead motioning to the ladder installed nearest her perch and made my way there.

Most people didn't feel comfortable invading the eagles' privacy—they *were* enormous raptors capable of lifting entire thousand-pound seals—but a few starry-eyed folk had hung out enough that they'd earned invitations. One such person sat on the far side of the tower where one of the white-tailed sea eagles roosted, though he himself wasn't present. I gave him a nod as I reached the top of the ladder and caught a glimpse of him. He returned a belated wave.

Scout, with one strong flap of her wings, descended to the edge of the tower to meet me.

"I've got a proposal for you, a charaid," I said to her.

The golden eagle cocked her head as I explained, looking for all the world like an oversized dog for the expression of curiosity on her face. But where a dog might have only been pretending to know what was going on, Scout latched on to every word out of my mouth with an exuberant readiness to help.

Steps we could take together. I let out a breath as I finished running her through my plan for the day, already certain of her eagerness to join me. Despite knowing of her agreement, the confirmation chirp she gave me drew a grin onto my face.

"Knew I could count on you," I told her. "First stop is the crafting centre for supplies and an updated map of what we're working with. Then it's into the hills with us."

I waited for scout to turn around so I could fumble my way onto her back, but she cocked her head at me again, first one way and then the other, as if she were waiting for something.

After a moment or two of me standing in front of her awkwardly trying to suss out what she wanted, she leaned down and nudged me with the smooth curve of her beak.

Friend-bond-connect.

She wanted me to use Tàthadh.

It *would* make everything significantly easier throughout the day, to have our thoughts and feelings more accessible to one another. Especially if we found trouble, which, let's face it—I was wont to do every time I stuck my head outside of the house.

"As you wish," I told her with a flourishing bow.

I gathered spirit into the weave for the skill, and with it came a wistful bloom of excitement. Excitement to share this experience with her, wistfulness that it was something that had an end mark. Unlike my bond with Sailean, through the skill Caidreabhas, with Scout the bond was only temporary. I didn't yet have the capacity to form another permanent bond, and for the first time as I spun threads of spirit and cast Tàthadh to tie me to Scout again, that lack rankled.

It was difficult to stay down for long, though—not when a giant golden eagle could tell you to jump off a tower so she could catch you.

A moment's rush with my brief free fall turned to dual joy and elation as her powerful wings bore us upwards, high above Oban and out over the harbour where we'd fought the kraken.

The wind smelled of the sea, fresh after early morning rains had washed through the town, and the tide lapped against the harbour, just past its zenith and on its way back out.

Upturned faces watched us—familiar or not, the eagles were still cause for awe—and Scout circled the harbour once before coming to land in the Tesco carpark near the ionad-siubhail where someone missed a step on their way to use it, tripping over their own two feet at the sight of Scout swooping down from the sky.

I slid down from her back as soon as she touched down and wasted no time trotting over to the crafting centre. She'd wait there; I felt her settle in and go back to preening her feathers.

My eyes scanned the crafting centre, seeking the familiar shape of Angus, who liked to come down to craft early before it got busy. My first glances around returned no sign of him, but there were a few people I recognised about. One of them, curiously enough, was Finn.

He must have felt me coming, because he had his back to me when I noticed him and turned the moment I recognised him.

"Madainn mhath," he greeted me, then glanced over at Scout. "Big plans for the day?"

"You could say that." I took one more look around in case Angus had been sneakily crouching down behind a table—something he did sometimes when overwhelmed by people badgering him for things—and decided he'd either turn up or not. "Instead of hitting two birds with one stone, I'm going to see if this friendly bird can help me progress two objectives in a day."

I really wanted that metaphor to work, but despite trying again, it fell flat. Hmph.

Finn listened thoughtfully as I told him about the quest

update; he hadn't gotten the Blood From a Stone quest, but his eyes narrowed when I mentioned the pointed clue the system had given.

"I don't think it's as impartial as it seems at first glance," he murmured.

"What, the system?"

"Of course."

"You must have missed what it said about Bawbag," I told him wryly. "Impartial, it was not. Practically called him a wanker, painted a target on his head, and loosed the hounds."

"It does seem to have an agenda," Finn agreed. "I'm personally thankful its agenda seems to value life on this planet, even if to them we're a heap of bogey-mining cockroaches who don't know our arses from our elbows."

The image of a cockroach with a nose it *could* go plundering for bogeys lodged itself in my brain with unpleasant alacrity.

I shook it off. "Anyway, I don't suppose you could point me at what I need to enact today's plan?"

"You know, I can," Finn said with a winsome smile. "In fact, I'll do one better. I'll join you."

"What?"

"Don't worry; I don't expect tandem flying with Scout. Duan will be happy to take me." Finn motioned out over the harbour, where a large winged shape was soaring in over the green hillocks of Kerrera.

"Duan's one of the sea eagles?" I asked. I couldn't help but smile at the name—trust the Bàrd of Mull to name an eagle for an ode or a rhyme.

Finn nodded without looking at me, already moving to one of the covered pavilions where the crafting materials were stored. I followed after him, listening as he briefly gave me a rundown on what he'd been using to expand the communications network from Lochaline up to Kilchoan in Ardnamurchan. We'd had nowt but eerie silence from that remote bit of the mainland. Even the Muilich up in Tobermory, who could flash a light and be seen in both Drimnin *and* Kilchoan, had had no contact for the first weeks of the ascension.

It had turned out Ardnamurchan had been hit with an absolute plague of ascension mutated sea lice, of all bloody things, and they'd chased everyone on that side of the Sound of Mull inland for days. Why they'd hit only the Ardnamurchan side and not the Mull side was anyone's guess.

"It's thankfully simple enough," Finn said as he reached a large wardrobe and opened it. "The trick is dividing territory and each going in a line like spokes on a wheel so you always know you're in range of the last one without too much overlap. We wasted a lot of materials the first couple weeks while we were learning that lesson."

Inside the wardrobe was fitted with shelves of crystal towers, mostly quartz, though a few seemed to be tinged other colours. It looked a bit like a black market new age rock stash.

When I said so, Finn snorted. The beautiful bastard could manage to look dazzling even when being derisive.

"Since quartz is just silica, we've gotten most of this from the sand mine in Lochaline. There are a couple miners over there whose affinities are off the charts impressive when it comes to refining quartz. I'd say they're having a blast, but we don't make explosion jokes to miners." Finn winked at me and handed me what looked like a large bandolier to load up with crystal towers. "One of these each ought to do for the day. How far are you hoping to get?"

"How far is the network now?" I countered.

Finn made a noncommittal noise. "I take it you're wanting the mainland?"

"Aye."

"We'll have to go look. Island-wise, we've covered everything between Islay and the Uists, and Samuel plans to head to Skye today. It would be nice to make contact with Dunvegan and see how they're getting on. I'm a bit worried that there's not been word from them yet."

"Last I heard, we'd made it up to Fort William on the mainland, but not yet to Mallaig. Maybe once we get folk up there, someone will have news from Armadale in Skye." And just like that, the crushing weight of everything we couldn't just hand wave with magic came pressing down again. I cleared my throat. "Unfortunately, my goal today is to reach towards the Central Belt. Crianlarich has been sorted, but we'll have to see if they got any farther than that."

"Leaving Kintyre to hang, eh?" Finn gave me a rueful smile that said he understood that crushing weight all too well.

We were both quiet for a moment as we filled our strange holsters with magic rocks.

Once mine was full, I went on.

"For now, anyway. We'll have to trust that Kintyre is doing at least as well as Ardnamurchan was. It seems our indifferent Atheani acquaintances"—at Finn's blank stare, I hurriedly clarified—"the aliens aimed themselves back southeast. If they're heading for population centres, that could get messy."

To his credit, Finn didn't add an "assuming there's still population in those centres," though I know he must have been feeling that familiar fear as much as I.

One thing at a time.

I hefted the full bandolier of crystals. "Let's go find that map so we can divide and conquer."

FOURTEEN

As it turned out, it was an easy division of labour. No one had gotten any farther than Crianlarich, so Finn was to start there and work northeast towards Loch Tay and Aberfeldy, and I was going to make my way Lomond-ward.

One might say he was to take the high road and I was to take the low road.

Before too long, we were airborne. Scout and Duan may have been different species of eagle, but they seemed to get on swimmingly as they carried us over the hills Eilidh'd been hunting raindrops and then followed the glens, avoiding the roads we'd stuck to on our own journey. The advantage of travelling how the eagle flies as opposed to how the numpties trundle.

We stopped briefly in Crianlarich to update our sword-wielding gran Raonaid on the Murray boys' status. The eagles caused quite a stir when we landed—enough of a stir that I had to Purifire an arrow and Spèird-yeet a bolt of spirit a pair of alarmed villagers aimed at Scout. When we yelled down at them to back off, their yelps of shock and chagrin quickly devolved into bickering as the couple, who *had* to be long married, turned to accuse each other.

Finn and I landed to a quickly hushed spat of "I *told* you they ride eagles in Oban, and you didn't believe me" cut off with a "Not now!" I had to disguise my laughter by aiming my face at Scout's feathers as I slid off her back.

Scout, for her part, seemed to decide it was most prudent to get back out of missile range. I couldn't say I blamed her. She'd come back and get me once I'd finished what she called, from the impressions in her mind, *two-legged squawking time*.

Raonaid came out of the hotel as we went to seek her out, which would have been nicer if she'd greeted us with scones or even a basket of chips—instead, she came bustling out with a half-plucked chicken in her hands. Not, I should add, the size of the one that nearly ate Iain. This bird, alas, had lost the ascension size lotto.

I still hadn't had the time to find Helen, and I didn't think I'd find that time today.

"Well, aren't you lads just a picture?" she crowed, motioning with her free hand, which dislodged a small flurry of downy feathers that had been stuck to her skin. "Come in, come in. Cockaleekie soup soon, if you're hungry! We've seen the aliens again!"

That last, she called over her shoulder just as we were coming through the hotel's glass doors, and Finn almost smacked right into the door because he missed a step just as I let it go.

It took a few minutes before we could pin Raonaid down long enough to elaborate between her practically flinging tea at us and her own barrage of questions, but she gave a dismissive sniff when I finally managed to ask.

"Oh, they came through again, what was it? Yesterday?

Day before? Three of them, plain as day. Old Rog, he tried to stop them to talk, but they blasted him right out of their way."

Raonaid paused for a moment there, looking pensive enough that my alarm crept back up until Finn asked, "*Blasted* as in exploded or *blasted* as in relocated?"

I shot him a grateful look for the clarifying question, and Raonaid started as if he'd flashed her his six-pack abs. Her face turned pink, spreading out from her cheeks to the pale skin of her neck. It made me wonder how much she'd blush if he really had given her a peekaboo.

"Oh! They knocked the wind out of him is all. Sent him flying about ten yards. Landed in a gorse bush, poor lamb. I think it was his pride bruised more than anything. Or punctured, as it were." Raonaid gave us a smile. "People dying isn't *quite* as unremarkable as all that, for me to report it so cavalierly."

That was...good to know. I busied myself with my cup of tea.

Raonaid tried to get us to stay for lunch, especially Finn, much to my amusement, but I was on a dual mission. I left him and his abs to fend for themselves and slipped away back to the Murray house where I had done my best to nuke the anomaly's insidious spread before it could really take root.

Yet again, the ascension's speed at healing the earth astounded me. I walked up to the small wooden bridge between the houses, seeking out the significant burnt patch, only to find fresh green grass already growing.

I wasn't sure how this part of my plan would work if the land and its recovering flora had already made such strides. Gingerly, I stepped onto the regrowing grass.

Standing felt safer, which made me feel a bit foolish, since I had cleansed the entire space with literal fire.

Nevertheless, I didn't want to make more contact with the ground until I made sure the corruption was indeed no more.

One pulse of Connection showed me nothing but healthy growth with no abnormalities, but even so, I stood there a few moments longer, allowing my spirit to relax, flow, permeate my surroundings.

It took a few breaths to pull myself into the current of it. With each soft push of Connection, I grew more certain. Spirit explored through the new-grown blades, through the sod layer, into the roots. It sought out the minuscule connections with fungi from mould to puffballs, even—a discovery that amused me—the mycelium of a healthy crop of liberty caps.

No corruption.

I lowered myself down to the grass, still a bit tentative, and splayed out my fingers on the plush carpet. Sitting on it wasn't ideal for the plants, but grass was resilient; it would recover from my weight.

With skin in contact with the grass, I let my fingers push through between the blades to find where they met the soil. From there, I opened myself again to spirit through my heartbeat-timed pulses of Connection. But this time, I tried to settle myself in the awareness of my other skills.

Faicte 's Neo-Fhaicte, the Seen and the Unseen. This skill was meant to give me insight into the bridges between awareness and the unnoticed.

Gu h-Ìosal was the complementary skill to Gu h-Àrd. Where the latter whispered *As Above*, Gu h-Ìosal answered, *So Below*. It connected me to the earth, the planes inhabited closest to the land and within the land itself.

Then there was Taobh a-Muigh, another duality with its sibling skill Taobh a-Staigh—these two worked together for internal and external context. It was Taobh a-Muigh, the world outwith my own self, that I turned to now. The skill helped me latch into the myriad interconnected threads of ecosystems, dependencies, symbiosis, into the push and pull of relationships between different species across the breadth of life and all its forms.

All three of these skills were passives; they had no trigger, no launch button. But I had learned that "passive" didn't mean they were so ephemeral they only worked in the background. To the contrary, with awareness and the mindful use of spirit, I could feel where they drew my attention, suss out the tiny intricacies of how they worked both alone and in tandem.

It meant that, as I continually cycled spirit through my meridians and utilised Connection as a catalyst, I could sense where these new grasses fed off the nutrient-rich ash of the dead. Taobh a-Muigh focused my attention outside myself rather than getting caught up in where spirit flowed in and out of me, where its swirls looped and curved like a rollercoaster's track, dizzying if I allowed myself to be distracted. Taobh a-Muigh kept my attention trained outwith those loops, instead seeking out where the filaments of Connection met something interesting or unexpected—which they did.

I felt a smile curve my lips as all of these things working together allowed me to delve deeper into my first glance of new growth and see it for what it really was: a resurrection.

My Purifire had burned away the corruption, yes. It had vaporised so much of the surrounding foliage, down to the organisms living in its sphere, but it hadn't killed everything. Plants were hardy things, meant to survive even forest fires, drought, any number of other challenges.

Some of their seeds remained, and those had germinated and grown.

But the real shock was the fungus.

I had noticed for myself that the fungus here had seemed to resist the corruption's influence; now the exploratory tendrils of spirit confirmed it beyond any doubt. Something about the mycelium had shut itself off to the corruption in a way I'd not seen from anything else. Even the ùruisg's apparent resistance paled in comparison.

Under the earth here, the mycelium had somehow made itself impenetrable to the anomaly's blight. Fascinated, I found remnants of it, evidence buried beneath me where I sat.

The corruption was hungry. Everything had the filaments of spirit; call them strings, call it whatever, but they ran through all of us. Everything, living and non-living, every atom, every particle. But the anomaly's influence did something to it. Consolidated those filaments, those strings. Made them writhe, made them wriggle in search of something—anything—they could latch onto.

Something in the book I'd absorbed clicked: arcane maladies required something to hold on to.

Unlike viral and bacterial pathogens, which sought a way *inside* the body, arcane invaders needed to find purchase somehow. They acted like velcro, like infinitesimal hooks.

The mycelium under this patch of grass?

It had somehow realised the trick to preventing that corruption from gaining its foothold.

It had smoothed out its filaments of spirit. So small were normal spirit filaments that when lain out, flattened, they became like a seal's dense outer coat, insulating the fungal body from the invader.

Nothing for those grasping hooks to catch. No loops. No stray strings to grab.

I probed through every layer of earth I could find. Delved into the negative space where my Purifire had burned away the root systems of grasses, weeds, you name it. That negative space ought to have also included the mycelium—but it didn't. Those intertwining threads of fungus beneath the earth remained, inexplicable. I'd been so intent when I burned it of eliminating the corruption that I had missed that the fungal network had survived. Not only that, but it seemed as good as new.

Which meant also that this fungus—or, more correctly, these fungi all entwined together—were the first organisms we'd encountered to have personally been in physical contact with an infectious anomaly and escaped its touch.

I'd thought it strange that, with the corruption in the roots of the grass and permeating through everything, that it hadn't leapt at the chance to shoot through the networks of fungal bodies, so dense beneath us that in every square foot of earth there would be hundreds of miles worth of its intricate lattice of communicative, adaptive network.

Trees had symbiotic relationships with fungi that allowed them to communicate where their own root systems couldn't reach—everything under the ground lived, talked, breathed by the connections made possible by an type of organism so common yet still so woefully untapped in terms of our understanding. And here, here in this half sphere I'd purged of just about everything else but the dirt and stones themselves, the remarkable fungi illuminated something for me.

I'd assumed the mycelium to be resistant, but that was not even the half of it.

The mycelium seemed to be *immune*.

CHAPTER

FIFTEEN

I had gathered some other items after Finn and I had raided the crystals, and I put it to use as soon as I tore myself free of my deep meditation on the miracle, well, under my arse.

My mind was afraid to hope, but my heart? Gods, but it leapt with the possibility that maybe, just maybe, the fungi here had given us a breakthrough that could allow us to help those who had been afflicted by the anomaly's corruption.

I needed several things for this to give me viable information. I was no biologist, but I had taken enough science labs to know the basics of the scientific process. First, a sample of the mycelium from the affected area here, as well as a sample of the dirt and the grasses' roots. It struck me as odd to feel a little guilty peeling back the new-grown sod to cut loose a few threads of fungus and root, even though I knew both grass and mushrooms were resilient fuckers— they'd be back in business in no time, especially with the ascension's help.

Second was that I needed to get samples from farther

away but still connected to this bunch in a direct line. Or, in the case of the fungal jungle under my feet, a wibbly-wobbly, curvy-swerve-y radius.

That didn't take too long. I only had to walk a few metres to get the second batch of samples. I labelled each of the glass vials with a brief push of spirit to etch the surface. Another ascension marvel—who needed a jaw that could cut glass when a thought would do it?

The third batch of samples would have to wait until I reached my next pitstop.

I heard the unmistakable—and hilariously seagull-esque—call from Scout above me as she chittered her excitement. She reflected back my own; through the bond of Tàthadh between us, she had been privy to everything I was feeling. As a creature of the air and crags and trees, I felt her fascination with my meditation as she winged her way to a suitable space for me to rejoin her.

The world of the ground was foreign to her. Sure, eagles might land on a beach to pick at carrion washed in on the tide. They might land for other reasons, too, but they weren't forest animals to burrow into the earth or even to scratch at it for food. Scout had no understanding of what went on under my feet, and until today, I didn't think she'd cared.

I made my way over to her, tucking my samples into my inventory. My mind whirred with the possibilities.

Don't get your hopes up, ya bam.

My mental self-chiding sounded suspiciously like Iain.

Clambering on to Scout's back was a lot less graceful when I couldn't just leap off of something and have her catch me. Her feathers were slippery, and even when she cushed down like she was incubating an egg, I slid right off her twice before she took pity on me and used her own magic to give me a bit of traction.

I could see the small faces of some of the neighbourhood kids pressed up against the windows of the nearest houses to watch me, and I clung to what remained of my dignity when their squeals of laughter reached right through that glass and into my embarrassed soul.

There was no way I was staying surly for long—not when the world fell away beneath us. Scout chittered again as we climbed, her fierce joy at being airborne enmeshed with her curiosity at seeing an entirely new part of the world. She'd spit her life mostly around Mull, sometimes travelling up and down the Sound of Mull, but the most "inland" she'd ever been had been that island and neighbouring Ardnamurchan. Once or twice, she'd ventured as far as Loch Awe, but no farther.

Today was a day of new experiences for both of us.

Our next stop wasn't even a village; it was barely a pulloff from the A82 at the Falls of Falloch, but Finn had insisted it was the most logical place to set up the next communications point.

Seeing the A82 dotted with abandoned cars still struck me with unease. This was the closest to Glasgow I'd ventured since the ascension, and the traffic here was a bit denser than I would have expected.

Scout had to circle for a minute or two before she found a place she could safely land. With her wingspan, the heavy tree cover surrounding the road made things awkward. Eventually, she alit on a hillock a bit back from the road, leaving me to make my way to the other side like a decisive chicken.

A turnoff from the main road looped sharply back to the

left from where I entered, expanding into a carpark for people visiting the falls.

I walked down towards the footpath leading to the falls, figuring that was as good a place as any. Unlike cell towers, the communications points didn't need high ground to function. Whether they tapped into ley lines or power lines or some other esoteric imagining of spirit channels, I had no idea. So long as it worked, I didn't need to understand it, not when I needed to keep my brain geared towards something altogether more urgent.

I unbundled the bandolier of crystals I'd filled in Oban, removing one and rolling the leather back up into its cylinder to replace in my inventory. The next part reminded me of the ionadan-siubhail. It seemed apparent that magic operated very much on having local ingredients—at least when we were using it to create something locally geared, like travel points and, apparently, communications points.

That meant I needed to find some native wood. Not difficult in the dense trees surrounding the river.

It didn't take me long to find a nice hazel that happily donated a branch to the cause. Finn had shown me what to do, but even though crafting was something I'd explored already, I still wasn't quite prepared for the way the branch of hazel engulfed the quartz tower when I patterned my tentative push of spirit the way he'd taught me. At first, I thought the wood would cover it completely and I'd essentially end up planting the branch in the ground like a fence post.

But after the wood had curled itself around the crystal, small fissures appeared in line with the grain, pulling apart to reveal the crystal.

I continued feeding my little trickle of spirit into the branch, felt it guiding and coaxing the wood to continue shaping itself into the formation best suited for the task. When it finally finished, I was left with what looked like a wood-and-crystal sceptre, the grains of the hazel emphasising the crystal's point and forming irregular but intricate patterns. I couldn't quite understand why until I selected a spot right at the edge of the carpark where a boulder half submerged in dirt marked the start of the footpath to the falls.

The moment the base end of the unwieldy sceptre touched the earth, threads of my spirit still swirling around it to guide its purpose, the quartz crystal within lit up.

The staff elongated, bringing the crystal's housing about to chest level.

It didn't glow brightly enough to hurt my eyes—or even enough to make more than a lousy impromptu torch—but it exuded a steady light, soft and gold-white.

Now was the kicker where I was either going to rejoice in my success...or look like an absolute tit using a rock and a stick for a microphone in an apocalypse.

Somehow the rockie-talkies felt less egregious.

"Crianlarich, this is Calum at the Falls of Falloch. Am I talking to a rock or is there a person who can hear me?"

I waited for a moment, only to hear a thunk and a crash and a "Bloody hell!" sounding from my rock-stick combo.

"You all right there, pal?" I asked into my shiny new landline rockie-talkie. "I didn't just interrupt a liaison or give someone a stroke, did I?"

A burst of laughter followed, and a moment later, the sound of someone clearing their throat.

"All alive and accounted for," came the voice of a man I didn't recognise. "And no one, I feel the need to report, is in flagrante delicto. Just clumsy. Me. I'm clumsy. Bashed my sodding knee into the bloody thing."

I let out a relieved breath—I think as much for my not having interrupted someone mid-coitus as for my success.

"Right. That's one down," I told him. "With a little luck, you'll hear from me again soon."

"Well, hurry up. The other lad's already on his third."

Damn it, Finn.

"Och, I had a late start. For science." *Yes, Calum, that makes you sound cooler.* "I'm going to go plant another stick in the ground."

Nailed it.

❖

We made our way southward, with Scout opting to stay airborne and give me a chance to stretch my legs. Which is to say "run along the A82."

My next stop took me to the old pitstop, the Drover's Inn, the inside of which hadn't changed its decor since the days of Bonnie Prince Charlie. To my surprise, the inn was open, running a much reduced menu, but they had somehow levelled their staff to the high teens. I popped inside out of politeness to see how they were getting on, and between a bowl of potato leek soup with the best damn bread I'd had in weeks, folk told me how they've fought off murmurations of enormous starlings, a gang of pit bull-sized grey squirrels, and an ongoing invasion of rats of a size that has become all *too* usual.

Inside the Drover's Inn, the soot-blackened stone and dusty wooden furniture has a lived-in feel that came with a palpable sense of cosiness. As I ate, I ran them through the basics of what had been happening in Oban and warned them about the anomaly. They were shockingly well-informed about that, since they'd been sending folk up and down the road Lomondside with news and gathering the same in return.

As efficient as they'd been in navigating the ascension —not without losses of their own—the whole inn broke out in cheers when I told them why I'd stopped there. Everyone from the chef to the guests came out to watch me make another crystal stick microphone.

The cheer that went up when we connected to my new pal in Crianlarich made the initial burst inside sound like a lacklustre huzzah; it was so loud that I felt a wave of amusement from Scout even though I couldn't see her. Apparently, she could hear us.

Ken, the inn's proprietor, tried to convince me to stay for a few days, but I excused myself with the hope that soon, it wouldn't take days of walking to jump between Oban and Glasgow. Laying the communications ground-work was, of course, only the first step in reconnecting Scotland.

Before I went too far, though, I paused to take more samples of plants and fungi that would serve as my control when I returned to Kilmelford to test the anomaly's effects.

Scout followed my path from above, her literal eagle eyes trained on anything that could pose a threat to me, but I made it to the end of Loch Lomond at Ardlui without inci-dent. Then Ardvorlich. Then Inveruglas's pyramid. Tarbet. Firkin Point. Inverbeg.

Stop after stop, I found birch or oak or pine, rowan or hazel or willow. Those trees staked out our foray south, drawing a line of connection all the way from Oban and the islands to the Trossachs.

Naturally, after things going smoothly all day, as the sun began to sink towards the horizon in the late evening of early summer, Scout sent out a blaring alarm in the form of a whip-sharp lash of spirit moments before an enormous, resounding *crack* split through the quiet of Loch Lomond's Culag Beach.

I spun just in time to see full-grown trees at the edge of the loch swaying, one of them lurching with more cracking until gravity took over, and it came crashing to the ground with...an all-too-animal roar.

My first inane thought, fully divorced in logic from my knowledge that Loch Lomond was nowhere near Loch Ness, was that Nessie had finally decided to clamber onto land to pay us a visit.

But no, as I spun towards the source of the sound, it was no dinosaur-inspired reptilian creature that came flailing through the copse of trees it had already half destroyed.

My first thought was *Is that a bloody kangaroo?*

It took a handful of shocked seconds for me to process that I *did* know what the mammalian—or marsupial, as was more accurate—monster was.

A wallaby. A goddamned wallaby.

Once upon a time, about four score and seven years or so before this, our current apocalypse, some bored landowner had imported a family of the Australian animals to Inchconnachan Island in the middle of Loch Lomond, where they'd quite happily propagated for the past century.

And now, it seemed, one had made a break for the mainland, in a very real and literal way.

I heard a few yells break out in alarm from the beach,

which was a short distance to the north along the shore and out of the rampaging fur ball's path. I stood in a small oval of asphalt for cars to turn round in. Another strip stretched parallel to the A82 for beach visitors to use to park, but the giant wallaby had taken the scenic route, seemingly out of a hatred of local flora, if its path of destruction was any measure. Limbs cracked, torn free of tree trunks. The surrounding trees were mostly slender birches, nowhere near strong enough to withstand such an onslaught.

My own heart gave a startled leap when whatever mechanism in my brain responsible for trigonometric calculations caught up with the sheer size of the creature.

A normal wallaby was only about three feet tall, much more compact than some of their kangaroo counterparts that looked like they could box Mike Tyson and come out on top even before the ascension granted them steroidal superpowers.

This big bastard?

The bloody *Godzilla* of wallabies.

Dripping wet, easily twenty feet tall, and in a very, very bad mood.

It came barking out of the brush, thumping a hind leg to shake loose an entire tree branch caught in the joint of its hip. Each thud came accompanied with more cracking as smaller sticks and branches split under the weight of the foot, and my enhanced awareness of spirit through my passive skills meant that each concussive strike reverberated through my awareness both in sound and sensation alike.

The sounds it made were a coughing spat, like some overgrown mix of a sea lion and a fox, all against the backdrop of shuddering underbrush and cracking sticks and limbs where the tree—the *entire tree*—it had felled shifted the rest of the way down to the ground with gravity's pull.

And it wasn't just a near T-rex-sized marsupial. The crashing of breaking wood and the hoarse chattery barks only momentarily preceded the wind bringing me an all-too-familiar odour of rot.

I swear, if the anomaly had taken full hold of Loch Lomond's legendary wallabies, I was going to kill the anomaly extra dead if I ever got the chance.

High above me, Scout fed me images of the thing's progress. It didn't yet seem to be aware of me, nor had the alarmed shouts from the beach a hundred metres away drawn its attention.

Yet.

While I had a moment, I gritted my teeth and cast Keen Eye, just to see what I was working with.

Anomalous Wallaby

Caught in a wave of spirit upon Earth's ascension, this non-native marsupial was first driven mad by its sudden and extreme growth, which drove it away from its fellows and into the loch, where it managed to swim to the next island and collapse. It is unclear where it made contact with the anomaly's corruption, but after days of near-comatose exhaustion, the wallaby woke with a driving need follow the anomaly's mysterious imperative.

As you have already established through hard-won experience, anomalous creatures are vulnerable to Purifire, but this creature is unlikely to be susceptible to control measures that would more easily affect smaller anomalies.

Great.

Just great.

This thing was like the enormous killer rabbit Eilidh and I had fought up north, but this time I was alone, it still had fuck-off flippers of death in the form of thumping feet, and I'd just watched it knock down an entire tree.

Not only that, but we'd long-since established the creatures' interest in...me.

Which meant I was the likely reason it had come lurching out of the loch like a goddamned creature of the Black Lagoon.

Even as I thought it, the wallaby seemed to shake itself, cocking its head first to one side and then the other as if trying to better hear something outwith the frequencies of my own hearing.

It wasn't half as cute as when Scout did it.

I reached out to pull Brac-Meanmna from inventory, feeling the living weapon flare to life as it recognised the threat. With every new encounter of the anomalies, Brac-Meanmna's hatred for them seemed to grow, like the unique staff had made it a personal mission to challenge and confront every instance of corruption it could find on the Earth.

If it could fly, I had little doubt the staff would be scouring the planet for targets, but for now, I had just provided it with a whopper of a foe.

I needed to slow it down.

My best bet was Purifire, and like I had developed Fist of Flame by combining that with Spèird, my force spell, I'd also learned a few tricks back when we'd first fought Lord Bawbag.

Gathering spirit and channelling it through my all-too-eager staff, I spun threads of Purifire into a lasso. The wallaby finally managed to shake its foot free of the offending tree branch caught around its hill, and it almost rendered my yet-uncast spell useless when it bunched its legs beneath it and leapt.

The damn thing had bottoms made out of springs. It bounded a full ten yards towards me, and I loosed my spell so fast that the flash of blue-green Purifire that lit up in a circle around the monster left strobing afterimages behind my eyes.

Ring of Fire encircled the wallaby, and it let out a rage-filled roar, hoarse and grating, as the flames licked higher and caught the end of its tail like a telltale pocket monster, if the wee butt-flamed lizard in the famous franchise had been bitten by zombies and was covered in oozing, rotting flesh.

Sparks of Purifire pinged from the wall of flame to the wallaby, igniting stray bits of flaking-off fur. It was far too much to hope that the fire would really take off, but the wallaby beat its burning tail against the grass and gravel beneath its feet, instinct forcing it to curl inwards.

"What the hell is that thing?" Someone bellowed the question from somewhere to my left.

"Giant wallaby—whatever you do, don't touch it. It's diseased and will infect anything it bites or claws!" I wasn't sure my harried warning would accomplish much, and the last thing I wanted to do as seconds slipped away was remove any hope of help.

I had Scout high above, of course, the eagle circling and assessing the situation from her vantage point.

"If you've got any ranged skills, I'd be very grateful for the assistance!" I called out to whoever would listen. "Anything you shoot through the fire should make your projectiles more effective—Purifire is one of the few things that can actually hurt these monsters!"

To my surprise, almost before I'd finished speaking, bolts of spirit came flying out of my peripheral vision, punching right into the wall of blue-green fire and hitting the wallaby in the flank with visible flares of detonations.

The creature's answering scream threatened to grate my eardrums like cheese. I shuddered, drawing on the ambient spirit around me to coax what aid I could from the wild magics in preparation for Ring of Fire to drop.

But I didn't have to wait for my temporary prison to peter out. Oh, no.

The anomalous wallaby pounded its paddle-like feet against the ground, sending shockwaves through the earth —and then it bunched its legs beneath it again and bounded into the air.

This time, it wasn't aiming for lateral distance but vertical, and I'd be damned if it didn't succeed.

Leaping almost ten feet straight up, the beast didn't have to go *through* my Purifire walls surrounding it. It could jump right the fuck over them.

No time to carefully weave my next tapestry of spirit; I lashed it together and loosed Tairm, throwing myself in what I hoped to god was the safest direction, to my left where my unseen ally seemed to be.

The wallaby came down with thump that seemed to ring the earth like a kick drum—or maybe that's just how it felt as the concussive vibration of its landing travelled through the ground and into my feet. For a moment in the aftermath of its collision with the ground, I thought my spell had somehow failed.

But I'd no need to worry.

Tairm was a rallying cry aimed at the land itself, and the land answered.

All at once, roots from the fallen tree erupted from the ground behind the wallaby, lashing out across the intervening metres with the precision of a sniper.

The wallaby screamed as sharp, spirit-hardened ends of the roots embedded themselves in the marsupial's hindquarters like a cavalcade of needles ready to stitch the hapless creature to the earth itself in a sick suture.

More bolts of spirit flew in from my left, though I still couldn't see the caster.

I cast Fuaran on myself to replenish my flagging spirit reserves, taking advantage of the handful of seconds where the wallaby's concern was focused on dislodging the Tairm-launched harpoons from its arse.

Scout's screech above got my attention in time to see her winging along the shoreline with an enormous branch of her own dangling from her talons.

Fire-leaves-fall.

I could tell she was in a rush from the cobbled-together words, but I caught the gist of what she wanted in the split second before she flew over the wallaby's head. With a burst of urgency from her mind, she dropped the branch from fifty metres up.

Guided by Scout's own threads of spirit, I cast Purifire, igniting the falling bough that probably weighed as much as an entire small tree.

It lit up in a flare of heat that reached me a second before it streaked downwards at the wallaby, which was still screeching as it wrenched itself free of the roots. Gobs of corrupted flesh fell with wet plops onto the ground, stealing my attention.

Only for a split second, but that was enough.

The wallaby had felt the gust of heat from the Purifire falling, saw the change in light—and knew the danger.

Before I knew what was happening, a wall of force slammed into me, sending me flying through the air.

I came down hard, slamming into the trunks of a tight-grown copse of new-growth birches only to bounce off and hit the floor. Brac-Meanmna clattered to the asphalt of the meagre carpark, half on the surfaced plane and half on the grass.

Fire rained from the sky.

It took me a few precious milliseconds to realise that the wallaby, like the anomalous Eurasian lynx we'd fought only a couple weeks ago, had access to skills.

Its blast of energy left residue fizzing and sparking through the surrounding atmosphere like it had charged the particles in the air with Spèird. But it hadn't been directed; it had detonated like a grenade, and its force had torn through the burning branch above, sending chunks of teal flame—bits of wood and dried leaves somehow still attached from the last autumn—falling through the air.

Scout's idea had been a good one, but the wallaby had its own defence. It was only pure dumb luck that some of the falling debris had landed on the creature's fur, distracting it with the desperate need to stop the spread of Purifire that eagerly burned through the patches of corruption-rotted flesh and matted fur.

I scrambled to my feet, snatching Brac-Meanmna from the ground. The staff practically leapt into my hands, eager to attack.

The sound of someone—or multiple someones—crashing through the brush behind me made me spin.

A middle-aged couple probably fifteen years older than me came stumbling out, no weapons visible in their hands.

"Don't let it get close to you," I warned them, sizing them up with alarm that they had no armour, nothing but loose clothing and gumption. "I wasn't kidding about the disease it carries. It's fatal and incurable."

"We'll run away if it comes at us," the man said glibly. "Till then, we reckon you could use a hand."

"Appreciate it," I said shortly.

To buy us time while the wallaby was again distracted by being on fire, I cast Dubh. My spirit reserves were replenishing slowly with Fuaran's increased regeneration speed, but even so, I was starting to worry about my longevity if I ran out of oomph.

Dubh rooted me in the balm of comforting darkness, but for the wallaby, it robbed it of its sight.

"Hit it now! Purifire's best if you have it!"

I took my own advice, aiming Fist of Flame at one of the still-smouldering patches of bloody, diseased fur.

The wallaby let out a howl that probably would have been a squeal on a smaller version of the animal, but even as it flailed, pounding its feet against the ground as if that could somehow stop the burn, my unlikely compatriots loosed more bolts of spirit at the creature.

No Purifire, which made me wonder what their skills were, since it was a foundational skill in the Arcane tree.

I didn't have time to puzzle it out; as if the pain had finally tipped the creature into full-on rage, the wallaby again bunched its powerful legs beneath it to leap.

"Look out!" My best guesstimate, aided by my appropriately named passive skill Tuairmse, gave me a possible path of the wallaby's trajectory, but unfortunately did not give me the ability to project that to my comrades.

Because of that, my hurried attempt to leap out of the way collided with their momentary floundering. I caught the man by the back of his shirt, hearing it rip, and his wife yelped as my shoulder crashed into hers.

A wave of wet rot stench preceded the wallaby's landing right where I'd just been standing.

I gave up on elegance and shoved the couple out of the way, pushing them to the ground just as a flash of swinging tail came hurtling into my periphery.

Not a moment too soon. I hit the floor between the two of them just as the tail flew over the tops of us, missing us by inches.

The odour of singed fur commingled with the anomaly's sick scent, rot and disease layering together in pungent putrescence.

"Move, move, move," I said as I shoved myself up and gritted my teeth.

Spirit came together through the focus of Brac-Meanmna, the staff flinging Spèird at the wallaby's flank.

We were fortunate; the thing did not seem very smart. The information the system had spit out with my use of Keen Eye *had* said the animal had gone mad. Maybe that had mitigated some of the threat.

The mental image of a falling boulder intruded, and my head snapped up to see Scout dropping rocks from high above.

Apparently unwilling to try the branch trick again, she'd resorted to the tried-and-true method of letting gravity take control of heavy things to brain thine enemy.

The first one struck the wallaby's flank, but the second —oh, that one hit home.

And by home, I mean head. It smashed into the wallaby's head from above at terminal velocity, and though the blackness of Dubh had worn off, the rock stunned the wallaby anew.

With half a second to catch my breath, I saw that the creature's backside was riddled with punctures and shredded flesh from Tairm's onslaught of roots punching through its hide.

I had enough spirit for only a couple more uses of my skills, and I knew what they had to be.

Fist of Flame punched right into the largest open wound just at the crook of the wallaby's hip.

The enormous marsupial spasmed at the impact, its powerfully strong leg straightening to thump once more at the ground—but that only served to increase the agony.

As it spun to face me, its beady eyes weeping pus and its mouth lolling open, I poured as much spirit as I dared into one more cast. Part of me wanted to cast Tairm again, to loose wild magic upon this beast to devour it before it could spread its corruption.

But I didn't need the unpredictability of wild magic. Right now, I needed precision.

I formed Purifire and Spèird into a javelin, a slender, deadly weapon, and I launched it with everything I had left at the wallaby's weeping eye.

And then I held my breath.

The couple behind me, to their enormous credit, had recovered and were hurtling more bolts of spirit to riddle the wallaby's flesh.

My vision flashed gold.

You have killed an anomalous wallaby.

I could have kissed every god who ever existed in imagination or reality.

CHAPTER
SEVENTEEN

I desperately wanted to have Scout fly us right back to Oban after the wallaby battle, but I hadn't yet accomplished what I meant to. That told me I would be spending the night Lomondside.

The couple who had bravely joined in the fight were called Maria and Tom. They had been walking the West Highland Way from north to south when the ascension hit, and after a few nights of being cornered by a flock of engorged ducks—*not* a phrase I found in any way appealing—they had opted to stay put. Neither of them had progressed past level six, an alarming thing to me, but maybe a worse shock for them when they learned I was level twenty-seven.

Reckon news of the kraken also did some psychic damage to their worldviews.

I stayed just long enough to give them some advice, and since they had both taken to magic like an engorged duck to water and mayhem, I also crafted them each staves from nearby birches and showed them the basics of ascension crafting. The way their eyes lit up like weans on Christmas morning told me that they'd do just fine—especially since catching the crafting bug meant they would gain some levels.

There was just enough daylight for us to make it to Luss before Scout would need to roost for the night. Partly because she felt my apprehension about the state of Inchconnachan's other wallabies and partly, I think, due to her own curiosity, she winged her way out to the islets herself to have a look. She also promised not to eat any of the wallabies, which I thought was very big of her.

Luss was a small village that catered to Loch Lomond's tourists with a campsite, loch tours, canoe and kayak hire—the lot. I wasn't surprised to find people about. Since the shift in my stature and physiology, namely my ears getting pointy, I had taken to keeping my hood up to conceal them. As a result, I probably looked like I was cosplaying a rogue from a fantasy role-playing game, but I couldn't much be arsed to worry about that when there were aliens about and I looked like I'd breezed in from sending a halfling to chuck a ring in a volcano.

But the tall, dark, and mysterious look also attracted attention.

"Where you coming from?" someone called out to me as I passed the Loch Lomond Arms hotel.

He was the epitome of a stereotypical rural bloke, including a flat cap and tweed jacket, but both cap and jacket were well worn and cared for, rather than brand new and matching in a way that'd mark him for a tourist. He'd pale skin turned ruddy from the sun and hair gone steel grey under the flat cap.

"Oban," I called back, "but I'm here to help get all of us back in contact. I've got a communications point to set up, and once that's done, you'll be able to chat to just about every village between here and Oban, and likely by now all the way to Aberfeldy."

The man who'd spoken let out a low whistle and beckoned at me to come closer, calling out over his shoulder into the hotel, "Oi, Mick! Bloke out here says he's rebooting the mobile service."

"Erm, no, not even a little bit that," I said hastily. "It's literally a rock and a stick and some magic."

That earned me a squinting sideways look. "You sure you haven't got a screw loose up there, mate?"

I was tempted to call Scout to fly me right out of here and see how they felt about a giant golden eagle swooping in from the loch.

"If you give me a few minutes and name a central location, I'll show you I'm not mad," I told him, but just for the sake of brevity, I conjured a ball of Purifire in my palm, which he rewarded with a raised eyebrow. "Magic's real now, yeah? You on the same page?"

"Och, aye, but none of the tech works, so I got my hopes up." He shifted his weight, both hands in his pockets where he leaned on the door frame. "A man can dream."

"You miss social media that much?"

From his demeanour, I guessed he was the sort of lad who liked a bit of cheek and banter, and his answering grin told me I was right.

"Don't you know, I was a big star on the TikTok. Americans love a kilt," he said with a wink. Then he looked at me quizzically. "You said you need a central location?"

"I *can* put this communications point up a tree or something, but I figured it'd be nice if it were accessible to anyone who might want to chat to someone up the road." I paused at his thoughtful nod. "Got any ideas?"

He seemed to take the question very seriously. After a

moment, he nodded again. "Aye, reckon over at the Faerie Trail."

"The what?"

Normally, talk of faeries would not fill me with trepidation, but since I'd just fought a kaiju-sized wallaby not an hour ago, I wasn't exactly predisposed to get on the bad side of the Fair Folk. There were plenty of reasons we treated them warily since well before magic had run roughshod over modern life. In an ascended world? I'd a brownie in a cage, a glaistig for a pal, and would not put it past anything else otherworldly to turn up and start mischief.

He pointed over the road to an open space where I could see a mostly empty carpark and some green grass. "Just at the head of the carpark there. Central enough, open and flat so if anyone has trouble walking, they won't have too hard a time."

"Good shout, pal. Cheers."

"Mind if I tag along? Mick's stuck looking after the regulars—either that or he thought I was taking the piss about the mobile service."

"Whatever would have given him that idea?" I asked him innocently.

My new friend grinned. "Dinnae ken, dinnae ken. Come on. I'll show you where it is."

It was barely a two minute walk, so his pointing would have done the trick, but I used the short journey to ask him how Luss had fared. Much the same story as Crianlarich and Tyndrum. They'd gotten mostly lucky not to have anything unmanageable, and Bawbag's bullshit hadn't made it this far south, so aside from talking folk down from panic attacks and suicide attempts—*that* made his face darken, rightly so—they'd been hanging in and hoping for news of a return to normal.

"Hate to break it to you, pal," I said to him, "but this is the new normal, I reckon."

"I know," he said, taking off his flat cap to scrub his hand through thinning hair. "Problem is, a lot of folk are in denial and don't want to hear anything about planning for a future where we have to adapt from here."

"Once we get things up and running with the communications and ionadan-siubhail," I said, pausing at his confused look. "Travel points. If you find this rock and stick routine a farfetched idea, you might have a tough time wrapping your head around portals."

He blinked at that. "Oh. Erm."

I had a feeling he was back to scepticism about my sanity.

No better way to illustrate the point than to show rather than tell.

A few trees lined the roads on either side of the carpark, so I detoured a few steps back the way we'd come without trying to further convince him.

By now, my routine was down to an easy art as I approached an oak tree, extended my spirit to it, and asked for a branch it thought might fall.

Mr. Sceptic raised his eyebrow even farther when a branch—suspiciously free of many outcropping twigs or leaves—fell into my waiting hands.

I was beginning to understand why his forehead had a crease in that one specific spot.

At least he didn't balk when I pulled my leather roll of now-depleted quartz crystals from my inventory, though that did instil me with some questions on the limits of his suspension of disbelief.

I worked quickly, shaping the wood around the crystal easily after my practice of the day's work. Blue eyes narrowed watching me, which made me a little nervous that he was about to ring a klaxon and sound the alarm that I was a witch.

It wasn't like he'd be wrong, but I really didn't fancy dealing with an angry mob, and all the villages so far had been so chill, I think part of me was just waiting for one place to house a cult or cannibals or any number of other horrors the world of video games had prepared me for. You know, the idea that people give up all memory of civility the second the power goes out. Outwith airports and people stranded on public transportation, that did not seem to bear out in life.

"What's your name?" I asked the bloke, more to break the silence than anything else. I did care to know, but my brain was struggling to catalog all the people I'd encountered in the past few days. "I'm Calum Green."

"Bertie," he answered. "Bertie MacDougall."

With the structure done, all that was left was to plant it. The carpark was shaped like an arch, with a semicircular fan of parking spaces at the northern end. I beckoned to Bertie and walked to the zenith of that semicircle.

"Tell me if you still have doubts after this," I said under my breath, spinning spirit into the oak-and-crystal sceptre.

Bertie watched with narrowed eyes as the thing elongated. It rooted itself down into the earth with the quartz crystal shining out through the waving grain of the oak at its head.

When it was done, I cleared my throat. "Hello, there, Crianlarich! You lot still with me?"

"Eyyy!" came a chorus of none-too-sober voices,

followed by someone slurring, "You owe me a tenner. Cos it's not ten yet."

"See, Bertie," I said. "Now you have the power to experience drunk people both in the pub here *and* up the road at the same time. So much better than the socials." I spoke up a bit louder. "Say hi to Bertie MacDougall of Luss!"

The chorus of *Hi* and *Hello* and *Hiya* almost drowned out Berties response, made worse by someone bursting into song with "Loch Lomond" in the background.

"Right, I think that's my cue to stop for the night. I'll get the last few tomorrow, Crianlarich," I said, unsure anyone at all on the other end was listening. "Make good choices."

All I heard in response was a very off-key "…and the moon comin' out in the gloooooooamin'!"

I withdrew my tendril of spirit before the chaos of the impending chorus, turning to Bertie to see how he was processing this unmundane return to something somehow completely normal, and he opened his mouth, holding up a hand in seeming confusion just as the rockie-talkie in my bandolier pinged.

"Two ticks," I said to him. "Rhona?"

"Chan e," said Eilidh's voice. "Mis' a th' ann, air ais san Òban. Càit' a bheil thusa?"

I couldn't stop the smile from creeping across my face. "Luss! Agus tha thu gam ruigsinn!"

Bertie was staring at me as if I'd grown a second head. Eilidh was home in Oban, and the communications network had officially expanded. I couldn't even be upset at the wallaby incident—today had just become a banner day. If the rockie-talkies could reach this far now, Scotland was this much closer to being able to talk to each other again.

Pulling the softly glowing rockie-talkie out of its pocket in my bandolier, I started to hand it to Bertie.

Before letting go, I said, "Eilidh, I've a sceptic here. Mind saying hello and where you're, erm, calling from?"

I couldn't hear her response as he took the crystal since it had left my position, but imagining her derisive snort was all too easy.

"You're *where*?" Bertie said, holding the crystal in front of his mouth like he was about to eat it.

"She's in Oban," I said, genuine happiness plastering my face with an unstoppable smile. "And just like that, Oban to Loch Lomond has communication restored."

Seventy miles. We'd gone seventy miles, and that wasn't counting wherever Finn had ended up. I ought to have asked the drunken louts in Crianlarich, but the moment I thought of it, I realised I wasn't sure I would have gotten any kind of coherent answer. Might have said Norway, for all I knew.

Bertie stared at me open-mouthed as he passed the crystal back. "You were serious."

"I didn't come all this way to take the piss, mate. We've been working our tails off from Islay to Barra and back to help each other survive this."

His mouth fell open a tiny bit farther at that. "Barra? As in the Barra on the other side of the Minch?"

"Boats still work, mate. Well, not the motors, not the way they did a couple months ago, but Bertie, we have magic now." To illustrate that—and because anomalies be damned, I was in a cracking mood all of a sudden—I spun some glittery sparkles of Purifire in the air. "Brave new world, my friend. Reckon you can be ready to join us in it?"

Bertie peered at me as if trying to make up his mind whether or not I was even real. After a moment, though, he laughed.

"Tell you what, lad. Ask me again after a few drams at

the Arms. We'll make up a room for you, and you can regale us with stories of this brave new world. Reckon you've got more than a few."

I clapped him on the shoulder and let him lead the way back towards the hotel.

Through my bond with Scout, I got a distinct sense of contentment—she'd found the wallabies in fine form, living their little wallaby lives without corruption.

Another bit of good news for the day. I'd take it.

My good mood still hadn't worn off the next morning, buoyed by Bertie and his mate Mick's reactions to Scout's enormous form landing in the middle of the Faerie Trails carpark.

Scout very graciously gave me footholds of spirit the first time instead of making me use her feathers as a slide again. A small crowd was gathering closer to the main road of the village, and I needed to get moving before I got mobbed.

"We'll be in touch, Luss!" I called out as Scout beat a hasty retreat into the air just as some kids started running in our direction. "Talk to your neighbours up north!"

I wasn't only eager to finish my route today for the sake of getting communications extended closer to Glasgow, though that *was* a priority. If Eilidh was back in Oban, she and the others would soon be waiting on me and Finn to arrive so we could combine our components and craft the Resplendent Throne.

While that thought still intimidated me about as much as me bletherin' into a rock had done for Bertie—a lot—it was a step we needed to take. I thought I was even ready. Or if not completely ready, I was at least ready to *be* ready.

Scout kept her focus on seeing any threats that might appear below us as we flew southward along the shore of Loch Lomond. The weather had remained dry, if cloudy, but now the sun came out, chasing away the remnants of the morning haze. We only had a few more stops to make. First at Duck Bay—I was never going to hear the word "duck" again without hearing the nightmare fuel of "engorged" before it—and then at Balloch, where Loch Lomond ended. I had one crystal left.

We hadn't planned for me to go all the way to Glasgow, but we *could* make it to Dumbarton Castle on the River Clyde, which was about as far as the last crystal would stretch.

As it happened, Dumbarton Castle had company when we arrived.

Atheani.

CHAPTER

EIGHTEEN

S cout let out a loud trill when she spotted the
Atheani, and while they were running away from the
castle proper—jeezo, they were *fast*—it was clear their
visit had not been as peaceful as their disdainful trip to
Oban.

That fact became evident when we saw a whole crowd
of about twenty humans chasing them.

There was no way the humans would catch them. Not
with the length of Atheani's strides. But from the yells and
frantic movement, they damned well meant to give it a
proper go.

The Atheani had no reason to turn back. None. Even
when Scout and I saw them, the distance between the
aliens and the humans giving chase spread out farther than
could be recovered. I wasn't even sure if the humans could
have caught them on motorbikes.

Which is why when the Atheani stopped and wheeled
on the humans, my heart dropped into my stomach.

I felt the pull of spirit—enormous, breathtaking like the
sea pulling back from the shore before a tsunami—and

with every thread of Tàthadh between me and Scout, I screamed, *Bank away!*

It was a measure of Scout's trust in me that the eagle did not hesitate. She twisted midair into a sharp dive back towards Loch Lomond, pumping her magnificent wings so hard I could feel her strain against my body as well as her desperation through our bond.

Had we been even a half a heartbeat slower, the detonation of the Atheani's magic would have incinerated us.

They did it with barely a *thought*.

The entire group of humans who had been chasing them? Vaporised.

Instantly.

And the Atheani simply turned once more and sprinted away, leaving nowt behind them but fire and smoke.

"They said we were thieves," the woman said to me in her soft Glaswegian accent, her voice still numb with shock. "They said we stole their magic."

"Isht," I hushed her, wiping soot from her face.

She was the single survivor.

All because she'd tripped and fallen down. About as pure an example of dumb luck as it came, depending on who you asked. Survivor's guilt was also a hell of a thing to cope with, as I well knew.

Scout had practically thrown me to the ground when we turned to see her struggling to rise in the middle of the road. It had been a wee while since I had had to use Beannachd Shlàinte, but I was thankful I had it in my repertoire.

I wasn't sure this woman would have lived, otherwise. She wore all black, what looked like military surplus but clearly adapted for our current apocalypse, and the only reason I suspected she was of Somali descent was the patch sewn into the shoulder of her tattered jacket, a riff on the *I Heart NYC* genre of souvenirs, but hers said *I Heart Somalia* and was accompanied with the sky blue flag with its single white star. One of the few flags I'd found easy to remember in my world geography class, partly because it looked like it could be pals with our azure flag and simple St. Andrew's cross.

Her skin was light brown, her black hair a tangled mess of blood and shrapnel, and even now, I could hear yelling as people approached—I presumed they were her friends or comrades.

"Who the fuck are you?"

The demand came from a scrawny ginger man covered in freckles so thick that he looked tan in the morning sunshine.

"Easy, pal, I just healed her," I said, backing away with my hands in the air.

"He's telling the truth," my patient said, coughing as she looked up at me with a look of warring exhaustion and gratitude.

"I saw the explosion from the air," I said as the ginger man came closer, others catching up and drawing weapons.

Out of prudence, I used Keen Eye to give me an idea of how far into the shit I'd be if they turned hostile. Ginger was level fourteen, but he seemed to be the highest.

"Ike, he's level twenty-seven," someone cautioned him from the crowd of newcomers.

"I'm here from Oban," I said quickly. "I've been establishing lines of magical communication all the way down the road from there, and my friend has done the same between Crianlarich and Aberfeldy by now. I have the supplies for one more this run, so I figured the castle would be a good bet. I just wanted to help her when I saw what happened. Those Atheani came to Oban too, but they were less...combustible there."

Ginger and the others looked me up and down as if trying to decide whether I was full of shit or not. I could feel Scout not far away, but getting on her back would be difficult if this lot tried to play rough.

But the fight seemed to have gone out of Ginger as he knelt by the Somali woman.

"You okay, hen?" he asked her.

"Aye, thanks to this lad here." She let her friend help her up, making eye contact with me. "Thank you."

"Nae bother," I told her. "I'm just glad someone survived that—nuke."

"If it was a nuke, we'd all be toast, pal," Ginger said, then blanched. "Jeezo, I hope they don't know about Faslane."

Faslane was where the UK kept the nuclear submarines. Near Scotland's largest city, because Westminster didn't feel safe with it near English cities.

Bless this mess we called a "union of equals."

But then I brightened. "Actually, I wonder if the nukes would even still work. Guns don't."

"Guns don't?" Ginger asked just as my impromptu patient asked, "How do you know?"

"Someone did manage to make one go off with magic by accident in the first couple days of the ascension, but the few other times we've seen them tried, just...nothing. Just click. No boom," I said. "So maybe this ascension achieved global nuclear disarmament."

How was that for a silver lining?

I didn't have all day to talk ascension philosophy, however. "Are you all staying up at the castle?"

"Aye," Ginger said warily. "Why?"

I held up my hands again. "I just wanted to ask if you want me to connect you to our communications network. I'm not sure when someone else will get down this far to expand it, since the islands are cut off from supplies, and we've been focusing on making sure people in the Hebrides have, you know. Food. But it'll only take a minute, and I don't need anything from you. And as a bonus, there'll probably be a horde of rowdy, drunk Crianlarich folk to entertain you on speakerphone if you get bored."

"It would be good to know we could send word of those —what did you call them?" Patient Woman asked.

"Atheani," I said. "And while we're on the subject of threats, I have some other warnings I'd like to pass on, in hopes that you'd let us know if any of them crop up here or in Glasgow."

That earned me thoughtful nods, and if they looked at each other a bit warily, when Ginger reached out to shake my hand, I thought perhaps I'd made a new cadre of allies —however reluctant they might be.

Much as I didn't want to be the bearer of bad news, I hoped providing them with a supply of awful renditions of "Loch Lomond" sung from forty miles away might be a nice stand-in for the fallen algorithm's endless scroll of dumbassery.

I gave myself an hour with the people at the castle before Scout and I made our escape. The castle was built against the similarly named Dumbarton Rock, an imposing "hill" of moss- and grass-covered stone overlooking the Clyde Estuary where the river widened in anticipation of meeting the Irish Sea.

There was a lovely wee park between the water and the castle, and it was there I had placed the communications point.

My instincts were telling me I needed to get back to Oban. I had information burning a hole in my pocket, both about the anomalies and fungi's resistance *and* about the aliens.

Any hope I'd had that they might just be bored and peaceful had ended with that show of gratuitous violence. If they had that kind of power, they had no need to worry about a bunch of early-ascension cave-humans chasing after them with the relative equivalent of pea shooters. They'd annihilated the humans in cold blood.

That was something everyone needed to know as soon as possible. So far we'd only seen groups of three Atheani at a time, but that didn't mean there weren't more. I hadn't been able to see the three in Dumbarton clearly enough to tell if they were the same ones who had paid us a visit in Oban; we'd been a bit distracted trying not to get blown up.

It was a relief to leave even the outskirts of the city behind again with Scout winging north, a sensation that grew stronger with every passing mile.

This time, we didn't need to follow the road, since we weren't stopping in any more villages, so we cut overland, tracing Gare Loch and cutting over Loch Long and the Arrochar Alps. On a day where the sky was clear and blue and the hills vibrant green with the rejuvenation of early summer, seeing the Cobbler's rugged, saw-like shape from high above it with Beinn Ìme behind it made something in my soul sing.

I could feel Scout's apprehension melding with mine as we passed into Kintyre, then over Inverary and soon, Loch Awe.

The sense of urgency grew stronger. Now that the glow of having completed something important had faded with distance, the pressing weight of everything else waiting in Oban settled once more on my shoulders.

As if in response, Scout increased her speed.

"You don't have to push yourself too hard," I told her aloud, knowing she could feel my meaning more than hear the actual words with the wind. "I'm just being an anxious git."

Scout chittered a response so snippily that I thought she might actually be grumbling.

"I appreciate your haste," I added in a hurry. "I just don't want you to hurt yourself for my sake."

From the surge of exasperation I got in reply, I decided to prudently shut my gob and let her navigate her own limits like the giant sapient eagle she was.

The sun had just passed its zenith when we arrived back in Oban, and I was unsurprised to see Eilidh and Rhona both waiting for me in the Tesco carpark when Scout came in for a landing. And they weren't alone, I saw as I got closer. Sailean was pouncing something too small for me to see a short ways behind them, but at the sound of wings, the kitten lost interest in her prey and bounded towards us.

She launched herself at me almost before my feet touched the ground, climbing me like a scratching post until I cradled her to my chest.

"Missed you, wee toot," I said to her, ignoring Rhona's muttered, "What are we, chopped liver?" and instead moving around to Scout's front where she could say hi to the kitten as well, which she did.

The eagle lowered her head to Sailean, who head butted her beak in what I was beginning to think was their special bestie greeting.

"Tapadh leat," I said to Scout, reaching out to give her a scratch at her shoulder where her wings met. "I'll tell Catrìona to bring you an extra fish tonight if you like."

For all Scout's bravado and sulk about my telling her not to push herself, I could feel her exhaustion through our bond, though she stoically tried to hide it.

Normally, she loved to catch her food herself, but her relief at my promise permeated through me, so strong she couldn't keep that under wraps.

I heard Eilidh murmuring into her rockie-talkie about fish and grinned at Scout. Between the two of us, we'd make sure she was spoiled rotten.

The eagle huffed and launched herself into the air again, heading straight for her alcove back up at the tower, but she didn't release our bond like she usually did. Puzzled, I let it lie and turned to greet Eilidh and Rhona properly.

One kiss on Eilidh's lips and another on Rhona's forehead, and my own exhaustion hit me like a giant wallaby foot to the face.

"I was going to say we should fetch the others and get the throne crafted," I said, unable to repress the face-splitting yawn that invaded with my last word.

"But you're not going to do that, because Samuel's in Skye, and Finn made it to Pitlochry, and neither of them will be back until tomorrow," Eilidh told me perfunctorily. "Allow us to make an executive decision, a luaidh: go to bed. Go directly to bed. You're not to get up again until you've had eight hours of sleep."

That was an order I was all too ready to obey.

CHAPTER
NINETEEN

It wasn't often in my life that I'd slept so hard I woke up wondering what day it was, but when I woke the next day—I was fairly certain "morning" was long gone—I lay there for a moment in bed with my head swimming from a bizarre dream about getting stampeded by perfectly normal wallabies and had to check my internal system clock to know where I existed in time.

Eight hours, Eilidh had said. Eight.

By the looks of it, I'd been out for fifteen and a half.

A budding crick in my neck also told me I'd barely moved. Maybe setting up all those communications points had drained my energies more than I had thought.

I swallowed, star fishing in the middle of the bed since Eilidh was long gone—I had a vague memory of her coming to bed but zero recollection of her leaving again—and formed a mental list of the day's priorities. My first order of business was to get as many of our core leadership conglomerate in one place to share what I'd learned, but that was not something I could do on an empty stomach.

Downstairs, I found Catrìona had set aside a veritable

smorgasbord for me, which felt a wee bit like being a golden retriever rewarded for performing a series of tricks.

But hey, muffins.

I hovered a bit over the basket of goodies, everything from fresh fruit to magically sealed and cooled cheeses and meats, and decided choosing was for weaklings and took the whole basket with me when I left the house.

The afternoon passed in a blur of meetings, some rougher than others, but once I met up with Eilidh and Meeksy down at the harbour for an early dinner, the basket was long since empty and tucked into my inventory, and my to-do list had stretched a few pages longer. I was all too happy to tuck into the lobster roll Meeksy handed me.

"Where's Iain?" I asked Meeksy as I gave him a quick one-armed hug to avoid smushing lobster on his neck. "I haven't seen him since we got back after finding Kev and Aidan. Except for when he was kicking my arse."

"He's been running mad," Meeksy said, and Eilidh gave a fervent nod of agreement. "I haven't seen much of him myself."

"Does it count if he literally sprinted by me to catch a boat?" Eilidh asked.

"Only if he slapped your ass on the way by," Meeksy said, then paused. "Actually, he's only allowed to do that to me."

"I was going to say," Eilidh agreed. "I don't care if I'm not his type. Nobody gets arse-slapping permissions unless I say so."

"A sound rule," Meeksy said sagely.

We moved a bit away from the seafood shack to sit on the concrete ledge of the pier. All too soon, my lobster roll was only a memory. I suppressed a burp before daring to speak.

"Has Finn made it back yet?" The final big item on the list for today was the Resplendent Throne, but that was moot without Finn.

In all my own running amok through the past few hours, I had yet to catch a glimpse of the man. I knew Samuel was in town since he'd come through when I was briefing Angus and Meeksy about the anomaly experiments I wanted to stage.

Eilidh shook her head. "I think there's some trouble in Perth."

"Perth? He made it all the way to Perth?" Apparently all my meetings had not been as much of a two-way information share as I'd hoped. "I thought he was in Pitlochry."

"He was," Meeksy assured me, "but he rang through a couple hours ago, just long enough to tell Angus he'd be a bit longer."

That suggested we weren't going to manage to craft the throne tonight. Damn.

"Eilidh!"

I recognised that voice. I turned to see young Andy, the teenage kid Eilidh and I had encountered near Kilchurn Castle not long after we'd met up ourselves. He seemed to have been going full tilt for a while, though I couldn't tell which direction he'd come from.

And whatever had him running our way was probably going to back burner any plans I'd had for the rest of the day anyway.

"Hey," Eilidh said to him, alarm creeping into her voice. "Something wrong?"

Andy skidded to a stop a couple feet away from us, breathing hard. "There's one of those rift things in Connel."

"Did you run all the way here from Connel?" I asked him, but he shook his head immediately.

"No, used the teleporter hingmy, but I had to run to the Connel one from where the rift was." He sucked in a few deep breaths. "Can you come back with me?"

"Did something happen?" Eilidh's own instincts seemed to be sending up warning flares, because she stood up and brushed crumbs from her hands. "Did something come out of the rift?"

"No, no, worse," Andy said, then blurted out, "People vanished into it and no one has come back."

Not much could get us moving as quickly as people vanishing through a dimensional rift.

Then again, we weren't sure what the rifts actually were. For all we knew, they just transported people around Earth.

I didn't believe that, not really. The few brief glimpses I'd had of the rifts had also come with unfamiliar smells of alien air, foliage we'd never seen in our world.

Andy led the way as we stepped out of the ionad-siubhail in Connel, breaking into a run straight away.

My stomach wouldn't thank me for going right to jogging after eating, but if I boaked, I could always replace the lobster roll.

I hadn't spent much time in Connel since we'd fought the vicious snake monster that was the beithir, and those memories did not make visiting more appealing. It was too easy to look out at Loch Etive and see Rhona's parents in the water, stumbling only just saved from death. Many people that day didn't have the luxury of so close a shave—they'd just died.

Andy picked up speed as we ran east along the loch on the A85, which had now been cleared of all cars.

"How far is it?" I asked him, understanding now why he'd appeared in Oban so winded.

"Primary school" was all he said in answer.

That wasn't far, but it also clued me in to why he seemed so urgent.

Fuck. I really hoped it wasn't kids.

It was only another couple hundred metres to the school, and we covered that distance quickly. I pulled back to let Andy take the lead, and he led us just past the school itself to a passing place where a fence and a stile gated off a path down to the edge of the sea loch.

A handful of people stood gathered around the stile, tension evident in their stances as they stared down towards the water.

One of them, I recognised.

"Eliza," I said to her.

She turned, her face going slack with relief as she recognised us.

Eliza was Angus's wife, a slender English woman with milk-pale skin and a curtain of silver hair that framed her face when she wore it loose, but today, she had it pulled into a plait over one shoulder, though it wasn't quite long enough to be secure, and stick-straight bits stuck out from where they'd escaped the braid.

"It's already gone," she said before any of us could say anything else. "It just vanished, like someone had zipped it up from the other side."

Andy's gangly teenage frame slumped in defeat. "It's just...gone?"

"You're sure people went into it," I said slowly. "On purpose?"

Eliza shook her head, and the trio of people behind her shot me angry looks.

"Not on purpose, I don't think, but I wasn't here when it happened. I was in the school with the kids and heard an uproar." Eliza glanced over her shoulder at the folks behind her. "Sean is the only one who saw it happen."

There was only one man in the trio, and I assumed that had to be Sean. He had dark hair that was even curlier than mine and an almost cherubic face despite the bolt of grey at his temples that suggested he was probably older than me.

When he spoke, he had a distinctive Irish accent. "They didn't just leap through a fuckin' hole in the air—it opened right where they were walking and I couldn't do anything to stop it."

That sent a chill wriggling its way up my spinal cord.

"Did you see what happened after that? Could you still see them through the rift or did they vanish?" My mouth suddenly felt very dry, and while the running had not made me vomit up my lobster roll, I wasn't entirely convinced this conversation wouldn't accomplish what the sprint had not.

Sean was just shaking his head, but I didn't think it was in answer to my questions. It felt like he was struggling to parse his own memories.

I glanced over at Eilidh, who stood beside Meeksy close enough that their shoulders touched. Both of them seemed to be making an effort to keep their expressions from showing how unsettled they felt, but I'd known both of them for years. That simple contact of old friends, the reassurance in proximity—it told me they were paddling this boat right alongside me.

The next thing Sean said made me feel like a kraken had

slapped the proverbial oar right out of my hand and dragged it under the surface, leaving me to flounder.

"I was calling for them over and over," he said, his voice growing distant. "They couldn't hear me. I don't think they could see me, either. I could see them at first."

Andy piped up. "They blurred after a few seconds," he said. "It was like some sort of fog covered them."

"And they couldn't hear you," I said slowly.

I thought of the rock chucked through the rift we'd discovered a few days back, how all of us waited for the sound of it striking earth. That sound had never come, even though the rock had to have landed somewhere, assuming there was gravity on the other side.

Eilidh met my gaze when I looked her way again. "Sound doesn't travel through."

"But physical items and people do." I paused. "And smells."

My brain wanted to explode with everything that was happening, and I couldn't shake the feeling it was all connected.

There was no way I'd be able to explain the physics of it. I also didn't think it mattered. We could leave that to the scientists in a few decades after we'd survived this one.

"Was it kids?" Meeksy asked quietly.

It was the question I'd been too afraid to ask, because I dreaded an affirmative answer.

Sean, thankfully, shook his head. "No. It was a couple of the swingers, you know, those people who came up from Glasgow. I only knew one of them a little—Sammy."

Sammy.

The name sent a shockwave through me, because I knew her a little. She was the first of her group I'd met, a lovely and warm woman with brown skin and a friendly smile. What was her husband's name? D.D.

"Was the man she was with white? Medium build"—I wracked my brain to remember—"with brown hair? Kind of face that shows all their stories in the lines?"

Sean shook his head again, this time more slowly. "She was with a white man, but he was younger, no lines on his face yet."

Fuck.

"Eliza," I said, "can you get on the rockie-talkie and ask Angus to find a man called D.D. and bring him here?"

If the person Sammy'd been with wasn't her husband, that meant we had to break to the news to him that his wife had vanished into a rift and might never make it back to this world.

CHAPTER
TWENTY

Even though I'd gotten arguably two full nights' sleep in one the night before, I felt as if I'd been put through a wringer and slowly cranked into my bed by the time Eilidh and I made it there well after midnight.

Telling someone their spouse was probably dead? Yeah, that was on my list of things to never have to do again, if I could avoid it. The sound of D.D.'s wailing sob would haunt me for the rest of my days—and if the ascension's hints were to be believed, the rest of my days would be a long, long time.

"Do you get the feeling everything's about to go tits up?" I muttered into her neck as we curled up together with Sailean—who had spent the day with Rhona—kneading up a storm on the duvet.

"Bold of you to assert that things are not already demonstrably tits up," Eilidh said groggily. "I thought I'd feel better after I got my portion of the throne crafting recipe, but now..."

"Feels a bit futile?"

"It feels like a Hail Mary." In the dark, I couldn't see

much more than her silhouette as we lay there. Eilidh sighed. "It might be worth it. I think it *should* be for the system to make such a big deal out of it. It doesn't seem to have much of a sense of humour beyond the puns. But it's hard to look at this throne from our ignorant angle and see anything but a probable large chair."

"What if it's a toilet?"

"What?"

"The throne. The Resplendent Throne. What if it's the most spectacular toilet anyone in the universe has ever seen?"

"A loo fit for the gods?" Eilidh snorted, then paused. "Do gods even need a loo?"

"I guess if we ascend to godhood, we can answer that question ourselves." If we couldn't be irreverent about our own potential deification, what could we be irreverent about?

"If we have done all this buildup and fuss for a toilet, I'm going to find a way to channel my inner Karen and complain to whatever manager I can find at this Ascended Alliance." Eilidh yawned with the last word, triggering an answering yawn of my own. "I don't think it's a toilet."

"Neither do I," I said after a moment. "What do you think it is?"

Eilidh was quiet for half a minute or so. I listened to the slow rise and fall of her breath, feeling it lull me.

Just as I decided she might have fallen asleep, she answered me.

"I think it's the next step in our ascension."

"Ours personally?" I wasn't sure what made me follow up with that particular question.

Another pause. "No," Eilidh said slowly. "Not just ours personally."

"Then whose?" I hadn't been expecting a denial, especially since the blueprints had been so tailored not only to us personally but to our friends. It certainly felt personal.

That time, the pause stretched out even longer than the first had. Eilidh's breathing, however, no longer held steady with the deepening rhythm of approaching sleep. Instead, her inhales were shallow, her exhales not total.

When she spoke, her voice held the same steel she wielded with such certainty in her claymore.

"The whole world's."

We came downstairs the next morning to find Finn waiting for us, sipping from a mug of coffee across the table from Catrìona.

"Morning, you two," I said to them, trying to disguise how odd it felt to see them in Catrìona's kitchen.

Sailean had abandoned us in the wee hours of the morning, and now she sat with Finn on the bench at the table, her tummy very round and probably full of sausage.

I swear, that cat was going to turn into a bowling ball if we weren't careful.

"Morning," Finn said, and Catrìona echoed it.

"No boat today?" I asked her as I squeezed past Eilidh to start our coffee, motioning at her to sit down.

Catrìona shook her head. "More pressing business. Finn wants me to organise reinforcements."

That woke me up far more than the cup of coffee I was anticipating.

"I don't like the sound of that," Eilidh said before I could.

"You shouldn't." Finn's voice was more monotonous

than I'd ever heard it. He usually spoke with expression and feeling, even if he was a rather reserved person.

The shift in his demeanour made me almost more worried than his words had.

"Explain," Eilidh said.

She was not known for her patience first thing in the morning, especially before her coffee. I hastily finished our cups and brought hers over to her, which she took with both hands and held it in front of her face like the aroma could form a buffer against the impending bad news.

Finn finally answered, his words clearly chosen after careful deliberation. "It seems the anomalies have infected a grove of trees."

His words made my blood turn to sap in my veins.

Eilidh and I locked eyes.

"Catrìona," I said faintly, "did you catch him up with everything I learned?"

"He just got here," she told me, an apology in her tight-lipped smile that didn't reach her eyes.

"Tell me," Finn said.

I let out a slow exhale, my mind already reordering the priority list for the day. "Eilidh, will you get Meeksy?"

"I think he's in Kilmelford."

"He can go back as soon as we're done. We need him to start on the experiments today. Fast." I did not think it was the caffeine making my body feel jittery. Naw, that was good old-fashioned fear.

Finn watched me closely, and I had no desire to hold him in suspense. I started talking, and as I ran through what I'd discovered in Crianlarich, that flat look on his face grew more and more pronounced.

This was going to be a long, long day.

Oban sprang into motion through the morning. With every person or group who came and went out of the Whyte House, the tension levels in the town ratcheted up another level.

We had Meeksy take all the samples I'd gathered and prepare them for exposure to the anomalies contained in Kilmelford. That meant we wouldn't have our most valuable healer with us when we left Oban, but it did mean we had one of the people I trusted most on the planet in charge of an experiment that could give us our first desperately needed breakthrough on the anomalies. On how they spread, how to fight them. Hell, if it took dosing people with mushrooms to cure the corruption, I'd find every liberty cap hunter in all of Argyll to cultivate those magic wee shroomies in every field between here and Perthshire.

If only it were that simple.

Catrìona gathered everyone she could find—veterans of Blàr Ghaineamhain who'd fought Lord Bawbag, survivors from the fight against the beithir in Connel, all our most experienced fighters, scouts, and healers.

And we sought anyone who had levelled Purifire past level seven or eight. We needed people who could create and hold a shield of the stuff if we had any hope of fighting a fucking *forest*.

Just the thought of it chilled me to the little ribosomes in my cells. There could be no doubt about it at all—the corruption was spreading, and it was very literally taking root.

Rhona we sent to Iona to fetch Samuel, who had gone home for the night, expecting a day or so to wait for Finn's return, and Ealasaid had gone with him.

Anyone who didn't fall into the above categories but had magical crafting ability or had experience with the ionadan-siubhail? They got sent out immediately with orders to stretch our network as far east as they could get before we had to march. Scout, who had sensed my growing anxiety through the bond she'd not yet relinquished, came in with her own plan: she rallied the eagles to transport these crafters.

Every moment we could save, every hour of walking overland turned into a quick jump with ionadan-siubhail—that could prevent the anomalous trees from further infecting the land around them.

And at this time of year when their pollen dusted the world around them yellow, the chances that the wind could be spreading the corruption farther afield with every passing second were too high for me to even attempt to comprehend. If I thought about it for too long, I would freeze up. Crawl under a duvet and wait for the heat death of the universe.

Okay, maybe not quite that dramatic, but this situation had gone from bad to worse, and then the "worse" had caught a fucking arcane plague.

Despite the urgency of the moment, or perhaps because of it, while the rest of Oban prepared to march into battle, the six of us prepared to craft a mythical item I truly, *fervently* hoped was not a toilet.

It went unsaid that if things went poorly in Perth, this might very well be the only shot we got at crafting the Resplendent Throne until others somehow unlocked the Pantheon affinity.

My task, apart from the antlers, was the Purifire reliquary.

Part of me thought I'd stalled in its creation out of

reluctance to take up the mantle that seemed determined to throw itself over my shoulders. I never, not once in my existence, would have thought to aspire to godhood. But here we were, the only six people in Scotland to have unlocked the Pantheon affinity and the only people, it seemed, who could make a mythical chair go.

I pulled up the list again.

To craft the Resplendent Throne, you must gather the following items and assemble the following participants:

   -Native wood from the community of the pantheon

   -Native stone from the community of the pantheon

   -Triune waters from the community of the pantheon (Varies by region. For Earra-Ghàidheal, this consists of: seawater, fresh-water loch, rain)

   -Purifire reliquary (additional blueprint unlocked)

   -3 donated animal offerings from sapient, willing participants

   -Guth iomadh-fhillte, aon òran air a ghabhail

Finn already had the water from Loch Ba he'd promised. We had the wood, the stone, the water, the animal offerings. And even as I sat in the Whyte House kitchen with a small pile of raw quartz in front of me on the trestle table, Catrìona herself was playing the dual role of army recruiter and Gaelic choir wrangler.

Oddly enough, I think she would have preferred to conscript people until the cows came home over trying to round up thirty Gaelic singers to have them sing at a glorified chair.

The Purifire was all me.

I was alone in the house, everyone else busy on their own personal missions.

The blueprint for the Purifire reliquary had already absorbed into my psyche; I had no need to look at the instructions to know how to do it. But part of the instructions themselves ran contrary to every bit of frenetic movement of the day, requiring a calm I wasn't sure I possessed even when I *wasn't* in a state of existential terror.

Even so, I knew what I had to do.

It felt simultaneously unbelievable and appropriate to be doing this at a kitchen table where I'd passed so many meals in the company of people I loved over the years. Mum and I had come here for dinner together more times than I could count before she died. She and Catrìona had been as close as I was with Iain; the table here had seen mischief, tears, laughter, crumbs, the occasional blood.

When I began to thread spirit into tendrils, binding the filaments and plying them together, all of those memories came with it.

The blueprint had given me the pattern of the lattice; all I had to do was follow it. I could see its shape overlaid in my vision, the reality of glowing threads of spirit melding with the image.

The quartz in front of me was in chunks and clusters, all pure but without structure like the towers had been. The structure was what I needed to build.

As the lattice of spirit expanded, the flows of its threads twined together, looping around one another and turning back in on themselves. It reminded me of wicker art, the reeds all layering together, softened and pliable as they were worked but sturdy and solid once they dried. Just like that, the spirit I continued to feed began as something pliable, shaping itself to the design in my mind, but the more it built upon itself, the established sections grew into immovable fractals.

And the quartz on the table responded.

The vibration began almost too low to notice, a thrum that could have existed outwith my ears' ability to sense the frequency. As it built, however, it became impossible to ignore.

As the vibration intensified, the raw quartz on the table began to fracture.

Some of my crafting study surfaced as the fractures grew more frequent. The cracking sound of breaking rock punctuated every breath I took. To the untrained eye, the conchoidal fractures of quartz might seem to lack the symmetry of a mineral like pyrite that, when dropped, would always break into cubic forms.

The manner of the quartz lay closer to flint or obsidian. Such a fracture was what created the stereotypical image of ancient arrowheads or hand axes—conchoidal fractures could allow for stone to be honed into something sharp enough to cut wood, pierce hide.

Here on the table in front of me, the chunks of quartz varied in size from the general shape of my closed fist to something closer to pebbles. The largest pieces fractured first, flakes falling away with little percussive snicks and cracks. As the pieces grew smaller and the flakes turned to small mounds, those also began to fracture.

Smaller and smaller they went until the table seemed covered in translucent fish scales. From there, they grew even smaller, the snicks and cracks softening to a whisper. And when the stone had broken down until, at a glance, it most closely resembled sand or table salt, those tiny pieces almost shuddered in front of me as they lifted from the table to float upwards until they met the lattice of spirit I'd carefully cultivated.

The effect of what was likely hundreds of thousands of scale-like pieces of quartz was dazzling even in the artificial light of the kitchen.

And that wasn't even its final form.

Despite the very solid-appearing design of spirit hovering in front of my face, it wasn't solid. If something had crashed through the centre of it, it would have dissolved, and I would have had to start over.

That wasn't going to happen.

I slowly breathed out, watching the mesmerising shimmer of glittering crystal and magic.

My breath eased out, calm flooding my senses as the lattice of spirit and crystal slowly rotated in front of me.

I pulled more threads of spirit now, form the ambient spirit around me and from my own well, allowing them to coalesce in a pattern I was intimately familiar with—Purifire.

Its green-blue hue swirled and licked at the air, flames both powerful and infinitesimal.

I fed it into the lattice, starting with the heart.

The moment the strands of Purifire touched the painstakingly constructed lattice of raw spirit and quartz, the entire lattice ignited in teal as vibrant as the waters of Iona.

What had been a rotating disk slowly elongated from the centre outward, forming into a point at the heart of the lattice. As the point drew away from the plane the lattice had occupied, it formed a cone. It began to swirl like a potter's clay on a wheel, the lattice blending with the myriad fragments of quartz and Purifire as it stretched, the wide end drawing in until what hovered in front of me was an oblong, symmetrical shape like a marquise-cut diamond, an oval that had contracted at both ends into points.

I caught it in my hands.

It warmed my palms, the glow of Purifire swirling within.

The quartz, no longer tiny fragments but a solid structure, still gave off glitters that refracted light into rainbows.

A Purifire reliquary.

The power within it would pour into the Resplendent Throne.

CHAPTER
TWENTY-ONE

By unanimous agreement, the six of us took all of our materials up to McCaig's Tower. It seemed like the right place to craft something that could prove so central to all of our lives and the future of our community, and it wasn't so *literally* central that our semi-secretive mission would prove a distraction for the hundreds of people working to prepare for the battle beckoning from Perth.

Ealasaid walked beside me, her arm in mine. Eilidh and Rhona were in front of us—Sailean perched on Eilidh's shoulder—with Samuel and Finn bringing up the rear.

I hadn't seen much of Ealasaid since the kraken battle. She'd been so busy in Mull, but I had no idea what it was she'd been working on. For all I knew, she'd been on holiday.

I didn't really think that was the case.

"Tha dragh ort, a ghràidh," Ealasaid murmured to me. "Dè tha dol?"

Giving her a sideways glance, I let out a sound that was half sigh, half chuckle. I ought to have expected that she would see right through me. The cailleach was in tune with many things, and since she'd adopted the lot of us as her magically bonded grandchildren—well, Samuel was closer to her age than ours—it seemed that Ealasaid had indeed taken her role in our little fledgling group of punters to heart.

She knew I was worried, and somehow I didn't think she'd let me answer her question with an excuse or a deflection.

"It's all a bit overwhelming," I said in English. "It's hard to feel like we are making any progress when the threats keep piling up like this."

Ealasaid tightened her arm in mine. We'd reached the enchanted pathway leading to McCaig's Tower, which I still couldn't look at too closely due to the enchantment doing the heavy lifting to make the nearly seventy-degree angle of the climb flat to those walking on it. But Ealasaid gestured ahead of us at the path and the tower itself, where three of our golden eagle friends and one white-tailed sea eagle—not Duan; I didn't know this one's name—perched, preening their feathers in the afternoon sun. Behind them, Craobh an Òbain rose, its branches visible over the tower's encircling stone.

"Seall air na rinn sinn." Ealasaid took hold of my hand and squeezed it as she pointed out one of the most tangible accomplishments of our community's ascension. "We have done the impossible many times over, a luaidh. How can you look at all of this and not marvel? If you had told me, when you rescued us from that monster's corral, that we would be going up against invaders from another world and a contagion that would make ebola look pretty, I would have backed slowly away and then run in the opposite direction. It's madness. Miraculous. Look, m' eudail, at what we've already done and ask yourself: if we could do all of this weeks ago when we're all practically weans in swaddling clothes, what miracles are we capable of now, today?"

The others had slowed, clearly eavesdropping, and I felt a hand on my shoulder from behind.

I turned to see Samuel, the gentle monk who had devoted his life to serving all people in Iona. His mercy surrounded him like a blanket, reaching out to embrace anyone near with the kind of unconditional love that could only be called divine.

"Set aside your fear for an hour, my friend," he said to me. "I will do the same. Let us see what the Resplendent Throne holds for us, and when that hour is up, we will ask ourselves once more what feels possible, just to see if our capacity for imagining our expanding abilities has grown. Like this tree. Like this town. Like this group."

I swallowed. Nodded.

I didn't trust myself to do anything else.

He was right. And I didn't miss that he had also admitted his own fear. That, as much as anything else, helped me walk with steadier steps.

I wasn't sure I'd ever really get used to turning up somewhere apparently empty-handed only to blink and see a wealth of materials coalesce before my very eyes.

The six of us had emptied our inventories of the materials we needed for the throne, much of it large and ungainly enough that pre-ascension, it would have taken heavy machinery to transport and not our own two feet and a mystical inventory.

When I'd read "native wood," I'd imagined planks, processed lumber. What Finn had produced from his inventory, however, was more or less an entire goddamn tree. It must have fallen in a storm, judging from the root ball showing signs of breakage even though it still held a large amount of dirt. Now it lay under the shadow of Craobh an Òbain like our mythical tree stood vigil over her fallen brethren.

Samuel had brought us three entire blocks of raw and rough-hewn Iona marble, its green-flecked faces retrieved from the century-dormant quarry in the southeastern corner of the island. Each had to weigh at least a tonne in itself. I had not tested the bounds of my inventory ability, but presumably, neither Finn nor Samuel had, you know, needed to power lift entire trees or hunks of bedrock to stash it away for travel.

Maybe in a thousand years, I'd have enough time on my hands to sit down and try to learn enough about ascension physics to understand how all this could work, but my little hamster brain was too focused on the task at hand today.

Rhona and Eilidh placed their bottles of water on top of one of the marble blocks, and a moment later, Ealasaid's decanter of water from Loch Ba joined theirs. It seemed Finn had let her do that gathering. Feeling strangely unsteady, I moved forward myself and produced the antlers and the Purifire reliquary I'd created, which still glowed and glittered, casting wave-like light patterns on the rough marble. Scout's feather came next, then Eilidh reached up to her shoulder to give Sailean a gentle stroke before pulling the wildcat pelt from her own inventory and placing it next to the feather and antlers with reverence.

"All that's missing now is the choir," I said.

"They're on their way," Finn murmured. "It's not just the Oban choir, either."

"It's not?" Eilidh's head swivelled to look at him.

He shook his head, a small smile on his face that, even without explanation, hit me with a pang of wistfulness.

"Word spread," he said. "From Barra to Aberfeldy."

There were something like forty Gaelic choirs in Scotland, if my fuzzy memory from childhood mòds held true. I knew there was a Barra choir, an Islay choir, a Portree choir in Skye. Taynuilt and Lochaline, Mull and Lochaber. There were more choirs in Lewis and Harris, too, but I didn't think we'd gotten that far afield yet. Same with Sutherland and the Central Belt. We'd not yet reached Glasgow or Edinburgh or Aberdeen—or Inverness.

"How many—" I began, but the sudden lump in my throat caught hold of me, and I had to break off to clear it. "How many are coming?"

Finn met my eyes with a look that told me he knew exactly what I was feeling. "Best I can tell, at least two hundred."

Two hundred.

Two hundred.

For some reason, those simple words struck my heart with a jolt of pure, raw emotion.

Even putting aside the surprise and relief that so many had survived this long in the ascension world when our Gaelic community was an ageing one, that was a tremendous number. I remembered standing with Mum on Saturday mornings after the frenzied week of music competitions we called the Royal National Mòd when the massed choirs from all over Scotland joined to sing through that year's repertoire, the different-sized choirs showing off their own categories' competition songs all together, not for prizes or acclaim, just for the joy of singing. Even in the years where Mum had practically had to drag me to the junior choirs I'd reluctantly sung in—or worse, my short-lived attempts at the occasional solo competition—the massed choirs, sometimes as many as a thousand singers, had stirred something in me, a sense of belonging all too fleeting.

And now they were coming here. Today.

Not all of them, but two hundred voices felt momentous.

Even as I tried to find words, I heard the soft sound of voices approaching and turned to see the conductor of the Oban choir, a longtime friend of my mother's, walking into the tower with several others at her back. Catrìona was with her as well, and—to my surprise— Iain.

The Oban conductor was called Julie MacInnes, a tall, vibrant woman, statuesque but with a warmth that poured from her smile when she spotted me and came up to take both my hands in hers.

"Sin thu, a Chaluim," she said to me in greeting, then switched to English. "Your mum would be so proud to see you today."

Damn it. I was never going to be able to speak coherently if people kept saying things like that. I barely managed a nod.

"Who knows," she said after a moment of squeezing my hands. "With all the magic in this world, maybe something will reach her spirit, wherever she is."

I had to close my eyes.

For a self-described pathetic himbo hamster with exactly one emotion, I was doing a fairly good impression of a feeling person.

Iain and Catrìona met my gaze as Julie moved on to Eilidh and Finn, but it was Rhona who flew into my arms like a small brunette face hugger, though thankfully she didn't throw herself at my face. She did, however, practically suction cup herself to my ribcage.

"Air," I reminded her as she squeezed what remained in my lungs right back out.

"Shut up. I'm trying to comfort you."

I obeyed, stifling a laugh because I didn't have much breath to let it escape. I wrapped my arms around her shoulders to give her a pat.

As minutes passed, more and more people poured into McCaig's Tower. The eagles, uncomfortable with this many people or simply giving us space, winged their way out over the harbour to hunt.

Familiar faces dotted the crowd, Gaels I knew either on sight or by name. There were the MacKinnons from Jura, speaking quietly to a MacKechnie bass from Morvern, some of Catrìona's cousins from Mull and a Barra tenor I'd actually met at uni and hadn't realised he still sang with the Barra choir. It hadn't been my world for a long time, but nevertheless, the more faces I recognised, the more I realised that it had always been just the one world all along; the only thing that changed was our place in it.

Now the only thing to do was wait.

No matter how momentous the occasion, one bit of levity helped me avoid dissolving into a puddle of goo: Gaels still ran on GMT.

Not Greenwich Mean Time.

Gaelic Maybe Time.

It took over an hour and a half for the tower to fill up with choristers, most of whom had not been to Oban since the ascension and most certainly had not seen our miraculous tree. I moved among them hand in hand with Eilidh—once Rhona had released me from her death grip of aggressive moral support—mostly watching them marvel.

That hammered home Samuel's point. Sometimes it took seeing our own accomplishments through the fresh eyes of newcomers to grasp the extent of it. McCaig's Tower had transformed from a funny wee busywork project for Oban's masons, a hollow shell of rock. Now it was a beacon on a hill overlooking not just our town of Oban but the surrounding islands. Its gargoyles were enormous eagles of legend; at its heart a tree that nourished all beneath her branches with knowledge and peace.

The soft glow of the tree's countless shimmering lights cast the whole of the space in an ethereal halo.

Samuel was right.

We had already moved mountains.

What we did today was simply the next logical step, wherever it might lead.

It was time for us to do just that.

All around me, the others in our strange wee group of unlikely leaders moved towards one another. Finn, Samuel, Ealasaid, Rhona.

Eilidh.

Me.

The time had come.

TWENTY-TWO

A hush fell over the gathered crowd without us needing to say anything. That alone was cause for surprise, if not alarm—we Gaels were a chatty bunch. Getting us to shut up was often a feat.

Out of the corner of my eye, I noticed that Meeksy had arrived at some point, which gave me a moment of relief. He and Iain both deserved to be here as much as anyone.

In silence, the gathered choirs spread out around us. I wasn't sure if Finn or someone had instructed them in what to do. Maybe no one had.

I couldn't take the time to count them, but I had the strong suspicion there were more than even the two hundred who had seemed so beyond my expectation only an hour ago.

As moments stretched out, spirit stirred.

At first, it seemed to swirl in small eddies around myself and my companions at the centre of this circle.

The choirs enfolded us, Craobh an Òbain sheltering us under her branches. The dying oak lay silent, uprooted but not yet gone. His summer leaves were drying but still green; I could sense life yet within his veins and roots and boughs. He held no fear upon him of moving past this threshold. How could he, when all trees knew their falling simply returned them to the forest, spreading their essence through the thousands or millions of life forms nourished by their passing? Something of his spirit remained, melding with ours, with the earth beneath, with the majestic heart-tree a shield to guard and guide his transition.

Quieter was the stone. To that ancient marble, even the trees were fleeting presences. It cared not for winds that might scour its face, nor for the shift of plates that might bring new stone to the surface in new forms. Patient. Certain.

The Purifire reliquary glowed brighter, and swirls of mica and sediment moved through the phylacteries of our triune waters. Sea water that contained the remnants of stone and crystal worn to sand over ages untold, loch water steeped in the ancient peat of millions of years' life cycles, plants and animals and fungi and everything in between. Peat was our fuel, the smoke in our whisky, the heat in our winter homes.

And the rain, the rain, the rain.

As I watched, Eilidh's jar of rain from the slopes of Cruachan Beann shifted, mist rising from the surface. The phylactery was only half full, and that mist condensed into tiny clouds, gathering at the top of the vessel.

Triune waters, all one word in Gaelic. All uisge. Even the rain—we had no word in Gaelic for rain, only called it simply "the water." An t-uisge.

And then, like the first drop falling from a Scottish sky, somewhere in the crowd of choristers someone began to hum.

It began as barely more than a murmur, a single voice amid hundreds.

Almost too quiet to hear, it was spirit where that voice resounded, clear as day.

Another voice joined, far on the other side of the circle. And then another.

One melody, picked up voice by voice around us.

Spirit responded. The eddies and stirring swirls I had noticed built with every additional thread of melody resonating through the crowd.

Where we stood at the centre of this space, surrounded by voices, that melody built quietly. Familiar. I knew this song, but its name eluded me. I could hear my mum humming it while she tended to an injured owl, her voice as calming to the wildlife she rescued as it was to me.

Music had always been a special kind of magic.

Now, amplified by literal magic, those voices spun a tapestry of resonance that I felt across the surface of my skin, as palpable as a touch.

I turned slowly to face the others. Eilidh stood by my side on my right, Rhona on my left. Ealasaid faced me with Finn on her left and Samuel on her right. Together, the six of us formed two smaller triangles.

It had been some time since the kraken, since our combined spirit had melded to destroy that threat to our lands and lives.

All the fear and apprehension I had felt about the uncertain wisdom of taking the time to do this in the face of the dangers converging on us from all sides—it slipped away, pried loose to dissolve the moment my unconsciously offered tendril of spirit met the others' at the centre of our smaller circle.

The choir had fallen into a lull at the end of the short,

repeating tune they hummed in unison. But at that precise moment, their wordless song began again, this time splitting into four-part harmony that bloomed in a mandala of expanding spirit with our six united threads at the heart.

Guth iomadh-fhillte, aon òran air a ghabhail.

A many-layered voice, one song sung.

Behind Ealasaid, the fallen oak lifted into the air.

Moments later, the Iona marble did the same.

Everything happened as if in a dream.

The six of us slowly stepped backwards, remaining in our circle but increasing the space between us. Our commingled spirit rushed in to fill that space as the old oak rose above our heads with a soft patter of soil dislodging from its uprooted base.

Heavy blocks of marble encircled it above our heads, suspended in the air, a perfect triangle with the tree at its centre.

Once more, the choir reached the end of the short tune, the harmonies holding as they began again.

Chills broke out over my entire body as I finally recognised the melody.

Ò, Rìgh nan dùl, 's nam feart tha shuas...

Spirit rose with the elements around us, stone and wood alike blooming into light as the exposed roots of the dying tree touched the lattice suspended between the six of us, fed and grown by the choir's voices.

O, king of the elements and forces above...

I felt more than saw the influx of spirit travel up the root system into the trunk of the tree, sensed it as it climbed to the level of the oak's first boughs and spread, spread, spread through the myriad branching forks to the leaves.

Do bheannachd gràsmhor dòirt a-nuas...

Light grew warmer, a soft breeze rolling off the tree

above us as it slowly descended. That warmth washed back into me, replenishing me even as I continued to spin my own spirit into maintaining the weave.

Your gracious blessings pour down...

Light and warmth spilled out from the tree's sheltering branches, suffusing the entirety of the inner tower with a reverent stillness.

Le 'r tìr 's le 'r teangaidh soirbhich fhèin...

That sensation built, growing, gaining strength as it reached the edges of the tower itself and continued to expand.

Upon our land and our language...

Dimly, I was aware of Craobh an Òbain. Without thought, the tree seemed secondary to the proceedings, but that could not have been farther from the truth.

While its trunk stood outwith the smaller circle I made with Eilidh, Rhona, Finn, Samuel, and Ealasaid, its roots had grown downwards and outwards, spreading beneath our feet. I knew to my core without testing or probing that those roots formed the foundation for the entire tower itself.

'S bidh clann nan Gàidheal fo sgàil do sgèith.

As the massed choir reached the final line of the simple hymn, they once more swelled into a hum with the last chord, voices splitting further to eight distinct parts.

And the children of the Gaels will dwell under the shadow of your wing.

And the oak and marble touched the ground in our midst.

The oak began to change, the roots condensing, the branches slipping back into the trunk.

Around it, the marble grew fluid, almost seeming to melt from its rectangular blocks to flow against the earth, grasses parting and drawing back like a carpet to accommodate the stone.

The choir continued to hum, this time a single clear soprano voice rising above the rest with the lyrics as they repeated.

Her voice ached with the simple invocation she sang, and spirit poured through our gathered masses to guide the flows of mouldable rock and branch. First marble carved out a wide circle, flattening and forming a level surface. Even as I watched, divots appeared at regular intervals around the circle, further smoothing out into ramps that seemed to blend themselves into the earth beneath.

Then, like petals unfolding from a flower's bud, between each ramp the marble reached upwards in an arc to create six perfect half circles.

I lost track of myself as the song continued to rise and fall around us, other voices taking the melody against the accompaniment of humming that drifted from one side of the circle to the other and back in quiet encouragement.

The energies suffused my entire being, permeating through even my sense of self, as if spirit had transcended even using the normal channels and meridians in my physical and energetic bodies, instead simply filling the empty space between the particles of my atoms.

The oak split.

My attention had been so focused on the marble that I had missed the shifting tree's descent until it passed into my field of vision, six root-like shapes emerging from the remade cohesive whole to reach out for each of the marble semicircles.

When rock met wood, the oak fanned out, extending beyond the boundary of the semicircle and curving inwards.

For the first time since we'd begun, I saw a throne begin to take shape.

Not just one throne.

Six.

The oak moulded itself into seats, graceful arms, high-backed leaves of wood expanding.

I had long since lost track of the waters and the animal offerings and the Purifire reliquary, but they appeared now.

Much like the tree had hovered with the trio of marble blocks encircling its roots, the blue-green glowing reliquary now slowly lowered over the precise centre of the marble dais. The three vessels of water, though, instead of hanging in stasis, floated in a circle to orbit the teal flames.

The choir began the hymn again, over three hundred voices singing the lyrics together in exquisite harmony.

As their volume slowly rose from a soft sigh to a growing, yearning intensity, the glass holding the triune waters dissolved into motes of spirit. The water seemed to funnel into itself, three sources combining and then splitting once more into too many threads to count. Those threads plaited themselves together like the layered voices of the choir singing this throne into existence.

Once again, the water split into six, like flowing spokes of an enormous wheel, and the Purifire reliquary flared into brilliance, cascading like liquid flame to meet the intricate plaits of the triune waters.

Almost too quickly for me to observe, the six thrones... unfolded.

I couldn't see what had become of the antlers, the feather, the pelt. But even as I thought it, I felt them, just the barest impression of their presence, their shape, before spirit gently took them back.

Somehow, my view of the thrones encompassed all of

them, unobscured by my physical vantage point's restriction.

Antlers sprouted like branches from one, a fan of swords and claws from another. A third expanded with wings that seemed to shelter the whole of the tower despite not moving. A fourth flared into the shape of flames; the fifth poured forth like water. And the last, it crackled like forked lightning against a backdrop of clouds.

Above us, the eagles had returned, circling on the warm updrafts of spirit in helical patterns. The glow from our magical endeavour lit the undersides of their wings.

The choir's mighty voice rose in volume one more time.

Ò, Rìgh nan dùl, 's nam feart tha shuas
Do bheannachd gràsmhor dòirt a-nuas
Le 'r tìr 's le 'r teangaidh soirbhich fhèin
'S bidh clann nan Gàidheal fo sgàil do sgèith

All at once, the world ignited with golden light, so bright I thought a sun had birthed itself in our midst.

But it wasn't coming from a newborn star.

It was coming from me.

From the six of us.

TWENTY-THREE

World first!

In the Highlands of Argyll in the west of Scotland, the community have crafted the Resplendent Throne.

Upon activation, the Resplendent Throne shall empower the community, enabling them to connect to other ascended communities ranging far outwith their homelands for the continued ascension of Earth.

Because their crafting of the Resplendent Throne also involved others from different communities joining with them in support, this is also considered a unique divine feat.

All involved communities not blended with that of Oban will now receive a quest to support them in their own community ascensions, have such milestones not already been met.

The sound of cheers and joyful sobs broke through my dumbfounded reading of the notification. My brain had hung up on the words "after activation," but right now that was beside the point. I read on feverishly, still lightheaded from the completion of the throne, among other, more confusing things.

Communities who performed this unique divine feat will receive:
    -Experience equivalent to:
    —3 levels if below Level 10
    —2 levels if below Level 20
    —1 level if above Level 20
    —0.5 levels if above Level 30
    -+20 Mind
    -+10 Spirit
    -+6 Pathos
    -+6 Will
    -3 skill points

You must accept these rewards in order for the Manipulation increase to take effect. Do so with caution in a safe place.
    For being the first on Earth to craft the Resplendent Throne, all participants receive, in accordance with and proportional to the feat accomplished:
    -Mark of Esteem: Mark of Invocation
    -Boon: Glòrmhor
    -Unlock: Faith affinity or
    -+1 to existing Faith affinity
    -1 item (class and affinity dependent as ascension permits)
    -Unique skill: Athchuinge. Conveys the right, in perpetuity, to petition pantheon of this Resplendent Throne once activated
    Private: As an initial member of this community's pantheon and having unlocked the Pantheon affinity, you have unlocked a unique skill that can only be used upon activation of the Resplendent Throne. In addition, you have unlocked a perma-

nent skill that is available to use now and in perpetuity, so long as your throne remains in your living community.

-Unique skill (unavailable until conditions met): The Reverent Creed

-Pantheon skill unlocked: Toghairm

My mind reeled as I read through the messages. If all of this was just from the crafting of the throne, what the hell would happen once we activated it? The thought was somewhat terrifying.

I also couldn't help but notice that it called me one of the *initial* members of this barely hatched pantheon. Did that mean there would be more of us?

We still had so far to go. Danger waited in Perth; indeed, all of Oban was preparing for us to go to war.

I hadn't even chosen my level twenty-seven specialisation yet. Something still stopped me; it was not a choice I wanted to feel forced into.

The rest of my notifications would have to wait. The hubbub around me increased with every passing moment, and when I blinked away my screens, the tower had turned to reverent chaos.

It sounded like an oxymoron even to me, but it was the only way I knew how to describe what I saw.

The choristers seemed drunk, and I didn't think it was from taking shots of Drambuie before our otherworldly ritual. Just steeping in the density of spirit we'd fostered with our collective energies seemed to have been enough to make everyone tipsy—or maybe that was the jump in levels.

I had no idea where Sailean had been through all of it, but now the cheeky wee bugger was curled up in what I presumed with some trepidation was my seat on this collective throne.

Which was not, much to my relief, a toilet.

I would have been a fool not to notice that each of the seats corresponded to one of us. The tiny ball of wildcat kitten lay in the one that had formed antlers. Or branches. Or both? The back of the throne was beautifully patterned oak, its design coaxed from the wood's shifting growth, and the antlers rose from the top corners, splaying out with the channelled magnificence of the Monarch of Glen Etive, who had gifted me his own for freeing him from Bawbag's puppetry.

Next to mine had to be Eilidh's from the fan of swords. The blades were still oak, forming a shape like the suit of spades eponymous symbol. Everything about the form of her throne rang out like justice, like will made reality.

On my other side, Rhona's. Where Eilidh's justice could not reach, Rhona's pathos and vengeance could. Our teenage ban-sìthe thrived in electricity and quicksilver shifts of her energies. She struck fast like lightning from a darkened sky, and her throne reflected that, billows of stylised clouds carved into the wood with forks of lightning coursing through them that seemed as if they might come to life if I gazed upon them long enough.

The cascade of water next to Rhona had to be Samuel's. He flowed with the patience of the river, but I'd also seen his power. His mercy would slake the thirst of the penitent; his wrath would wash away the foes who dared threaten his flock. His throne, much like Rhona's, had an elemental feel to it that suited our soft-spoken monk.

Beside it, Ealasaid's throne had unfurled wings.

Those wings stretched out like the antlers on mine, pinions curving in to cradle the headrest of her seat, upon which was emblazoned a pair of crossed hammers that framed a single eye.

That, more than anything so far, gave me pause, because I knew too well what it meant.

A' Chailleach, Scotland's creator. Said to have one eye, deep blue skin and silver-white hair with rust-coloured teeth, a' Chailleach's wicker basket she carried on her back had scattered lumps of earth that made our islands. Some believed that she bathed in a well of youth at the winter's solstice as the dark began to recede, and as the days grew longer, she grew younger.

If Finn was to be believed, that well of youth was Loch Ba in Mull.

Perhaps that was why it had been Ealasaid to fetch the water from Loch Ba.

And, of course, the final throne was Finn's. The flame of inspiration, its rippling shapes almost palpably warm when I let my gaze linger there.

Simple. Clear. Purposeful. Much like Am Bàrd Muileach himself.

I felt him coming before I turned to see him, Finn himself, approaching me. He had a rockie-talkie in one hand, which he tucked into a pocket as he drew closer.

"They've gotten the ionadan-siubhail as far as they can," he said. "Just got the message. We'll have to march to Perth from Aberfeldy."

I did a double take at that, glancing at the sky first and then at my system clock. Bloody hell, the creation of the Resplendent Throne had apparently gone on for five hours.

"We need to go, don't we?" I asked him quietly, not needing his hesitant nod to confirm it.

But his nod confirmed something else.

What we'd done here today hadn't been for us, not really.

It had been for *them*.

The three hundred people who had travelled here via the networks we'd built, the communities we'd been nurturing both since the ascension and before. Finn more than I had—I wasn't arrogant enough to say that my work held a candle to his own. But now we were on the same team, in a way more profound than I quite knew how to describe.

The throne, well. Assuming we managed to make it out of this next battle alive, we would likely sit on it, all six of us in our respective roles, whatever those roles may be. But the real magic today was in those who made it possible. Who lent us their spirit, their song. Finn had been right about that, too. The song, "Athchuinge," was one almost all Gaelic choristers knew. It was little surprise the name of their new skill had been born from its title.

It meant *invocation*.

No one had sat idle whilst we were crafting up on our little Argyll version of Mount Olympus. Oban was a veritable hive of activity when the six of us came down the mountain, but despite the busy bustle of folk hauling supplies and funnelling in and out of the Tesco carpark where the ionad-siubhail sat, when eyes sought us out, the movement slowed.

Time seemed to slow as our neighbours and comrades watched us as if we'd somehow been marked.

I stubbornly, one might even say belligerently, kept on

in denial that that wasn't the exact thing that had happened.

"Will everyone else be ready for us?" Eilidh asked, looking around at the catch in people's gait when they spotted us and swallowing as if she found it as unsettling as I did. "It seems like things here are still gearing up."

"They're ready," Finn said. "We can't wait longer. If we need to fall back, we'll have reserves ready to join us. With a little luck, we won't need them."

"I'm not sure a 'little' luck is all we're going to need," Rhona muttered, flinching as she caught someone staring at her.

She stroked Sailean, who she held against her left shoulder. The kitten, who not too long ago had protested being left behind, seemed to have decided that prudence required her to make her choices with wisdom. I wasn't sure if kittens' prefrontal cortices were anything like ours, but if such things existed for them, I wondered if hers was developing impulse control and long-term consequence decision making.

Sailean wasn't going with us—a relief to me—but she was determined to soak up every stroke, pat, and cuddle she could before we walked into battle.

"Remember what I said to Calum before we crafted the throne," Samuel's soft voice said from behind me. "What might be possible now that you may not have considered a few hours ago?"

Rhona turned to look at him. I could almost see the scales in her mind tipping this way and that as she tried to balance his words with her fear.

But I felt certain his point had landed, if for no other reason than that it had landed for me.

We'd prepared our people as best we could, and not

only that, the inclusion of those from other communities had allowed those communities to follow in our footsteps. If Samuel's optimism proved misplaced, we would have at least established our successors.

Most of our goodbyes had happened up at the tower. Meeksy had already run back to Kilmelford, and Iain had gone ahead to Aberfeldy, as had the handful of folks from the choirs who would be joining us as fighters.

It didn't take too long for us to get Sailean situated back at the Whyte House and make our own way to the ionad-siubhail, geared up for battle.

Now, when we stepped inside and pulled up the map of potential destinations, it had expanded vastly from the initial three. I counted eleven, and Finn gestured at the line of them stretching from Tyndrum to Aberfeldy.

"One day's focused work," he said softly. "Pushed our best to near exhaustion and ran us out of supplies for more, but we can deal with that once we are out of the weeds."

None of us had to say it; the effort had been worth it. Not only had we linked more and more places to active communication, but now we could jump almost to the other side of the country, as well as out to the islands.

Without wasting any more time, I selected Aberfeldy on the map, and Oban fell away.

CHAPTER

TWENTY-FOUR

The relative peace we'd experienced in Oban—strange looks notwithstanding—dissolved the moment we stepped out of the ionad-siubhail in Aberfeldy.

Angus met us, talking a mile a minute about the progression of the corrupted grove in Perth, how they'd already sent people ahead to try their hand at at least containing the spread until we could get there. It'd outgrown the ability of the local mages to keep it quarantined.

Any remnants of the ecstasy of our magical creation afternoon quickly slid into grim resolve.

If Oban had seemed busy, Aberfeldy was a hurricane of movement.

We had no military training, no one marching lock-step to the southeast, just the frenetic buzz of people who knew what was expected of them and intended to do it, come hell or high water.

If we couldn't destroy this corrupted grove, hell might very well come to call.

We had barely arrived in the town before heading right back out of it, this time on foot.

The hastily made ionad-siubhail was in Victoria Park, so we had to jog through much of the town to get to open land again.

Angus came with us as far as the Moness Resort. "Follow the A826. There'll be scouts posted along the way to direct you and relay back information. There are about five hundred fighters either already in Perth or en route. You'll probably catch up to them on your way. Don't stop to talk to them. First priority is gauging the current status of the situation."

He didn't wait to see if we understood, just took off at a lope back towards the town centre.

I took a deep breath.

Ealasaid glanced over at me. "Well, a chàirdean, what are we waiting for?"

With that, she was off running, and we had the good sense to follow.

As Angus had said, we did encounter multiple groups of reinforcements heading south. They moved at a jog, conserving their energy since they didn't have our levels, and it seemed they'd been briefed well; none of them tried to get us to stop, only greeted our appearance with whoops and encouraging cheers.

I didn't trust myself to allocate my attribute points whilst running, but I hoped we'd have at least five minutes once we arrived at the corrupted grove for me to do that. I was hanging onto skill points until I sorted out my specialisation bullshit, but I didn't want to go into this battle without at least upping attributes. New skills I wasn't familiar with might throw me in a fraught battle, but an extra couple points in Agility or Constitution could literally spell the difference between life and death.

The sun had begun its downward journey back to the horizon, and while the eastern part of Scotland tended to not be as wet as the west coast, today, it had flip-flopped. Oban had been glorious, sunny, blue skies and warm breezes, but Perthshire sat under a dense, crouching layer of pregnant clouds.

It meant we would likely be fighting in the dark.

Perth itself was thirty miles from Aberfeldy, which wasn't too terrible a distance with our ascension-boosted attributes. What might have once been a gruelling, full-day forced march or a several-hour literal marathon for the likes of Ronald now could be covered by even low-level people in two to three hours tops. We were much faster.

It only took us a little over an hour to cover the distance, and though pushing it like we had did leave all of us winded—except for Rhona, the little show-off with her Stamina well over a hundred—we were all glad we'd made the effort the moment the city came into view.

Perth was a good-sized city by Scotland's terms. It greeted us with a downpour, but we'd long since come up with ascension remedies for that typically Scottish problem —our armour kept the rain off. The heavy showers did, however, still obscure our visibility.

The city's name came, most likely, from an old Pictish word for a copse of trees. It was heavily wooded for a city, making it a popular destination for folk looking to enjoy autumnal foliage.

Usually, trees made me feel peaceful, but considering what we were about to do, the knowledge of just how established the root systems of the city had grown over the centuries only layered on more worries about the anomaly getting a worse foothold if we failed.

They blanketed the banks of the River Tay that ran through the city, spilled out in parks and green spaces, lined roads, hills, fields.

Scouts occasionally flagged us, directing us through the city by the most efficient roads.

It was bizarre, being in a city again, especially one where this far into the ascension, they hadn't done half of what Oban had to integrate our new abilities. I couldn't judge; I had no context for what Perthshire had faced or how many people they'd lost. Even so, having to manoeuvre ourselves around long-abandoned cars that had died in place in rush hour at the end of March was a strange shock to the system. In Oban, we'd used all of the vehicles in the town for crafting materials. Here, they'd just been left to rust.

The thirty-mile run from Aberfeldy had passed in a flash compared to the dash through the city of Perth. Maybe it was having to dodge vehicles or simply the dread of what we would have to face, but the streets dragged out, depleting my energy each time I had to sidestep another car.

"Next order of business after we kick some arboreal arse is having a chat with the Perth folk about how to maximise ascension efficiency," I muttered to Eilidh as we had to change course yet again where a car had stalled out halfway between one lane and another mid-turn.

"I'm sure they'll be delighted to hear how annoyed we are," she murmured back, then chuckled, throwing me a sideways glance. "Though if we do succeed at kicking arboreal arse, as you said, they will owe us something. We could always ask them for the boon of their own self-interest."

"I like the way you think."

"I know." She flashed me a tight grin.

About a hundred metres ahead of us, another scout appeared, waving a small ball of glowing spirit to get our attention.

When we reached her, she motioned at us to stop.

We slowed to a walk a short distance from her but didn't stop.

"What's going on?" Finn asked. "We're meant to circle round to Kinnoull Hill Tower."

"Not anymore," the woman said curtly, though I didn't think her brusque tone was meant to be rude. "The anomaly has spread—it's moving north towards the monastery. That's where you're needed first."

Fuck.

I did not like the sound of that. Neither, it seemed, did Finn. Not that any of us would think this was good news.

"How far has it spread from where it was contained?" he asked.

"Two hundred metres," the woman answered, then pointed in the direction she wanted us to go. "You better hurry."

Finn had blanched at her answer, and he didn't wait for any farewells. He took off running.

Knowing we were getting close to the anomaly's range set me into metaphysical motion as well as the now-frantic pace of our near sprint. I pulled Brac-Meanmna from my inventory and held it over my head where its specialised claws could take hold of the grip between my shoulder blades.

If I couldn't stand still to meditate and breathe, I could

time Connection to my breath and strides as we ran. Running on its own could be meditative.

With my skill having improved as much as it had, its range had increased. I usually refrained from stretching it to the boundaries of its efficacy because there was no need for it unless I was on watch or seeking a threat.

Right now was a combination of both.

I started with smaller radii, pulsing Connection with every fifth step along with my breath, counting off the rain-wet slaps of my boots against the tarmac. Spirit returned nothing with the limited radius, so I expanded it bit by bit with each cycle of pounding feet and heart and breath.

The River Tay appeared before us, a bridge giving us our means of getting across. I still felt nothing as I continued to expand Connection with the rhythms of our running.

Just as we reached the eastern side of the river, at the outermost edge of my awareness, I felt it.

It was as if Finn had picked me up and chucked me over the edge of the bridge into the river; the shock of encountering the anomaly nearly made me miss a step and fall flat on my face.

Never, in all the times I'd encountered a corrupted being, had my use of Connection come against a *wall* of corruption.

All the other instances had been discrete, single animals usually. The closest analogy I had to this was the patch of grass in Crianlarich, but even that had felt more like spreading tendrils than an established curtain or barrier.

"Wait," I said to the others.

"We can't stop," Finn said shortly.

"The corruption—it's like nothing I've encountered so far," I said to him, honouring his wishes and continuing to run, but my mind was racing faster than my feet. "I think there might be something else going on here."

The alarm of the discovery had left me reeling even as I sorted through and discarded possible explanations.

"You'd said it was a grove," I went on after a moment. "I don't think it's as simple as that."

Could this be something worse than an infected grove?

Could this be the source of the corruption itself?

The thought nearly bowled me over, but I doggedly kept up my running pace.

I almost couldn't bring myself to continue using Connection. Every pulse, every cycle of spirit and breath and heartbeat and pounding feet made me want to recoil. Where my spirit encountered the anomaly's corruption, it flinched back. Because the anomaly was sticky like a spider's web, and it was ravenous to ensnare anything that came within its orbit.

Something about this was even more wrong than what I'd found in Crianlarich.

If this truly was the *source* of the corruption, the anomaly itself, I didn't think even a fully trained army of mages would be enough to root it out.

I kept that thought to myself, but both Eilidh and Rhona glanced at me every few steps, worry writ large across their faces.

Another scout met us at the junction of the A85 and Hatton Road, sending us onward with a yelled, "Hurry!"

We picked up the pace even more, tension ticking upward faster and faster with every new warning.

With sickness sloshing in my stomach, I continued to track the edges of the corruption with Connection. The breadth of it almost took my breath away as we ran at a full sprint down Hatton Road.

The sky was beginning to darken, the sun only barely above the horizon but fully blanketed in clouds, and while Connection sketched out a hill in the direction we were aiming, the low-lying cloud bank also obscured that from view.

Finally, with all of us now panting, we saw what would be the last scout on this journey. He waved both arms at us from the entrance for cars that led back under some trees, which I took to be the monastery grounds.

Sure enough, upon closer approach, the gateway bore a sign saying "St. Mary's Monastery and Church."

We came to a stop. My stamina stat was not too shabby, but I still felt like I might have a heart attack. I gasped a breath, missing what the scout said at first, and when I squinted up at him, wiping a sudden wave of sweat from my brow with inside of my right bracer, he repeated himself.

"In the church. They'll brief you, but you'll need to get ready. We've been losing ground fast."

"Anyone infected?" I asked, alarm spreading through me like nerve pain would spiderweb out from a cluster when struck.

"Not yet. Not that I know of. Everyone's been taking as many precautions as possible, but they're also not updating me. Situation's changing—fast. Catch your breath. There are potions waiting as well to help you get some energy back. Follow me."

The combination of lactic acid and adrenaline was not a pleasant one-two punch.

The uppercut came when we approached the entrance to the church only to see a trio of mages holding a Purifire bubble around a fourth, who was grimly handcuffing himself.

"One infected," the scout said after a beat. "Fuck."

I couldn't have said it better myself.

CHAPTER
TWENTY-FIVE

I wasted no time. Despite my legs protesting at the return to running, I bolted from my companions, aiming right at the mages, who were breathing as hard as I was.

"Do you have any containment cells prepared?" I asked them urgently, eschewing any attempt at basic politeness.

"Not here," a woman said, using her elbow to brush her brown hair out of her face where it seemed to have come loose out of its ponytail. "We've haven't been using this as a base until this afternoon. Until now, the thing's been contained to the south side of the Kinnoull Hill Woodland Park, a small area around the tower. Originally, it was just one small copse of pine trees."

"What changed?" Finn asked, appearing beside me, his face more intense than I thought I'd ever seen it even when facing down a monstrous cephalopod that had a tendency to impale people with venomous spines.

The woman shrugged. "Not a sodding clue."

She had dirt smeared across her face, and without hesitation, I ran a net of Purifire over her just to be safe. The woman jumped as the spell cleansed her from head to toe.

After a moment, I did the same to the other two women with her. The man in the bubble looked up at me with a self-deprecating smile that didn't reach his eyes.

"Probably safe to assume that wouldn't help me," he said.

"Aye. I'm sorry, pal. More than I can say."

"Everybody's got to go somehow," he said, his fatalism surprising me until he rolled his eyes. "At least that's what they tell me. Just—try to wipe this shit out. Feels like the time I got a botfly in Nicaragua, but, like everywhere. All at once. Every inch of my skin."

The smile that accompanied that was...unhinged. And I did not think that was the anomaly talking. Yet.

The others had gathered around us, and Rhona looked about ready to boak.

"How far away is your containment centre?" I asked the women.

"As the crow flies, about half a mile, but that half a mile is right through the affected area." The brunette who I'd first spoken to bared her teeth.

Behind her, the two others, both blond, exchanged a glance and quietly excused themselves, jogging into the church and calling out for extra backup.

"And if you have to go around it?" I glanced at Finn as I asked the question, already doing the maths in my head, calculating risk, calculating out how much spirit and energy and time we would waste trying to build triage containment here if the anomaly was growing fast enough that it caught everyone on their back feet.

"Closer to two miles."

Finn nodded, probably doing the same maths I was. There was no answer I liked.

"They hadn't set it up yet when I was here," he told me. "It was next on the list."

"You should go inside and start working with them on a contingency plan, as well as some way to evacuate anyone living within a mile range of this place," I said, hating every single word out of my mouth. "Send someone out who can take us to the site so I can get an idea of what we're dealing with firsthand."

"I'll deal with the contingencies," Eilidh said. "You need Finn's context on how this thing has changed. Samuel and Rhona can help them transport our lad here to containment, and Ealasaid—"

"Ealasaid will go with the boys," Ealasaid said, her tone brooking no disagreement whatsoever.

"Aren't you all very organised?" This voice came from our handcuffed Patient Zero. "My heroes."

I really, really hooped this bloke was just a dick.

Otherwise, the corruption had taken hold far, far faster than I was prepared to deal with.

We'd come for a battle, but I somehow thought we'd already lost.

Gosia was the name of the woman who had been speaking to us, and she ended up coming with us back into the forest to the front line of this shitstorm.

"How did your pal end up infected?" Finn asked her. "No one should have been in range."

"He did something stupid and reckless," Gosia replied

bluntly. "The thing was expanding, and he ignored the call for a new line of Purifire shielding to try to blast the nearest infected tree himself."

"And the blast didn't help, I presume?" I asked, horrified but somehow fascinated by the utter disregard for his own longevity.

"Depends on what you mean by 'help.'" Gosia paused. "He did not expect the explosion to flash-boil the sap in the tree's trunk. It made a frag grenade of corrupted sap and wood splinters. The rest of us got the shield up just in time, but he was behind the line."

"Does this numpty have a death wish?" Ealasaid muttered, earning her a sardonic smile from our guide.

"I wonder the same thing," Gosia replied.

We had passed around the perimeter of the monastery grounds, and Gosia led us along the row of deciduous trees separating the campus from the adjacent neighbourhood.

Gosia caught me looking at the houses through the foliage. I couldn't see much but the roofs and the occasional flash of window with a light in it, but that was plenty. Her face twitched with what I thought was guilt. "We should have thought to evacuate them sooner. Things changed very quickly, but that is not an excuse."

"We're all doing the best we can here," Finn said. "Blame me if you like, for leaving you to go back to Oban."

From the way he said it, I did not doubt for a moment that he was in fact blaming himself.

We walked in silence for the next minute. I needed to use Connection again, but the very thought repelled me. I would need to get over it the moment we got to the current line of scrimmage. Until then, I gave myself the short-lived grace to preserve my frayed nerves for a few more precious moments.

Very short-lived, as it turned out.

No sooner had we reached a line of evergreens running perpendicular to the deciduous border of the housing estate than I caught the unmistakable glow of Purifier through the trunks of the dark forest ahead.

Gosia blanched.

"It's already moved closer, hasn't it?" Ealasaid gave Gosia a shrewd look. "How much closer?"

"Fifty metres," Gosia said.

Finn was shaking his head, whether in denial or confusion, I didn't know. Maybe both.

"None of this makes sense," he said. "It should not be spreading that quickly. At this rate, I'm already thinking we need to burn the whole forest, and I don't think we have enough people to do that."

Nothing in the book I'd absorbed about arcane epidemiology had prepared me for this situation. Not for the anomalies at all, obviously, but this was beyond my ken in every possible way.

"The only thing I can think of—" I broke off, mirroring Finn's head shake and unsure if I myself was in denial or confused. With three pairs of eyes on me, I blew out a breath and forced myself to continue. "Meeksy hasn't gotten a chance to really gather any actionable data on this, so all I have is my own observations, okay?"

When they all nodded, Gosia frowning while she did it, I gave her a brief mirthless smile.

"I don't have time to fully explain, but we're conducting experiments on the anomaly's impact on plants, and by chance, I discovered that fungi seem to be resistant. Plants also seem less preferable to the anomaly than do living beings, in that the corruption either ignores them or infects them slowly. With me so far?" I waited again until they all confirmed with a bob of their heads again. "The only thing that makes sense to me here is that there is something else going on in addition to the anomaly's presence. Plants are most definitely living things; that part isn't in dispute. But the anomaly seems to gravitate mostly to living beings that are mobile. Or the corruption does."

"You're talking about it like they're two separate things," Gosia said. "Are they two separate things?"

I nodded, as did Finn and Ealasaid, though the latter looked thoughtful, as if she were examining the opinion more closely after having surprised herself.

"I think there is the anomaly, and it *causes* the corruption." I hesitated before going on, gritting my teeth to send out another pulse of connection to see if it would change my next words. Nothing came back to dispute my conclusion. "When we were running here, I thought maybe this was the anomaly itself. Not just a corrupted copse of trees but the actual cause of all the corruption. Now I don't think so."

"You're saying the trees seem to be getting infected like they're animals and not plants." Ealasaid looked at me with slightly narrowed eyes that I didn't take to be doubt, only consideration.

"Yes," I said. "And there might be a way to see if I'm right, but I'm going to have to get closer."

Not just physically. I needed to delve deeper into Connection than I probably ever had before. I didn't think Keen Eye alone would do the trick.

After all, it'd be far too easy if I cast Keen Eye and got back that we were surrounded by dryads.

❖

"You're sure about this?" Finn asked me. "We'll cover you as best we can, but we can't account for every variable. Another numpty could have the bright idea to drop a bomb on the pathogen and make another biological weapon."

"I think that bloke is, himself, a class-A biological weapon," I said. "Absolutely breathtaking lack of self-preservation."

"Or he's working for the anomaly," Finn agreed. "But I don't think he's that kind of numpty."

We were, momentarily, on our own. We stood a short distance away from the boundary of Purifire the locals had reinforced with some of our people, but I wasn't going to be staying behind this line of safety. Oh, no. My bright idea was a bit like a bunch of billionaires with no credentials deciding to go to the bottom of the sea in a tin can. I couldn't even take the piss out of those blokes anymore, not with what I was considering. Not even considering. Planning.

I paused for a moment before answering Finn's initial question. Eilidh might kill me for taking this risk, but she'd sent a runner to let us know she was personally overseeing evacuations of the nearest neighbourhoods, so I'd either be alive to ask for forgiveness or too dead to care.

"I don't think there's any better choice," I said to Finn finally. "We can't fight this thing if we don't know what we're up against, and there is a non-zero chance we can't fight this thing, full stop."

"I promise not to tell Samuel you just binned his inspiring pep talks," Finn said, but I got the feeling he didn't disagree with me. "I felt a lot more optimistic before we got back here, and I wasn't exactly feeling confident about our chances when I left."

"I promise not to tell Samuel you needed his inspiring

pep talks as much as I did," I replied. "Let's get it over with. If I die, tell Rhona to learn necromancy and bring me back so she and Eilidh can kill me themselves."

"I'm not going to let you die," Finn told me.

"That's the spirit."

Ealasaid had gone ahead of us to prepare the front line shield holders, and she waved us closer without looking over her shoulder to even make sure it was us coming.

I gave her a tight-lipped smile as she grabbed me by the shoulders and positioned me in the middle of a small circle made up of herself, Finn, and four of the fresh relief fighters who had arrived from Aberfeldy only ten minutes before.

The first layer of Purifire mesh made me shiver as if it were cold instead of hot. I acclimated quickly, opening myself to spirit and trying to draw my own inner layers of backup measures in case plans A through F went tits up. I wrapped my own familiar weave of Purifire around me like a second skin rather than a cloak. Cloaks had way too much wiggle room for parasitic fuck-off pathogens to weasel their ways into. No, thank you.

The second mage seemed nervous to the point of being jittery. His weave frayed away twice before he managed to calm himself down enough to make a proper bubble, which made me all the more diligent about pulling my own mystical blankie tighter.

Ealasaid added her own layer to the ones the helper mages had slathered over me, and I felt better just knowing she was there. Sometimes even grown-ass men needed their gran, honorary or no.

Her version of the bubble threaded in not only Purifire but a shielding spell I thought she must have learned from Meeksy. Either that or it was just farther up the Slàinte skill tree than I'd explored. The combination felt like getting tucked into bed by someone who made sure the blankets cradled you, snug to every side and sealing in the warmth.

Finn waited until another two mages had added their own layers to my ultra-armoured bubble of nope before he added his. Like me, Finn seemed to think that even the word "bubble" left too much to chance. With his weave of Purifire, he treated it like fucking shrink wrap, the mesh he'd woven so tight that it practically snapped over me like a full-body condom.

I really wished I had not had that thought.

My traitorous brain notwithstanding, the addition of Finn's extra layer of protection put my mind at ease. I had expected my nerves to kick off the closer I got to the moment of truth, but instead, a wave of calm washed over me. I was here, under the close watch of people I trusted not only with my life but with my community's lives. With Eilidh's life. With Rhona's life. And Ealasaid and Samuel and Finn as well. Everyone here was in the best possible hands, despite the unpredictable and unprecedented circumstances.

"Sin thu, a luaidh," Ealasaid murmured to me. "Deiseil is deònach?"

I smiled a crooked smile at the familiar Gaelic phrase for *ready and willing*.

Not quite trusting myself to look her in the eye, I nodded instead and signalled to the shield bearers that I was on the move.

And then I walked straight into the corrupted hornets' nest.

CHAPTER

TWENTY-SIX

The world fell away as I stepped through the line of Purifire they'd staked around the border of the anomaly's influence.

My first thought was that it was strangely loud in here, but that was only until I tried to blink away something obscuring my vision and realised that it wasn't something alive making noise.

All around me was a swarm of...something.

Midgies were the obvious first guess in Scotland, but I knew the way the highland midge swarmed. They seemed to bounce off every stray current of air around you, like tiny styrofoam balls in a wind tunnel. Midges were so easily tossed about by the tiniest breeze that a low-level wind was usually enough to keep them at bay.

Whatever this was, it wasn't midges.

I wasn't even sure it was a life form.

All I knew was that it wasn't the buzz or drone of wings an insect would make. No high-pitched whine of a mosquito, no flinch-inducing racket of a cleg.

No, the sound came not from the particles themselves

but from the particles colliding with the Purifire mesh seven layers deep covering my whole body.

It was the noise of their incineration.

By the thousands. Every passing second.

All of a sudden, it no longer seemed like overkill. In fact, I could probably set myself on fire like a human torch of Purifire and still be *under*reacting by a significant margin.

Great plan, Calum. What was that you were saying about Mr. Blow Things Up? That he was a class-A biological weapon of a numpty?

Switch my arse and plonk a dunce cap on my heid; I deserved any lecture or fight that came from Rhona and Eilidh learning of this decision.

I'd blame it on exhaustion, stress, anything, but as I ventured deeper into the dead zone, serenaded by particles of I-don't-fucking-want-to-know self-immolating against my multi-layered prophylactic personal protective equipment, I knew with increasing certainty that I'd made the right choice.

I did not like the sudden gut-deep acceptance that this, quite possibly the stupidest choice I'd ever made in my life, was also the best choice for our ultimate survival.

It was now or never.

My first pulse of Connection this side of enemy lines lit up like I'd struck a match whilst submerged in a powder keg.

A full-body shudder wracked me as my expanding spirit no longer had to search for relevant pings of information. We were literally buried in them.

My powder-keg analogy suddenly seemed far too appropriate.

Each step I took made my skin crawl even more. I no

longer doubted the poor sod's botfly metaphor; it was, in fact, even more on the nose than the gunpowder.

I didn't think the particles swarming me were actually alive. They pinged on Connection because they were tainted, but they had no spirit signature. While I hadn't exactly done an in-depth study of ascension mycology, all of my passives were constantly cataloging my surroundings, the things I noticed and the things I didn't. And I had poked at enough mushrooms to know that their spores *did* have spirit signatures. They were living things. Tiny balls of genetic material that could self-propagate once they landed somewhere appropriate.

A flash of insight lit up in my mind.

My own thought had hit on something in that book, *Ascension Epidemiology and Arcane Contagions.*

I stopped walking, dazed.

Life followed similar patterns the universe over. The primary pattern of those, foundational to the rest, was the basis of evolution: life adapted to the environment. One of the others, much further along in the tree of universal truths—or the closest thing to universal truth—was that life evolved to become more complex. The smallest forms of it, the oldest forms of single-celled organisms and amoebas, bacteria, viruses, protozoans, you name it, they were still little balls of genetic material.

That wasn't what had stopped me short.

For one long, surreal moment, I found myself creating a mental negative image of everything I'd learned so far about the anomaly.

I had been so caught up in trying to figure out what it was that I'd forgotten a perspective that just now, felt like the most vital aspect of this entire question.

We all had been approaching it like it was a repeat of

the COVID pandemic. Which, fair. We were all a bit trau-matised by the thing that had swooped in and taken a mahoosive bite out of the prime of our lives. It made sense that we would all be looking at this like a pathogen. I'd even called it a pathogen more than once.

But here, in this dead zone so rife with the anomaly's corruption that, had I not been wreathed in multiple layers of Purifire, I would have it baked into my lungs just breath-ing, for the first time I adjusted my perspective not to look at the shapes the corruption drew. Not the parallels to zombie films or ebola or anything else of the sort.

Instead, I had to seek out the negative space.

It was in that negative space that I found the first answer after asking the wrong questions over and over and over. It came in the form of an answer to a different question entirely, one I hadn't thought to ask because frankly, it sounded daft.

We'd been asking what the damn corruption was.

We hadn't considered how much we could learn by instead asking what it *wasn't*.

And what it wasn't?

It wasn't life.

It wasn't hungry.

The corruption, by itself, may have grasped out at everything around it, but for the first time in all of this mess, an epiphany burst into pure, radiant brilliance in my mind.

It drowned out the incessant hum of all the particulates bashing into the arcane bug zapper I'd built around myself.

I'd observed the corruption reaching, grasping, seeking contact and something to glom onto, but I hadn't consid-ered whether or not it actually had agency.

The *anomaly* had agency. The anomaly had desires,

wants, goals, emotions. I was pretty damn sure the anomaly wanted us all to suffer and die.

But the corruption itself? This thing the anomaly seemed to leave in its wake? It wasn't sentient or sapient. It was like a magnetic charge.

Or no. No, I had that backwards too.

The corruption was like tiny iron filaments.

I'd thought that once before, that those filaments hungered.

So close to the correct answer. I'd just come at it from the wrong direction. The filaments weren't alive; they couldn't help themselves. The anomaly was the polar equivalent—it pushed. It could influence them the same way you could push two poles of a magnet away from one another without them ever touching. But flip them the other way around, and *snick*.

They'd click together. The anomaly and the filaments were the same polar charge. The anomaly craved something, something its residue clung to, reached for. Something that attracted it because it was the polar opposite, the thing a magnet needed for that physical form of attraction to work.

Life was the magnetic pull.

Once those tiny iron filaments stuck to life, the anomaly could control it.

I was just about to refocus myself on my task at hand and prepare to delve deeper into the forest when I heard shouting in the distance.

Eilidh.

She was calling my name.

I couldn't just run back to her. Not in my spirit-dense hazmat suit and not trailing clouds of these particulates that would attach themselves to life at any cost, even if it drove them into the Purifire to disintegrate.

In my horror-world of this hellscape, I hadn't realised quite how far I'd walked. It had only seemed like I'd been walking for a few minutes, but as I made my way back, that constant drone in ebbs and flows accompanying every crunch of dead earth beneath my feet, I realised the system clock had me gone for over an hour.

Picking up my pace, I tried to project some sense of calm, something she would instinctively feel through whatever mysterious ties of spirit helped us locate one another without looking and identify one another by feel alone. Something told me it wouldn't work. Not here. Not with the debris of the anomaly clouding the air.

As if the word *air* had jolted a brand-new horror into my brain, I stopped stock still and looked up.

Oh, no. Oh, fuck-fuck-fuck.

We ought to have caught it. Tired minds made mistakes, and we had all made a damn big one.

It might have seemed sensible to build a fence around a radioactive pit. But if that radioactive pit were spewing uranium dust into the atmosphere?

A fence wouldn't cut it.

I started walking again, pulsing Connection with every step as I walked to seek out the edges of this mess and also the limits of its upper reaches.

My own range had expanded well beyond the necessary radius to encompass the corruption's perimeter. That part made it feel almost like a relief that it was finite, discrete.

The problem was these particulates.

My earlier thought that they were like tiny styrofoam balls in a wind tunnel had been all too apt. It would only take the slightest breeze to send them soaring up and over the edges of our Purifire fence.

We had enough people to cover the perimeter—barely. With the growth, it had stretched to almost a square kilometre at my best guess. Almost all the way to the A90 on the far side of the park. We most definitely did not have enough people to make a sphere that large the way I had in Crianlarich with a couple cubic metres of space.

I walked back towards my people as fast as I dared, knowing that I'd have to emerge carefully and go through a decontamination process to make absolutely sure nothing had escaped. The only reason the single layer of "fence" around the corrupted park had held was, if I had to hazard a guess, because there was enough life within that box to attract the corruption filaments.

If my hour inside that glimpse into hell had seemed like only a few minutes mired in my mental processing, the walk back of barely a kilometre felt like hiking from Moscow to Seoul.

The moment I got within shouting distance, I called out, "Eilidh! I'm safe!"

I heard her anguished reply, barely more than a shout, and that sent chills into my heart. She wasn't upset that I'd gone in here alone; much as I joked about getting yelled at, I knew she trusted my judgement.

Something else must have happened.

Something bad.

As soon as I was close enough, I yelled to one of the mages. "Get Finn if he's not nearby! He's going to need to hit me with a Purifire flamethrower when I get out of here."

"I'm here, Calum," Finn said, his voice blessedly close but laced with tension.

I made my way to the border of Purifire. "If you and

Eilidh can make a decontamination bubble for me to step into, I'd be very grateful."

The alarm that filtered through the surrounding mages —with their single, flimsy layer of Purifire "protecting" them from an extinction-level threat—made me pause to close my eyes for a moment and breathe.

There was nothing I could think of right now that would solve this problem. We weren't going to be able to fight this with an army; these weren't corrupted ents we could blast with Purifire or stick with the pointy end of an enchanted sword. Unless we could contain it well enough to do a controlled demolition, an implosion instead of an explosion where no debris could be tossed into the wind, anything we did to disturb this space would instead set off a biological weapon that could consume all of Scotland. Hell, with the trade winds and the Gulf Stream, it wouldn't be a far cry to think we could send the anomaly's corruption to Norway.

Eilidh's face when she stepped close enough for me to see her had gone whiter than its usual pale hue.

She looked like I felt.

What the fuck had happened when she was evacuating people?

She was here, and she was safe—beyond that, answers could wait.

"Get me the fuck out of here," I said to my friends. "Please."

Eilidh and Finn, despite their obvious urgency, took their time crafting the weaves of the decontamination bubble. I appreciated every excruciating minute even as much as I hated counting the seconds when I knew none of the particles had made it through the layers of protection. They were small enough that they could float just out of reach of the Purifire and drift, unnoticed, through the air to latch onto any nearby life. As my friends primed the proverbial flamethrower, I noticed that Ealasaid was notably missing.

Where Rhona and Samuel had gone after they'd gotten the infected bloke to containment, I didn't know. Maybe they'd run into issues.

I thought I would have to shift the language I'd been using to discuss the corruption. "Infected" didn't sound right after my epiphanies and revelations in my hellwalk. It implied pathogens, and while maybe the distinction wasn't vital to the average person who would need to protect themselves, we'd been looking at it like an opportunist when it had no agency. It was just the sleeper cell. It wasn't even nominally alive like the simulacra Bawbag had employed as spies, though in some ways, they had behaved in similar ways. They also had had the creeptastic, grasping-waving frond thing going on.

Neither Eilidh nor Finn spoke as they worked until Eilidh let out a heavy sigh and nodded at Finn. "That should do it, Calum. You can step into it now."

They'd built it so the edge closest to me actually sat inside the fence line, as it were, which meant there were no chances of gaps.

"I hope the rest of you were paying attention to what they did," I said as I stepped into the bubble. "Since I'm going to suggest every single one of you who has been near this mess gets a go in one."

That caused a stir and more than a few murmurs.

Once I was fully encased in Finn and Eilidh's decontamination bubble like a matryoshka mage in all my many prophylactic layers, they released the weave.

It was like they'd interwoven a million rubber bands on

an enormous flat loom and then yanked it off the pegs all at once. An eye-watering amount of spirit hit me from all sides at once, and I was relatively certain that after that, every inch of me would have been sterilised to the point that you could eat off my arse cheeks without encountering a single bacteria, virus, dead skin cell, or tiniest particle of dirt.

My eyes literally watered with the shock of it.

"I think he's clean," Finn said dryly. "Which is the good news."

"And the bad news?" I asked as Eilidh threw her arms around me. I caught her up, relieved beyond measure to feel her solid presence in my arms. "Did something go wrong with the evacuation?"

"There was no evacuation," she said into my neck. "Because there was no one to evacuate. Every house between this chunk of forest and Murrayshall was empty."

TWENTY-SEVEN

I froze with my arms around Eilidh's waist. "What?"

"No people. No bodies. Just...clothes. Like the pop culture fantasy of the what the Rapture would be like. Clothes just lying where people should be." Eilidh finally pulled back, looking sick. "Whatever did it moved northeast."

"You think something did that. What could do something like that?" My brain was now running like a hamster wheel and getting nowhere.

Then again, it dovetailed with one of the more nebulous thoughts I'd had tonight.

Eilidh was shaking her head. Not in a way to negate what I'd said, but with the distinct sense of *Not here*.

Belatedly, I realised we were the subject of every nearby mage's attention.

I cleared my throat. "Right. I've got to rally the troops and I suspect make some very difficult decisions. Everyone here needs to spread the word. Decontamination bubbles like you just saw for everyone here every quarter of an hour and *especially* if you venture anywhere near other people."

The unease in the air intensified with my words.

"Are you—are you saying we're not safe even on this side of the fire?" Someone asked this from about twenty metres down the line, where all I could see of their face was a ghostly glow.

"Yes," I said bluntly. "That's exactly what I'm saying. Unless you can make yourselves bubbles—make them skin tight, not a bubble leaving air space—and keep them up indefinitely, every fifteen minutes. At the very extreme least, it might be prudent to make yourselves a face mask. Just make sure to cover your eyes. Any mucus membranes or open wounds, even a hangnail. Act like the floor is radium and it's shedding particles."

That did not go over well.

"What changed?" Finn asked, his voice low and worryingly flat.

"Perspective," I said and pointed up, where about twenty feet above the ground, the Purifire fence ended.

Both Finn and Eilidh's heads had snapped up to look, and I felt more than saw as they understood what I meant. They each immediately encased themselves in Purifire. Well, Finn used Purifire. Eilidh had her own skill, every bit as effective, that haloed her in gold.

The other mages followed suit the moment they saw my companions do it, and I did the same, also imbuing my bubble with the tiniest thread of Spèird to hopefully repel any particulates that drifted too close without propelling them at anyone else.

"I'd rather be safe than risk this becoming ground zero for an unmitigated disaster," I said, hopefully loud enough for people to hear me. "We'll send someone back shortly. Spread the word. If you get tired or low on spirit, get the rotations of relief on a quicker timetable until we can figure out what to do."

I started moving away, all too cognisant that I was leaving a nightmare in my wake, but my instincts said it was better that way. We'd already seen one person make a spectacularly bad life choice, and along with all the other problems, we were going to have to check every single person who had been in and out of the church in the last two hours or had been at the site for corruption.

As we walked back, I talked fast, running through what I'd learned and what I'd seen in there. Finn's face grew darker and darker as we walked, paradoxically illuminated by the glow of his thin veneer of Purifire even as his expression grew to resemble a thunderhead about to erupt into a torrential storm.

"You're sure?" was all Eilidh said.

"As sure as I can be," I told her. "It tracks with what I've seen. I think it even helps explain the fungus."

Finn's turmoil cracked for a moment as he looked at me. I'd told both of them about the fungi before, but until I'd said it out loud, I wasn't sure if I was on the right track.

My mind sifted through the observations I'd made, how the mycelium I'd seen had smoothed out their filaments of spirit. Initially, I'd assumed that was something the fungi simply did. Whether in response to a threat or simply the natural state of things, I couldn't say without further exploration. But now I thought it might be a more canny defence mechanism than it appeared at first glance.

"I think the fungi have somehow figured out how to play dead," I said after a long pause. "It's not fully effective, I don't think, but it repels enough. By the way they smooth out their energy field, for lack of a better explanation, I think it neutralises their radius of attraction."

Trying to piece all of this together was going to do my head in.

"Whatever all this means, we cannot leave things like this here," Finn said. "Not an open field of radium, as you put it, not when the wind can just blow it everywhere. We need to find a way to contain it."

"We don't have enough people," Eilidh countered, but I heard the exhaustion in her voice. "Even with the reserves, that's what, a quarter mile, squared? Plus the vertical space, even if it doesn't make a full cube."

"It's about a square kilometre to the best I could measure," I told her. "And you're right. We don't have enough people as it stands. Even if we emptied out Oban, it might be too late by the time we got them all here."

But Ealasaid's words had popped back into my head, seemingly of their own accord.

Look, m' eudail, at what we've already done and ask yourself: if we could do all of this weeks ago when we're all practically weans in swaddling clothes, what miracles are we capable of now, today?

"I have an idea," I said suddenly. "And if we do this right, we might also help Perth achieve a community ascension they desperately need."

The next few hours passed in a dizzying daze. The scout relay that stretched between Perth and Aberfeldy got a workout as we sent out an SOS. And we didn't just include Perth and Aberfeldy. We included the entire trail we'd connected to see who might answer the call.

In the meantime, every capable body above level fifteen who were already in Perth thinking we would be attacking the corrupted trees, we gathered to give a crash course in arcane synergy.

Samuel led that particular charge with Ealasaid and Rhona helping him provide object lessons.

If there was anything we had learned in Oban, it was that individuals might be powerful on their own, but when we joined forces, we created feats far beyond the sum of our parts.

By the time the sky was starting to lighten—this time of year, around half four in the morning—we had stationed our most capable higher-levelled mages at equal intervals around the still-growing perimeter of the corrupted park.

Their job was not to reinforce the fence but to extend it upwards, curving it with strategically woven-in threads of Spèird to funnel any escaping particulates back down into the dome.

We had nowhere near enough people to actually create a dome, but if we couldn't do that yet, well, at least we could play damage control until we figured out a more decisive plan.

I was about ready to drop. We'd had an exhausting day even before we'd left Oban, and the day had stretched through its allotted twenty-four-hour period and was officially eating into the next one.

Eilidh and I got a quarter of an hour to breathe once we'd gotten the new recruits pointed in the right direction, and after a newly habitual Purifire cleanse, she slumped against me on a pew in St. Mary's Church. We were in a small chapel off the main church, out of the line of sight for anyone coming in the door.

"You know," she said, her voice coming out scratchy from hours of talking to people, "I naively thought this might just be our usual high-stakes, blood-pounding battle to the death against a foe we never would have imagined facing. I did not expect to walk into fucking *Silent Hill*."

She swallowed, and I squeezed her tighter to me, letting her slide down to curl onto the pew with her head in my lap.

"I know," I said. "Tiree feels like it was a million years ago at this point."

"God, right?" Eilidh turned her head to press her cheek into my quadricep.

For a moment, I thought she might scream into my leg just to let out some emotion, but instead, she just groaned.

"This is bad," she muttered, letting out a sigh I felt through the bit of my armour where my tasset ended at the edge of my thigh.

Her breath warmed the under-layer, leaving it cold as the small bit of moisture evaporated.

"I think that about sums it up, aye," I said to her.

I closed my eyes for a moment and leaned my head back against the wall, the image of the Resplendent Throne popping into my head unbidden. I couldn't stop the guffaw that burbled out of my mouth, an unfortunate half laugh that sounded as ridiculous as it felt.

"Is something funny?"

I felt Eilidh's head turn as she twisted to squint up at me, only one blue-grey eye visible. A small lock of auburn hair had fallen across her forehead. I pushed it out of the way.

"Hilarious, actually," I said. "You know we've got a divine throne now? A throne for us. We're the divine ones. We actually built a mystical six-seater throne because we're the closest things to real gods in all of Scotland."

Another laugh hovered dangerously close to the

surface, and I quivered with the effort it took to keep it from escaping.

Eilidh, of course, felt the movement. "We are in a church."

For one arse-backwards moment, I thought she was scandalised that I'd declared our divinity in a Catholic church, but then her shoulders started to shake as well.

"Best gods ever, probably," I said. "Much omnipotence, very divinity, wow."

"Jeezo, that's a meme from the archives," she complained. "What are you, a Millennial?"

"That's *divine* Millennial to you. The you who is also a divine Millennial."

She snorted, then pushed herself up to sit, rubbing at her eyes with the heels of her hands.

"If we make it home to Oban, I swear to me, I will smite anyone who interrupts my week-long nap," she said, still with her palms covering her eyes.

"Someone's coming," I said absently, my habitual short-range pulse of Connection encountering a person not far away.

It was Gosia, who looked about as harried and knackered as we felt.

"There you are," she said. "Your friends are upstairs in the dormitories. It's going to take a couple hours to make the final preparations you asked for, so anyone who hasn't had a chance to rest is supposed to get some sleep."

We were moving before she could say another word.

When someone knocked—not gently—on the door

exactly two hours and three minutes later, I sat straight up in bed.

"Calum, it's Rhona. You've got to get out here."

Shit.

Those words also had Eilidh flailing to a sitting position, her hair a messy nest of waves half covering her face.

"We're awake," I said.

This was decidedly not what an alarm clock was supposed to mean. Not a punch of dread to the throat. Maybe some nice tunes on the radio or a slow build of a pleasant digital melody.

"Are you?" Rhona asked, her voice growing a wee bit shrill through the door. "I don't hear Eilidh."

"I'm awake, m' eudail," Eilidh said groggily. "We're getting up. You can come in if you want to make sure. We're decent."

"I don't have time. Samuel and Ealasaid are getting Finn, and Gosia needs my help right now. Don't fall back asleep."

"We won't," I assured her. "I promise, we're up."

I got out of bed with an audible creak of the bedspring, which I was sure Rhona had heard.

"What exactly is happening out there, Rhona?" Eilidh called. "Did something change with the containment?"

"No, but it could," Rhona said. "Someone just came in from the scout relay and said they've seen the ali—I mean the Atheani. They're still on the outskirts of Perth but the scouts said they're on a direct collision course for the park like they're tracking some sort of homing beacon."

Eilidh leaped to her feet in one fluid move. "We're on our way. Tell everyone *not to engage or pursue*."

She'd beat me to it, and for good reason.

All I could think of was the Somali-Scot who'd been the

only survivor at Dumbarton Castle when the Atheani detonated an arcane blast in cold blood.

She'd never even told me her name.

The only thing I could think of that would be worse than striking a match from the inside of a powder keg would be a blast like that in the vicinity of our quarantined park.

CHAPTER
TWENTY-EIGHT

I wished Scout were here.

It hadn't made sense to bring the eagles here—the risk of them getting corrupted was too great since their primary means of attack was talons and beaks.

With plenty of toxins, the distinction between venom and poison mattered. If it bites you and you die, it's venomous. If you bite it and you die, it's poisonous. But with the anomaly's corruption, I did not think that distinction mattered. It bites you, you die. You bite it, you also die.

But as her name proclaimed, she was a fantastic scout, and with the bond she'd yet to release, it was as good as seeing through her eyes.

I simply hadn't thought there would be anything of dire enough importance to need to track from the air.

Silly, silly divine Millennial.

Eilidh and I managed to be out the door in about three minutes, taking the path back through the corridors of the monastery to the church at the fastest speed we dared when our heads were still swimming with exhaustion and sudden movement after being dead to the world in the deepest stage of our sleep cycles.

We found the church packed with people. Angus stood at the pulpit—or next to it—looking well-rested and alert.

At least one of us was those two things.

His rangy body released some of its visible tension when he saw us, and he beckoned at us to hurry.

There were enough people that we couldn't run, so we squeezed through the throng as best we could. Most people, once they realised who we were, did their best to clear a path, but it was six in the morning and I couldn't blame anyone for not having the best reflexes when almost everyone had bags under their eyes and shellshocked expressions on their faces.

We made it to Angus relatively quickly, and he pulled us aside, turning away from the crowd.

"The Atheani were only spotted about ten minutes ago, but they're fast. Our scout relay can't keep up with them. It's likely they're almost to the park already, so we need to decide what to do," Angus said without preamble. "If they're really headed for the park, after what you saw in Dumbarton, getting in their way could be beyond disastrous."

"I don't love the idea of just letting them through, but we can't beat them there to enact what we've been putting in place all night."

I hated those words as they came out of my mouth. Why the fuck were they even here? Could they somehow be tracking the anomaly?

"What if we got everyone in place with orders to let them through if they try?" Eilidh asked slowly.

I stared at her. "Are you suggesting what I think you're suggesting?"

"No," she said vehemently. "I am absolutely not saying to just let them through to get corrupted—I'm not *that* out of it even on two hours of sleep. Call it a contingency in case they aren't headed for the park. Mobilising quickly will just get this over with faster if we're able to enact our original plan. And if not, maybe we can draw them away somehow. Or attempt to reason with them. They are intelligent beings who understand our language. I'm not expecting them to be reasonable, but they might hesitate to do anything genocidal if they think they could also accidentally plague themselves."

She was right, and it was better than pulling all our people off the park and risking the corruption further breaking containment.

"I think we should what Eilidh said." I swallowed, and she gave me a tight-lipped smile and squeezed my hand. "Let the six of us try to intercept them. If we can buy you all enough time to take care of the park problem, then that's a win-win."

"And if they blow you all up?" Angus countered.

"At least they'll have to do it outside the radius where the explosion could loose that corruption on everything in the path of the Gulf Stream," Eilidh said sweetly.

He gaped at her.

"You heard the woman," I told him, turning as I felt the approach of the four other people we needed for our part in this plan. I waved to Samuel and Ealasaid, signalling them to stay put.

"Angus?" Eilidh said.

"Fine," he said. "But if you all die before you sit on that sodding throne we just went through all the trouble of building, I'll use my special skill to bring you back from the dead and kill you myself."

It was so close to what I'd thought Rhona and Eilidh would say to me about venturing into the park by myself that I couldn't help but chuckle.

"You think I'm joking," he said, his salt-and-pepper eyebrows knitting together.

"Love you too, Angus. Get the troops moving."

I heard him mutter a few choice words under his breath, but then his voice boomed out through the church's optimal acoustics, making all conversation stop dead.

"Everyone briefed, now's your moment. Your first job is to clear a path for Calum and Eilidh so they don't have to blast you out of the way." He paused, and everyone hastily split to let us hurry through. "As soon as they're gone, that's your cue. Battle stations, double time. We've got one shot, and our pals there are going to give us the best chance we have, so don't fuck it up."

As far as pep talks go, I think I preferred Ealasaid's and Samuel's.

"Are you out of your mind?" Rhona hissed as we made a break for what I desperately hoped was the most likely route the Atheani would take to get to the park.

"It was my idea," Eilidh answered coolly, falling into step beside Ealasaid. "And in Oban, they implied they were looking for people of consequence. We may be more consequential to them now, especially if they got that global announcement about the Resplendent Throne."

"I'm not sure them thinking we are people of consequence is necessarily a good thing," Samuel said, "but our priority has to be keeping the corruption contained at all costs, even if that cost is our lives."

"Well, that went full martyr, a charaid." Ealasaid's tone exuded exasperation. "We aren't helpless, and the Atheani aren't fools."

"That's what I said." Eilidh motioned at one of the scouts as we approached. "Best route to intercept the Atheani?"

"Motorway," the scout called back immediately, "but you'll have to hurry. They passed Craigend just now."

I wasn't going to stop to ask how the relay was getting these messages, but Rhona looked over as she ran and saw my expression.

"Crystals," she said. "Brandon and George spent the night distributing crystals tuned to our links to everyone in the scout relay, and we have people who came in from Stirling to help, so the relay stretched south—that's how they spotted the Atheani. Aberfeldy folk have been working all night to get communications points in. That was what Gosia needed my help for—we got Branklyn Garden just over the river right after I woke you up."

"That fast?" I asked, to her harried nod. "What would we do without you? Cracking work."

"Aye, well, the rest of you had your hands full enough last night, it seems. I'm going to scout ahead."

With that, Rhona blurred out of sight. I wasn't sure I'd ever get used to the way she could simply cloak herself in shadows or bend light to vanish like she did. I used magic heaps of times per hour and it still amazed me.

The clouds from yesterday had started to clear, as if the lovely weather from Oban were making its way east to us, but I could barely enjoy the crisp dawn air. Having our adrenal systems in constant overload could not be healthy or ideal for our ability to function.

"What's the plan?" Finn asked, breaking his silence. "Talk the Atheani into leaving the park alone? Stall them?"

"Yes and yes," Eilidh answered. "We try reason first, and if they respond to that, we talk and hope they don't kill us for interrupting them."

"Excellent," Finn said under his breath. "I love to court death before breakfast."

"Don't we all," I said. "Best plan we have on short notice."

"Oh, I agree." Finn looked over at me and gave me a savage grin that still managed to look devastatingly handsome with his perfect white teeth, even with the bags under his eyes from the lack of sleep. "If the alternatives are risking nuking Perth or throwing ourselves on a live grenade—"

"We're not throwing ourselves on any grenades," Ealasaid interrupted him. "Stop it with the martyrdom. Just because you got slapped with a label of divinity doesn't mean you go nail yourself to a cross."

Samuel, our resident monk, tripped over his own two feet, and Finn caught him by the arm, righting him before he could fall.

"Thank you for that," Samuel said, and I honestly wasn't sure if he was talking to Ealasaid or Finn.

Theological questions about how our friend the monk was managing to reconcile his faith with his impending divinity could wait until after we tried to sweet talk the aliens.

We got lucky.

Rhona flashed back into view in the middle of the bridge over the river, and she pointed back the way she'd come.

"They're coming. Get off the bridge."

Right as we reached the western side of the River Tay, the Atheani came into view, rounding the side of a stalled-out lorry in the middle of the motorway.

To my eyes, it seemed they were indeed the three we'd seen in Oban, and I thought it very likely that they were also the three I'd seen in Dumbarton. Two with coiled hair pinned to their scalps, one with long plaits worn loose.

They spotted us immediately and didn't stop.

"There's a volatile danger ahead!" I yelled out in their language, my hands crossing and pushing away from my chest in the added layer of signing to compensate for my inability to form all of their phonemes. "We came here to warn you!"

I didn't know if it was the best greeting, but I figured getting the danger bit right out in the open could be seen as a good faith effort at diplomacy—unless they thought I was lying and decided to blow me up where I stood.

But to my surprise, they slowed, staying some distance away.

"You again," one of them said in English, the one with the loose hairstyle, the same who had spoken to me in Oban. It seemed unfair that their physiology was compatible with our language when ours was not compatible with theirs. "Why are you here?"

"We were asked to help contain a very dangerous substance that has the ability to infect lifeforms and has no cure," Eilidh said, her voice ringing out with the undertones of truth from one of her skills.

I had a similar skill I could use to get their attention, but

I was afraid Òran na Cloiche might be seen as manipulation.

"She is telling the truth," one of the other Atheani—
with hair coiled and pinned at the scalp—said in their
language. It seemed Eilidh was not the only one present
with such abilities. The Atheani switched back to English.
"You assume we are going to this danger. Why?"

"It is directly in your current path," I told them bluntly.
"And we are very serious about its volatility. We are
concerned for the safety of this community."

Two of the Atheani made a noise that, surprisingly, the
Clach-Cànain translated as a derisive snort.

"You doubt that we would protect our people?" I asked.
"Why?"

"We have seen your kind," one of the Atheani who had
snorted said. "You are weeks into your stolen ascension,
and your people cower in their homes. They hide from one
another, sometimes fight one another."

My mind had stuck on *stolen ascension*. "You say we stole
this ascension as if it was not a mistake," I said incredulously. The folk of Dumbarton Castle had said the Atheani
called them thieves. Suddenly, that clicked into place. "We
know we were not meant to ascend, but we had no choice
in it. The matter was settled before it began. You can blame
us for being imperfect, but you cannot accuse us of
stealing."

"It was your planet that was supposed to ascend,"
Eilidh said, her voice ringing out in a strange resonance I
hadn't heard before. When I turned to look at her, her eyes
stared right through the Atheani as if watching something
unfold on a cinema screen. "You blame us even as you prove
your own unworthiness."

Oh, no.

I felt everyone in our group tense with her words—except Eilidh herself, who seemed to be in some sort of trance.

But the Atheani did not react, only watched us for a moment before turning to one another in what I thought was telepathic communication.

"If a thief steals a precious gem but drops it in your basket at the market and you keep it, you have stolen it," one of them said. "You are thieves. But we acknowledge that it was not your hand that took our promised ascension from us."

One of the other Atheani murmured something aloud to the speaker, something I couldn't hear, but the hand gesture was one I understood.

It was their polite equivalent of pointing, and the Atheani had indicated all of us.

"You presume that our path was to continue to the source of this danger." The same Atheani spoke to us again. "Why?"

"We don't presume to know where your planned destination is," Samuel said slowly, "only that had you continued on the trajectory of this road, you would have encountered the danger."

The Atheani seemed to consider that for a moment.

"Then you are mistaken," their long-haired speaker said. "Our trajectory was to track the notable power in this region, and we have found it here where we stand. In fact, this power came to us."

The tension in my shoulders grew stronger as the meaning of that sank in. I didn't think they meant the M90 motorway or the River Tay, and since we were the only reasonable definition of something that had come to them directly, it seemed they had changed their minds since our encounter in Oban.

"What is your intention regarding this notable power?" I chose my words very carefully. "You have deemed everyone here inconsequential."

"It seems we were premature in that evaluation," the Atheani said. "You, collectively, are the first of your kind to touch the reality of the ascension."

CHAPTER
TWENTY-NINE

B ehind me, I could feel Finn's growing resolve, along with Rhona's. Ealasaid and Samuel had the air of being on high alert, but neither of them were preparing for a fight.

That left myself and Eilidh.

And Eilidh was still in her strange trance.

The Atheani still had not answered my question, and I was not sure I wanted to risk repeating it.

"Our intentions were to observe you," the main speaker said after a pause that stretched out long enough for my stomach to churn with the anticipation of imminent attack. They exchanged another long look. "You have mentioned this danger is near. Do you intend to allow it to remain a threat to your people, or do you have a plan to neutralise it?"

I glanced at Ealasaid, then at Samuel. Ealasaid had one hand on Finn's arm as if to calm him, and she gave me a small nod.

Time to roll the dice. "Our people are moving to neutralise it as we speak. They may have already done so."

"And you are not with them," one of the other Atheani said, incredulity rife in their tone.

Eilidh, still in her trance, chose that moment to speak again. "We deemed you an escalation of that threat. We came in hopes to avert that escalation."

It felt like all nine of us present, the six ascended elves and the three Atheani alike, held our collective breath.

"Ah," said the main Atheani spokesperson. "You predicted our trajectory would take us directly into this threat just as your neutralisation attempt was to begin. Because we are unknown to you, you feared that we would interfere with your attempt, and in doing so, not only disrupt but potentially cause this danger to spread. Is this correct?"

"You are not entirely unknown to us," I said, if we were all telling the truth. "I saw you, in Glasgow, murder over twenty of my kind who posed no threat to you. This also factored into our decision to intercept you."

Another pause followed my words.

"Ah."

That was not the reply I was expecting.

Were they *embarrassed*?

"Our apologies," the Atheani spokesperson said, which one of the others echoed in their own language.

Which my internal magical translator clocked as sheep-ishness.

Oh, god. They were. They were actually embarrassed.

"I don't suppose you care to explain." The surreality of the moment increased when I looked over at Finn, who looked like he was about to throw something at *me* rather than at the Atheani.

The Atheani exchanged another uncomfortable look.

"We will," the spokesperson assured me. "But I think

perhaps it would be best to do this after you have seen to the danger."

Oh.

"Thank you," Finn said quickly. "We need to hurry."

It was my turn to feel sheepish.

"Duilich," I apologised to him in Gaelic.

"We will join you, to help or to observe, if you please." The Atheani voice surprised me all over again.

"I think observe," Samuel said. "The corruption is as dangerous as we have said, and already once today someone has fallen to it because they acted in ignorance."

That was a polite way of saying "dumbass recklessness" if I ever heard it, but Samuel tended to be polite to a fault.

"If you're coming, follow and keep your distance when we arrive at the park," Finn said. "We will send word ahead that you are there at our invitation."

All three of the Atheani inclined their heads.

"Trobhadaibh." Finn's tone made it all too clear that this was an order.

He turned and loped back towards the bridge. I took Eilidh's hand, and the moment I touched it, she seemed to snap out of her trance. She stared at me, wide eyed, as if she was waking up from a dream.

"We need to go," I told her quietly. "Follow Finn."

Eilidh shook herself and did just that. We all took off after Finn, matching his pace. I knew for a fact that the Atheani were far faster than we were, but they kept their speed in line with ours, hanging back enough that I felt certain they were honouring Finn's leadership.

Rhona glanced back once at me, motioning with a quick hand gesture that she was running ahead again, and she slipped into an appropriately wraith-like blur a half second later.

"Tell me," one of the quieter Atheani said to me, making me miss a step just as we reached the end of the bridge. "Why is it you do not paint yourselves blue? We heard that this was the custom among your people."

That made *Ealasaid* miss a step, though she corrected her gait so smoothly that I wouldn't have noticed if she hadn't been in my direct line of sight.

"Erm," I said, floundering. "I—don't think we have ever done that. Except for Blue Man Group, but that's their thing."

"Do the people of this land not paint themselves blue when going into battle?"

I could have sworn that the Atheani, who was indeed painted blue, was floundering as much as I was in consternation.

"Woad," Eilidh said, coughing. "A very long time ago, another tribe of people lived here. They used woad, a native plant, to sometimes do this. But I think it is a matter of debate whether this practice really existed and to what extent."

"Oh."

The Atheani who had asked again seemed so embarrassed that I had to wonder—but didn't dare pose the question—if the reason they had painted *themselves* blue was because they'd somehow unearthed some very outdated information about tribal customs of the ancient Picts.

There was no time to further explore this line of questioning, because we were quickly approaching Kinnoull Park's southern edge, and from the heady pull of spirit tangible even where we ran along the motorway, Angus had succeeded in getting everyone in place with as much haste as he'd promised.

Rhona reappeared moments later, waving at us to stop. "The Atheani should stay back here. I warned the scouts, but there's not enough time to get the word to everyone that our new acquaintances here aren't a threat. They're ready to start. Angus is holding off until we give the go ahead."

Finn had run on a short distance farther than we had, and he was talking to one of the scouts with a rockie-talkie in his hand.

"I've told them to go ahead. We need to do this before it spreads any farther," he said, gesturing to the northeast. "Since we left, it's progressed."

I could tell the Atheani trio's interest was piqued, but they seemed to be able to appropriately gauge our social cues enough to recognise that now was not the time to ask.

That the corruption had spread more in that very short time sent another spike of anxiety jolting through me. I triggered Connection, expanding my range as far as it would go, and sure enough, a pocket had bulged out on the northeastern edge of the previous perimeter, like I'd once seen happen with a rubber ball when squished by Catrìona's car in the moments before it burst.

The one small tiding of comfort was that with the influx of volunteers from Perth itself and beyond, our people had encircled the affected area completely. The increased spirit capacity and the scattered higher-levelled mages who had gotten the crash course in synergy had expanded the fence into a full dome. I hoped rather than believed they had completely contained the corruption. While selfishly, I was thankful the wind was blowing from west to east, there was no good or safe direction for the wind to blow those particulates. Nowhere would be safe from their corruption.

"If you three can stay back here, we'll come back once it's done," I told the Atheani. "I look forward to getting to know you all properly, with fewer misunderstandings between us."

That earned me a small smile from their spokesperson and from the poor soul who'd asked me about the woad.

Finn beckoned to us to join him, glancing back at the Atheani as if warily waiting for them to try to join in.

"We should stay on this side," he said to the rest of us. "This originated near the base of the tower, and it's possible that first spot will have the deepest-rooted corruption."

He was on a mission, and I didn't blame him—it seemed far too evident that Finn blamed *himself* that the corruption had spread this much from its initial point. I hoped he knew at least intellectually that this was in no way his fault; there was more going on here that circumstance had not allowed me to investigate.

The Atheani remained where we had left them. I wish I could say it gave me confidence, but there was too much at stake here for me to feel calm.

Already, the entire area surrounding the park pulsed with spirit, pouring off those who had come to lend their energy to those guiding the endeavour. This first tier of volunteers was the largest, low levelled and without the control needed to directly participate in shaping the precise exercise of magic we'd need to safely destroy all traces of the anomaly's corruption here. Their job was to channel their spirit, pushing it towards the second tier.

The second tier consisted of people we'd appointed to funnel the first tier's raw energy to the third tier, key mages over level twenty who formed the inner circle closest to the

Purifire dome that had been a simple flimsy fence only a few hours ago. These mages in the third tier stood with intense focus, their staves acting as a point of entry where the raw power could be concentrated rather than rushing into the delicate lattice all at once.

It was more than possible for the people present to do this without us. Almost preferable, in my eyes, seeing as how such an accomplishment would empower the communities present in myriad ways. At the very least, it would demonstrate to them that they could accomplish such things—the same important lesson Ealasaid and Samuel had impressed on us all with the crafting of the Resplendent Throne.

Even so, I don't think any of my companions planned to stand idly by while people knew we could help. They could see us; therefore, they needed to see us as partners, not examiners.

Because we were significantly higher levelled than most of the people here and had more control over our use of spirit, we carefully melded our flows directly into the tributaries flowing out of the second tier to the third. The mages over level twenty could handle that influx; we'd spaced them out well enough that we knew they wouldn't get overloaded.

The six of us fanned out just south of Kinnoull Hill Tower under the trees off the motorway. Samuel would direct our threads of spirit through the needle that was the tier-three mages. All I had to do was draw on my spirit and feed it through to him. I opened myself to spirit, feeling the rush of energy as even the ambient spirit around me, buoyed by such a powerful density of magic around us, leapt to the task.

Concentrating entirely on my breathing and keeping my flow of spirit steady for Samuel to manage, I tried not to think about the fact that there were barely twenty meters of woods between the motorway and the start of the corruption.

I also tried not to think about the fact that it had been over fifty when I'd made my way out of the mess. Barely four hours had passed since then. The speed with which the corruption was spreading rang every alarm bell I had rigged inside my mind.

A golden flare arced through the air away from the monastery. That was the agreed-upon signal to begin.

And begin it did.

Until that moment, the potent energies surrounding the perimeter of the corruption had acted only to maintain the dome of Purifire and Spèird so that it wouldn't degrade. A quick cast of Connection told me that the places where it had spread had not caused a retreat so much as ballooned out between the tentpole mages, as it were, those who stood at intervals to hold the line.

Retreat would have become inevitable had those ballooning sections continued to grow; it was all too easy to think of a mage getting trapped between two of them that converged around the patch of ground the mage occupied.

At least now that was moot.

Now, the task began in earnest.

A collective gasp—and a few startled grunts—went through the gathered channellers when the tier-three mages began to draw on the tier-two funnels.

This was nothing like the crafting of the Resplendent Throne or our mythical birlinn. It was nothing like Craobh an Òbain or the ionadan-siubhail. Those had carried an air of necessity, but they also built themselves upon our shared awe, the wonder of using magic to create.

Here, despite the thrill of such immense amounts of spirit electrifying the air around us, the atmosphere sank with the weight of the potential consequences if we failed. This was a trial by fire, in both a literal and metaphorical sense.

The tier-three mages' first job was to turn the dome into a sphere. They slowly dipped the flowing rivers of spirit into the earth, extending the circle downwards.

Minute after painstaking minute passed as they sought the depth the corruption had reached under the soil, where it had hitched a lift on beetles and earthworms, where it had burrowed into the dirt like a grub.

I lost track of time through the process, my focus entirely on my breath and the ongoing flow of my spirit adding itself to our task. Inch by inch, the upside-down bowl grew until it more closely resembled a rounded amphora, until the open space at its head drew together to finally seal itself off into a closed sphere.

The result was breathtaking enough to the naked eye even in the daytime. Glowing like a blue-green sun, the sphere stretched just over a kilometre in diameter.

Now came the tricky part: the tier-three mages had to begin compressing that sphere evenly from all sides at once.

I held my breath while they began, jittery nerves intruding when the sphere wobbled first once, then twice and a third time, before steadying itself once more. Then, almost imperceptibly, the sphere began to shrink.

The point of the methodology was for the same reason Finn had wrapped me in skin-tight Purifire when I'd ventured into the danger zone and then made the decontamination bubble compress the same way. By forcing the corruption's particulates into an inescapable wall of Purifire, they would be vaporised.

But it was a slow, tedious process. Which made it that much more dangerous.

Exhaustion was the biggest threat to me personally. Both Eilidh and I had only slept two hours, and I would have been surprised if the others got any more than that. I cast Fuaran over our small group to aid in our spirit regeneration. The cool wave of energy washed over me, raising gooseflesh on my arms, but almost as soon as it started, it retreated into the drag of the ritual's weight.

I realised it was good no one had insisted we take our places with the tier-three mages. My mind could hardly cope with the mere act of channelling my spirit for someone else to use; the thought of actively being responsible for hundreds of people's magic with stakes this high made me nauseated.

Minutes turned to a half hour; a half hour lengthened into an hour, which stretched out into two as the enormous sphere shrank, step by step and bit by bit.

We had also agreed that no one would step forwards to close the distance, just in case the ground remained dangerous.

It carried its own risk, having people wield spirit when it would become more and more difficult to see what they were doing, but after walking through the corrupted forest myself, I knew it was the right decision.

The sphere continued to shrink, retreating from view until it was barely a blip in the distance.

But there was one thing we hadn't counted on.

The size of the park and the nature of the corruption had infected creatures around us. Just because we hadn't seen them yet didn't meant mean we wouldn't—and the amount of spirit and gathered life was like an electro-magnet to draw the filaments of the anomaly's corruption.

We realised this when, on the other side of the park came a burst of screams.

CHAPTER
THIRTY

S amuel turned to me. "Calum, you and Eilidh go! Now!"

With as much speed as I dared, I pulled back my spirit, feeling Eilidh do the same.

We took off running towards the sound of screaming. While we had reserve mages around the enormous circle, they were meant to step in if someone strayed too close to losing control.

Tired brains made mistakes.

I added this one to the list.

Eilidh seemed to sense my train of thought. "We've done the best we can with crisis after crisis piling on top of each other," she said. "Everyone here knew there was a risk."

I would have to figure out later whether or not that made me feel better.

The uneven terrain slowed us down, but it was not difficult to follow the sounds of frantic fighting.

Even as we drew near, I reached once more for my beleaguered spirit reserves, not bothering with anything but Purifire because I needed something both powerful and guaranteed to be effective.

Finally, through the trees, I was able to spot the commotion.

Grey squirrels. Anomalous grey squirrels.

The damned things were not abnormally sized, just normal squirrels that had fallen prey to the anomaly's poison.

But even a normal angry squirrel could do some damage if cornered. These ones were far worse than anything rabid.

The squirrels were a flurry of squeaking teeth, barely visible with the speed of their movements, and the clinical part of my brain had to immediately prepare for the inevitability of condemning the three people fighting them off to containment and probable death.

Eilidh began to glow gold as she prepared her stun, and I slammed the butt of my staff into the forest floor with a cast of Connection to locate every bushy-tailed rodent in the vicinity. With a sick wave of bile, Connection pinged on not only squirrels in our midst, but incoming voles, field mice, even a blasted *adder*.

"Eilidh, now!" I drew as heavily on my spirit as I dared when the familiar sunburst of golden, cleansing light exploded out from Eilidh's triggered skill.

Another pulse of Connection confirmed it had stunned the wee deadly beasties, and I let loose the lattice of spirit I'd formed into a trap net, Purifire and Spèird together.

That net harnessed every anomalous creature in its path and scooped them into a squeaking, writhing pile.

Without missing a beat, Eilidh fell upon them with one powerful leap, her claymore's heavy slashes cleaving through half the pile at once as she followed with another stunning overhand blow that reverberated through my feet.

That had been easier than expected; Connection informed me that they were all dead.

By now, I knew just what to do. Harvest for the petrified hearts. Burn the whatever remained.

I didn't trust the flash of gold in my vision to tell me we'd gotten them all until my own skill came up with only living creatures who belonged here.

Except now we had three people touched by the corruption, and unfortunately for them, they had the same luck as poor Aidan Murray. One puncture of the skin was enough, and all three of them were bitten bloody.

"I am truly, truly sorry about this," I said to them, "but until our friends are finished here, we don't have time to get you to a safe containment space."

One of them was already a quaking mess, eyes blinking owlishly as blood from a gushing scalp wound dribbled over her brow ridge.

Three controlled fists of Spèird, and all of them were out cold. I highly doubted they'd expected that, and the smattering of gasps from others around us said the onlookers, at least, had not.

"Purifire cleanses, every last one of you. Now." I didn't give them time to worry about the people I'd just knocked unconscious.

Eilidh was already grimly pulling temporary containment cages out of her inventory, which we'd so far not had to use.

I helped her manoeuvre the poor sods into their enchanted boxes. It wouldn't hold forever, not against humans.

"They won't be in there for long," I said amid the

flashes of Purifire as people belatedly followed my order. "We need to move and try to avoid any other surprises like that. If you've got a problem with how I've handled it, feel free to come yell at me after we've cleaned up this mess. And if anyone lets them out, you'll be joining them, because they will almost certainly spread the corruption to you. There will be no chance to find a cure for this if we don't contain what's inside that sphere today."

Somewhat surprisingly—or maybe not—the only response I got was a series of shaky nods.

One glance at Eilidh and we were off again.

We hadn't gone two hundred meters around the perimeter when she let loose her stun again, barking my name just as Connection revealed another inbound band of anomalies, this time coming from the northeast.

My mind filed that tidbit away, the direction.

This group was rabbits, and unlike the enormous thumpers from hell we'd once battled in Argyll, these ones were your average garden-variety fluffers. Like the rodent-reptile gang, they were so recently corrupted that they looked normal at first glance, aside from the blood-thirstiness.

Once again, I employed my Purifire-Spèird net, and once again, Eilidh sliced them through with her burning sword. Set 'em up, knock 'em down. We'd caught this bunch before they got their teeth or claws in anything, but it felt like only a small victory when upon immolating what was left of the harvested carcasses, we heard more screaming—this time from two separate points around the circle.

More from the northeast.

I liked that common factor less and less.

Eilidh triggered another skill I hadn't seen, and she

blurred forwards like a golden comet, leaving me to catch up with only the power of my own two feet.

Her skills seemed to have levelled up in a powerful way. I hadn't had a chance to talk to her about how she was managing her own progression, nor had I brought up my own in days. Hard to have chit-chat time about the future when the present was biting us both consistently in the arse.

Figuratively speaking, thank god.

Though when I reached her, the present *was* literally biting someone else in the arse.

My blast of Purifire was not alone—other mages joined in this time, shortening the work considerably. By the time we got to the second point, the anomalies had already been dealt with, and all we had to do was clean up.

I'd just cast Connection again when a cheer went up behind me.

What had been a heavily forested park now had a naked circle of burned turf branded into its centre.

They'd done it.

They'd fucking done it.

"Oh, my god, we've triggered a community ascension!" A young woman practically squealed this news, pumping her fist in the air awkwardly because she had a staff in her hand. "A *mythic feat*!"

I hurried to help Eilidh with the shellshocked newly minted corrupted. Just two, one of them the unfortunate soul to have ended up with the ignominious story of contracting the corruption via rabbit to the arse.

They didn't protest, only asked how they could keep people safe. And they didn't hesitate to climb right in the containment cages themselves.

When they were safely sequestered, I murmured a thank you for their bravery just for their ears.

Then I turned to the murmuring circle, for the first time able to see everyone who had turned out here to help with this monumental task—indeed a mythic feat. Perth's community ascension was hard won.

"Well done, Perthshire," I said, calling on my skill Òran na Cloiche just to hammer home how genuinely earnest I was about my proclamation. My words boomed out over the now-barren park. "Well done, you absolute legends."

Part of me thought the Atheani might not be where we left them, but when Eilidh and I finally made our way out of the celebrating throng, we could see them standing there like big blue statues.

We paused before going to meet them, and I caught hold of Angus's shoulder. "We're going to check on the Atheani before they get skittish and vanish, but there are three corrupted people in containment cages on the north-west edge—"

"Already being handled," Angus said, cutting me off. "Say hello to the aliens for me."

That was a minor relief, if for no other reason than I didn't really want to face them when I'd made the impulsive decision to knock them out.

Tired people make mistakes. And I was, demonstrably, a very tired people.

Making our way back to the M90, Eilidh and I exchanged a glance that I thought meant we shared a certain amount of surprise that the Atheani were still there;

they stood stock still without fidgeting, watching everything with unreadable expressions on their faces.

"You did well," their spokesperson said when we approached, tossing their head to throw the long plaits of their hair over their shoulder. "You have introduced yourself, Calum Green, and we will do so now, out of respect. My name is Tinea, and these two with me are Saro and Sathia."

Sathia was the one who had shyly asked me about why we didn't paint ourselves blue. Saro had scarcely said anything, except to inform Tinea that Eilidh had told them the truth during her trance-like state.

Eilidh introduced herself, her stance still wary.

"What will you do now?" I asked Tinea, who glanced at Sathia and Saro, who stood impassively without seeming to answer.

"I think we have seen enough here," Tinea said. "We will find our way back to our world. It is rare for one of the outer worlds to become accessible, but the ascension made it possible. We were sent to ascertain, if possible, how it came to be that your world ascended and ours did not. But you have said it was—what was it?—a mistake."

"A very large one," I muttered, "to say the least."

Tinea cocked her head at me. "How is it you know this?"

That, at least, I thought I could show them. Maybe. "If I want to share a system announcement with you, can I do that?"

"I cannot say either way," Tinea replied, again glancing at the others, who looked just as mystified.

"Worth a try," Eilidh said.

Every notification I'd ever received stayed somewhere in my memory. It only took a thought to pull it up. I hadn't looked at it in ages, probably because it qualified as traumatic.

Somewhat gingerly, I tried to send it to the three Atheani—and from their immediate twitches, I thought I'd succeeded. I read it again, just for the good old "hindsight is 20/20" kicks.

Greetings, human.

Due to extenuating circumstances, Earth shall begin to ascend ahead of schedule by approximately 10,329 Earth years. Because Earth is not prepared to ascend, we regret to inform you that the process is likely to cause mass casualties, as Earth had, until now, only trace quantities of spirit, and fewer than 0.005% of inhabitants display any affinity for its detection, let alone its gathering and use.

We are unable to provide assistance, as even with our advanced technology, we would arrive too late, and astral projections are incapable of providing meaningful aid.

We apologise for the inconvenience.

Ascension begins in one minute.

We wish you fortitude.

Short. Sweet. Damning.

Somehow, after everything, the message smarted even more.

I wasn't quite prepared for the Atheani to begin cursing in their language—quite fluently, too. I'd met a fair few Weegies who would give such a performance a standing ovation.

"This is what they told you?" Sathia asked, pure scandalised. "Nothing else?"

"Nothing else," Eilidh said with a mirthless smile. "Doused in petrol and kicked right into the fire with an 'oops, sorry, try not to die.'"

"I did get a primer on manipulation resources," I said

after a moment's pause. "But even that was offered as a bit of an afterthought. If we hadn't had the exceptionally bad luck to stumble on the quests we did, we'd probably still be level nine or ten with no idea what's going on."

A sudden commotion, very near us just off the motorway's hard shoulder, made all of us turn just in time for a blur of a human shape to hurtle over the shallow ditch, followed closely by a second.

The Atheani reacted with razor-sharp reflexes, snatching them right out of the air.

"Drop them!" I shouted frantically. "Drop them and get away!"

I pulled hard on spirit even as Eilidh sprang into action but I heard dual sounds of surprise and disgust from Tinea and Saro and knew, knew deep in my most primal instincts, that it was too late.

My blast of Spèird sent the two corrupted humans hurtling away, and Eilidh followed, bellowing for backup and more containment cages.

Sathia was backing away from their fellow Atheani, dawning horror stretching her features slack as she correctly gauged my and Eilidh's reactions and put together exactly what had just happened.

"Tinea, Saro," I said, panic creeping up my throat and almost freezing my tongue against the roof of my mouth. "You mustn't move."

I didn't know if I could render them unconscious with a single blow; I didn't know if I should try, knowing they could easily blow everyone in a hundred-foot radius sky high in bits.

Tinea turned to me, cocking their head to the side. "Why mustn't we move? It is only scratches."

Sathia murmured something in their language, something I didn't hear but didn't need to.

Saro froze, reaching out to touch Tinea's shoulder.

Everything around me seemed to slow to a stop as I saw what was about to transpire and could do nothing—nothing—to prevent it.

I'd seen the Atheani in action.

I didn't even have time to blink.

A burst of spirit sent me soaring backwards. I landed with a crack of breaking bone and the sounds of others crying out as they collided with trees and tarmac.

Desperate, I rolled my head to seek out Sathia.

The gentle Atheani stood there, mouth open in a perfect O of shock.

"Sathia," I said in their language, "if you follow them, you will all die."

"They can spread this—this danger."

It was not a question.

"Yes. They can and they will."

"I am sorry, Calum," Sathia said in English. "If this is true, then they are my responsibility now."

Those words hung in the air like a curse.

"Sathia, please." This came from Eilidh, her voice a bruise of supplication. "We will need your help here, and you would need our help to know how to—"

"I am sorry," Sathia interrupted, then went on more quietly, "I hoped we could be friends."

Then the Atheani was gone, a gust of wind the only evidence of their departure.

That and the compound fracture of my left arm.

CHAPTER
THIRTY-ONE

C onversations eddied around me without coalescing into coherent speech my ears could process.

I sat in the monastery's dining room just off the head of a long table. My arm had been healed, but my mind still reeled.

I couldn't even come up with the energy to take the piss out of my own rhyme.

Just when I thought we might have made a trio of powerful allies, instead our anomaly problem got turned up to eleven.

Samuel sat with Rhona at the other end of my table. I couldn't see Finn but sensed he was in the room, hidden somewhere in the din and the milling bodies. Eilidh had gone to make absolutely certain that the corrupted individuals really were contained this time, and Angus had unleashed a rage I never would have believed him capable of if I hadn't seen it myself. I wasn't entirely sure the gaggle of middle-aged mages—some of the tier-three folk who had helped guide us to victory, even!—would ever recover from the tongue lashing. If a normal tongue lashing were the average, humdrum whip, Angus had flayed them up one side and down the other with a cat-o'-nine-tails.

Even Gordon Ramsey and Simon Cowell would have turned tail and fled from that tempest; how the mages managed to stay vertical and not dissolve into sludge on the spot was a mystery I'd never solve and didn't care to.

I myself had nothing left, no chastisement or berating, no energy and no will to do anything but sit in a fugue state and wonder how the fuck things had gone so wrong so fast.

Tired people make mistakes.

And that was just it—every single one of us was beyond exhaustion. We'd left fatigue far behind.

Now we had solved one large problem only to gain two physically smaller but arguably much more dangerous problems like this anomaly was a sodding hydra from hell.

"Breathe, Calum" came Ealasaid's voice.

I wasn't sure where she'd come from since my back was almost against a wall, but our resident cailleach had appeared by my right shoulder and pulled up a chair beside me.

When your divine gran tells you to breathe, you breathe. So I breathed.

"Good," she said, conjuring a small ball of golden light that she held in front of me. "Inhale as it grows brighter, exhale as it dims."

I obeyed.

It took an embarrassing number of cycles for it to really have an effect, but hair by hair, I started to calm down.

"It feels like every time we accomplish anything, a new sinkhole opens up beneath our feet and sucks us in," I said to her, my voice a strange and distant monotone even to my own ears.

Ealasaid sized me up, looking me up and down. She still

wore her finger-width-thick spectacles on a chain around her neck, and even though she didn't need them on her face anymore, I still got the feeling that she was using them to look into my soul.

She saw me glance at them and plucked them off her chest. She slid them onto her face, where a piece of red wool lint dangled from the frame over her left eye. The eye was magnified to about twice its usual size by the thickness of the glass.

"You know what I see, m' eudail?" Ealasaid asked me.

"Blurry glass with bits of fluff stuck to it?"

"Exactly."

"I beg your pardon?" She was the one with the glasses, but I squinted at her as if it would somehow clarify what she meant.

"Sometimes, we get so used to a certain way of seeing the world that we keep looking at it that way, even when it stops making sense." Ealasaid removed the spectacles again, letting them drop back to her chest. "Things are always changing, a ghràidh. Listen to an old cailleach when I say that fighting that change is the fastest way to misery and despair."

I couldn't fault her philosophy there.

To my surprise, she took hold of the heavy gold chain and pulled it off over her head, letting the spectacles dangle. They turned this way and that in front of us, light glinting off the lenses.

Then she grasped the glasses between her palms and threaded spirit through the rims, the lenses, the earpieces. The space between her hands began to glow.

Tongue tied, I couldn't quite make my mouth move to ask what she was doing. Even if I'd been able to, I wasn't sure she would have answered.

The light faded.

When she lifted her hands to my eye level to reveal what had been her spectacles, her aged fingers unfolded like a chrysalis opening.

A delicate crystal and gold butterfly sat in the palm of her hand, swirls of spirit dancing in the translucent glass of its wings. The wings opened and closed with each twist of spirit.

"Thoir dhomh do làmh, a ghràidh," she said to me.

I held out my hand as she'd asked, and the butterfly crawled across her palm to mine, settling in the crease of my fingers.

"Ealasaid," I said to her, overwhelmed, "you wanted to keep those."

"They served their purpose long ago. Maybe they have another purpose to serve now, if for no other reason than to remind you that change"—she reached out and thumped me on the back of the head—"sometimes requires us to become soup before we learn how to fly. It's okay to be soup for a time. Just don't forget that eventually, you have to let that part of you fall away. You've bigger things to become than soup, lad."

Then she wandered away, leaving me with an enchanted butterfly quietly opening and closing its wings in the palm of my hand.

It was Eilidh, fittingly, who helped me figure out how to break out of my chrysalis.

We'd decided to stay a full night in the monastery to regroup, debrief, and fucking get some sleep. The door had closed behind us, leaving us with blessed silence and the chance to collapse for the first time in what felt like a month.

Somehow, my lizard brain chose that moment to say, "You haven't told me what you chose for your level twenty-seven specialisation."

Eilidh blinked at me, understandably thrown. "We didn't talk about it?" She frowned. "I guess we didn't, because I don't remember you telling me what you chose, either."

"Because I didn't."

"Oh, thank god you didn't tell me. I was terrified I'd just forgotten somehow."

"No, I mean I didn't...choose. I haven't chosen a specialisation yet." I gave her what was probably the most awkward smile of my life, made worse because my tired mouth was so dry that my upper lip stuck to my tooth and didn't fall back down when I let the smile drop.

Eilidh just gawped at me. "You're taking the piss. Tha thu really a' tarraing asam, a bheil?"

"Tha mi *really* an da-rìreadh," I told her wryly, which sounded dumber out loud than it did in my head when my brain helpfully garbled it into an unnecessary and incorrect translation of *I am really in really*. I winced. "I got overwhelmed. Well. I mean, that's just the general vibe lately all day every day, but I looked at the suggested specialisations, and they were each *just* enough off that I couldn't justify any of them."

"Let me see them. Buail thugam iad." She made a *come at me, bro* gesture with both her hands and flopped on the edge of the bed.

I thought that sounded like an excellent idea, so I dropped myself right down next to her.

Pulling up my possible specialisations, I flung them her

way, as requested. And I read through them again myself, because I hadn't looked at them in several aeons, if I were going on how much I'd aged in the past week.

Dìleab an Daghdha—For those who have chosen to walk in the footsteps of the draoidhean of old, this class elevates the draoidh to the role of acolyte under the Dagda, an Daghdha, the father-god of the Tuath Dè Danann.

Just as an Daghdha led in the image of divine masculinity, so would you follow his legacy, lending your strength to the fertility of folk and fields, spiritual guidance, wisdom, and magic.

Dìleab an Daghdha is a class that seeks the support of all for the benefit of all. In combat, their skills guide the flow of the battle outwith the primary struggle where they are able to observe and funnel allies to victory and foes to defeat. As Dìleab an Daghdha, you will unlock the Dìleab an Daghdha skill tree and gain a permanent +10 to Spirit and +5 to Will.

Wilder—For mages who have unlocked the specialised Wild affinity, this class offers a chance to harness chaos...or to revel in it. Wilder mages are those who follow their primal instincts in their Manipulation abilities, leaning on Pathos and Will and raw power to achieve the effects they desire.

Not for the faint of heart, the Wilder class demands the mage surrender to patterns they may not be able to predict. Its abilities are some of the most powerful for an ascending mage, but it is a class that prioritises instinct over order, intuition over planning.

In combat, the benefits of having a Wilder on your side are legion; the impact of surprise in the heat of battle cannot be overstated. Wilders are sometimes looked down upon by more stringent disciplines for seemingly lacking structure, but the actual class is full of nuance and the need for deep roots of control in order to utilise its boons. If you choose the Wilder class specialisation, you will unlock the Wilder skill tree and gain a permanent +7 to Will and +7 to Pathos.

Làmh Lùgha—Perhaps contrary to first assumption, the Làmh Lùgha class does not refer to acting as the ancient god Lùgh's hand in the world. Rather, as a Làmh Lùgha, you channel the attributes of Lùgh himself.

Lùgh was, in Irish folklore, the epitome of the oft-misquoted adage "A jack of all trades, master of none, but oftentimes better than a master of one". When Lùgh arrived in Tara to join the Tuath Dè Danann, he had to present himself as having a skill that would be useful to the king, but each skill offered had already found representation in the king's service. It was not until Lùgh cannily enquired whether any of the king's devoted can lay claim to all skills at once that he gained entry, earning renown for his abilities as a smith, a master crafter, a hero, a tradition bearer or seanchaidh, a mage, a harpist, a poet.

Within the Làmh Lùgha class, you gain a permanent +10 increase to Spirit, but in lieu of gains to Will and Pathos, you will unlock the following skill trees with an additional three skill points per tree: Bàrdachd (the art and power of verse), Masterwork Crafting, and Ceartas (Justice).

"Oh, for fuck's sake," Eilidh said when she'd finished reading. "That's just...sneaky. Finn *said* it was sneaky like that."

"Wait. Finn said what?"

Eilidh heaved a sigh, shaking her head. "I haven't talked to him about level twenty-seven, but he was telling me about his level nine specialisation. Did you know he went the route of a whole new class?"

"What? No." At this rate, I was going to be sporting a perpetual Shocked Electric Pocket Mouse face. "Where have I been for these discussions?"

"In your own little Calum world," Eilidh said, waving her hand as if to say that was beside the point, which it obviously was. "I ought to have brought it up sooner, but the apocalypse has been...apocalypse-ing. Either that or the universe has conspired for me to deliver this news at the precise right moment so you can ascend to godhood at my side and we can take over the world."

"Eilidh."

She had the good grace to blush. "It's possible I'm a little punch drunk."

"No, it's good, I'm rolling with it. Stuff me into the cannon, aim me at the world, light the fuse, and boom. We'll take it over. But tell me what to do with my life first."

"We are definitely in the right mental space to make major, inalterable decisions," she said in a sombre tone. "I ought to make you sign an indemnity waiver."

"Tell me what to do with my *life*."

"Okay, so Finn said pretty much the same thing happened to him at level nine. His first class had been a nature something. Rogue-like. Nature's blade? He didn't love it, so he worked his arse off to reach level nine so he could specialise into something that felt like him." Eilidh paused to take a breath. "But when he looked at the *suggested* specialisations, they were all disappointing and underwhelming. I think he got something really random, like, fish-related random."

"What."

Maybe it was the butterfly from Ealasaid fluttering around in my inventory where I'd stashed it, but now that I'd stopped moving, the world wouldn't stop spinning.

"You'll have to ask him if you dare. The point is, he got so annoyed that he went combing through all the classes he could possibly choose. Or not *all* of them, since I think they're just a hair on the countable side of infinite, but he spent days sorting, trying new searches with different parameters—"

"You can set search parameters?" I asked, turning to stare at her.

"Did you not even—never mind. Not important. Yes, you can absolutely set search parameters. And here's the kicker: you can tell it to narrow the search by affinities both unlocked and *potential*"—she held up her hand to stop me from interjecting with another inane question—"and on top of that, you can filter by rare and unique classes available to you."

"Oh, what the fuck."

"That's what I said." Eilidh made a face. "We really should make that public knowledge, actually. Before people have to wait until level eighty-one to do it again."

"You *think*?" My mouth did not want to close. An entire anomalous squirrel could dive in there with room to spare. I snapped it shut and shook my head. "Tired minds make mistakes."

"What?"

"Nothing. Or—not nothing, just the general thematic irony of this entire week."

Eilidh paused, considering that. "Aye, that's terrifyingly true, actually."

I gave up on existing vertically and fell backwards onto

the bed. The room spun around me, a veritable carousel of hungover feelings without any of the fun bit of getting drunk first.

"I want nothing more than to pass out for two days straight, but I think this revelation might be the jolt of adrenaline to the ticker that keeps me wide awake long enough to become god," I muttered.

"I'm not saying it'll be that easy, but..." Eilidh hesitated, then sheepishly went on. "I'm not *not* saying it, either. This is my new class."

I only had to take one look at it before reaching up above my head, feeling around until my hands found a pillow, and promptly shoving it against my own face to scream.

Eilidh's level twenty-seven class?

Cridhe-Cheartais.

Heart of Justice.

THIRTY-TWO

Y ou have chosen to seek an entirely new class.

Not an option for the faint of heart or the weak in spirit—literally or figuratively—this can seem like a daunting option indeed.

However, it is well-known in an ascension that circumstances change dramatically and without warning, even in worlds prepared for the ascension in ways Earth lacks. To illustrate this, we have calculated that in a normal ascending world, people choose a new class at Level 27 approximately 3.2% of the time. On Earth, that statistic has risen dramatically to 11%.

Because this decision is the final class choice you will make before you reach Level 81, you are advised to consider your options with great care and remember not only the ascension directive but also a piece of advice we hope you will find bolstering: thrown as you were into the ascension process, it is still an unparalleled opportunity for you to become not just who you could be, but who you long to be.

The practical aspects are myriad, but if you have reached Level 27 on a planet with as many unpredictable effects as Earth, you have already proven yourself up to the task.

Seek and choose based on the truest desires of your heart.

Sodding...rift-cursed, corruption-shat *arse wobbles.*

I could not come up with swears inventive enough for the cavalcade of emotions that Plinko'd down the levels of my brain from the animalistic Id to my apparently divine Superego, hitting every single rung in my pathetic hamster cage's ascension ladder on the way.

Eilidh, prudently, removed herself to the small sofa on the other side of the room and let me take out my frustrations on the mattress with my fists. My very manly hissy fit was neither effective nor satisfying, since I had just enough presence of mind to remember that unlike myself, the bed was not an ascended deity-in-waiting—probably—and if I hit it as hard as I wanted to hit it, I might just reinvent the meaning of *Bedknobs and Broomsticks* by smashing the bed into kindling suitable only for a hand broom. With today's luck on my side, we might just punch through the floor, through a rift, and land in a literal hell dimension.

I was well aware that my toddler tantrum was exactly that, but at this stage in the game, I *was* a suddenly six-foot-three infant who'd been handed enough responsibility to make even poor Atlas back away slowly with a, "Naw, pal, a'm sorted, cheers."

(Atlas, in my mind, hailed from Govan.)

If anyone had a right to be peckish, peevish, and in dire need of a nap and a cry, I reckoned it was the six of us. Finn had been slowly dissolving in a morass of guilt for the past several days, Rhona remained staunchly in her stoic bottle-up-until-inevitable-explosion classic avoidant state, Eilidh'd gone full cheerful nihilism, Samuel'd volunteered to die for the cause, and poor Ealasaid probably wanted to batter each and every one of us but instead had made me a beautiful little butterfly out of the glasses she'd worn for thirty years and told me to metamorphose my sorry arse out of soup and into something nicer.

All that said, the scream-into-pillow trick had helped.

Once I'd read through that, had my little internal scream and my little external scream—round the second—I read on and promptly felt like even more of a numpty.

Because the options for classes are as wide ranging as the stars and vary so vastly from culture to culture, in order to narrow down your potential choices, please select an affinity from your list of unlocked affinities. You may choose more than one for optimal search parameters.

If you have not yet unlocked the affinity you wish to explore, select Other.

 -Coimhearsnachd
 -Faith
 -Healing
 -Justice
 -Nature
 -Pantheon
 -Synthesis
 -Staves
 -Wild
 -Other

I'd forgotten about the Faith affinity. Maybe that explained my ongoing crisis of same. That one would get tabled for now.

It was high time to stick this bullet right between my teeth and give it a good, hard chew.

I selected Pantheon.

You have selected Pantheon. Do you wish to further refine your results?

Yes or No

That was going to be an immediate yes from me.

Do you wish to add an affinity or skill tree to search parameters?

Yes or No

Another yes.

After a few moments of deliberation and navel gazing, I added Wild and Nature.

It kicked me back through the tree, asking if I wanted to further refine the results, and I hesitated.

This was one of those now-or-never moments. Eilidh had said a couple very important things we needed to send out messengers to every village in Scotland to make public. Two of the little tidbits in there were things that gave me a little thrill. First was that we could refine not only by affinities we had unlocked but by affinities we currently showed *potential* to unlock.

When I reached the affinity list again, I selected Other.

· · ·

Have you unlocked the skill tree related to an affinity you wish to pursue?

    Yes or No

Maybe for the first time all week, the little spike of adrenaline was excitement, not fear.

    I selected Yes.

Please select the appropriate skill tree you wish to use to filter class options. All existing affinities omitted at your previous request.

    -Arcane

    -Draoidh

    -Tàthadh

Moment of truth. I selected Tàthadh.

    It asked me once more if I wanted to refine results, and since I wanted to cut through all the bullshit, I selected Yes once more. This time, it took a bit of hunting. I had to select No a few times, Yes a few times, No again, No again, and finally, I got the prompt that excited me the most.

Would you like to exclude options for which you do not meet necessary prerequisites?

Yes, for the love of all the gods. Which I supposed was supposed to be us.

    At long last, a list popped up.

Immediately, I was actually grateful that I'd panicked and waited this long. If I had opened it earlier, I would have probably taken one look, packed my mental bags, and gone on holiday to the bottom of the sea.

There were indeed near-infinite options, it seemed, if this was my refined search results. A few were annoyingly generic, like—with one hundred percent seriousness—*veterinarian*. Likely because of the Tàthadh skill tree, which was all about making pals of animals, but I had slightly higher ambitions than a class I could have taken at the University of Strathclyde with no magic needed.

Maybe the system truly was taking the piss. If so, its humour was certainly dry enough to be appropriate to the people inhabiting this little group of islands.

A few other classes showed up haloed in gold, denoting them as rare classes. I scrolled and scrolled, looking for something I don't think I could have described if someone paid me in anomaly-killing skills unlocked.

But then I saw it.

Not only was it perfect, but it was a pun.

An Duine Uaine.

The Green Man.

An Duine Uaine—This mythic class must be sought and will not show up in search parameters to those who have not unlocked the Pantheon specialised affinity and met prerequisites as follows:

-Willing reciprocal bond(s) with sapient animal(s)

-Synthesis affinity and demonstrated use of synthesising skills from different skill trees

-Coimhearsnachd specialised affinity at Level 3 or above

Many in history have aspired to divinity, but no true god has need of proving themself by any means but their own deeds and the legacy they build in the world around them.

An Duine Uaine, known otherwise as the Green Man, is an archetype established in many of Earth's cultures as well as cultures and peoples in other worlds. Characterised by an intense belief in justice and the value of all living things, An Duine Uaine is also known for respecting the awesome and unpredictable forces of nature.

A nurturing figure at heart, An Duine Uaine forms an integral aspect of an ascended pantheon, cultivating the bonds between language and land, living creatures, and the elements.

An Duine Uaine also exists in seemingly paradoxical duality. In combat, this class is a fearsome foe as much for their unpredictable uses of wild magic as for their openness to solving conflict by non-violent means where possible.

Because this is a mythic class with stringent prerequisites, you will receive permanent bonuses of +10 to Mind, +7 to both Pathos and Will, and the unique skill: Fìor-Uisge, which allows you to guide others—humanoid and animal alike—into unlocking skills organically without the use of skill points.

This was it. This was me.

I confirmed my choice without a single hesitation, and it felt like coming home.

The problem with going full avoidant on my notifications for so long was that I had let an absolute mountain pile up over the past few days. The physical exertion gains alone made me blink, but they paled in comparison to the jumps from the Resplendent Throne's crafting and my new class.

In my exhausted state, I needed to narrow down all chaos to the chaos of my own making. I dismissed all the basic notifications, chucked my two floating attribute points straight into Constitution, and stared at my updated stats in one fell swoop. Even that barely felt digestible, but seeing my new class beneath my name?

It made some of the panic, the anxiety, the overwhelm fade. Not completely, of course, but like the draoidh class had made me feel at level nine, this felt like the right step. Like I truly had a shot at being the man I'd kept buried within me most of my life.

Name: Calum Green

    Age: 36

    Level: 28

    Class: An Duine Uaine (Mythic Class) (Further class specialisation at: Level 81)

    Affinities: Nature (Level 24), Healing (Level 9), Synthesis (Level 14), Staves (Level 21), Faith (Level 1)

    Specialised Affinities: Wild (Level 18), Coimhearsnachd (Level 9), Justice (Level 4), Pantheon (available with activation of the Resplendent Throne)

    Marks of Esteem: Life, Connection, Justice, Passage, Invocation

Alteration:

    Strength: 53

    Dexterity: 60

    Agility: 73

Mind: 191

Regeneration:
  Constitution: 57
  Stamina: 111

Manipulation:
  Spirit: 157
  Pathos: 69
  Will: 71

Boons:
  Blessings
  Làmh na Glaistige
  Glòir a' Ghiuthais
  Blàr Ghaineamhain
  Glòrmhor

My eyes had nearly bugged out of their sockets when I'd seen the leaps in Mind, Spirit, and Stamina from all the goddamn running and Connection-ing.

And apparently good old-fashioned Gaelic stubbornness counted for something, because I'd organically gained two points in Will in addition to the hefty thirteen-point gains from the Resplendent Throne bonuses and from my new class.

I was bordering on overload, so the unique skills, I only skimmed. Athchuinge was a bit moot, considering I was a member of the pantheon it granted perpetual rights to petition, but I supposed if I ever needed to grovel after doing something legendarily ill-advised, I could at least get some of my pals to talk to me, as well as my partner.

Not an ability I planned to abuse. Also an ability I hoped no one did or I'd never get a moment's peace.

Who was I kidding? What was *a moment's peace* anyway?

The Reverent Creed was the other unique skill, which we couldn't touch until we'd activated our shiny new six-seater throne. Every time that particular eponym for the Resplendent Throne popped into my head, I became just a little more grateful that it was not, in fact, a six-seater toilet. Though that might be a good joke for April Fool's Day next year, and who wouldn't appreciate a pantheon who could have a laugh at their own expense?

I was already counting my giant chickens before they hatched. The proverbial cart was running laps around the plodding horse.

There were two other unique skills. One of them, Toghairm, was a bit confusing. I think it allowed me to summon people before the Resplendent Throne, which sounded a bit more monarchical than I fancied. But if I was reading it correctly, it also seemed to allow me to...summon myself?

I think that meant that no matter where I was, once we had activated the Resplendent Throne, we would be able to go home.

Immediately.

From anywhere.

It wouldn't matter if we had an ionad-siubhail or a giant golden eagle who was a very good sport—just a thought and poof. Oban.

It wasn't entirely fair to make Finn and Samuel commute, but at least they had the ionadan-siubhail.

Islanders—always getting buggered in infrastructural concerns. Even when they got to become gods.

We'd really have to figure that one out.

There was one more unique skill, and this one was all mine. Fìor-Uisge.

Ever since I was a child and Mum would take me out into the hills, one of my favourite things to do was to fill my bottles from our mountain springs. If there was anything in Scotland we had in abundance—besides bams—it was water. And our freshwater was the sweetest I'd ever tasted.

Fìor-uisge, in Gaelic, meant freshwater or spring water. But the very literal meaning was *true-water*. It also carried a lot of poetic weight in our songs. One of my favourite songs, a Mull song, had a line about it:

Chì mi fìor-uisge nam beann
Tighinn na dheann leis gach màm

I see the true waters of the mountains
Bursting forth down every hill

The skill brought that to life.

Fìor-Uisge (Level 1)—As An Duine Uaine, you have the power to nurture seeds that wait only for a nudge to grow. This can cover myriad situations, from coaxing land to come back to life and helping seeds germinate...to helping the members of your communities awaken their natural skills and inclinations without use of a skill point. As a unique skill, Fìor-Uisge is neither passive nor active, but as you develop your relationships with your world and its inhabitants, you will also develop your instincts in finding exactly what needs water to bloom.

For that, I already knew exactly where to start.

THIRTY-THREE

E ilidh and I didn't make it downstairs the next day until well past what could even qualify as lunch, let alone breakfast or even brunch.

We'd both held off on confirming our major stat allocations until bedtime, counting on—rightly—the knock straight into unconsciousness that came along with heroic, mythic, and divine feats.

It wasn't my favourite way to fall asleep, not by miles, but we got it over with and woke up bleary eyed but miraculously, magically rested and rejuvenated.

Worth it. Absolutely worth it.

Especially since we'd slept through most people's departures, giving us a blissfully quiet dining room.

Our ill-defined afternoon meal consisted of an array of pastries suitable for high tea, leftover tattie scones from breakfast, a bowl of soup, a dram from Angus, and a trough of fresh strawberries, which made up approximately sixty percent of my food intake.

While we ate, we hashed out logistics for the coming days, as well as finally making some clear-eyed decisions about how to put our new communications network to best use. Beyond our desire to spread the news about class specialisations and the system's desire to be a sneaky little git about finding the right ones, we also decided to put out the word about Ronald. We'd been all hands on deck here for the past couple days, but all the scouts who had been combing every corner of Argyll for the man seemed to have lost him.

Gosia, it seemed, had a good knack for public relations, and Eilidh half-jokingly suggested we put her in charge of press releases—but the moment it was out of her mouth, both Angus and I were nodding along, because we had plenty of existential threats and warnings and general information to pass on to people that we hadn't been able to share for weeks now.

That meant our new, very sensible pal got drafted into the PR-my. When I said that out loud, Eilidh almost choked on a strawberry at my pun, but Angus just looked at me like he had moved me several notches down on his list of tolerated people.

For the first time in days, I was in an absolute belter of a good mood, and I was sincerely planning to make it everybody's problem.

There was, of course, plenty of less playful discussion on what needed to come next. That and the eerie Not The Rapture discovered upon the evacuation attempt, which I'd frankly forgotten about in all the calamity.

When Angus brought it up, he did it in a roundabout way.

"One thing I've been wondering whether to mention," he began hesitantly, "is a rumour that's come up more than once since we did our big push to expand communications. I wrote it off at first because it sounded absurd, but the details matched up too well the second time after what Eilidh found trying to evacuate people."

That got my attention. "What sounded absurd, exactly?"

"That Leeds is haunted." If Angus had said it any more dryly, his tongue would have shrivelled into biltong.

"Haunted," Eilidh said slowly. "Like classic ghosts haunted or a more esoteric interpretation?"

"I don't mean haunted by the human condition and our obsession with our own morality, no. I mean literal ghosts, but not just random spirits. Ghosts well-known in Loiner folklore." Angus held up his hands like he'd no horse in the race, just reporting the news. "Nelly Longarms in ponds, Jenny Greenteeth in the river. Jack-in-chains terrorising the suburbs."

"How'd we get news from Leeds?" I asked, perplexed.

We'd had trouble getting Tobermory in contact with Kilchoan, and they could literally see each other across the Sound of Mull if they stood on their respective piers and waved.

"Refugees," Angus said with a shrug. "Apparently. This came in both via Dumbarton and Dundee."

That made me do another double take. "We've got communications connected to Dundee? Are you sure Eilidh and I only slept fourteen hours and not a fortnight?"

"Folk get motivated when they get a taste of hope." Angus shrugged again.

"You're full of the pithy one-liners today," Eilidh muttered. "And here you gave Calum the stink-eye for a pun."

Angus ignored that. "The point is, there's more to the Leeds rumour, and it reached me by two quite disparate channels. One of the things that has been swirling around the grapevine is that thousands—I'm not sure I believe their numbers—of people disappeared into that old ruined abbey, and when a group of adventurers not unlike your-selves went after them, all they found was clothing, laid out just like the people had evaporated straight out of their outfits. Well. Clothes and a whole horde of ghosts."

I was tempted to say something about "out of their outfits," but I couldn't bring myself to make that pun. Not when Angus looked like he was trying to decide whether to say something else.

Instead, I just said, "That all sounds worth listening out for."

"There might be more. No one mentioned the term *anomaly* by name, at least not through the rumour mill, but there were just enough little things sprinkled through, like ghosts that made people sick. Again, hearsay." Angus looked increasingly unhappy, the corners of his mouth turning downwards every time he stopped talking even though he seemed to be trying to keep a stiff upper lip.

"Well, that all gives us plenty to add to the worry pile," I said, more blasé than I meant to sound. "Would you like to accompany your friendly neighbourhood pantheon on a wee field trip, Angus?"

Eilidh hid a small smile; she knew what I was up to. Angus, on the other hand, didn't quite seem capable of following my sharp turn into brand new territory.

He stared at me blankly. I wasn't quite sure if he was more stuck on *pantheon* or *field trip*.

Eilidh slid her chair back and stood, leaning over to give me a kiss on the cheek before she went off to gather the others. Angus gave her a half-hearted wave that didn't even aim in her direction since he was giving me bombastic side eye.

"You want to go on a field trip?" Angus asked the question as if I'd casually suggested popping out to the moon.

"Aye. Just the six of us and you. I'm going to give you all the chance to marvel at my new unique skill."

"How thoughtful."

"I'm very generous. If it fails miserably, rest assured that you can take the piss until the day we die. Which I'm told might be never, so hey, free pass to take the piss forever." I grinned at him. "What do you say?"

"I say I'll take the piss out of you till the end of time whether you like it or not, but you've piqued my curiosity, so lead on, Green Man."

Either I would get to perform a miracle with my own two hands or I'd have very dirty hands and very amused pals.

I knew a win-win when I saw one.

❖

The "field trip" destination wasn't far.

So close, in fact, that when I led Angus to the burnt-out perfect circle we'd cleansed yesterday, he scowled at me and said, "You sure you didn't haul me out here so *you* could take the piss out of me?"

"Nope, I'm the one either about to show my entire arse or make you believe the sun shines out of it," I told him, secretly sweating to my toes because I truly had no idea if Fìor-Uisge would even work like I hoped it would.

"Get tae fuck, Calum," Angus said. "I have no desire to see your buttocks in any form."

Though I was walking away already towards the centre of the burnt-out circle, I swore I could *hear* his eyes rolling.

Made me worry, just a little, that he'd pull a delicate wee tendon if he kept that up.

The others were on their way. Without looking, I could tell Finn was walking with Rhona on one arm and Ealasaid on the other, and Eilidh was in deep discussion with Samuel.

It was another minute or so before they came into view, and I turned around just to check whether or not I was drunk on my own flights of fancy or actually able to see them before they were within physical line of sight.

Sure enough, Finn came first with Rhona and Ealasaid, and just behind them were Eilidh and Samuel. Neither looked up, but Eilidh waved.

A smile tugged at my lips.

Not just me, then.

"I hear you found my misadventures useful, a charaid!" Finn called out.

"Is iad a bha," I answered. "So useful we decided we ought to tell everyone in Scotland, in fact! I thought you might like to see the fruits of your labours."

"Is that what you're calling your arse now?" Angus asked loudly.

Rhona looked back and forth between the three of us, then craned her neck to catch Eilidh's eye. Eilidh shrugged.

"You know what? I don't want to know," Rhona announced.

I tried to tune them out. This was going to either make me greet from joy or make the lot of them greet from laughing so hard they passed out.

Again, I knew a win-win when I saw one, but I truly hoped it would be happy greetin' in an awe-and-wonder sense.

Even if it didn't do what I hoped this time, that didn't

entirely mean it wouldn't someday. That would make an eternity of jokes worth it.

Allowing their playful banter to drift into a blur of sound, I carefully cast around with Connection before I put my skin anywhere near the ground.

The combined efforts of all of those people had done what they were meant to; I could find no trace of the corruption. Not in the epicentre, not in the middle where my friends gathered, and not even at the edges where I'd feared tendrils might have escaped.

One of the many little knots of tension I had been carrying all week loosened. Not enough to vanish completely, but enough to give me some respite.

Content that I was safe to touch dirt, I crouched easily, placing both of my hands flat on the ash-sprinkled soil.

The jumps in my stats overnight bloomed into evidence as I reached for spirit. I had never found it particularly difficult to channel spirit, but now, it was if the energies sought me as much as I sought them. That thought pinged something in my awareness, something to file away for later discussion or debate. For now, though, I tried to enjoy the simplicity of my hands in the soil and spirit flowing through me, circulating through my meridians and channels, moving like breath in and out.

All around me, the entire wide circle where we had carved the anomaly's corruption out of existence seemed dead at first glance.

Like the grass patch outside the Murray home in Crianlarich, though, this land was anything but.

Resilience.

That word whispered through my mind like a soft breeze.

That was what I'd learned from that much-smaller

patch of grass, and that was what I was meant to nurture here as well.

Resilience.

As the skill had told me, Fìor-Uisge didn't have an active or passive label; it was both and neither. I knew from use of my other skills that such terms were meant only as a benchmark anyway. A way of conceptualising something to get people to trust their own intuition.

I chose to trust mine now.

I worked my hands into the soil until they were covered in rich, black dirt. The earth would leave its traces under my fingernails, in the cracks in my skin. That gave me no pause. I left traces of myself on the earth wherever I went, whether I meant to or not.

Resilience.

Something within the earth whispered back in response to that word. I continued to breathe with spirit, allow it to pass through me and return to the earth. Over and over, round and round.

I kept it up as minutes grew fluid, drifting into one another like waves at the shoreline.

But beneath my hands, the black dirt remained black.

Even just yesterday, the me of the past might have become frustrated. I'd be lying if I said I felt no frustration at being cut off from where I wanted to be within this space, how I wanted the roots of my spirit to reach into the soil and draw forth fìor-uisge, both in the sense oof my new ability and in a literal sense.

Time continued to stretch.

Resilience.

A small ripple of worry surfaced in my friends the longer I crouched at the centre of this feat we had helped bring to life in a location we knew from personal interaction was on its way to death.

Except there was no finality to death, not really.

All that died nourished new life in some way. Even if death did come calling, nothing was ever destroyed or created.

There was only cycles.

Like breath, in and out of my lungs.

Like spirit, drawn through the earth and into my third eye.

Like the love that drove each and every one of us to try.

Perhaps, just perhaps, that whisper of resilience wasn't just for the soil under my palms.

Maybe it was for me, too.

The moment I thought it, something shifted, and I smiled as shoots of perfect green burst through the rich, nourishing black of the soil.

They yearned skyward, wedging themselves between my fingers in their quest for the light.

Then it wasn't just shoots close enough to touch me. Spirit poured into the earth, and the earth took that fioruisge and returned it manifold.

When I looked up, I was crouched in the middle of a bower of transcendent green.

Part of me had hoped that I would leave trails of verdant greenery in my wake, but when I walked on wobbly legs away from the centre of that circle that, a mere forty-eight hours before, had struck dread deep into my soul, all I had to do was see through Eilidh's eyes to know that this?

This was enough.

This was only the beginning.

She met me at the farthest edge of the green shoots as I lightly brushed soil from my palms, and she cupped my chin in her hands, stood on her tiptoes, and kissed me.

"Seall," she said, gesturing at me to turn and look behind me. "Seall na rinn thu."

Look what you've done.

A strange thing happened as she took my hand and I felt the others moving closer to us. For just a moment, one brief glimpse, there and gone again as it vanished into excited chatter, was an image of me, leaves spread out around my shoulders in all the shades of the year's changes. From my head sprouted antlers, stately and imposing, and flowers bloomed in cascades where my breath landed on fresh buds.

A fancy, a flicker, a fever-dream—I couldn't say.

My steps grew steady as we returned to the monastery.

THIRTY-FOUR

The light interlude of peace and levity soothed all our spirits, I thought, especially when it came time to make up our minds on where we would go next.

"We don't even know if we can face the threat of corrupted Atheani," Samuel said when we gathered in one of the monastery meeting rooms that night. "That isn't to say we shouldn't try, but we've witnessed their abilities, and I suspect that's only a fraction of what they're capable of."

"What I saw in Dumbarton was certainly enough to give me the fear," I said bluntly. "They seemed embarrassed about that for some reason, but without knowing what the reason is—and with the corruption eating away at any chance to find out—we're simply not strong enough to face them."

"We don't have to face them. Not yet." Eilidh was chewing on her lip when I glanced over at her. "But it would be good to know where they are."

"Are you suggesting we should follow them and try to

avoid their notice?" Finn pressed his knuckles into the base of his skull, which I'd learned meant he had a migraine coming on. "It's risky."

"They went northeast," Eilidh said, and this time, I managed to catch on to what she was saying.

"You think they're following something themselves," I said. "What do you think they're following?"

"I'm not sure."

Rhona exhaled audibly through her nose. "You said that the emptied neighbourhoods moved northeast from here, where the corrupted forest began."

I'd been debating whether to give voice to my own suspicions of the past few days, and while I wasn't convinced speaking up was the right answer, necessarily, the bottom line was that none of us really knew where to aim. If we could at least say, "We're going northeast to see what's there," that would potentially be a start.

"I think Calum is having a thought," Finn said.

"Is it that obvious?" I asked.

"No. You're not as dumb as you look, but on occasion your face makes a show of putting two and two together, and I think that's adorable."

"Love you too, Finn," I said.

He blew me a kiss. I made a show of catching it and shoving it in my pocket, to which both Eilidh and Rhona sighed, but it was Ealasaid who spoke up.

"Sometimes I miss smartphones," she said to no one in particular. "Those two would go viral in a heartbeat."

I cleared my throat, since we were wading into territory that made me glad Eilidh was very secure in our relationship. It probably didn't hurt that her class was very literally the Heart of Truth, so she had every right and reason to feel confident.

"The thought Finn so observantly noticed," I said, "is something that's been on my mind since my questionable decision to wade into Anomalous Chernobyl in the back garden here."

I paused, considering my next words carefully. I was a bit grateful that Angus had left us to go back to Oban and his wife Eliza, because I wasn't sure if I was anywhere near the mark on this hypothesis, and a smart-arse remark about the idea itself and not my himbo hamster identity would hurt the feeling I had on reserve for venturing tinfoil-level ideas with little more evidence than a hunch and a guess.

"I think it took a day or two to settle to a point where it became a viable thought instead of a passing inkling," I went on wryly. "And to say we've been a bit distracted is an understatement. How many people do you reckon we had helping us yesterday to cleanse that section of the forest?"

"Several hundred," Eilidh said hesitantly at the same time Ealasaid said, "Two thousand eight hundred seventeen, all told. It takes quite a few people to encircle a sphere with a circumference of three kilometres, and we did that and then some."

Whatever thought I'd been about to express flew out of my head at the precision of her figure.

I had to shake myself out of wondering at the numbers, because it didn't ultimately matter; Ealasaid's answer had more than supported my point.

"Okay. It took almost three thousand people to generate the amount of spirit it took to cleanse that space of the corruption. Even if we shrink that down to the original footprint of the grove—"

"The original footprint was still almost a square kilometre," Finn said quietly. "That's why I was so alarmed. It grew, but only in one direction."

"That is an enormous amount of energy to magically affect that space," Ealasaid said. "Calum, say what you want to say. I think you have all our attention, a ghràidh."

"I think whatever left the corruption there expended all that energy to do so." This was where it ventured into tinfoil territory. I swallowed. "I think all those people who vanished were the means of replenishing it."

"I didn't expect everyone to jump on board that fast," I said to Eilidh when we were getting ready for what was likely to be our last night in a proper bed for a while.

"Two plus two equals four," Eilidh answered smoothly. "If you'd just started shouting, 'Four! Four!' with no context, you might have gotten pushback, but when you show us a two and another two and count it out on your fingers like you did, it's a little hard to argue."

"Well, when you put it like that," I muttered.

Eilidh fell silent as she pulled back the duvet and crawled into bed. Her next words sounded like she chose them very deliberately. "Bawbag used people like that. As fuel."

I hadn't actually put *that* together. I let out a low whistle. "You're absolutely right. If Leeds is proper haunted, we better not be chasing Bawbag's vengeful ghost into Aberdeenshire. We already killed the bastard once."

That earned me a wan smile. "I think that's one nightmare we can safely lay to rest. No pun intended."

"You better intend that pun." I slipped into bed beside her, my whole body draining of tension in one long sigh.

The other part of my apparently very good maths skills had been weighing on me, because I wasn't quite up to voicing that part.

"There was one other thing," I said, scooting down and pulling Eilidh to my chest where she nestled into what felt like her comfortable nook in the crook of my arm with the top of her head resting against my neck.

"What?"

"I think we're on the trail of the source of the corruption itself." I blurted it out so quickly that it came out in a nearly stream-of-consciousness run-on, and Eilidh's breath stilled against the bare skin of my chest.

But what she said in reply, barely above a whisper, was almost worse than if she'd laughed in my face.

"I think you're right."

We all rose earlier than we'd intended, ready to go as the sun was creeping higher in the sky but about to vanish behind a gathering bank of clouds.

Gosia met us on our way out the door of the monastery with a large wooden crate filled with six bags of food.

"As a thank you," she said gruffly by way of greeting. "This is from our community. If Oban ever needs our help the way Perth needed yours, I hope you will send word."

Without any further comment—and without answering our surprised chorus of *thank you*s—she thrust the crate into Finn's arms and strode away with crisp, brisk efficiency.

The whole crate vanished into Finn's inventory. He grimaced. "We can go through it later. And I think we should perhaps have some more people come to Perth to help them get their feet under them."

"I'll ping Eliza," Rhona said shortly. "I'm going to scout ahead anyway. I'll let you know if there's any trouble."

"You know the route?" Eilidh asked her.

In answer, Rhona pointed, marched that direction, and slipped into the next morning shadow in her path, out of sight.

"How is she the youngest of us and also somehow the scariest?" I wondered aloud. "Is it just the fact that she chose the class ban-sìthe or does she just like being creepy?"

"Yes," Ealasaid said sagely.

Situated where we were on the eastern edge of Perth anyway, it didn't take us long to leave the city behind. Rhona reappeared only once every mile or so to let us know she was still alive and looking out for us, but other than that and Eilidh pointing out where the trail of missing corpses and empty nests had led a few nights before. "Empty nests" were what she was calling them, and I understood what she meant all too easily.

Growing up with a mother who rehabilitated wildlife, I'd learned many of the signs of predators, and one of the saddest to me as a wean had been when Mum found a meticulously crafted nest lined with snatched bits of wool from sheep and downy feathers and soft grass and the empty shells of eggs with no chicks peeping to be fed.

Clouds rolled in, bringing with them the heavy drops of an early summer shower.

We passed the Murrayshall Country Estate where Eilidh pointed out the last few places she'd checked when tracking the spate of empty houses.

"I would never have gone in someone's home, but in the

first housing estate just next to the monastery, I saw a front door open and a business suit in a puddle in the threshold," she said. "And right next door was a car with a dress and a string of pearls on the driver's seat, shoes on the floor, earrings on top of the dress. A thief would have taken the jewellery. We started going door to door and in almost every house, we could see clothes fully visible in the same way, just like someone dropped out of existence in their birthday suit and left everything else behind."

"Gosia has been trying to compile a list of the missing," Ealasaid said from behind me. "I suspect that is why she struggled to say goodbye to us."

None of us were really sure how we would be able to follow the path of something that, as far as we could tell, was completely invisible and could pass through a city unnoticed except by the emptiness and corruption it left behind it.

We needn't have worried.

As Eilidh and I had learned all the way back in March, when it came to the anomalies, we didn't much have to go looking for them.

They always seemed to find us.

Rhona was very good at her self-appointed job. When a small, controlled bolt of lightning sprang up three hours into our trek northwards, it came from a poultry farm just off the A94.

"This is the universe's revenge," Eilidh muttered in horror when she noticed the signs for the farm.

"For eating chicken?" Samuel asked.

"No, for taking the piss out of Iain for almost getting eaten by one," I explained. "In his defence, the chicken was the size of a two Shetland ponies stacked on top of one another."

"I respect your strangely American approach to measurements," Finn murmured. "Somehow I understand exactly how big that chicken was."

I had my focus glued to the place where Rhona had sent up her lightning bolt, and I pulled Brac-Meanmna from inventory, murmuring a greeting to the living weapon. It was the first time I'd held my staff since my class change and jump in attributes. I was not prepared for the almost greedy way the weapon latched onto my spirit and seemed to guzzle down a good ten percent of it.

"Oi," I said, startled, "if we have to fight and you've turned into a spirit vampire, we're going to have a problem. Especially if we have to fight an entire farm of anomalous chickens, however big they are."

Brac-Meanmna gave a little guilty twitch. I held the staff out behind me for it to take hold of its usual place.

"Oh, god, I hope we don't have to fight an entire poultry farm. I'm sorry, Iain." Her apology came out morose, almost as if she were begging forgiveness from the dead.

I almost asked her if she happened to have developed a chicken phobia, but I stopped myself, remembering how I'd first encountered her. She and her lovely grandmother Mòrag had been fighting off a moose-sized seagull that had already killed Mòrag's husband. It struck me very belatedly that her laughter about Iain's chicken encounter may have been a desperate coping mechanism.

No army of anomalous chickens descended, however, and the closer we got to where Rhona had sent up her flare, the more worried I got that I'd misinterpreted an SOS as a warning.

Before I could say anything to the others, though, the reason for the warning came barrelling across a field, hooves pounding the grass and churning up great clods of sod and grass.

"Thighearna," Finn muttered, sounding every bit as dismayed as I felt.

I cast Keen Eye just to make sure this was the object of the warning and not a potential victim trying to get away.

No such luck.

Anomalous Highland Bull.

CHAPTER

THIRTY-FIVE

There were few animals in Scotland more beloved than our signature heery coos, as they were most affectionately known. Tourists loved them, locals loved them—I'd never met someone who saw one of the shaggy, long-horned animals and said, "You know what? Fuck those cows."

They were adorable. Gentle. Half the time, you weren't really sure if they could see you with all that hair in their faces. They looked like they belonged in the heyday of emo, except you couldn't see them without the damned things bringing a dopey smile to your face. And the calves were every bit as cute as you would expect.

This one was not a calf.

I was very thankful it was not a calf.

But other than that, I couldn't quite think of another example of livestock I would be more reluctant to kill than a heery coo.

Except this one was huge, enraged, and corrupted. Their enormous horns could be dangerous when the animals were their usual placid selves if they got startled.

This thing was three hundred meters away and closing quickly.

Ealasaid made an unhappy noise, and Samuel's lip curled in distaste.

"I take it back," Eilidh said mournfully. "I will trade this cow for the entire poultry farm."

Barring any better ideas, I grabbed Brac-Meanmna from where I'd just placed the living staff on my back.

"Help us do this quick, and I won't snipe at you for siphoning my spirit," I muttered, feeling the staff flare to life with alacrity. "The rest of you, be ready."

I hadn't tried to cast any of my normal spells yet, and when I reflexively pulled, wove, and loosed my familiar lasso of Purifire called Ring of Fire, I was not prepared for the near exponential increase in power.

It didn't just lasso the beastie; it slammed down a circular wall of blue-green flames with the anomalous bull galloping full speed ahead. The term "ring" fell into obsolescence, as the structure far more closely resembled a cylinder.

The woeful creature struck the barrier running as fast as its hooves could carry it, and the resulting combination of the crunch of shattering horns and the scream of the corrupted beast smashing itself headfirst into the single most effective weapon against it, well.

I wasn't the only one who blanched.

Finn launched a javelin from where he stood with the grace of an ancient Olympian, and Samuel called down a lightning bolt of his own in the centre of the ring.

Eilidh didn't budge, only looked at me with the closest thing to a pout I'd seen on her face in a long time. "Do you need me to go kill it?"

"We've got it," I told her, rubbing her shoulder as I passed her to leap over the fence.

My words were the truth. Between Ealasaid loosing bolts of silvery projectiles through my Ring of Fire and Samuel and Finn combining Finn's javelins with Samuel's lighting, the fight wasn't much of a fight at all.

We moved on quickly after harvesting the bull. I was all too happy to see its corpse vanish and to cleanse the earth beneath it with Purifire.

Rhona met us another quarter mile or so down the road. "Sorry I didn't come help," she said quickly. "I found something you should see."

She led us to an old church just off the right-hand side of the road. A driveway cut in to the church, but Rhona stayed on the main road, pointing at a wrought-iron fence separating the churchyard from traffic..

It took me a moment to see what she was pointing to, but when I did, I forgot to breathe for long enough that my heart gave a little stutter in my chest as if saying, "Hey, loser, *air*."

Or maybe it was saying *hair*.

What Rhona had led us to was none other than a familiar-looking plaited lock of hair that looked like spun silver, carefully cut and wound around the metal spike at the top of the fence like a calling card.

Instinctively, I cast Connection, probing it for any sign of corruption. There was none.

"Sathia," I said slowly.

"She knew we'd follow," Eilidh said, staring at the lock of hair. She turned to me, a confused look on her face.

"Why would she let us know? Why would she leave a trail?"

"She's not corrupted. Not yet, at least," I said. "Or she wasn't when she left that, but it can't have been long ago."

I walked up to the fence, checking the plait one more time to be safe, but there was not even a hint of the corruption's grasping filaments to be found. When I reached out a finger to touch the hair, it was perfectly dry, though the grass around it was wet, probably from the same passing shower we'd been caught in earlier.

"Sathia's still nearby," I said suddenly. "The hair's dry, but the grass and the fences are wet."

"The question is whether or not she's alone," Finn said, and Ealasaid nodded her agreement.

That was my cue.

Connection, my trusty radar system.

With a literal lock of hair to use to seek out a specific spirit signature, it ought to have been a simple enough thing to the hair's owner. The others waited, pretending patience, while I pushed my signature spell as far as it could go, but it came back with nothing. Not a hint of Sathia or the other Atheani anywhere nearby.

"I can't find her," I said after a moment. "Either she can hide from Connection, which is a thought I don't particularly like, since it implies her corrupted companions likely can as well...or she is fast enough to get out of range within minutes. Another thing that doesn't bode well if Saro and Tinea are out here too."

"Or," Ealasaid said, walking over to pull the hair from the fence and holding it gently in her hand, "Sathia is warning us to stay away. She seemed like the most level-headed of the three of them. If she took the time to leave something recognisable for us to find of hers, we ought to ask herself what reason she might have to do something like that and then escape as quickly as possible."

"That might be right," Finn said. "She may be warning us away from her fellow Atheani because she is afraid they'll harm us, especially corrupted as they are."

"Calum, we should tell them what we were talking about last night," Eilidh said suddenly. "If we're right—"

"Right about what?" Rhona looked back and forth between us, a perturbed expression on her face as if she were annoyed at being left out of our speculation.

"We suspect we're tracking the real, original source of the corruption," I said, another thought dawning on me that I hated so much, I wished it hadn't even occurred to me. "And I think that's what the Atheani might be doing now too."

I reflexively triggered Connection again, out to its fullest distance.

"But two of them are already corrupted," someone said, and I wasn't even aware of who.

The voice distorted, vowels drawn out like we were trapped in a film and someone had hit a button to turn it to slow motion.

It hit me like I'd swallowed an entire ice block, my stomach suddenly frozen with fear so cold and heavy that I couldn't move.

My body began to shake without my permission, a low-level tremor quaking me from head to toe.

A strange rushing began in my ears. White noise. My left ear popped like I was in a plane taking off, and added to the sound of that staticky nothing was a high-pitched drone like tinnitus but strangely undulating. It gave me the sensation of a tiny outboard motor shoved up into my ear against my eardrum but suspended in midair, rotating slowly.

I swayed on my feet, a cold sweat breaking out over my cheek.

"Ei-Ei-lidh," I stammered out, my body twitching as if I were about to have a seizer.

"Calum?"

Her voice sounds like it's coming at me through water.

All at once, the fog cleared like someone had slammed down a soundproof door the way a blade would drop on a guillotine.

My equilibrium had tilted so far with the impact of whatever had just happened that I pitched over, my right leg twitching hard enough that my right foot caught on the back of my left angle, and as commotion broke out among my friends and hands caught me by the upper arms, I realised something.

I'd reached out with Connection and something had grabbed hold of my spirit and pulled. Whatever that guillotine had been, whatever it was that had cut off the trap like slicing through a kraken's tentacles all at once—it had, without any doubt in my mind, saved my life and every single one of our lives.

My body still shook with irrepressible tremors, but where I felt as if I'd been hooked up to a live wire, I felt something else.

"Sathia," I said through chattering teeth. I was so cold. Why was I so cold? "Sathia is coming."

She wasn't just headed our way; Sathia was moving at a speed I thought might be able to outrun a cheetah.

Then again, at the moment, a snail could probably outrun me, so my sense of proportion couldn't be trusted.

"There," Finn's voice said, disembodied in my senses.

God, what was happening to me?

"Oh, fuck," Rhona whispered. Her voice seemed to come from two places at once.

A jolt of spirit seemed to plunge into my spine like I imagined an epidural would.

"*Fuck!*" I barked, spit flying from my mouth as I almost spun off my feet even with Eilidh gripping my arm tight enough that I thought there was a distinct possibility she'd take the whole arm off.

Brac-Meanmna.

My living staff. I felt a surge of emotion, panic, resolve —but above all, a desperate need for me to do something. It wanted something.

That surge hit again, enough that Eilidh yelped as if she'd stuck her hand on a live wire.

"My staff," I managed to get out, twisting through the still-constant shudders.

My hand closed around the staff, and it leapt free of its grip between my shoulder blades.

Immediately, my world steadied.

And narrowed to a pinpoint focus.

Sathia.

For her to not have reached us yet, I must have felt her from *miles* away.

But she wasn't alone.

Behind her, like a tornado of pure terror, came a wall of anomalies.

They ballooned behind her like shrapnel tossed in a cyclone's radius of destruction.

And through the lingering connection that she'd made to me when she severed the anomaly's grip on my spirit, I heard her voice ring out inside my head.

Run.

CHAPTER
THIRTY-SIX

I must have gasped out the word to my friends, must have communicated to them somehow, because suddenly we were all moving, almost tripping over each other.

Something of the utter heart-stopping terror that had threaded its frozen fingers into my ventricles, filled my arteries with ice—something of that must have bled out into my companions. With the bond we shared, I never knew how much transferred, how much any of us knew about what our collective destiny passed between us.

Brac-Meanmna in one hand and Eilidh's in my other were the only things that kept me mobile, kept my head pointed up and my feet finding safe footing on the ground.

In that strange dual vision, I saw Rhona stop, turn, and scream. Spirit erupted from her with a jagged frequency so sharp that had it been aimed at us, our ears would have ruptured from the inside out.

The clouds above turned black, roiling with Rhona's spirit and Samuel's in a dance of danger and electricity that lashed out behind us like caltrops the size of a small village.

My mind slowly recovered with each pounding step—or was it each pounding beat of my heart? A constant drumming, a relentless rhythm. Golden fire kindled beside me as Eilidh turned to meet my gaze and pressed her hand once against my heart with a shock of heat and resolve that pulled me onwards and allowed me my first full breath in what felt like years.

The shockwave as Eilidh released her stun flattened the fields on either side of the road. The pure golden flames flashed outwards from her body, engulfing Sathia without scathing the Atheani but tearing through the cloud of screeching anomalies at her back.

An enormous wave of spirit rolled over us as we ran, and our steps grew lighter, longer, strides lengthening until we seemed to skate over the tarmac as if it had been made to give us a space to dance.

The others felt it too; for every one of us who spun to call down death to our pursuers, another twisted to sprint forwards until the ebb and flow of our movement swirled with the perfect poetry of currents in a river rushing wildly over rapids.

It washed away the remnants of the terrible fog that had lodged its claws in my mind and heart, chased the cobwebs from my vision, and my living staff exulted.

Brac-Meanmna hungered to strike, and I indulged it.

Tairm made a torrent through my spirit as I loosed the spell in the centre of our maelstrom of complementary magics. In the midst of farmland as we were, my wild magic became dual tornados, one on either side of the road, tearing into the summer grasses, drying them, honing them into thousands of darts that launched themselves into the clouds of anomalies flying fast enough to be gaining on Sathia.

Which meant they were also gaining on us.

Sathia had slowed herself to continue her relentless assaults on her pursuers, and we lent her our spirit in the form of wind to support her speed. Her power and control made mince of the seemingly endless clouds of corrupted crows, starlings, robins, magpies, sparrows, shrikes.

My fury rose with every fallen bird, every small life stolen to feed this anomaly that hungered to devour our homeland. Brac-Meanmna amplified that anger, spinning spite from the spirit all around us to rain down hailstones honed to deadly points, each piece of ice an arrow aimed at our enemies.

And Finn.

His dark mood over the past days had shuttered something in him, left him distant. Colder.

But now, faced with an army of anomalous birds, all that rawness he'd bottled up came unstoppered.

The still-healing scar along his jawline had paled with the tension of his clenched teeth, but I *felt* it loosen as he gathered himself.

And Am Bàrd Muileach began to sing.

I recognised the song, but I didn't know it—or I thought I didn't.

Finn's deep blue eyes, as blue as his island's waters, bored into me though we were not even facing each other. Just as I could see Ealasaid borne aloft on a wave of frost far behind me, just as I could see Samuel running with corded muscles at a full sprint as he pulled down lightning bolts from the black and roiling sky—Finn and I locked eyes.

Spirit whipped through the air, wild, alive.

It built from Eilidh's shining sun and Rhona's lightning-wreathed moon howling through the night, pulling Ealasaid's cold of winter with Samuel's summer heat, long days stripped to the waist on the deck of a fishing boat revelling in the storms that struck fear into the hearts of sailors.

My wild chaos.

Finn's fire.

The song that poured from his rich baritone was as raw as the wild magic leaping from soul to soul, and it didn't matter that I didn't think I knew the song. The waulking song's rhythm matched the pace of our frantic flight, the vocables' vowels and heavy howling consonants twisting and turning with each of us who spun to twine spirit into ruin for our pursuers.

With every syllable Finn sang, the rest of us answered. Waulking songs were work songs—they were sung to the thuds of tweed on tables, women's hands softening the wool with each concussive blow. This waulking song used that rhythm for us to dance through the dual warring storms of death.

We made our survival the labour of our hands with the magic we pulled from the air itself.

But it wasn't enough.

Even buoyed by what had to be Sathia's magic—none of us could have soared over the land as we were without help—we were going to be overtaken.

Then Ealasaid yelled out one word: "Toghairm!"

Confusion caught me even as I cast a wall of blackness into our wake and Eilidh loosed another stun.

"The throne hasn't been activated!" Rhona yelled, her voice contorting the moment she finished to rise in a piercing howl that felled anomalies by the score.

"Chan eil e gu diofar!"

It doesn't matter.

Tired minds make mistakes. Tired minds make muckle fuckin' mistakes.

As if Ealasaid had flung the image outward to all of us, I saw the text again:

Private: As an initial member of this community's pantheon and having unlocked the Pantheon affinity, you have unlocked a unique skill that can only be used upon activation of the Resplendent Throne. In addition, you have unlocked a permanent skill that is available to use now and in perpetuity, so long as your throne remains in your living community.

-Unique skill (unavailable until conditions met): The Reverent Creed

-Pantheon skill unlocked: Toghairm

Toghairm was already unlocked.

"Sathia!" I screamed our ally's name into the raging wind. "To us!"

I couldn't tell who reached her first, only felt a resounding, bell-like tone as all six of us triggered Toghairm in unison.

In an instant, we were tumbling to the soft, familiar grass under the sheltering branches of Craobh an Òbain, a tangle of seven people's arms and legs and bits of debris that had gotten caught in all the gale.

A cry of alarm went up from whoever was in McCaig's Tower and unfortunate enough to have the daylights scared out of them by having their bumbling pantheon come tumbling out of thin air.

I didn't think Sailean was *ever* going to let us out of her sight again. The kitten had been glued to my shoulder since she sensed our sudden reappearance and had pelted out of the cat flap at the Whyte House like a bat out of hell.

Two days had passed since we'd—almost literally— blown back into Oban, and we still had a whole lot of explaining to do.

I'd taken to sitting under the branches of Craobh an Òbain with Sailean, Sathia, and a rotating cast of our pals.

I knew, without any doubt in my mind, that the presence that had come so close to destroying us was the anomaly itself.

Sathia had abandoned their siblings to save us.

In the past two days, Sathia had done some of their own explaining. Some basics in the form of cultural differences, like that my instinctive impression of them as a genderless people was correct; the Atheani had no concept of it. Others things were offered because Sathia knew Earthlings were likely to be curious—like that for the Atheani, biological sex was immaterial, and their form of reproduction entirely, well, alien in our eyes.

But Tinea and Saro—those were Sathia's family. Born of water and blood, as Sathia told us softly.

They also explained that their siblings would likely never surrender to containment. From there, we all agreed to table that particular discussion until a later date. It wouldn't get kicked down the road forever with our new understanding of the anomaly and its danger impressing urgency upon us anew, but at least for now, we could give our new friend the time and space to grieve.

Oban buzzed constantly now, with people arriving all day to explore, to learn, to see how our community had grown and thrived, and people from Oban ventured out, too, to share where help was wanted.

Our frantic push to connect more of Scotland had bloomed more every day. Glasgow and Edinburgh down to the borders down south, Inverness and Ullapool and all the way up to Stornaway in Lewis and Kirkwall in Orkney.

Poor Shetland was in the mix, but people all over the country were placing bets on whether we or Norway would manage to fight our way through the sea monsters to reach them first. We thought our kraken had been bad.

The real dark spot amid growing good news was Aberdeen.

Many of us across Scotland pre-ascension may have taken the piss out of the grey granite city, but anyone who bothered to visit and look around could tell you—when the sun shone on Aberdeen, their world shimmered.

No one had heard from anyone within a fifty-mile radius of our Doric friends' home city.

Whatever awaited us, one thing was clear: we had to grow stronger. We had to learn everything we could from each other.

We had to ascend.

Or we would die.

That cheery thought cast a shadow over us regardless of our daily triumphs, and every day, news of more anomalies cropped up. Iain and Meeksy practically lived in Kilmelford now, and we were having to build yet another containment zone.

I was just making my way back to Kilmelford from visiting Helen in Crianlarich with Sailean—I'd *finally* made it to her a few days after we made it home from that frantic flight through Perthshire—when I heard a "Yoohoo, Calum!" and turned to see Raonaid coming out of the hotel, waving at me with a cast iron skillet.

"Hiya, Raonaid!" I called to her. Sailean mewed, starting to purr. She had decided she loved Raonaid. "We're just on our way out, but I'll stop back—"

"There's someone here to meet you, lad, and I think you'll want to come in." Raonaid seemed to realise she was brandishing a hefty piece of cooking paraphernalia at me like a weapon and gave me a sheepish smile. "I've got fresh scones and cream."

Well, I couldn't say no to that, could I? It would just be rude.

I trotted away from the ionad-siubhail and up to the hotel, pausing to kiss Raonaid on the cheek. "How are you getting on?"

"Oh, you'll see," she said enigmatically. She shooed me inside. "In the dining room, as usual. I've got to go get the tuna."

She hurried off, still clutching the cast-iron skillet in one hand, leaving me to wander across the lobby wondering why she was hunting for tuna whilst carting around a frying pan. I turned to Sailean as I walked into the dining with a frown. "Did you and Raonaid plan a tuna caper?"

Sailean mewed plaintively. She did like tuna—she was a cat—but sausage was the real way to her heart.

I stopped short when I passed over the threshold, because there was a young blond man and an array of unfairly attractive people, nearly all of different races but every one of them beautiful, all sitting comfortably around two tables pushed together.

But despite my initial shock to have invaded the first ever Crianlarich modelling expo, it was an all-too-familiar face that had brought my feet to a halt on the low-pile carpet, a face attached to a string-bean body that looked even more gaunt than it had the last time I'd seen him.

We'd put the word out that we were looking for Ronald over a week ago, and now here he was. That young blond man with 90s pinup boy hair falling straight into his face had our elusive quarry by the scruff of the neck.

Literally—he had his hand clenched over the back of Ronald's scrawny excuse for a cervical spine.

"Erm, hello," I said, for lack of any cleverer ideas.

"Good afternoon to you," the lad said, his accent placing him somewhere around Manchester-Leeds-Sheffield. The rangy blond Englishman gave me an amused smile. "You must be Calum Green. Props on getting a whole colour. I'm just the bastard of one."

I raised an eyebrow at him in confusion while Ronald squirmed in his grip, looking—as usual—like someone had taken a piss in his lemonade.

"Erm. Hi," I said again, still trying to wrap my brain around whatever was happening here. "Bastard...of a colour?"

"*Calum*," Ronald forced out through gritted teeth.

He'd kept us running long enough, and it was his damn fault Alison had spent the last month in a containment cell in Kilmelford, getting skin-crawlingly creepier by the day. Aye, that was Ronald. So I ignored him.

This cheeky English bloke seemed to make the same choice. "You're Green. I'm Grayson. Anyway, I've been interested to meet you," he said, with a wave of his free hand as he jostled Ronald with his other one. "I heard via your very exciting magical grapevine that you've been looking for this."

At that, a small, excited trill cut through the air, and something cat-sized and winged launched itself from the table right at my face.

Instinctively, I ducked, and there was another trill I could have sworn sounded embarrassed.

"Oh, for fuck's sake," Will Grayson said. "You can't just

dive-bomb people and kittens. They'll think you're trying to eat them."

Sailean, though, was wriggling and squirming her little way down the chestplate of my armour, so I pried her off and held her out so she could get a better look at...whatever it was.

Which, when the creature poked its head out from behind an amused-looking Black woman's elbow at the table, I still wasn't quite sure.

Deep teal—almost dark blue, like the seas around John O'Groats—scales, gleaming golden eyes. Definitely wings.

And Sailean veritably yeeted herself out of my hands, landing on the floor and using the hapless Ronald as a launchpad to get herself up on to the table, where she came nose to nose with...

"Trudy," Will said, sounding exasperated. "I'm not really cross with you. Obviously the kitten likes you."

"The kitten is Sailean." My voice sounded faint even to my own ears. I cleared my throat. "It's nice to meet you, erm, Trudy."

Sailean's purr vibrated loudly enough for me to hear it from where I stood, and Trudy made another happy trill, reaching out to boop her nose against the wildcat kitten's.

"I'm sorry," I said. "Is Trudy a—"

"Oh, ha. Yes." Will scrubbed a hand through his hair, which immediately fell right back into his face. "Trudy's a baby dragon. She's been very keen to meet you."

A Note from Mati

How do I love thee? Let me count the ways.

After the year I've had, I cannot tell you how good it feels to be actively creating again. I know I've harped on about it for pretty much the entirety of the last year and a half, but yer boy's been put through the wringer, pals.

Thank you so very much for continuing to support me and for reading my books. Getting back to writing after so much grief last year has been healing, and particularly the scene in this book with the massed choirs singing "Athchuinge" is a tribute to a very dear friend we lost in the world of Gaelic music last year, the inimitable Kirsteen Menzies MacLellan. You can hear the Dingwall Gaelic Choir sing this song on their record *Cabar Fèidh* with Kirsteen herself singing the solo verse.

Kirsteen's late father, Hamish Menzies, was the long-time conductor of the Dingwall Gaelic Choir, and she took over the helm of that choir after his passing a few years ago, later founding the Black Isle Gaelic Choir and leading them to great success at the Royal National Mòd.

Kirsteen knew the power of music to heal, to create, and to bond a community as more than just the sum of its parts. It's a secret we all too easily forget, that simple magic of voices in harmony. If you fancy contributing to the legacy she left us, a donation to the Black Isle Choir (Còisir Ghàidhlig an Eilein Duibh) or to breast cancer research would warm many hearts. I plan to donate a portion of the proceeds of this book in her name around the time of the mòd this autumn.

The Reverent Creed is, as I suspect you'll notice, a bit shorter than the first three in the series. I hadn't planned to do it that way, but as the last year has evidenced, sometimes you execute a daring quadruple axel in the Winter Olympics, and sometimes you leap, spin, and...eat shit. That I managed to finish this book at all is a bit of a miracle to me, and I really hope you've enjoyed it!

I promise to make it up to you with the next book, *The Penitent's Cry*, which will be out in December and is up for preorder now. I'd say it would be sooner than that, but autumn is the busiest time of the year for me and much of the Gaelic world—any Gaels reading this book will have a solid idea of why, especially considering certain references! —and I don't want to make promises I can't keep!

I reckon you'd rather I am able to safely get a book written and ready than have to sacrifice my health and risk burnout again when I'm just getting my groove back. For transparency, part of the reason it's been a longer wait for these ones has been financial. Bluntly, the covers are expensive, and my artist is worth every sgillin ruadh (every red penny), so I don't want to cut that corner just to save money.

Anyway, I'll be working away on the final two books in this series over the coming months, and in the meantime, you will hear from me sooner than December with a new series with covers done by the same lovely lass who did the *Terra* miniseries covers. The first few chapters of *Death Spiral* follow this note, so I hope you'll check it out! I'm super excited to share it with you. It's got some fun Easter eggs for fans of this series, and without giving too much away, it's more fully in progression fantasy than LitRPG, but it's a rollicking, world-jumping adventure with a very cranky Gael and a mystery animal companion who definitely thinks oor plucky protagonist is *his* pet and not the other way around.

You can find the preorder link for that here or at the end of the sample.

Once again, thank you for reading. I'm so pleased to be telling stories again.

Trudy + Sailean 5evaaaaa! (They're going to drive Scout absolutely bonkers.)

Mati

DEATH SPIRAL: CHAPTER 1

There's something about waking up with your heid in someone's backwash to make you take a wee inventory of your life choices.

A puddle of stale beer. The tang of sick. A discarded vape with glittery lipstick stuck to the mouthpiece.

Not, demonstrably, the bedfellows I'd have chosen.

"Good. You're up."

The booming voice—several hundred decibels too loud for my poor tender heid, by my estimation—triggers a split-second urgent decision: boak here or dash to boak in the loo.

I decide to chance it, flinging myself from the club's sticky, stinky floor towards the nearest WC. It's a risky manoeuvre for all but the most seasoned professionals, but I am nothing if not the consummate Platonic ideal of a functional alcoholic.

Trying not to let myself see the full-on *Trainspotting* level of loo as I retch into basin, I unfortunately feel my head begin to clear.

"Fuck," I say through the bile and drool. I spit into my porcelain chalice.

Two things I wish I'd known when I got punted into a magical world as an eight-year-old wean and subsequently spat back into this one as a thirty-year-old in a teenage body:

1. Ye really cannae go home again.

2. Ye lose yer magic but keep yer memories of it—and your constitution.

It's been ten years since I got slammed back into a gangly sixteen-year-old meat suit I'd long since grown out of. But it came with some unexpected downsides in addition to the obvious. The first I discovered was that it takes a *lot* of drams for me to forget, and the forgetting wears off the second the sore heid kicks my face in.

Double whammy. Condemned to a life in exile on a magic-less rock after saving the only fucking world that was ever really home and I have to slap fight my paycheques to afford my unhealthy coping mechanism.

Earth.

I hate it here.

"All right in there, pal?"

I flush the toilet, cringing at the wetness of my bare and tattooed forearm. I'm far too much of a realist to pretend it's water or even vomit. Nope. Defo pish. Not mine.

"Aye, just gave the loo a wee clean," I call back to Ailig belatedly.

"Did ye aye" is the predictable response. "Get yer arse out here when you're done playing janitor. Got you a fry up. And wash your goddamn hands!"

Hands? I'm already planning to scrub up to my feckin' armpits.

Ailig, owner of this fine establishment and the one person on this sorry rock who both knows and believes my life history of getting the reject end of the isekai stick, is a damn good friend.

He's a Leòdhasach, but we won't hold that against him. Much.

"Madainn mhath," he says when I emerge, arms still dripping from the elbows since the hand dryers here are about as effective as having a drunk pal breathe on your wet skin.

"Droch mhadainn," I mutter, correcting his good morning to a much-more-appropriate dismal one.

"Don't look at me, mate, I tried to drag your drunk arse upstairs. You were having none of it. Said you deserved to sleep with the rubbish."

I close my eyes with a resigned sigh. Aye, sounds like drunk and despondent me. I'm lucky one person puts up with me. "Fair play."

"Ever the maudlin drunk," Ailig says as if he heard my thoughts.

"Alcohol is a depressant."

"That explains why you're never your old chipper self."

"What, was I ever Sammy Sunshine?"

Ailig gives me a look, one I'm not prepared to deal with. He wipes the moment of honesty—the one that says "aye, used tae be"—off his mug with the will of good-old Gàidhealach stoicism and says, "You're a cheeky wee git is what you are. Come on."

Of the two of us, he's the wee one—he barely broke five feet by eighteen and now is only a few inches taller after a late growth spurt I'm convinced was born of pure pigheaded stubbornness. Also, I should say, a common Gaelic trait.

By contrast, I'm tall, rangy, and ginger to his short, muscular stature and dark brown hair. When I got unceremoniously chucked back to Earth, I took out my rage on Ailig's bullies. Went from stranger to bestie in three KOs flat.

His family stayed next door to mine—a boon for my Sgitheanach parents, who desperately wanted other Gaelic speakers about and who just as desperately wanted me to have friends who spoke the language outwith our Gaelic-medium schooling. He and I happened to hit it off about three months before I fell through reality into a whole new world. By the time I came back, he was two ticks from suicide for all the bullying, and I had learned a thing or two about how to shut up bullies. Mostly with my fists.

I became the bad boy of Sgoil Ghàidhlig Ghlaschu—not exactly street cred—and Ailig and I took up where we left off and also took up weightlifting. Eventually, I told him my story.

As he fiddles with the keys to the janky lock on his flat above the club, I take a moment to be thankful.

My parents, somewhat predictably, didnae believe me. What Ailig accepted with a simple "Granaidh and Seanair were awa' wi' the faeries often enough. Who am I tae doubt our long and storied tradition of fucking off to the otherworld? Glad you're back," my parents took it as a decade-long abduction that triggered an exciting side effect of sparkling schizophrenia.

Not that I blame them. Their reasons for thinking that are the same as mine for giving myself alcohol poisoning six nights a week.

Ailig finally gets the door open with a grunt, and the

aroma of a proper full Scottish fry up chases away the residual odours of club loo and my own vomit.

Without asking, he goes and turns on a mix of the same music he plays in the club—all trad bands with an up tempo and often a healthy dose of electronica fused with the bagpipes and box. Folk have forgiven him for making the Teuchter Triangle—iconic Gael-heavy Glaswegian pubs the Park Bar, the Islay Inn, and the Snaffle Bit—into an awkward quadrilateral. Mostly because he's given Gaeldom somewhere to go when their licenses demand they close. Oor lad is open till three, charges fair prices, and funnels his profits into community investments.

He's something of a legend.

Elephant Sessions today.

"Deagh thagh," I say, complimenting his music choice.

"I know."

I pull a rickety stool up to the worktop, absentmindedly shoving aside an eclectic pile of Gaelic poetry books, spiral notebooks, and invoices that will—by some miracle—make it to Ailig's accountant in meticulous order.

I open the takeaway box he hands me and inhale. I could winch this black pudding. The wee cafe down the street gives us extra. I joke that the marag dhubh and Ailig himself are Lewis's best exports; Ailig always tells me my Isle of Skye sucked all the beauty out of its people to make the island as bonny as it is, so it left me with my ugly mug.

Besties.

I shove half a slice of my black pudding in my gob before Daibhidh's even sat down.

"Amazing," he mutters. "I'll never get used to that, how you can be boakin' one moment and shoving food in your mouth the next."

"Hangover cure," I say around my mouthful of marag

353

dhubh, then swallow. "Speaking of which, where's the Irn Bru?"

"Fridge, ya wanker. Get it yourself."

I do just that. Despite our havering back and forth, it's pure ritual at this point. When you tell a mate you spent thirtyish years in a fantasy world and got ripped away from the love of your life and thrown back into this one having only aged about eight and the pal *disnae* try to get you sectioned? Aye, that's no just a pal. That's family.

For that, I get him a can too.

He catches it without looking when I chuck it at him. Showoff.

We natter on while we eat. Elephant Sessions jams away in the background, and I feel time slipping away moment by moment. I'm sober and clear headed by the time my takeaway box is nowt but a greasy bit of biodegradable paper.

My time of reprieve ticks away.

Here we, here we, here we fuckin' go.

As always, the moment I'm alone, it returns.

It starts with a whisper at the edge of my mind, like a breeze too faint to really feel but that you can smell on the air, something that doesn't belong, something from *elsewhere*.

I call it my manadh, my ghost, because it haunts me.

Because here's the thing—after three decades of using magic daily, of painstaking lessons, of sweat and blood and worse, coming back to Earth could only strip me of the ability to use it. Magic is technically everywhere.

Earth, though, is practically a dead zone.

Only magic here is the ways in and out, and those have to be opened from the other side, in whatever world happens to find the key.

I used to be able to navigate them. Now I only sense when another reality presses against ours. I just can't use them.

The way home has always been here, like a pair of fucking ruby slippers, and unlike Dorothy, I'd need to do a whole hell of a lot more than just click my heels and wish.

Every day, day in and out. It's like starving to death in the middle of a feast that turns to sand every time you raise a bite past your parched and cracking lips.

Every day my manadh haunts me with the life I fought and bled for, with the whisper on the wind of Alaya's perfume on our shared pillows, with the tingle of creation in my fingertips that fizzles the moment I try to use it. Always lingering at the edge of my awareness, always out of reach.

Earth is torture.

So I go the fuck to work.

Work is grueling on purpose. Even though I'm long since grown and on my own, my parents still worry. To them, I'm still that eight-year-old wean who disappeared into thin air. They wonder—and cannot fathom—why I choose manual labour.

They can keep wondering.

They're both retired from their white-collar jobs and content to let me sweat so long as I don't start gibbering at the thin air that once stole me away. The first year after I got back was...bad for everyone.

Now I build things and knock them down—usually not in that order—and the thought of swinging a sledge-hammer is about all that drags me down the street from Ailig's.

Practicing meditation helps to an extent. It calms me down on one hand, but on the other, it makes it far too easy to hear my manadh. It's a trade off, a seesaw of give and take that I avoid when I feel that sparkler go off in my brain where the manadh gets too strong and use when I just want to punch someone instead of something.

I'm in the city centre this week on a demolition after a fire tore through yet another historic building. I stop at home just long enough to change into my jumpsuit and shove my helmet into my rucksack, and then I'm off.

Glasgow's subway is loud enough to drown out the manadh's incessant whispers. Most people hate it, but I appreciate the screeching of trains on rails and the clack-clack-clack that keeps my brain on track.

It's only two stops to the site, and the routine is such second nature to me that I plough into the turnstile when it fails to open.

Smartcard not readable. Seek assistance.

Ugh.

Buchanan Street station is a mess of commuters this time of day, and there's a queue behind me. I scan the card again.

Smartcard not readable. Seek assistance.

I give the middle-aged woman behind me an apologetic look and get out of her way. She scans her card.

Smartcard not readable. Seek assistance.

"The fuck," says someone nearby, and I look over to see a broad-shouldered bloke with a buzzcut at odds with his tailored three-piece suit just as he slaps his card against the reader.

He's not the only one—the entire mass exodus from the outer circle train has bottlenecked at the turnstiles.

No one's is working.

One of the station attendants is on his way over in his high-vis orange waistcoat, frowning. "None of them working?"

"Not a one," says the woman I tried to let go by me. "I've a train in five minutes I can't miss."

The attendant scans his own card on the nearest turnstile, but it doesn't open for him, either. Clearly unsure of what to do next, he looks over at the ticket cashiers behind their panes of glass, and they only give him a bewildered look. Folk behind us are starting to press against my back.

Naturally, that's when all the lights go out.

DEATH SPIRAL: CHAPTER 2

By the time I get to work with a scalding americano in one hand and a box of doughnuts to share in the other, I'm on time, but barely, and my entire body feels like the time I accidentally touched a live wire. Not a lot of juice—just enough to give me a jolt. It's "quadruple espresso on an empty stomach" level of yikes.

Other colleagues filter in at the same time, a few grumbling and dumping Greggs down their throats or gnawing on sausage rolls. Cynthia, one of the forefolk as we've taken to calling them, stumps my way in her steel-toed boots, looking like a sun-baked haystack with a short, wavy golden-blond mullet and tanned skin that makes strangers sincerely doubt her Shetland upbringing since they forget Scotland and Norway have passed those islands back and forth for centuries.

"Why's everyone late?"

I'm not sure why she's asking me since technically we're not, but she's not being aggressive. She's just gruff—used to being the only woman amid builders and ran out of fucks twenty years ago.

"Power cut at the subway," I say. "At least when I came through—they couldn't even get the turnstiles open."

"Still oot," says Jamie, a rangy Rangers fan I once saw deck his own mate for spitting on a Celtic fan, so he's all right in my book. Well. When he's not hawking a loogie like he is right now. He spits—not at anyone, since that's clearly against his code of ethics—and squints at his handiwork before clearing his throat. "Absolute pileup at Buchanan Street. Pure chaos."

Cynthia scowls in the general direction of the subway. "Anything else cut?"

She's clearly thinking about the sparks we're supposed to have coming in today to work on wiring where my one-man-demolition band has finished.

"Not that I know of, boss," I say.

"Good. Gies a doughnut."

I grin at her and hand over the box. She snags a caramel fudge and salutes me with it, and we get to work.

I'm in a completely different sector of the build knocking down walls when it starts.

The first is a small fountain of sparks when my sledge-hammer hits drywall. Not sparks as in the electricians who are coming this afternoon but literal sparks. And it's nothing major, just like the puff of glittery orange when a log pops in a fire pit. Except there's nothing combustible about chalk, which is pretty much what drywall is. Peering out from my goggles, I wait for the dust to settle before taking them off. My mask I leave on; even if the place has been checked for asbestos and black mould, I prefer to huff only stale, N95-filtered air, thank you. I don't want a lungful of chalk.

Even so, a wave of wooziness washes over me. I give an experimental sniff, but I don't smell anything that could indicate a gas leak I'd be unaware of. Any sparks in that case would be deadly far faster than mould or asbestos.

I blink to clear my vision. I occasionally get migraines, and the tension in my jaw suggests both wooziness and blurry vision could mean one is coming.

Footsteps intrude. "Stopping early?"

It's Jamie, squinting at me under his hardhat and goggles. He must have heard all the crashing come to a halt.

"Naw, mate, just had something spark and wanted to check. If I hit this chunk again, will you watch?"

"You sure you can hit the same place twice?"

"Har, har." I slide my goggles back on after ineffectually blowing on them through my mask to clear some dust off the outside.

Jamie stays well back as I swing the sledgehammer at the chunk of wall, and I hear the crunch of his sudden movement at the impact when another flurry of sparks flies up.

I turn to look at him. "Not just me, then."

"I'll get Cyn," he says.

He's the only one who can get away with calling her that, probably cos he and his wife always invite her around for Christmas and get her pished.

In the silence, my manadh begins to whisper.

"Not fucking here," I mutter under my breath. "Chan ann an-seo."

It usually leaves me alone at work, even in a lull. I crack my neck, digging my gloved hand into the hollow at the base of my skull as if the whisper is in there and I can knuckle it out. It gives the tension in my fascia a bit of release, but the whisper hovers, an unseen susurrus punctuated by the other sounds of builders on the crew.

It's only a few minutes before Cynthia and Jamie return, Cynthia carrying a dusty bag of detector gadgets from carbon monoxide to a Geiger counter I hope she's never had to use.

I move back to let her do her thing, and she crouches, which increases the sun-baked haystack impression because it makes her shorter and stouter.

After a few minutes of placid beeping and no alarms, Cynthia gets back up. "Should be good to go." She glances at me. "Sledgehammer?"

I hand it to her without question and step back with Jamie to give her space. She gives the sledge a swing, connecting with the same relative chunk of wall, which is hanging on by a thread at this point.

No sparks.

Just a puff of drywall dust and a crackle and thud as the thread gives up and looses a plate-sized hunk of plaster and wood to land on the floor.

"No sparks," she says. "You two taking the piss?"

"No, boss," I reply automatically, mystified.

Jamie just shakes his head.

Cynthia hands me the sledgehammer back. "Maybe there was just a bit of metal in that chunk to spark on. Dinnae ken. Give it another go while I'm here."

"Aye." Pausing to let her join Jamie, I try to shake off the whispers. My manadh still lingers, haunting me.

Imagining I can smash it with my hammer—an ongoing fantasy—I eyeball the next targeted section of wall and gie it laldy.

Jamie and Cynthia both yelp as a veritable explosion of

sparks bursts from the point of impact, and throughout the building site, every power tool in earshot sputters and falls silent.

"Right, Sam, we'll have to come back to this after I have Abdul check it more thoroughly," she says, then seems to hear the same sound—or lack thereof—I'm hearing. "Bollocks. Did the power go?"

"Nice one," Jamie mouths as Cynthia stomps off to investigate.

"I didn't do fuck all!" I mutter it under my breath, but I can't be sure. Not with the whispers crawling round the inside of my skull.

Just like that, I'm alone with my manadh again.

I make my way back to Ailig's on foot, since the only thing worse than the constant whispering at the back of my cranium is dealing with that in my barren flat. The subway doesn't even tempt me; last thing I need is to end up stuck underground because of a power cut, and when the button at a pelican crossing flickers before I even touch it, I grit my teeth and thank Past Sam for heeding that intuitive nudge.

What the fuck is happening?

It's only half ten by the time I get to Ailig's, and he answers the door with an enormous Sports Direct mug of steaming coffee in his hand and blinks at me.

"Bha an doras fosgailt'," I mutter, slipping past him as he holds the door open, nonplussed.

He looks over my shoulder as if he can see around corners to figure out why the main door to the close was open, but since he does not have go-go-gadget eyeballs, he surrenders to his own mortality and shuts his flat's door.

"Off work?" He asks the question as if it tastes like licking sulphur. "You all right, mate?"

"*I'm* fine," I say, thumping over to the kitchen with hard enough footfalls that Ailig winces, despite not having anyone living below him. "Power cuts all over the city centre."

"That stop you from hitting things with your cartoon mallet?"

I empty his coffee maker and throw in some more grounds, pausing to punch a couple buttons to get it percolating before I answer.

"Nope, the shower of sparks every time I hit something stopped me."

My back's to Ailig, but I can practically feel the man blink.

"Something's off," I say finally, still staring at the machine as if it will somehow give me answers.

"Manadh?"

A little pang in my sternum region—okay, maybe my heart—makes me turn to face my pal.

"'S e a bh' ann," I confirm. "It's worse than usual, mate. The power cuts...'s beag m' fhios. Only common denominator "

I let the sentence trail off, unsure if I want to voice the little nugget of nerves ricocheting off my diaphragm like a fuckin' bouncy ball.

Ailig just waits. He knows me well. Too well, honestly. He waits with the absolute patience of someone who knows they're my only safe port of call in a Hebridean gale. Steam curls upwards from his mug, and instinctively, when I feel a pull from somewhere over my right shoulder, I turn. Now it's my chance to stare like I have the vision of a Kryptonian farm boy to see through walls and over miles.

Which, of course, I don't. All I see is eggshell wall and the very 80s faces of Runrig in their heyday.

I may not have supervision, but I do have something else—or I did. Once upon a time in a faraway world. In the past ten years since I got dumped back on Earth, I haven't felt this kind of pull.

If anyone's coming with me to see what's got a hook in me, it's my best mate.

"There's something out there," I say, tearing my gaze away from the wall and the framed—and signed—poster of Runrig. "I have to go see what it is."

A flash of something indescribable passes over my friend's face, a spark lighting in his eyes before he takes a deep swig from his coffee and winces at the heat.

"Right, ma-thà," he says, sucking his teeth. "I'm going with you."

It's a bit surreal, after ten years of despair, to sense my first inkling of magic on Earth in Kelvingrove Park, for fuck's sake.

Don't get me wrong, the park's lovely and you're much less likely to get stabbed there in the 2020s than, say, in the late 80s, but pretty trees and statues of dead arsehole aristocrats don't really feel otherworldly to someone who's actually been to another world.

The park's quiet for late February despite the proximity of Glasgow Uni and the term being in full swing. We make our way down Kelvin Way's tree-lined pedestrian street, crossing over the River Kelvin, and I irrationally profess inner gratitude that there are no notable electric elements nearby to make me feel crazier.

The thing about being me is that even though I was there, even though I spent twenty years growing to maturity and living an entire life of magic and wonder, when no one believed me for long enough, I started to think I *could* be mad.

Now, though, my fingertips tingle. My skin feels like an unseen wind caresses it, and the part of me that once could effortlessly kindle a flame in the palm of my hand ignites once more. *Ignite* isn't quite the right word; more of a piddly spark or two. I made more with the sledge earlier. But it's there.

My pace quickens as the manadh's whispers grow nearer. I feel like a bloodhound on the trail of a juicy rabbit.

When I glance to the side, I finally realise what I'm seeing in the bounce of Ailig's steps beside me, in the light sheen of perspiration on his forehead: excitement.

He believes.

A lump appears in my throat, and I cough, looking away. All this time, there's been a tiny part of me that couldn't be sure he wasn't just humouring me.

I swallow, clapping him on the shoulder without a word.

We're close.

It's at the bandstand.

The bandstand sits empty in the winter months, and it's empty now as we approach. It always seems to appear out of nowhere, and today is no different.

I don't hesitate to jump the green fence, hearing Ailig clamber behind me.

My heart has taken up a competing rhythm with the nervous nugget using my diaphragm as a trampoline, and I suddenly feel such a wave of near-panic anxiety that wooziness follows on its heels. I hop up onto the bandstand's stage, awash in the memories of two disparate lives —one with the bandstand full of cheering concert-goers and the other, a whirlwind of magic and glory crowned with the touch of my beloved's hand on my chest like a beacon.

But then I see it.

Something I thought I'd never see again.

A rift.

DEATH SPIRAL: CHAPTER 3

Ailig reaches me only moments later, but I'm stood stock still, staring at the thing.

"Tell me you see that," I say hoarsely.

"See what?" he says in a shaky voice, and before I can cuff him upside the head, he goes on. "Oh, you mean that tear in time and space five feet in front of us, stage right?"

I bark a helpless laugh, and then it's all I can do not to fall to my knees and sob.

It's real.

It's here.

A doorway.

"Dè as ciall dha?" Ailig asks me what it means as if I have any clue under the sun. When I don't answer, he thumps me on the shoulder. "Oi."

My mind whirls, old thought patterns waking up after what feels like centuries of dormancy. I've shut it out for so long, so long, and now it's come to find me.

Or, more correctly, I've gone and found it.

In the Kelvingrove bandstand. Bloody hell.

"Gies a sec," I say to Ailig.

Alaya.

It's been so long since I've let myself think of her—millennia since I could bear to hear her voice in my mind.

As if her memory has been waiting to seize the first opportunity, remembered knowledge pours in, smooth like the honey of her contralto lilt, rippling through me.

"Hm, not to Earth," I hear her say all over again. "Or not easily, anyway. Travel between worlds is easiest in the inner realms where spirit is abundant. But out in the Death Spiral it's complicated. Most don't even bother philosophising about it."

This conversation happened in bed, one lazy morning with the amber sunlight pouring through the window, a sapphire morning sky beyond in the light of a burnished-gold star older than Earth's.

"Then I will not be returning to Earth," I remember saying, satisfaction buttressing my voice. "Good."

Her quiet sigh sounded content at the time, but now how many times have I heard the hitch, wondered if she was hoping her seer senses were wrong, wishing for the both of us that light-ning wouldn't strike twice in the same backward, magic-barren planet I came from.

"Whatever brought you here did so by accident." Soft words, soft touch upon my shoulder. "A byproduct of whatever magic they were attempting. The distance between Tìran and Earth is monstrous on planes both temporospatial and magical, an impossible chasm to leap by practical means and a gargantuan abyss by mystical ones. Far easier to open a door from one of the other outer ring realms in the Death Spiral to a neighbour, just like it is easier to toss a ball of wool across the corridor to a friend's outstretched hand than it is to launch it to Talavash."

We both snorted at that; Talavash lay on the opposite side of Tìran from our home in Ilyn; the comparison would be like kicking a football from Glasgow to Auckland.

I take a deep breath, shaking myself back to the present, to the rift in front of me and Ailig waiting by my side.

Because I know.

Maybe not what caused the rift, maybe not what's responsible for opening this door; *that* I may never know, like I've never found out why I fell through that first one so many years ago.

But I do know one thing.

Ailig voices it before I do.

"You want to go," he says, his words a whisper like my manadh. "You *need* to go."

My next breath catches on the returned lump in my throat. I can only nod.

"Fine," he says. "I'm going with you."

That's the other thing I know.

"You can't." It comes out gravelly, rough as rubble in my larynx.

"Fuck off, I can't. All these years—"

"I don't know how long this thing will stay open, so you need to listen to me now, closer than you've ever listened before." I stop to clear my throat again, where it feels like my lungs are trying to escape if my heart doesn't beat them both up to do the same. "The only places that door could go are Death Spiral worlds. It would have taken a supernova of spirit to punch through to Earth from anywhere it would be *safe* to travel."

Even as I speak, I know I'm right. The last two times I made a jump like this, the rift was solid around the edges, deliberate. This—this is a tear, like a ladder in a woman's stocking.

Ailig opens his mouth to protest, but I see his resolve wavering already. I barrel onwards.

"The Death Spiral is barely acknowledged. In Tìran, the

only reason I learned about it was because I was married to a seer." *Alaya.* I force the surge of wild hope down in my chest. Not the time. Not now. Maybe not ever. "All worlds exist in duality, the time-space physical dimension entwined with spirit, and in the metaphysical plane, think of it as a galaxy with a nexus of pure magic at the heart, everything spiralling inwards. The closer a world is to that nexus, the denser the magic. On the outer fringes? That's what they call the Death Spiral. Dead worlds, newborn worlds of ash and colliding rock, extinct worlds, monster realms. Earth not only exists on those outer fringes where there's virtually no magic, but Earth is an anomaly for the fact that humans have created magic-like technology."

"You've told me all that before, just not the Death Spiral bit."

"Aye, well, now it's important and not just academic," I mutter. The rift pulls at me, threads of spirit rippling at its edges like they're beckoning, a summons I can no sooner ignore than I could a heart attack. "Anything could exist on the other side of that doorway."

"And you want to walk through it without me." Ailig turns to look at me, clamping both hands down on my shoulders like he wants to shake the stuffing out of me. "A bheil thu 'n da-rìribh?"

A much softer way of him asking *are you fucking kidding me?*

"Tha," I answer in the affirmative. Earth has almost no spirit to speak of, droplets in comparison to an ocean. The world on the other side of this rift, though, it has a stream. And I've been here for a decade, dying of thirst. "I can defend myself in ways you can't, mate."

There's no Mordor analogy to be had here, no matter how poignant the idea of Ailig diving into this river when he can't swim its currents. His hands drop from my shoulders.

"Tha an cianalas orm ro mhòr," I murmur, knowing he will understand that, if nothing else.

There is no English word for the yearning of cianalas, no equivalent for the bone-deep drag of the undertow you can't deny. It's been too much for too long, a burden on my soul with a loss like a black hole at its centre. Inexorable. Inevitable. Inescapable.

My own manadh, my own ghost of a distant life finally calling me home.

Even so, I hesitate.

"I can take this risk alone," I say after a long silence, those tantalising threads of spirit reaching for me. "I can't take it with you. You're still part of this world, a charaid. I've been a spectre in it for far too long."

"I'm a veritable little mermaid," he replies gruffly, good-natured even in the face of this, the weirdest of all fucking days. "Or maybe I'm the prince and you're Ariel, cò aig tha fios."

"I'm sorry to disappoint you, but I'm spoken for." My words come out drier than I expected, and Ailig chuckles, but then he has to clear his throat before he can respond.

"If you ever make it home, send us a postcard," he says, and I know this is the closest we're going to get to a goodbye.

A wave of spirit startles me, just a ripple but practically a tsunami by Earth standards.

"Did something happen?" Ailig asks, looking at the rift like it might swallow him whole.

"Aye. My cue to leave, I think," I say, but I frown, suddenly uncertain.

The rift is shifting, the edges...not widening, not shrinking, but becoming somehow less tangible. If I'm going to go, I need to go. Now.

Something is happening on Earth right now. That wave of spirit felt far too intentional, if entirely impersonal. I don't have time to stop and figure it out. It fades after another brief moment, and I'm left at the precipice.

"What are you waiting for?" My mate's unease grows with each moment I linger, like I'm pulling off a glued-on plaster over an open wound with agonising slowness.

I suppose I should be merciful and rip the plaster off.

"Just felt something else," I say before I can stop myself. "Do me a favour, mate, and just...remember everything I've told you. About magic. Just in case."

"I've taken dutiful notes, ya bastard. Now go on. Thalla."

"One more thing." I pause and give him a crooked smile. "You know the Pleiades?"

Ailig frowns. "The...stars?"

"The Seven Sisters, aye. They don't look the same in Tìran, but they're visible. The same stars, just from a different angle."

My voice cracks on the last word, just like it did when Alaya first showed me, and I told her I knew those stars. Four hundred light years from Earth. A bare two hundred from Tìran. But the same stars, the same sky, the same vastness of space.

At that, Ailig yanks me into a bear hug, almost crushing me. The part of me not getting squished into a compressed cylinder wonders if I ought to bring him along just to crush enemies with his arms.

When he lets me go, I take a big breath.

There are no more words in either of our languages.

Spirit beckons, my manadh quieted for the first time in a decade.

I turn away from my oldest friend and step into the rift.

I hope you enjoyed this wee sneak preview of my next project.

You can preorder Death Spiral here!

LOVE LITRPG?

To learn more about LitRPG, talk to authors including myself, and just have an awesome time, please join the LitRPG Group!